Charlotte Mary Yonge

An Old Woman's Outlook in a Hampshire Village

Charlotte Mary Yonge

An Old Woman's Outlook in a Hampshire Village

ISBN/EAN: 9783337737658

Printed in Europe, USA, Canada, Australia, Japan

Cover: Foto ©Andreas Hilbeck / pixelio.de

More available books at **www.hansebooks.com**

AN

OLD WOMAN'S OUTLOOK

IN

A HAMPSHIRE VILLAGE

BY

CHARLOTTE M. YONGE

London

MACMILLAN AND CO.

AND NEW YORK

1892

CONTENTS

JANUARY

I MIGHT say, except for brevity's sake, an old woman's outlook through a keyhole, for all my life has been spent in one place, and one which can boast of nothing extraordinary; but then it has always been looked at with loving eyes; and though I have only a second-hand smattering of the knowledge needed to appreciate its interests, it seems to me that its very absence of peculiarities may make it serve to assist others to make the most of their surroundings, so as to find no country walk devoid of the homely delights that sustain and lift up the spirit—though it strikes me that my style is that of Mr. Bertram in *Guy Mannering*.

The New Year is coming in! Here, in South Hampshire, Christmas does not often come in conventional form, laden with snow. 'As the day lengthens, the cold strengthens,' is a very true proverb, but the lengthening is seldom perceptible till after Twelfth Day; and it is well for the poor that the severest weather should not often set in till there is a little less darkness. When I first remember, the families used to go to bed as soon as the father had come in, so as to save fire and candle; but better wages and paraffin have made a difference, and each cottage shows a cheerful light over its muslin blind, with the geraniums that flourish so wonderfully behind it. These years have done much every way for the labourers' families. The dark blue cotton, sprung from 'Nancy Peel's' parsley pattern, has given place to the serge, too often, indeed, shoddy, but warmer and less liable to catch fire ; and short sleeves no longer expose brawny arms and blue elbows. The red-cloaked black-bonneted old woman still existed in those old days. The scarlet cloaks were most enduring—one dame (wife to a man who had sailed under Nelson) measured her son's age by hers when he was at least eighteen. But they were scanty, and would not wrap, though they were far preferable to the gray duffle which the children wore, poor things ! over their bare arms ; and one woman, during their decay, pronounced to be so me-an. I remember a well-intentioned paper, where the extravagant woman is rebuked for buying scarlet instead of gray by some one who evidently did not know the true economy. It is dangerous to preach thrift without full knowledge. After the cloaks went out, there was a period of tartan shawls of all sizes, checked black and white, or black and red. But the jacket or ulster, though far less picturesque, leaves much less room for cold-catching and conceals some untidiness.

The thick white cap, with a lofty caul and crimped frill—very becoming when clean— went out through a course, first of white, then of black, net and flowers—the last sometimes so undesirable in dirt that a lady has been known to object, and be answered, ' Dear me, ma'am, 'tis only a little cap as I've worn more than a year!' Bare heads, if tidy, are better; but it is a pity to see women wearing their boys' caps. Ladies should bethink themselves of the harm a bad fashion does to their imitators. The bonnet, which we once were told was to serve as a hood, shutting us in with our book at church, has dwindled to the smallest span. I remember a good old dame, a survival, giving directions, in these degenerate days, that in making her new bonnet 'the moon'—that is, the crescent front—should be big enough. But I did not intend a dissertation on the fashions, but to remark on the improvement in the welfare of the poor. This is the worst month, however, for work, especially for the brickmakers, who are numerous.

This portion of Hampshire, between the chalk and the sea, was probably once a great estuary, and is a capital instance of the making of land described by Charles Kingsley in *Madam How and Lady Why*. The water has deposited high ridges of gravel, with here and there veins of sand, and beds of the finer particles which have formed clay. The gravel has become covered—in many places—with peaty soil, and is full of springs. The clay has no doubt been worked for many years—names of fields such as Potters, Pot Kiln, Kiln Lane, and the like, show where it has been used and exhausted ; and several fields still full of ups and downs have been thus used within this half century. The long thatched sheds where the yellow bricks, being dried before the kiln burns them red, show where the present workings lie, and here most of the boys are employed on first leaving school—not much, unfortunately, to their moral improvement.

Almost all the buildings are of red brick. An old red-brick house, with a tiled or thatched roof, is of a very harmonious colour; and at one time a fashion prevailed of setting the bricks within timber frames, arranged in herring-bone fashion. A few barns and houses still show this; but the thin red walls and the cold blue slate roof of modern cottage builders never do tone down, and are far too hot in summer and too cold in winter.

The early winter is far more often wet and misty here than frosty and snowy. Perhaps it is about one year in seven that is really severe, with snow enough to be a real inconvenience. Yet the glorious beauty of the snow makes one shrink from complaining, when the expanse lies perfectly smooth and dazzlingly white on the lawn, sparkling here and there with crystals, and only marked by the delicate little claws of the birds, or, mayhap, with the rosette-like pads of dog or cat. Or going further afield, with the trailing track of hare or rabbit, and, as I have seen round the hen-house, with the steps of the prowling fox. Each bough is laden ; fir and yew are meant to bear snow on their narrow leaves. The boughs of the yew are elastic, and those of the fir, the true mountaineer, are formed like the roof of a house, the tapering form of the tree like a spire, the seeds within the scaly cones shielded in their two years' growth from all injury. The holly, too, with its strong shiny leaves, crumpled up by their firm spiny border, is ready for resistance.   But the laurel, or that which we call a laurel, shows that it came from warmer regions, in Persia and the Caucasus, by the inability of its broad leaves to endure any weight of snow, which crushes and kills the branches.   It is by no means the laurel that crowned the classic victor.   That was probably the Alexandrian laurel (*Ruscus racemosus*)—much more convenient for the purpose.   Our laurel was only brought into Europe by a German Ambassador to Constantinople in 1574, and was a rarity in England in Evelyn's time.   It is really, as its fruit shows, a cherry, and its proper name is *Cerasus lauro cerasus*.   I always pity it when I see it labouring under a weight of snow.

To enjoy snow properly when it does come, especially with wind, behold the drifts, where they lie along a bank curling over like waves, in the most exquisite soft rolls, blue in the shadows, or perhaps rosy in the sun. Or again, see the icicles along a roof, in all their beauteous glassy pendant forms. The most beautiful of these I ever saw was along the edge of a hatch in the water meadows, where the stream must have splashed over and gradually dropped. They hung like crystal stalactites, many two feet long, and in all varieties of fantastic shapes, delightful to remember.

It is remarkable that what is most like descriptions of heavenly glory should be, though pure, most evanescent and often terrible, such as mountain and Arctic snows, and the iceberg or ice cavern. Ice in these parts is apt to be more of a pleasure than a pain. Skaters have now scarcely more than time to look out their skates; and the school-children, who begin at once, with hands in their pockets, to slide on the pools in the gravel pit, have the most fun after all.

For the most part the frost does no more than turn the water in the puddles into delicate white tracery over the top, a slanting bar, backed by white stars of spiculæ. I stand to admire them now, and smile at recollecting that destructiveness of childhood that used to delight in crackling up this 'walking ice,' as we used to call it, with our feet.

The six-pointed crystal formed by water is certainly one of the loveliest of forms, whether in the elaborate snow star one can catch on a muff, or in the marvellous tracery upon the window-pane. Or again, the deposit of a fog makes the world unspeakably lovely, when every leaf, every thorn, has its soft white border, and the branches of the trees stand out in crested whiteness sometimes against a blue sky. It is but for a short time; the sunshine melts the delicate efflorescence; it is crumbling and rustling down already, the only sound breaking the wonderful breathless stillness in which this scene of beauty has been formed in a perfection that almost inspires awe.

And the nights of this clear weather give the stars in the greatest perfection in which they can be seen in our climate. I am afraid the starry heavens are hardly studied, or even looked at enough. I have often known educated people, when told that there is a comet to be seen, come in quite contented, and full of admiration of the planet Jupiter. They will go out and take pains to look for a comet, which, with a very few exceptions, is a pale misty spot, when they never attend to the ordinary glories of the sky; just as they go to some trumpery exhibition, and leave the British Museum and National Gallery to country cousins. The Great Bear, who, as Pope makes Homer say, 'Never dips his burning muzzle in the main,' is always to be

had.   People know how to value him when
they come back from the Southern Hemisphere, and greet him as an old friend, when
again they see Charles's Wain, *i.e.* the Carle,
the husbandman's wain, or the plough.
Arthur's Wain is probably from Arcturus,
the Bear's Tail, as the Greeks called the
brilliant star, which is to be found by con-
tinuing with the eye the line of the Bear's
Tail.   Boötes is the herdsman, whose name
tempts us wickedly to talk of Arcturus in
Boots.   A Canadian lady having, apparently
on the authority of the constellations, ordered
bears' tails as the adornment of her sleigh,
was solemnly informed by her servant, in the
middle of a large company, that 'bears has
no tails.'   In fact, the names of Ursa Major
and Minor are said to be owing to a mis-
translation by the Greeks of their Arabic title.

Deneb, the double star, in what we may
call the Great Bear's hind leg, can some-

times be separated by the naked eye. The Pole Star, to which the pointers guide us, is small. In how many of the elder generation was not interest in it first awakened by Tommy Merton's being guided by Harry Sandford by the aid of the Pole Star when they lost their way?

And there is the family party, Andromeda, apparently marked by four great gold nails to fasten her to her rock, her mother Cassiopeia, like W sideways, near at hand, and Perseus climbing up to rescue her, his noted nebula just perceptible—that wonderful nebula, the delight of telescopes! Cepheus, the father, is hardly discernible. And turn round! There is glorious Orion, with his belt and his sword, and his bright shoulders and lion skin. So we see him; but the Northmen saw Frigga's distaff, and later he became Our Lady's Rock, the misty look of the nebula in his sword suiting with the idea of flax.   Glorious creature! ever, as the Greeks believed, pursuing the Pleiades, the nymphs changed into stars to escape him—the rainy stars, which with *Nimbosus Orion*, sailors dreaded.   How much has been said and sung of those seven tiny stars, and Alcyone the vanished one, once supposed to be the central star round which our entire universe of stars revolves, a notion which we are sorry to lose after connecting it (rashly) with the 'sweet influences of the Pleiades!' A moderate telescope reveals far more stars in the cluster; in fact, there are above seventy.   Then below comes the Bull's Face, a V lying on its side, with the glorious 'bright star Aldebaran,' shining at the end of one horn!   And above all other stars in our firmament glitters Sirius, the Dog Star, large enough to be a planet, but twinkling so much that he cannot be mistaken for one. He is almost flashing, and yet we are told that he is by no means the nearest of the fixed stars, and the human mind fails to grasp the idea of his size or his distance. A little girl once defined the stars as 'little sparks of God's glory,' and so indeed they are to us, all the more for these mighty discoveries! See the Milky Way, arching pale overhead, wonderful, an object of so many theories of science, with the Northern Cross, or Cygnus, in the midst. Our Cross is a Latin one; its longer limb makes the neck of the Swan. But we must not linger over the 'thousand eyes' of the frosty night. Here is the delicate blue brightening towards morning, with Venus in favoured years making herself a Star in the East; and by and by she fades into the gold round her, and the sun comes up. If mists hang on the horizon, he is round, red, and beamless; but often he comes with his flood of light, slanting, and making the hoar frost on the grass retreat with the shadows of the trees.

Now for the birds. Robins, of course, come to the windows, and so do clouds of sparrows—poor despised creatures, whom some one has well named the Irishmen of birds, with their noise and their squabbles, their boldness and ubiquity. When farmers had their own way with the Church rate, their extermination was paid for out of it. In an old church account-book, payments for 'sparer heads' and 'sprow heads' are often repeated in all sorts of spelling, together with 'marten-cats' heads' and 'poul-cat heads.' These two last were altogether destroyed, but the sparrows were unconquerable. In 1832 the custom was condemned by the curate, and given up; but an old retired farmer continued to shoot every sparrow in the place. He succeeded several times in reducing them to one, but always

by the next day that sole survivor had in-
duced a mate to come and dwell with him in
this Castle Perilous of Sparrowdom.

More favoured are the titmice. We hang
up a bit of fat, and these pretty little
creatures come in four species—the delightful tiny blue-cap with azure crest, the greater
one with the sulphur waistcoat and white
cheeks, the broad black, or rather purple,
line edging them, and running down his
breast—Ox-eye, as we call him here, bold-
spirited fellow; the marsh-tit, like blue-cap
gone into black and gray mourning; and
cole-tit, with white cheeks under his black
cap. These two last do not seem to have
the same power of hanging on upside down
as the two with yellow breasts, and are somewhat more shy. The charming long-tailed tit
never thus comes—I suspect he hybernates
somehow. Blackbirds and thrushes do not
appreciate crumbs, and puff themselves out

very disconsolately when neither worms nor berries can be had. Often a cock chaffinch comes, a grass-widower or *Cœlebs*, as his Latin specific name expresses, for his wife is gone to a warmer climate. I once met a whole flight of these delicate ladies on their way in the autumn; but it is not always the case in these southern counties that the females migrate. I have often seen them braving the winter, though in the North they never attempt it.

Kingsley says that wrens roll themselves together in a ball and sleep for the winter; but I have certainly often seen Kitty hopping about on a bank on warm days in the winter, perhaps come out to reconnoitre.

How many people fancy that the robin and wren are really mates, on the authority of the nursery rhyme! and how many more will aver that hen robins have no red breasts, deceived perhaps by the brown plumage of the newly fledged! Golden-crest darts about in the quick-set hedge. He is permanent here, and does not go North for his beautiful nest.

Gunnery, though somewhat checked, is too rife for curious birds, especially by the river. Some four miles hence there used to be a decoy, which I once saw. I do not know whether the institution survives in the north of England, but many people only know the word in its proverbial use. It can only be used in such frosts as are so uncommon here, that to keep up the skilled establishment is not worth while; and this is well, for it is a treacherous affair. When all other waters are frozen over, an artificial lake is cleared of ice to attract the water-fowl. Round this are arranged screens of reeds gradually doubled into a path, narrowed till they become a tunnel ending in a net.

Tame decoy ducks are trained to entice

their congeners into this fatal passage, and a clever little dog shows himself just enough to prevent a retreat, but not enough to cause the creatures to take wing. The victims swim on, led by the treacherous ducks into the net. The tame ones are taken out and , petted; the deluded victims have their necks wrung for the market.

When we went to see this great trap, many years ago, we were very cold, and very cautiously and silently were allowed to peep between the screens, where the birds were to be seen swimming, and now and then alighting on what was to be their Styx—and it was black enough! They were not near enough to be distinguishable, and of course we might not show ourselves, and could only be allowed to admire the dead; the mallard with his glossy green head, blue marks on his wings, and the inimitable fawn colour of his breast; the pretty little teal, with the green pocket and green streak over the eye, and the widgeon, with rust-coloured head and breast.

There are snipe and woodcock in the meadows, but my only acquaintance with them is when sportsmen bring them down. Nor do the fieldfares visit us much. I fancy the birds that come from the North for the winter stop before these southern counties are reached.

This is the sleeping time of vegetation. If the season is mild, violets can be gathered in the gardens, resolutely blossoming on every tolerably warm day, and the leafless jessamine on the houses still shows pale spark-like yellow flowers. These yield to frost and rain ; but the buds seem to be indestructible, and endure anything before they open. There are some of the 'steadfast Christmas roses' in gardens, to which their creeping roots have 'taken,' and where they are not disturbed in the time of their handsome green foliage ; and a primrose or two peeps out. It is possible to gather fourteen or fifteen garden flowers in some Januaries ; but these are almost all lingering remains of last year, not to be reckoned as the promise of the incoming season.

And 1890-91 was a winter to be remembered, with seven weeks of frost, five of unbroken snow, falling windlessly, and thus regularly, not in drifts, while the air, being still and clear, *felt* far less cold than it often does when the thermometer is lower. But the partial thaw, suddenly arrested, made the roads slippery beyond measure, and a walk became a story of casualties. Rooks came in black clouds to fields where food was provided for them, and rare birds appeared — alas! only to be shot by the unscrupulous.

It must be more individual character than

the species that gives ascendency among birds. At one window where they were fed, a water-wagtail acted tyrant, and drove off the others. At another, a hen blackbird made no scruple of driving off her own 'ouzel cock so black of hue, with orange tawny bill.' At another, a thrush ruled as long as these birds were brought by famine. And, usually, the little blue-cap showed himself more than a match for the much fiercer-looking ox-eye, whose bravery seems to reside in his colouring. Robins are often masters of the field. Is it true that they kill one another in the autumn? I used to be told so in my youth and thought it a romance; but like other traditions, rejected in the pride of one's younger days, I find cause for believing that ' 'tis true, 'tis pity; pity 'tis, 'tis true.' A labourer's widow tells us that her husband has seen them fight to the death in the woods; and they certainly never seem to increase in numbers, though they have broods of four or five; and a bed-ridden old woman has had a family of four or six walking about together on her quilt, but that was before the breasts of the young ones became red, and they were still at peace. It is well known that they cannot be kept in an aviary because they kill the other birds, and I fear the indictment must be accepted.

FEBRUARY

Eɴɢʟɪsʜ months do not by any means feel bound to act up to their traditional character, and at the outset February is often quite as cold as January; indeed, some of the most distinguished snows I have ever known began in February, or else were at their height on its first days, cutting off communication where there were deep roads to be choked, and making everything tardy.

And then the inevitable thaw, announced by avalanches from our roofs, drippings from our trees, drippings, alas, from all the weak places in roof or ceiling, floods in the cellar, and the roads, which had become a mixture of dust and snow, churned into a horrid yellow cream.

At last—
> Like an army defeated,
> The snow has retreated,

not here, to the bare hill, but under the shady banks, where it lies in lines till, as the sage declare, it waits for more to take it away.   And, in fact, the final clearing rain often does begin with snow.

> Come, wheel around,
> The dirt we have found
> Would be an estate at a farthing a pound,

is a song of Cowper's, often to be remembered in these days!   Gravel-mended roads are seldom now disturbed except by the break up of a frost; but there is a lane, leading to old brick-fields, which once on a spring day two of us found a quagmire of thick clay.   It was full on our way home; we tried creeping along the hedge sides, but slipped off, one of us plunging over both ankles, the other over one; so that when we emerged into the public road, in sight

—or supposed sight—of a carriage full of acquaintances, it was proposed to stand with the one best foot foremost!

Mist and fog are prevalent in our valley, hanging over the water meadows along the river. The Will-of-the-Wisp is sometimes seen over the wet meadows. I have once seen the pale dim light, and the children from the hamlet at the other end of the meadow speak as if it were not an uncommon sight. Far more frequent, however, is the bar of white, furry-looking vapour hanging over the grass in the evening, raised by the warmth of the earth and condensed by the cold upper air. For days together there will prevail a gray mist, not rain, not fog, near at hand, but a veil over everything. Dull, is it? Nay, come and walk along the raised footpath of our lane, and look towards the wooded hill, behind which the sun will presently set without being able to produce even a ruddy tint. No matter, it would only disturb that strange, still, 'silvery crape' that makes all the scene like a delicate transparency in shades of soft gray. Each hedge or group of trees is defined in gradually diminishing distinctness up to the pointed tops of the little plantation of larches on the side of the hill, which stand out in soft outline against the lighter tint of the sky.

Leafless trees are near, but Ruskin has taught us fairly to enjoy the beauty of the infinite, intricate ramifications of branch, bough, and twig, now that the foliage is gone. Nothing but doing as Ruskin recommends, trying to copy even a fragment of a tree on paper, makes one realise the beauty and intricacy of the forms. Of the inner wonders, the pith, the fibre, the medullary rays, the threefold bark, where resides so much of the life of the tree, there is no pausing to speak ; it is a deep and wondrous study, and the trees are asleep now, though a little angular russet bud at the end of each twig of the oak tree gives promise of awakening.

Nay, here is something awake. Dangling from the hazel twigs are the catkins, name formally accepted from the playful term ' pussy's tails,' though they are far more like what in some countries they are termed, ' lambs' tails.' What a wonderful provision there is for the protection of blossoms coming out so early without a leaf to shelter them. Look at these tails hanging in one, twos, and threes, so as to cover the hazel bushes with their own pale yellow tint. Each is a succession of scales, properly bracts, which roof in the tiny stamens. Long ago these were produced, then closed up tightly, now opening, but so that each scale is a protection to all below it, and the number in each catkin is so profuse, no doubt on account of

the numerous perils of such early blossoming.   The dust of the pollen on a sunny
day comes powdering those who gather
them.   But where are the pistils, the future
nuts?   Look below, close on the branches.
See a scaly bud, very small, but surmounted
by a crimson crest of tiny threads.   This is
the germ of the nut, the crimson threads
are the stigmas held up to receive the widely
scattered pollen.

Hazel is from the Saxon *hasil*, a covering
for the head, an allusion to its helmeted
state, as is the generic name *Corylla*, from
the Greek *karos*, helmet.   *Avellana*, the
specific name, is the Italian word in use,
and the origin of the surname Evelyn, well
fitted to our first writer on forest trees!

What is that sound of chopping in the
wood above?   There is a clearance going
on!   The underwood is all being levelled
with the ground.   Is the wood to be sacri-

ficed?   Oh no, it is only the periodical copse cutting.   In these southern counties the copses are regularly cut, some once in five years, some once in seven, some in nine.   Old labourers can, or used to be able to, tell the exact time for each copse in the parish.   Men, expert in the work, hire a copse from its owner, and employ others. See them at work up there.   A sort of hut, or shanty, is erected with sticks, and roofed over with chips, which shine out white. Here the tools are sheltered, the men eat, and sometimes have a fire close by.   The underwood is cut down, and, as it lies prone, a rapid selection is made.   Some is tied up in faggots for burning, the slenderer branching stems are laid aside for pea-sticks.   Others are selected for being woven into the wattled hurdles here in use for sheepfolds; but the more important are cut into even lengths to be made into hoops.   See, a huge sharp

knife is fastened between two posts set upright in the ground.   The stick is applied to
it at the butt end, drawn along, and, *presto*,
is split in two, the white interior contrasting
with the bark.   Another dexterous movement bends the cleft piece into a hoop, the
smooth white part within, the round bark
outside.   Then, as the hoops are finished,
they are built up, one upon another, into a
kind of tower-shaped pile, quite symmetrical,
and varied outside by the brown hazel stem,
the gray ash, and dark birch, but all white
and smooth within.   The chips lie around
in white piles, and altogether these 'hoop-
shaving' establishments are a very pleasant
feature in the spring, preparing the way,
too, for an outburst of primroses next year
before the brushwood has grown up.   The
hoops will travel far and wide to encircle
barrels.   In old times they used to go to
the West Indies to surround the sugar-

casks; but now they seem chiefly used for English beer.

It is the chief work of February, unless an unusually dry time sets in, enabling men and horses to 'get upon the land' to plough it.

Under the sunny banks, where the copse was cut last year, a few stray primroses are peeping out. Like most of the earliest flowers, they have a main stem underground, and only put up a short flower-stalk for the blossom. So it is with the Fair Maid of February, the snowdrop, whose bulb is an underground stem gathering nourishment for the flower—

> In vernal green and virgin white
> Her festal robes arrayed.

Up they come, the *perce-neige*, as the French well call them, the pure, white-pointed calyx first pushing up, then by and by, hanging in an exquisite oval drop on its slender footstalk, and then expanding the three white sepals, like wings, enclosing the three notched petals, touched with green, shutting in the six stamens.

Double snowdrops are a mistake, losing all the symmetry of the triads of the endogen. And those who are happy enough to have good clumps of snowdrops had better leave them alone as much as possible, they do not like being transplanted ; but where they find a really congenial spot they will spread a white sheet of blossoms on the grass-plat like a procession of clergy in surplices. Whether we may call them native or not is doubtful ; 'the river islet' of the *Christian Year* is on the Test, but I have only seen them apparently wild in deserted gardens.

Their comrade, the crocus, also an endogen with its nourishment in the bulb, is the better for being taken up, as its new bulbs form beside the old ones, and thus it gradually travels out of its situation. Those people who write to the paper on any complaint are always bemoaning the way in which the sparrows devour their crocuses. Perhaps they *do* take a course of saffron ; but a good deal of destruction may be prevented by feeding them. It is generally only the golden crocus that opens in February, the brightest of flowers, as it holds up its deep vase to the sun, raising that most curious and beautiful stigma in the midst, while the first adventurous bees revel in its gorgeous depths. The crocus will on cloudy days remain for a long time waiting, folded up, but when it has had a few hours of basking in the sunbeam, it has done its work, and is content to hang down under the next fall of rain. The purple, striped, and lovely white are somewhat later. The Nottinghamshire wild crocuses (*C. nudi-florus*) were the subject of a charming little poem of Mrs. Gilbert—the Ann Taylor of the Original Poems and Nursery Rhymes—a lament for the fields that were built over, yielding to the cruel defacement of nature by mammon.   She makes the flowers say—

We came, a simple people, in our little hoods of blue,
And a blush of living purple on earth's green bosom
    threw.

Purple, too, are the closely covered twigs of the Mezereon (*Daphne mezereum*), or Mazalion, as our village friends call it, entirely leafless, and with a strong scent, overpowering in a room when the tough bark has been conquered, and a spray triumphantly brought home as an announcement of spring.   In spite of the multitudinous flowers, the bushes will only show one or two red berries among the green leaves, specimens truly of what has been called the lavish waste of Nature.

1891 showed in February a delightful reaction from the snows of January, in days of April-like geniality.   Fog prevailed in the morning, dense white fog, and in London it hung so thickly all day that traffic was in difficulties ; but here, in the south, the sun licked it up by the middle of the day, leaving a few delicious hours of sunshine, setting the thrushes and robins to sing, and the ox-eyes to cry Peter, the rooks and the starlings to chatter.

But then came the knowledge of losses, ceanothus and myrtle that had gone on for years, and reached the top of the house, with leaves like tea, though their stocks will probably recover ; while evergreens are shaking off the leaves injured by the continued frost, which have had time to find out that they are dead and fall off at once, instead of waiting to depart slowly as their place is supplied.

And, oh, there must be mourning among the chaffinches of the North. No less than a hundred and thirty-nine frozen hen-chaffinches were taken out of one hayrick in the north of

Hampshire ; but these poor dames must have been overtaken by the winter on their way, and their lords will cry chink, and plume their ruddy breasts, gray polls, and white pockets in vain.

They are called chinks from their note, in some places copper-finches, as being bad imitations of bullfinches, who, handsome fellows, are to be seen questing about the buds for insects, and drawing on themselves unjust suspicion of preying on the buds instead of the grubs.

Little flies come out on the windows in the sunshine, and birds come too and tap on the glass in hopes of a meal, but alarming superstitious inmates, who think the tap a warning. Perhaps the story has been told before of the Devon doctor who was summoned in haste to a farm-house on the moor. He found an old man in bed, but in perfect health, and could only ask why he had been called in. 'Why, sir,' said the daughter-in-law, 'there came a little robin about the door. We knowed it was a call, and we thought it must be for granfer; so we put 'im to bed and sent for you.'

If you find a stray primrose or two, beware of bringing them home, for the first brood of chickens will be of the same scanty numbers. Those early broods of black-eyed balls of soft yellow down are careful comforts and matters of anxious pride to the house-wife. The sensible, motherly hen, all puffed out, with her bright black eye and red comb, uttering cheerful chucks to her lively brood, is a charming sight; but when the little speckled wings begin to appear, is the time of danger and loss in the broods.

My poultry-keeping days have long been over. They were in the time of my good old grandmother, who loved to potter after them in pattens long before the era of India-

rubber galoches.   It was likewise before the
era of fashion in poultry, when the hideous
Shanghae monster was unheard of, and when
the black Poland lady with her nodding top-
knot was not, as yet, too fine a lady to sit or
bring up her children, though, if her admirers
were to be trusted, she laid at least 366 per
annum!

No—our wildest ambition was for the
respectable five-toed Dorking, and we did
not prefer the flame-coloured, flame-tempered
game-cock, whom generations of 'natural
selection' have taught to dispense with the
tall fleshy comb, so open to attack.

Our kings of the yard—I never see such
true chanticleers now—had broad rose combs,
very like the flower that bears their name.
They had substantial metallic-black green
breasts and splendid tails, and wore long
handsome capes of hackles, each slender
feather white with a black streak down the

centre, and they moved with a stately pace and Louis XIV.-like grace and courtesy to their brown ladies. They were not amiable to their sons, especially when these last began to perpetrate ridiculous hoarse crows. But it is a happy ordinance of nature that these elders of the yard always go to bed quite early, in full daylight, and may be seen sitting in a row on their perch.

But there is as much difference in character in poultry as in dogs, or, to go further, in human creatures. We had one cock who undertook the care of the half-grown chickens when their mother cast them off too soon; and he used to take them under his wings in the nest at night. Our old Louis XIV. was most courteous to his train of ladies, while others drove them away with one favoured exception.

One hen, too, will be frivolous, always deserting her nest for amusement; another will be clumsy, treading on her chicks ; and a third will be kindly, hovering stray orphans like her own, while her neighbour resents proposals of adoption and drives off all interlopers.   I have heard of a partlet who must have been infected by modern notions.   Her first brood had been ducks, and when her next, of poor little chickens, would not take to the water, she drove them in and drowned them.   Does character grow by domestication, or is it only that we perceive it ? and is there as much individuality in the wild herds of animals, only we do not know them ?   Any way, happy are the memories of the proud discovery of the first egg of the season, pure and white, with a certain almost transparent look around its border when held up to the light.   Or still more delightful it was to detect under the thatch of a low outhouse, hidden amid dry oak leaves, a grand 'stolen nest' of at least a dozen eggs.

LEADEN skies, dry hard atmosphere, with a gray haze over the distance, such is the general character of March. The boys play at marbles, favoured by the hardness of the village street ; people's faces get a stern fixed expression, and their talk is of 'black east wind.'

But the Easter moon, the moon of moons, will soon begin to fill her horns. She often breaks through the haze at night, as the sun cannot do by day, the fact being that his absence makes more equality in heat (or cold) in the air, and therefore there is less opaqueness. The sun towards the end of the month is in Aries, therefore, of course that constellation is invisible now ; but in the winter it was to be distinguished by two large stars, one with a lesser one beside it, leading the zodiacal train. Just now, at night its opposites, Virgo, with her brilliant Spica, and Libra, are the most distinguished constellations. Libra, by the help of one star of its neighbour Scorpio, makes a kind of star-dotted anchor. It is a wonderful and grave thought that on that first Good Friday, the sun who hid his face at noonday, must have been in Aries, the Ram, named long ago in some strange uncomprehended foreboding of the Sacrifice.

Here, too, preparing for the Holy Week, are the withies, the silver buttons of their catkins expanding into the full, fragrant yellow tuft of stamens protruding from tiny scales — pussies and goslings, as happy children call them. They furnish the substitutes for palms, which our village children still wear on Palm Sunday. It is far from inappropriate when we remember that 'willows from the brook' were part of the prescribed booths, made by the Jews at the Feast of Tabernacles, though that was in the autumn. The willows then used were by their traditions to have smooth-edged leaves, resembling a smiling, good-tempered mouth, whereas a rough-edged leaf betokened ill-temper. In some counties, yew branches are used instead of willow, and the tree is called, in consequence, palm.

The yew's dark evergreen branches are all over covered with little buff, dusty balls, that is about every alternate tree, for the yew is diœcious. This is a great country for it. The deep green bushy trees stand at intervals in the hedges separating the fields from the chalk down, flourishing, though their trunks are in a state of dry decay, crumbling away, and sometimes with ferns nestling in their breasts.

A row of them at Brightstone, in the Isle of Wight, is said to have been planted by Bishop Ken, and the path beside them is called 'the Bishop's Walk'; but though the living was held by him, it is doubtful whether he ever lived or walked there much. Near at hand in these parts is the great mushroom-like yew of Twyford Churchyard of unknown age, and with a seat around its gnarled ruddy trunk. It might almost date from the enact-ment of Edward I. for the cherishing of the trees that were to supply the tough yew bows that made the English archers well-nigh invincible.

The glory of March is, however, in favoured places, the daffodils. They have come to be popular favourites now, though I remember when they were despised for being yellow and having no scent, whereas at present they are so much the fashion that the places where they grow need to be guarded from unscrupulous marauders, who pull up roots with the flowers, and it is even said that some farmers mow them on their first appearance to prevent the incursions of trespassers.

For my own part, they have been the delight of my life ever since the days of rushing down, in a funny little round frilled white tippet of checked cambric, to the hazel copse where they nodded in profusion, nay, still nod, or, as Dorothy Wordsworth called it, dance. That copse has pools of water, which encourage the daffodils to be much larger than those on a lighter, thinner soil. What peculiar beauty there is in the six pale petals and the deeper coloured bell, which old-fashioned botanists called the nectary. Call it what we will, the fairy robe, the folding of the bell, the crimping of the edge, and above all, the marvellous subdued glitter upon it, are unequalled, and render it more charming than its white, yellow - eyed congeners, whether called butter-and-eggs, pheasant's eye, or more elegantly, *Poetic narcissus.* It is curious that when cultivated into being double, it should become so much larger, as well as lose all its peculiar gracefulness.

The 'pale primrose' has a longer reign than the daffodil or than the sweet violet, purple or white, according to the soil, or sometimes of a curious undesirable pink. Like most blue flowers the violet 'sports' into white and pink, white being perhaps more frequent than purple, and forming the staple of those school - children's 'Sunday nosegays,' so charming in intention and theory, but in practice so often squeezed so tightly together as to lose their bright beauty, and have their own odours stifled in that of hot pews, whereas a white violet smiling on a bank in its freshness is a sight for sair e'en !

Not that this is a very favoured country

in the way of *Viola odorata.* We are not destitute, but they are few and far between, and in the clay soil copses where they grow, many a hope of gathering them is disappointed by the anemone bud. Otherwise there would be not a word to say against the beloved *Anemone nemorosa*—the wind-flower —or, as the village children unpoetically call it, 'smell foxes.' It is a more universal flower than even the primrose, starring the woods with delicate pearly blossoms, each standing simply between two delicately pinnated winged leaves, on the stem, rising from the roots which creep in an endless network underground. Here is a congregation all wearing a purple stain; there the whole party are pearly white. If they are pulled up from their junction with the creeping roots, they will last for some time in water. The garden shows their blue brother, the Alpine anemone, which is almost identical in growth ; also the gorgeous Pyrenean anemone, brilliant scarlet with a black or purple centre, so dazzling that more truly than the rose does its ' hue angry and brave, bid the rash gazer wipe his eye.' Whether it is the rule, I cannot tell, but here, if a garden cherishes the blue flower of the Alps, it seems alien to the scarlet pride of the Pyrenees, and *vice versâ*. The little *Anemone hepatica*, blue or pink, which peeps from the snow in Scandinavia, seems to have an affinity for cottage gardens—perhaps it is because it is less liable to be disturbed by gardeners. The little Banksia roses, which are not roses at all, but an Australian creeper, named after Sir Joseph Banks, are putting out their little uncalyxed buds all over the house, trusting not to be nipped by frost. In the hedges, among their heart-shaped, sometimes black-spotted leaves, rise the folded spathes of the arum. These will by and by expand into a hood, wherein arises a column, crimson or white, surrounded at the base by white beadings and little threads. These are really the flowers, one circle male, the other female, and the hairs between divide them and carry the pollen to the bare germs, which by and by will become scarlet acrid berries. The old nicknames are Cuckoo-pint and Wake Robin; but I knew them as lords and ladies in their coach, the red ones being lords, the white ladies. This is, however, a corruption of Our Lord and Our Lady. Devon makes it a lamb in a pulpit, and it is the English passion-flower with pillar, scourges, nails, blood, and a final arch of glory.

When I first saw the great white arum, properly a Caladium, I felt as if my beloved lady were there glorified, and it is in every way a suitable Easter decoration for churches, only it ought never to have been called a lily.

It grows all over marshes at the Cape ; and it is curious that, while the berries are acrid and poisonous (one of the many sorts is used to poison tigers), the tubers afford the best starch-powder or arrowroot, which is really arum-root !

The terrible storm of March 1891 held back the spring unseasonably. It is to be feared that the tendency to inflation, which calls a moderate-sized shop a mammoth warehouse, and a selling-off a tremendous sacrifice, will soon term every shower a blizzard ; but this really was one, and its doings on Dartmoor and the adjacent parts were really terrific, devastating woods, burying cattle, blocking up deep Devonshire lanes—so that supplies of food were cut off for three or four days, while travellers on the railway were in a still more piteous condition—weather-bound for twenty hours at a time with nothing to eat but, perchance, samples of Cadbury's cocoa, or Devonshire cream on the way to a friend.

Here the storm came in a comparatively exhausted state, but it was bad enough, and greatly interfered with March Confirmations. One clergyman came tandem, bringing as many of his flock as he could; but it was well that the whole system has been altered in these days of increased activity and earnestness, so that few parties of candidates have to go far from their own parish church.

An old man—he would be over a hundred years old were he alive now—used to relate that he first saw 'his missus' at a great Confirmation at the Cathedral; but he waited for her until he had two pigs in his stye: 'And then, sir, I knew I was a match for any woman!'

Triennial Confirmations at central parishes became the rule, but though the distances were not long, the expedition could hardly fail of being a somewhat excited and noisy one when lads and lasses had to make their way unguarded by their clergy ; and such a thing has been known as a boy pulling out the tail-board of the cart going up a hill, and letting the screaming, giggling girls down into the mud. Indeed, when Bishop Samuel Wilberforce began to confirm from parish to parish, an innkeeper possessed of an assembly-room threatened an action for thus preventing the ball that used to be given, when so many young people were assembled.

There is far better hope of a permanent impression being made where the gatherings are smaller, and the churches easily reached, so as to have room for parents and god-parents. Long did we hold out against veils, as a greater excitement, and possibly an encumbrance to unaccustomed heads ; but when caps became useless afterwards, and veils came to make a distinction between rich and poor, it seemed well to keep a stock of squares of tulle to lend on the occasion; and very fair and gracious is the spectacle of the bent heads under their white drapery.

I had written snowy—but in 1891 we had had too much of literal snow to wish to use the term figuratively. It lingered long in banks where it drifted, and kept back the spring. Nevertheless, a flock of no less than forty water-wagtails suddenly appeared walking on this little grass-plot one evening just after sunset on the 25th of March. They seemed to be too much tired to wag their tails, though a few made little flights after insects, and they gradually disappeared into the shrubs, where they roosted—and doubtless continued their journey early the next day. The wagtails of Southern England are stay-at-home birds, but those further north migrate even to Africa when their food of flies begins to fail them, and this troop must have been on their way home, since they came back in March.   They were pied wagtails; the yellow species, properly called gray wagtails, is not often seen here.   The yellow wagtail—so named—is more rare, and less yellow than the 'gray,' a pretty creature, not uncommon in Devonshire, though the pied species is far more frequent here.   Dishwasher is the Hampshire name for these pretty birds of graceful form and lively air; Lady Dishwash is their title in Kent.   They are *Lavandière* in France, and their Hindoo name has the same meaning.

The chalk downs which rise to the northward gave a charming place of exercise in my younger days.   There was a mile and a quarter of turnpike road first, but the down itself was exquisite enjoyment.   There were two pits, grass-grown, whose sloping sides were play - places; but best of all was the further side facing the river.   Subsidence had

formed the ground into a succession of ter-
races, the highest up being also the steepest
slope. Here some shepherd had cut out a
rude sun-dial in the short turf, and in another
place there was a magnificent giant in the
same style of art as was to be seen on barn
doors before the compulsory schoolmaster
was abroad. There was, moreover, a flight of
what were called steps, but were really holes
for the toes cut out all the way up the height,
affording fine training in climbing. Our
delight was to launch round flints from the
top, and watch down how many of the slopes
they would bound before they stopped on a
terrace. There was also a charming view
over the valley of the river—its rich, green
water meadows and the clusters of trees, the
church tower, and far on beyond, Winchester
Cathedral.

By and by the railway spread its length
as a chalk embankment along beside the

river, but at first it did not disturb the breezy solitude of the down, till a little station was raised with a corrugated iron roof to its stair-case, exactly like, when seen from above, the restoration of some hideous pre - Adamite monster, such as the plesiosaurus. And now the down is a thoroughfare, and villas and all other imports of a station have sprung up, and the free delight is no more—only remaining as a memory.

Those stones which we rolled down were, when round, no doubt fossil echini, or sea-urchins — shepherd's crowns as our people call them—the more perfect ones very like the present heart echinus, and with the same pentagonal star traced on the under side.

Besides these, our chalk produces the Cardium, much like the cockle-shell of the present sea-shore, and lamp shells (*Tere-bratulæ*), whose like is to be seen in existence still, bi - valves, with one valve curved over the hinge, and the other valve perforated to allow of a silken cable being put forth, mooring it to the rock. Some of the species are wonderfully like the classic lamp. These all are just rare enough to be treasure trove.

APRIL

In spite of its showery reputation, April is often quite as beset by Eurus as is March, and shares therewith not merely the grayness of 'black east wind,' called by the mysterious name of 'blight,' but also those enamelled days of intense brightness, when every laurel and ivy leaf absolutely glitters in the sunshine, and the small celandines open their many-petalled crowns, so as to be almost too resplendent for the eye.

The cold winter has painted the ivy leaves in a curious manner. Every variety of red and purple is to be found on (oh, forgive me! it has no more reasonable name) the parenchyma of the leaves, while the veins remain green, so that there is a beautiful regular pattern. These are the old leaves, ready to drop off in a quiet way when the new tender ones are ready to take up their work; but there is no leaf so cheerful in old age as the ivy. An eccentric creature it is, with that endless variety of palmate, pointed leaves while it is climbing, and the entire ones after it has reached the summit and become an 'ivy bush,' bearing in autumn its round heads of pale green blossoms, to be succeeded by the black fruit to become in spring the birds' staple fare, just when other berries are exhausted. The little claws on the stem, by which it mounts, have no familiar likenesses except in the Virginian creepers. There is the satisfaction in gathering wreaths of ivy, that it is a benefit to the tree to disembarrass it of its clothing.

I have just been to pay my annual respects to the Green Hellebore (*Helleborus viridis*) which is one of the semi-varieties of which we are proud.   It grows in wide-spreading patches from its creeping roots in a hazel copse, putting up its green drooping bells—little green Christmas roses — in fact, before its very handsome crop of root-leaves.   The so-called flower is really the calyx ; the corolla is only some tiny scales around the cluster of many stamens, which by their growth on the receptacle stamp it as of the poisonous race—a witch plant, indeed, though not so much marked as its brother *Helleborus fœtidus*, which has purple spots and is more rare.

This Green Hellebore grows in a close hedgerow, containing a path up which the Danes are said to have marched—if so, they must have gone in single file.   It turns out of another historical lane, which is said to have been the route of the cart of the charcoal burner Purkiss, when carrying the corpse of the Red King to Winchester.

So averred, on the authority of his grand-mother, an old farmer in the days when farmers wore long drab coats and leather gaiters. Not only he, but his house and farmyard are gone now, though the meadow still remains, the only one where grows the Greater bistort (*Polygonum bistorta*).

The hedgerow lane is a wonderful place for flowers; not merely the primrose and anemone, but the extraordinary varieties of violets. The dog violet and the sweet one have perhaps crossed, for here is an intensely blue one, not the regular purple colour, but with more of blue; here another rather large and of most delicate texture, with more of pink; here a small gray one (*V. calcarea*); none of them with the little white fringes that mark the true *Viola canina*. Six sorts are actually found in this one walk.[1]

---

[1] *V. odorata* (the sweet), *V. hirta* (the hairy), *V. calcarea* (the chalky), *V. canina* (the dog), *V. Riviniana* (the snake), *V. Reichenbachiana.*

Pant, pant! Cough, cough! That noise tells of ploughing. There is an engine at each end of the adjoining field, and a little plough travelling up and down between them in the furrow, apparently of its own accord. Happily there are some farms still left which afford the pleasant sight of the sleek horses plodding before their ploughs, all the better if there be a dappled gray to show out on the rich brown earth of a sloping field.

But the measured thump, thump of the flail on the barn floor, which warmed the labourer on winter days, and kept up his pay, that is a sound which the younger generation have never heard; nor have they seen the curious winnowing machine, with its four fans of canvas which used to revolve in the barns.

The threshing machine, with its engine and lengthy apparatus, makes its rounds among the farms, and its whirr is the familiar sound. The hostility to it as the enemy of the poor man's labour, which greeted it sixty years since, is an absolute matter of history. The machine-breaking did not affect these parts to any great extent, as well as I remember, but the Reform Bill riots made themselves felt. We were from home at the time, and only heard of bands of men being stirred up to go from house to house demanding food and arms, though they did not here do any actual mischief. It was said that here only two men avoided joining them, and of these, one went about his work as usual, the other hid himself in a wood. There was, however, much rick-burning in the northern division of the county, and in the general alarm the nurse of one family used to keep a quantity of pepper by her bedside, wherewith to blind any assailant!

There was an assize afterwards, where there were many condemnations. Years after, the brother of one of the victims spoke with remarkable acquiescence in his fate: 'Never could be quiet, sir. Best thing to do with such chaps as that to string 'em up.'

But it all was brought home to us, for our nurse was sister to two of the condemned. They were respectable men of some education, and their sentence was commuted to transportation for life — real transportation to Botany Bay, whence they used to write at intervals letters in wonderfully minute penmanship, all across the single quarto sheet, each word so small that they could scarcely be read without a magnifier, and the lines so close together that a black ruled paper had to be kept under the one in course of being read. Sometimes anecdotes were imparted to us, of which I only remember a story of a little kangaroo which jumped into a hunter's open shirt, taking it for the maternal pouch. Convicts like these two brothers were sure to thrive. One married, and probably his descendants are by this time among the aristocracy of Sydney.

Machines have destroyed much of the picturesqueness of farming, but in many respects they have improved the condition of the labourer, and especially of his wife. Yet perhaps the intelligence—not in books, but in common things—of the villager has not advanced so much as might have been expected.

Every one used to stay and do home work. Now the enterprising ones go away, leaving their less adventurous brother to follow the plough, so that the shrewd and thoughtful men who were devoted to the home agriculture, their master's right hand, and full of racy sayings, have become few and far between.

Still, there is more cultivation, and it is

to be hoped therewith more observation. The old-fashioned country lad was the most unknowing creature in the world as to the things around him. In the early days of trying to open peasant children's minds, I have heard of a blank book placed at a school, where the children were to record any observation of natural objects. One adventurous scholar set down—

'Saw the sun drawing water,' John Smith. Then followed—

'Saw the sun drawing water,' Mary Jones; and so on, to the bottom of the page, without a single deviation in these experiences.

'Have you heard the nightingale yet?' asked the clergyman of a boy here some forty years ago.

'Please, sir, I don't know how he hollers,' was the answer.

I have also heard that 'they birds hollered so that one could not sleep.'

They—the nightingales—are just come, the cocks singing to pass the time till the ladies arrive. Slender creatures they are, with whitish breasts, and ruddy backs as they open their wings. One year we had a nest close to the house, and the nightingale sang incessantly, from nine in the morning till about eight at night, and again from ten at night till eight in the morning. Then he used to come out on the lawn for his breakfast, and a John Bull of a robin as regularly used to charge the poor foreign minstrel, and, though smaller, drive him to a bush, where he sang a few notes, then tried again to get his worms. Some nightingales have much better notes than others. Bishop Samuel Wilberforce, a great bird lover, used to interpret their song into ' My heart is broke, broke, broke! I'm awfully jolly! I'm awfully jolly, jolly '—but this hardly accounts for the curious gurgling sound.

The cuckoo's curious mechanical-sounding note has likewise begun, and that of the Wry-neck, or cuckoo's mate, so very hard to see, as it always keeps on the side of the tree opposite to the spectator, or rather non-spectator.

And there is a delicate green veil over the woods, towards the end of the month—such a veil of tender greenery as April alone can show—every bush putting forth tiny, dainty leaves. The Larch trees show an ineffably lovely colour, and bear their future cones, in tiny crimson, among those pointed needles, which seem to make them like the Yew, a link with the great pine tribe. The Larch (*Larix europæa*) is not an English native, but was brought from the Alps in 1629. The Horse-chestnuts have cast off the gummy cases of their buds, and have pushed out their spikes and the pendant leaves, which have been so carefully cottoned up all the winter.

The pink Almond, the white Apricot, the rosy Nectarine, and blushing Peach all unfold their blossoms, happy if the frost does not nip them, though probably the fruit is all the better flavoured for an occasional interval in bearing.

In the hedges the Sloe, or blackthorn (*Prunus spinosa*), emulates hoar-frost, and relieves our minds as to the blackthorn winter having done its worst. Its thorns are held to be peculiarly venomous, and to make wounds difficult to heal.

The small Celandine (*Ficaria verna*) is twinkling in the hedges in starry constellations. The numerous petals have a most brilliant polish, but they close too rapidly out of the sun to be available for gathering.

And in the woods there are sheets of bright green Dog's mercury (*Mercurialis perennis*), golden rivers of King-cups (*Caltha palustris*) in every boggy place or ditch, and on the mossy banks, that exquisite thing the Wood-sorrel (*Oxalis acetosa*), red-stemmed, trefoil-leaved, white-flowered, with dainty purple veins—a perfect creature. And there is the first butterfly, all sulphur. Here, too, in the roads and around manure-heaps begin to appear creatures unwelcome to most—namely, snakes. They change their skins about this time. One may find the disused garment wound in and out amid the rough bents of grass by means of which the creatures have pulled themselves out, though no one has yet seen the operation. The old skin is perfectly transparent, with a network forming the pattern, and even a skin which has covered the eyes.

The poor Slow-worm, or blind-worm, so often killed as a snake, ought to be cherished, for its food is slugs. It is really no snake at all, but a skink, and perfectly harmless. It may be known by having a less developed head and neck, and, when young, a V upon its head.

The V is often supposed to mark the viper; but this is a mistake. The viper's mark is a chain of dark diamonds down the back. We call it in the country an adder— an odd corruption, or rather confusion, of the 'n' with the article; just as we have made an apron out of a napron, from nap (cloth), so from the universal word natron or nadre for a serpent, we have developed an adder. It is not often that the viper does much harm, though I have known a pony die from being bitten in the mouth, and suffocated by the swelling; and our poor old dog was for some days in a state of much suffering from a bite near the ear, but he recovered, though I suspect the injury was the foundation of his final illness.

Persons bitten have a good deal to go through. They should be kept awake, and ammonia and sweet oil applied as soon as possible, and no harm finally ensues.

As to the common snake, it too often suffers for the venom of the viper, as well as from the natural unreasoning loathing that fulfils literally the prediction, 'I will put enmity between thee and the woman, and between thy seed and her seed,'—the outward shrinking from the animal marking what should be the inward shrinking from the evil spirit.

But those who have patience to watch may sometimes see curious sights. I have seen a snake swim across a small pond, with its head just above the water; I have also seen one climb the trunk of a young oak tree —not twisting round, but zig-zagging its body, as it were.

Once, too, as a snake was crossing the lawn, it was pursued and driven, whereupon, in order to be free to move, it opened its jaws and emitted a frog, then wriggled away rapidly. The frog lay pulled out at full length, a ghastly spectacle, and we were just about to have it removed when—behold, it drew in first one leg, then the other, contracted itself into a respectable frog, and hopped off as if nothing had been amiss!

When I first remember, there was an old man who professed to eat adders. He used to send in a message that he had a nice one, and might he have a bit of bacon to boil with it? We suspected the bacon was the chief part of the viper broth. He lived in what was then the workhouse, a large, untidy brick house, which gratuitously lodged the aged and infirm, and indeed, whole feckless families, without the slightest supervision, and the parish likewise paid them enough for their maintenance. Those were the days of the old Poor Law. The hero of the viper broth was dead, luckily for him, before the days of Unions and discipline.   The feckless family had departed to Manchester, which was then crying out for 'hands,' and thence they wrote letters, where the first person plural was spelt 'whee.'   I should think a half-witted man born there, still an inmate of the Union, was the sole survivor.

The water-wagtail, here called dish-washer, comes tapping upon the windows in search of the insects within, called out by the sunshine, a performance very distressing to superstitious folk, who think the tap-tap is a call.   The same tapping is sometimes made by the little bird on the church windows outside, or in.   Has any one ob-served the different manners of birds captive in church?   Robins will take up their abode there, no doubt finding plenty of food, and behave with great propriety, and their song fits in, as St. Francis would have liked to hear his 'little sisters.'   Old starlings some-

times learn the way in and out by the roof,
come in and go out again composedly; but
when their young ones are hatched in the
ivy outside, every arrival of the parents with
food creates a wonderful chattering, hissing,
and commotion. When they fly, and first
blunder into the church, they dart about
in terror, and hammer at every space of clear
glass, but as they are clever birds they will
find their way out, if doors and windows are
left open. Blackbirds and swallows get
hopelessly confused, but happily their visits
are rare.

Starlings are some of our most beautiful
birds when seen close, with their purple
necks and green wings bedropped with gold;
but, like true English folk, they do not show
their splendours at a distance, and their form
is less elegant than the blackbird's, from
whom they may be easily distinguished, as
besides that we know 'the deep black yellow-

beaked cock, and his brown termagant wife.'
He hops while the starling runs, when both
are equally busy seeking worms on the shaven
lawn.   Stares, to use their old name, have
an infinite variety of conversational notes,
and must greatly enjoy society, as they flock
together in the winter, often in the train of
rooks, and at roosting time sit twittering and
chatting in the trees as if talking over the
day's adventures.   In the spring they pair
off for family cares, in holes or under
roofs, but apparently all join again in
autumn.

There is an old French fairy-tale which,
I believe, is one of those illustrated by the
curious sheets of coloured 'cuts' sold at fairs
from time immemorial, where Berniquet the
wicked boy is doomed, for acts of cruelty, to
be devoured by a starling.   At every stage
of his history all the birds cry out 'Berniquet for the starling!'   But he takes no

warning, and is finally eaten up by an enormous starling—a startling catastrophe!

There was another young gentleman called Brimborion, no higher than a boot, who was of a lovely complexion whenever he did a good action, and orange-coloured whenever he was wicked. Most of the stories were tragic, except one of a dear little Henry, who scaled a dreadful mountain to obtain healing herbs for his sick mother.

Does not every one cherish the memory of a few precious books of their youth, or even of some not valued then? I should like to see once more the square, green spelling-book, which began with columns of ‘B-a-t—Bat,’ and ended with a useful poem on English history, beginning—

> William the First, for his valour well known,
> By the battle of Hastings ascended the throne;
> His Acts were all made in the Norman tongue,
> And at eight every evening the curfew was rung,

> At which every subject, by royal desire,
> Extinguished his candle, and put out his fire.

Messrs. Griffith and Farren have reproduced some of these old friends, especially Marmaduke Multiply, with pictures appropriate to the rhymes that clenched the memory of the multiplication table.

> Five times six are thirty,
> She's tall as any fir-tree.

Tall and stately she walks along, in a light-green gown, and coal-scuttle, yellow bonnet.

> Ten times ten a hundred,
> How he got there they wondered—

the antecedents being left to the pictures. ' He,' in this case, is a donkey looking out of a sash window; 'they' are two children laughing at him.

But children are supposed to learn multiplication rationally by proof on the abacus frame, or by the 'gifts' of the Kindergarten, and mere memory and jingle are despicable. There is to be no more of the strain of attention over what one of Miss Edgeworth's beloved children calls 'a long ladder of figures' in long division. We are to work by reason instead of by memory. There is much good sense in this. Only how is the important lesson of application for duty's sake to what is distasteful to be learnt ?

The first school I remember was taught by the regular old dame of Shenstone's verse, in a high-crowned black bonnet, worn permanently ; a buff, spotted handkerchief over her shoulders, tucked into a checked apron. She presided over about a dozen children in her own cottage, as picturesque as herself, sitting in the chimney-corner with her rod. But the teaching was of the very smallest description.

Then came an attempt at another school

of a superior kind, in a house built for the purpose of mud, rough-cast and brick floored. Reading was taught and needle-work, for a penny a week, after six years old, but writing and arithmetic were extras, not encouraged, for there was a rooted belief that if maids could write, they would write love-letters. So, no doubt, they do, but they write a good deal besides which keeps up the bonds of family affection. This very March, on one of the first relenting days, I came upon an aunt sending a bunch of violets to her niece in a London service to be worn on her confirmation day. Who would have dreamt of such an attention when that girl's grandmother was one of the penny scholars ?

The boys went out to work so young that the wonder is that they learnt anything at all, and the eldest girl was always kept at home as nurse, growing tall, uncouth, and dense.

We have gone through the permission to learn the three R's up to their becoming a necessity, and that greatest R of all—Religion—for the sake of which alone we taught in old times, has a hard matter to hold its own.

MAY

NEVER did Wordsworth sing a truer or a sweeter note than in his address to May. True, she often sets in, as people say, with 'her accustomed severity,' and cold rain is falling, or east wind is blowing, and blighting frost has turned brown the green shoots of potatoes and pease, and made limp rags of the first premature endeavours of the oaks. Yet still there always are some perfect days of the poets.

> And what if thou, sweet May, hast known
>   Mishap by worm and blight,
> If expectations newly blown
>   Have perished in thy sight;
> If loves and joys, while up they sprung,
>   Were caught as in a snare:

> Such is the lot of all the young,
> However bright and fair.

Of all others, be the weather what it will, May is the month of singing of birds. The larks are quivering and shouting high up in the sky long before sunrise, the thrushes and blackbirds take up the strain, and though the nightingale ceases for an hour or two, and only resumes after his breakfast, the whole air is full of twitterings, chirpings, and songs. The turtle-dove groans, the wood-pigeon invites Taffy, ' Take *two* cows, Taffy! Taffy, take *two*!' the tame pigeon mourns complacently on our roofs, and the African dove coo-*roos*, bows, and laughs in our cages.

Each has its own voice. The turtle is a small creature, keeping in pairs, not flocks, and with the ring round the neck speckled with darkest green and white, so as to give a chess-board effect. It builds in low bushes, the proverbial untidy nest of the dove kind, and is much less common than that handsome and devouring creature, the cushat or wood-pigeon, the ring-dove proper, so called on account of the white collar very conspicuous on its gray throat, as it flies out with a great rush.

Shenstone wrote—

> I have found out a gift for my fair,
> 　I have found where the wood-pigeons breed ;
> But let me the plunder forbear,
> 　She will say 'twas a barbarous deed.

And it would have been an unsatisfactory one likewise, unless his 'fair' had uncommon powers, for the wood-pigeon is an untamable creature.　I have known one rescued, with an injured wing, almost in its infancy, bred up in the same cage with a number of doves, yet never ceasing to be terrified at human approach, and tumbling about in a one-sided way, quite distressing to behold.

Wood-pigeons are not plentiful enough here to be very mischievous, though there are enough of them for them to be considered as enemies by the farmer; but their residence in the ivy, their voices, the best of those of all our English pigeons, their beautiful forms, and delicate subdued colouring, make them great favourites with the no-farmer.

As to the mourning of a dove, that proverb is only due to its murmuring voice ; and the constancy of the widowed dove is equally a poetical fiction. The African dove does not mourn at all, but bows and goes 'majoring' about to very lively tunes of its own, and, moreover, indulges in peals of laughter, whence its specific name of Risoria, the laughing dove. It is very hardy, and, when there is sufficient range apart from villages, will fly about and nest in the trees, though too often molested by hawks.

The yaffil laughed loud.

Not that here we call our grand green wood-
pecker by that name, when he scuds over
the grass, and shows for a moment his red
head, and the green back that so perfectly
assimilates with the colour of the moss on
decayed stumps, his larder and his domicile.
The gray lichen evidently strikes the note of
colouring of his much rarer cousin ; whose
feathers, black chequered with white, I have
only once come upon, and that was in
Devonshire, where they call him the French
magpie.   In Norway and Germany he is the
Gertrude-bird, from a legend that a loaf was
refused to our Blessed Lord by a woman
named Gertrude, who was, therefore, trans-
formed into the black-and-white, red-capped
bird, and condemned to seek food between the
wood and the bark.   As Geir-Trude means
spear or war-maid, and was a Valkyr's title, it is
probable that, like the black, scarlet-crowned
thrush (?) of South America, it was once a

war-bird. The robin of the United States is a red-breasted thrush. So is the pretty whole-ringed ouzel of Devonshire riversides, while our proper thrushes—called in western peasant tongue 'drishes'—are the big, speckle-breasted missel, and the equally speckled song-thrush, which almost rivals the nightingale in some of its notes, and builds a nest neatly lined with mud compost, and lays eggs of indescribably lovely blue-green. The good old Warden Barter of Winchester used to tell a story of two valiant thrushes, whether song or missel I am not quite sure, who, thinking a peacock in dangerous proximity to their nest, charged him both together full on the throat, and knocked him down. The blackbird is really a thrush. The eggs of his rusty-brown wife are more variable, and less beautiful, generally spotted all over with brown. For two or three years this garden was tenanted by a blackbird with a white feather on each side of his tail, indeed we thought the feathers multiplied after the moulting ; but our observations were cut short in a melancholy manner.   Poor Mr. Whitetail, as we called him, was discussing worms on the lawn with his brown lady, when another ouzel-cock, entirely black of hue, appeared on the scene. The faithless dame could have had no taste for singularity, for together she and the new-comer chased Mr. Whitetail over the tall quick-set hedge, and we never saw him more!

May Day is sometimes all that is lovely and genial, when the children and their flowers are all that their ideal should be. Cold east wind does not matter so much to them, but showers make their rounds dismal work.   The custom varies a good deal, according as it has been fostered.   Once boys in Devonshire were licensed to drench with water from cows' horns whoever did not wear a spray of maythorn. I can just remember a lady coming in, indignant and dripping. In many towns there is a Jack-in-the-Green, attended by a rabble rout; in many villages, chiefly in the northern counties, a doll in the centre of an arbour of flowers is carried round and exhibited in return for halfpence, probably being a remnant of honour to an image of the Blessed Virgin on the opening of the month of Mary. In the south, however, it has often dwindled to small children wandering about with an untidy bunch of king-cups and cuckoo flowers at the end of a stick, quavering shrilly out—

> April's gone,
> May's come,
> Come and see our gar*land*;

and halfpence being thrown out till the stock of them and of patience was exhausted, and the whole affair discouraged.

We have found the best way in our parts to be to sanction the whole school going together under some efficient guardian with one general money - box, the proceeds of which, when divided, have always proved more satisfactory than those of individual effort; or, at one parish, all is spent in a general tea, which, of course, gives delight. We also encourage the best garlands with a special prize, and this promotes the keeping them beautiful. Last year a child named Violet had a small garland, a circlet entirely made of the snake violet from the copse. After it had made its rounds, it was set upon her brother's grave.

We also make a May Queen, not the fairest maiden, as in song, but the youngest girl in the infant school, who appears in a white dress kept for the occasion, flower-wreathed, as well as her hat.

The rathe primrose is on the wane before

May is over; but its sister, the cowslip, is in its prime, to my mind, the most deliciously scented of all flowers, above all when formed into a cowslip ball, or tisty-tosty, as in some places it is called, though in the midland counties the flowers are paigles. There is a rich softness in the petal; and no wonder they were Titania's guardsmen.

> The cowslips tall her pensioners be,
> In their gold coats spots you see;
> Those be rubies, fairy favours,
> In those freckles live their savours.

And such savours!

But our cowslips, beloved though they be, cannot compete with those of Berkshire and Oxfordshire in size. They are hardly ever found in Devon, being dependent on soil.

The woods are, however, the great glory. Here is a glade which, if shown in a painting, would be pronounced incredible, for the ground is purple-blue with wild hyacinth, the canopy overhead of young birch leaves is tender yellow-green, often lighter in colour, with the sun through it, and between the slender trunks are shining silver-white; the boughs—what can be seen of them—dark russet-red. The oaks are of every imaginable tint of brownish-yellow and green, no two alike, the beeches releasing their neatly-crimped leaves from their brown cases, the larches of unimaginable green beauty, and here and there comes out the tall white cone of the beauteous blossom of the wild cherry.

And in the hedgerows, on the heaths, wherever there is room, stretch the hawthorn branches, snow-laden, as it were, with their pure white blossoms, with rounded, pin-like buds, and within, the dainty stamens, dark as to the filaments, and with red anthers. The often gnarled and stunted old trees come out for the time in bridal splendour.

A flyman, who was used to spend his days in driving up and down streets, when once he had to take a lady home through a park in all its glory of maythorns, could not help, when setting her down, saying, 'Thank you, ma'am, for my beautiful drive!' A pinkish tint comes over the blossoms towards their fall; but I much prefer them to the pink and crimson thorns of cultivation.

The glory is not only of the thorns. The cherry orchards, where they are in favour, make white sheets. Pear trees, the largest of all both as to treasure and blossom, make splendid features, and the apple, with its deep pink buds and delicately-tinted petals, has the fairest of all the blossoms.

The gold chains of the laburnum, the rich clusters of the lilac, join their bright beauties. The Laburnum (*Cytisus laburnum*) came to us, in Queen Elizabeth's days, from Switzerland and Dauphiné, where it is sometimes called *Arc-bois*, and sometimes by the appropriate name of Beau Trefoile. Though the branches snap easily, to the discomfiture of those who strain after the drooping gold, it was used to make excellent bows; and though the outside wood is yellow, the inside heart wood is so black as to be called false-ebony. It is in curious accordance with the blackness of the seeds, and of the delicate dark pencilling on the standard of the flower. The Lilac (*Syringa vulgaris*) came from Persia, and Henry VIII. had it in his garden at Nonsuch; but it has been found growing wild in Transylvania.

Nor can I go further without a note of love to the Gueldres rose (*Viburnum opulus*). In the hedges it is graceful with its vine-shaped leaves, and corymbs of white flowers, small in the centre and fruitful, but wreathed round with large, handsome white barren blossoms. All honour to Gueldres, which

first seems to have shown these barren
flowers as snowballs.

> Her silver globes, light as the foamy surf,
> That the wind severs from the broken wave.

Snowballs are among the delights of
country childhood. To me they always
recall the remembrance of the ecstasy it used
to be to see the Whit-Monday procession of
the village club, when the two tall banners,
one of pink, the other of blue, glazed calico,
were decked at the summit each with a peony
and a snowball, and the Friendly Society
'walked,' as it was technically called. Each
member carried a blue staff tipped with red,
and had a blue ribbon round his tall hat, and
almost all wore the old white round frock.
The big drum was beaten lustily at their head,
a few wind instruments brayed, all the rabble
rout of the village stepped after them, and
it was certainly a picturesque specimen of
genuine village sports, perhaps the more so

because the procession was, at the best, straggling and knock-kneed and often unsteady. Yet it filled the childish mind with an exultation and delight which is droll to recollect now, and the enthusiasm of singing the 133rd Psalm, Old Version—

> O what a happy thing it is,
> And joyful FOR to see,
> Brethren to dwell together in
> Friendship and unitee.
>
> 'Tis like the precious ointment *that*
> Was poured on Aaron's head,
> Ran down his beard, and o'er his robes
> Its costly moisture shed.
>
> And as the lower ground doth drink
> The dew of Hermon's hill,
> And Sion with his silver drops
> The fields with fruit doth fill,
>
> Even so the Lord doth pour on them
> His blessings manifold,
> Whose hearts and minds sincerely do
> This knot fast keep and hold.

And oh! the odour of the church—a mixture of beery and tobaccoey human nature together with that of the fading young greenery of infant beech and larch boughs with which, even in those days, Whitsuntide decoration was kept up. Only very youthful and very rural nostrils could accept it as part of the festivity.

Afterwards there were banqueting and cricket on the village green upon the hill, and too much of that which was politely called 'breaking out at tide time,' popularly considered as a Saturnalia, not interfering with a character for steadiness and sobriety.

So it was a melancholy affair after all. The investment was anything but a safe one. The meetings for payment were at the public-house, and involved cups of beer each time, and when the elder members began to grow old and pressed heavily on 'the box,' the younger ones voted to 'break it up.' Too often this resulted in drinking it up; and men who had saved for thirty or forty years were left destitute of the provision for age.

Attempts were made to induce the men to invest in Government securities, but these were not quite comprehensible enough; and besides, the attraction of 'walking' and the gala day were lacking.   At the present time, the prudent are divided between the Foresters, who, as every one knows, keep their great day with green banners and ribbons, in great numbers generally at the county town, and the County Friendly Society, whose carefully calculated tables they have become better able to appreciate, and which affords them a holiday, band, procession, and feast, much more decorous and civilised than their grandfathers would have relished.

The hedgerows and the very grass in the fields are growing visibly from day to day, and the earlier sorts are showing their exquisite blossoms, the chaffy scales arranged in tossing plume, aigrette or spike, and hanging out their thread-like filaments and double-barbed anthers, too frail to be carried home in full perfection, though the actual skeleton will so long endure.

There is the Quiver grass (*Briza media*) known by many names—Quaker's, Quiver grass, Timothy grass, and in French as *Langues de femme*. So slender is its stem, as well as the branches, that it is not easy to detect it at first, but once stoop down to a piece and there is a whole fairy forest of the tremulous heads, each branchlet bearing a purple-tinted chaffy blossom, with the pale buff anthers protruding. They grow mixed with *Chrysanthemum leucanthemum,* the flower that in my younger days was contempt-uously called 'a great horse daisy,' more civilly an ox-eye, but is come into fashion as a moon daisy or even a Marguerite. It has not the crimson tips nor the blushing air of modesty of the real daisy, about which people quote poetry, though they exterminate it from their lawns till it is quite a treat to see it whitening some neglected plot.

But who would wish for a fairer though all too fleeting nosegay than can be made of ox-eye and bright rose campion, deepened with quiver grass, with here and there a spike of purple orchis (*O. mascula*), or paler meadow orchis (*maculata*), and the little brown-winged orchis (*Morio*), always with the striped wings, but with the lip varying from deep purple to pink or white. How wonderful the orchis is with all its kindred can hardly be told. It is one of the plants over which its admiring cultivators become nearly insane, and an occasional sight of the freakish wonders they import enlarges one's mind—the swarms of white and purple butterfly flowers, and above all, the pure white-dove flowers imported from South America.

The curious arrangement is nowhere better seen than in the purple orchis (*mascula*), whose black-spotted leaves are among the first tokens of spring, and which country-folk call by the unpleasant name of Dead Men's Fingers, probably on account of the tubers of the root. There may be seen the ribbed germ which looks like a foot-stalk, and whose stigma is the expanded lip, while under the real petals, which form a sort of helmet, is the single stamen, two-celled, and with an abortive one on each side. It is closed, but contains a sticky fluid full of pollen, which on provocation will burst out and communicate, not with its own germ, but with another germ in the spike in which the orchis proper always grows.

We cannot part from woodland haunts without a word of the bluebell. It may be correct, but is uncongenial, to call it a wild hyacinth, and if the slender hare-bell (*Campanula rotundifolia*) is the bluebell· of Scotland, England may be allowed her own *Hyacinthus nonscriptus*—this last odd name is due to the absence of the two letters AI for woe, which Apollo is said to have inscribed on the root of the plant that sprang from the relics of his friend Hyacinthus. Nothing can be further from sorrow than those rich deep bluebells hanging in such clusters on their stems.   There is a drooping grace in the bells, and in the whole outline of the plant, that puts to shame the cultivated stiff top-heavy hyacinth of Dutchmen and of gardeners, known by endless names, and fetching fabulous prices.   One stem, bending so modestly under its weight of delicately curved bells with their deep purple hearts, is worth all the prize yellow or green (?) beauties of a gardener's catalogue.

Mr. Wallace has said that in spite of the splendours of tropical plants, England is the country for real sheets and masses of colour, while M. Taine declares that the broad extent of bright hues is to blame for Englishwomen's gaudy taste in dress. Certainly I have seen a glade in a wood perfectly dazzling in its May dress. Above all was the delicate green gold of young birch leaves glittering in sunlight on black twigs, below were slender silver pillars of young trunks, and the floor was a sheet of deep purple blue-colouring, such as must be seen to be credited.

This year Whitsuntide falls in June, but there is another May Day not to be omitted, namely the 29th, which for some unknown reason is called in Hampshire and Sussex, Shik Shak Day, and when those who omit the wearing of the oak-apple are liable to the drenching which in Devon belongs to the 1st. I cannot help thinking the custom must be older than the Restoration Day of 1660. At any rate, every one in this country of oaks appears with the spray of young leaves, generally with the tassel of catkins above and the rosy oak-apple below.

What a curious fact it is that this same oak-apple should be the effect of some matter deposited with her eggs within the bud, stem, or leaf by one of the Bedeguars or Gall-flies, small four-winged insects. *Cynips quercus* is the formal name of her whose produce is the handsome oak-apple, delicately shaded with red, of historical association. It is full of little cells in which reside the larvæ of the gall-fly. There, unless loyalty brings them to an untimely end, they will live upon the fleshy part, become pupæ, and finally make their way out as flies. There are other gall-flies, one of whom prefers the leaves and produces a much smaller ball upon the mid-rib; another pierces the bud, and a pretty bunch, like unripe currants, is the result; and a third prefers the bark, where there arises a cluster of round wooden balls as large as the biggest marbles. These gall-flies should be the badge of authors and letter-writers, for their 'apples' produced in Asia Minor are or were, together with oxide of iron, the chief material of ink. People in the old days, before universal commerce, used to make their own ink. I remember one experiment, when a jug full of something very black was produced, but whether good to write with, I cannot say. Also I have seen a pond, with iron, no doubt, in the water, turned black by a fallen oak tree, the like of which may account for the invention. Another Bedeguar produces the pretty rosy mossy tuft on the dog rose, which we call the Robin's Cushion, but Hans Christian Andersen names the Rose-King's Beard.

We would not cultivate dull colouring at the expense of our meadows, white with ox-eye and cuckoo flowers; of our woods, blue with hyacinth, pink with campion; of our golden gorse, ever renewing the glories that brought Linnæus to his knees, nor even the lively bright-green sheets of dog's-mercury in the hollows of the woods.

Most of these have creeping roots, and so has the Convallaria kind. They are Ascension-Day flowers, ladders to Heaven, the pure blossoms drooping humbly, yet in steps ascending. Indeed the Solomon's Seal (*Convallaria multiflora*) is one of the many plants known to country folk as Jacob's Ladder. It is not universally found, but there is plenty of it here with its arching stem, alternate handsome leaves, with a graceful white green-tipped bell hanging from the sprig of each. Its more admired sister, *Convallaria majalis, the* Lily of the Valley, is found here and there, but is much more rare in the woods. On one hillside, where it is to be found, it has each pearly blossom ornamented at the bottom of the cup with a little red dot.

That wood, where likewise is found the curious Herb Paris (*Paris quadrifolia*), lies on the side of a steep down, on whose summit is a kind of brick tower, called the Horse Monument, bearing an inscription in honour of a horse which in a hunt leapt with its rider unhurt down a very deep chalk pit, and moreover won the cup at a race a few weeks later!

The lily of the valley is the prime glory of any old-fashioned garden where it has room to spread undisturbed; but where it grows wild, rapacious plunderers from towns fall upon it, and will soon make an end of it where it is not guarded.

What shall be said of those plunderers? It is cruel to blame poverty for its efforts, and hard to wish the dwellers in towns to lose their pleasures; but when the ferns that adorn the lanes are torn up without care by men tramping from the town out of work, and dropping frail fronds along the road, one can only wish for some protection for our beauties. But sweet May must not have a farewell moan. I take leave of her in the midst of her

> Modest charm of not too much,
> Part seen, imagined part.

JUNE

The leafy month of June! Well, it is the crown of the year, and all the leaves are fully out, but they have lost the tender light colour of growth, and the white petals of the blossoming trees come down like snow.

Perhaps it is the best augury when their fall is hastened by showers, for an over - dry late May and early June are apt to result in a break - up during the haying and harvest time. Roaming in the meadows is pretty well over. They have been bush-harrowed—namely, a construction of branches of hazel and thorn has been dragged over them, and then the gates are mended and fastened up with elaborate twists of withes, and woe to the trespasser tempted by the pink, white, and yellow heads that rise above the grass.

The borderlands are, however, very charming. Here is the river walk in full perfection. The way thither is along a lane, in the hedge of which towered, a year or two ago, a gigantic teasel (*Dipsacus sylvestris*), the daily delight of my eyes, till some barbarous boy, only bent on destruction, smote off its head, vainly armed with pointed spears. Who has realised the beauty of the teasel, or its perfect symmetry? This one was at least four feet high, and a perfect example of what Ruskin calls the secret of beauty, the combination of curve, straight line, and angle. The parts are all in pairs, and divide by two, the less common rule in flowers.

There is a tall, straight, perpendicular stem, ribbed and garnished with hooks, fair and white. Thence, at regular intervals, spring pairs of arms opposite to one another and curving upwards. At their base are two long leaves, pointed, following their curve, and joined together at the base, so as to form a deep cup around the stem, capable of holding water. In fine plants, such as my friend of the lane, the lower branches each send forth a secondary pair on a smaller still, preserving the same perfect order and regularity. Each branch, and especially the main stem, is crowned with a marvellous head. First there are four long, narrow-toothed involucre leaves, from which springs an egg-shaped head, compounded of circle upon circle of tiny flowers, every one within a stiff, chaffy calyx, terminated by a long bristle. Observe the wonderful design. Each of these bristles, *before it grew*, was so arranged and so supplied with sap, as to come to the exact length which would serve to form the outline of the prickly head, not one breaking out beyond or falling below the shapely oval, which is more pointed, like the smaller end of the egg, in the central one, the monarch as it were, than in its attendants.   Moreover, the flowers, all of one petal, four divided, with two thready stamens and one pistil, are delicate pale purple, and are so arranged as to bloom in successive circles, so that the head is wreathed continually with a band of soft light purple—like a fillet on its crown of summer glory, moving gradually downwards.

After this lovely garland fades, and with it the leaves, the stiff heads, stems, and scales still remain, as sceptres to be touched with silver for the winter king,

till storms, and the growth of their suc-
cessors, push them aside. They vary much
in size. I know an upland field, left
fallow under the depression of farming,
perfectly covered with small teasels little
more than half a yard high, as if inten-
tionally sown, so that one longs to make
them of use ; but the really valuable Fullers'
teasel (*Dipsacus fullonum*) has hooks at the
end of its bristles, so that no invention
of mechanism has ever succeeded in so
efficiently raising the nap on cloth. Three
teasel heads are, therefore, the arms of the
Clothworkers' Company.

We have been a long time getting past
the teasel, and here is more temptation
to linger at the wreaths of dog-rose that
stretch out overhead—bearing their delicately rosy buds. Like the tulip and the
hyacinth, the rose loses its grace under
the gardener's hands ; it is allowed no

arching wreaths, clad with sprays where the buds blush within the slender exquisitely formed calyx of the five brethren, two bearded, two unbearded, one bearded on one side only, as in the old Latin riddle.   Here is a bush growing just enough out of reach over a deep ditch or water-carriage to escape the eager hands of children, and to show its soft pink flowers in lavish beauty.   This is the true *Rosa canina*; but there is also much in the hedges of its trailing brother, *Rosa arvensis*, which is quite white, with darker stamens, and less graceful in growth.   I know also of a bush or two of true sweet-briar (*Rosa rubiginosa*) growing wild, betraying its neighbourhood by its scent, and bearing blossoms and buds of the softest deep pink.

Every ditch and waterway is bordered with forget-me-not.   In sentimental art the poor thing is hackneyed to death; but who can withstand the charm of the real blue flower, on that curving footstalk, which always presents a pair of full-blown blue flowers, the buds beyond them more or less pink. If we carry home a sheaf of it, and put it in a soup-plate or small bowl, it will live a long time, but the out-coming flowers will be less and less blue, more and more pale pink. This one is *Myosotis palustris*, the head of the genus, which numbers many more, generally looking like starved varieties. The name is Greek—mouse-ear—probably from the curling corymb; and the English name by which no one ever calls it, Scorpion grass, is no doubt from the very innocent little bristles that clothe the plant. In common with all its congeners of the great and beautiful *Boraginaceæ*, it has these rough stems and leaves. These plants all have five stamens in one five-lobed petal, and their colours go through the whole scale of blues, purples, and reds.

Here is another of them, the *Symphytum officinalis*, or comfrey, a large plant with handsome leaves and bell-shaped blossoms. Before our walk is over, we may collect specimens of every tint, from the darkest crimson down to white, not blue, but the scale is made up by the *Symphytum asperrimum*, a prickly comfrey which was brought from the Caucasus under the impression that it would·serve for fodder. Horses and cows really like it, but it never has made its way, perhaps because it is not of continuous growth, and there is no ‘cut and come again.’ A plant that we obtained has remained a shrubbery ornament, with brilliant blue bells, heading circling processions of deep pink buds.

Well, in spite of lingering, we have

reached the river at last. The walk is by
a canal along a towing path, and there is
the real river meandering about, sometimes
close to the path, sometimes leaving a
space between. Once the said canal was
the means of conveying coal, but since
railway times it is chiefly serviceable as
a means of watering those bright green
meadows, and it is the happy hunting-
ground of fishermen. Between the two
rivers lies a quaking space, sometimes fit
to tread on, sometimes not, but always
alluring, for here grows the big purple
Orchis latifolia, here the hoary Cotton grass,
here the odd red-calyxed *Geum rivale*, called
by the village children Granny's nightcaps ;
and there are the three colours of lovely milk-
wort, and best of all the handsome trefoil
leaves of the Bog-bean (*Menyanthes trifoliata*).
See what an unrivalled flower it is, the buds
tipped with rose, the five curving petals of

each open blossom covered with pure snowy fibres, out of which look the little black anthers. Once, amid the Red Rattle (*Pedicularis palustris*), with its rose-coloured labiate flowers and dark fern-like leaves, we used to have the charming violet-like purple butterwort with its long. spur, and rosette of pale yellowish-green leaves (*Pinguicula vulgaris*), our especial pride, but

> Now a Giant, plump and tall,
> Called High-farming, stalks o'er all,

and his tread has effaced alike the purple butterwort from here, and *P. Lusitanica*, the pale lilac one from another bog, so that they cannot be found nearer than the New Forest. Here is consolation in our charming nosegay, further illuminated by the bright divided petals of well-named Ragged Robin (*Lychnis floscuculi*).

Probably the fishermen are heartily wishing us further off, as they stand armed, for

> Here and there a lusty trout,
> And here and there a grayling.

The trout are in all their season and beauty of red-spotted sides, and the grayling is in his robe of glittering silver scales. They are feeding to the full on the May-fly, which was named in the days of Old Style, and is really a June fly. The air is full of it; aye, and towards the evening, the water too; Ephemeris, the creature of a day, it has fulfilled its destiny, drops, and is carried away by the stream. But it has had a long previous existence as a six-legged larva in a hole in the mud bank, and then as a pupa, whence it emerges as a very handsome fly, the larger species as large as a Daddy-long-legs, with a pale yellow body marked with dark brown, four lace-like wings, also spotted with brown, and their special ornament, three long whisks by way of tail. There is a smaller species, no larger, though much more

elegant, than the bluebottle fly; and it is
on these that I have watched the further
changes, to me the most astonishing thing I
have noted among the many insect marvels.
These creatures have a last change which
brings them to an absolute perfection of their
frame, which is so minute and exquisite, yet
for so brief a period.   Twice it has chanced
to me to walk to the river with a companion
wearing a crape mantle.   It was quickly
covered with hosts of these small white May-
flies (*Ephemera albipennis*).   In a moment
each seemed to have doubled; then away
flew one of the pair, leaving behind it what
proved to be an empty white skin, covering
wings and all, but left like a glove, while the
late owner came out more finished and more
beautiful than ever, wearing much longer and
more delicate whisks than before.   All the
Ephemeræ do this, the large one becoming
more polished after this last change.   And

all this for one day of dancing ecstasy, with no food as far as appears ; only this sublimated glory, to end in a few hours. Is it to give us a glimpse of how mortal bodies can be refined ; though like other pure and beauteous emblems, their perfection is so shortlived ?

Of course the rough stems and leaves of the sedges are the natural holdfasts of these May - flies, as they are of their relations the Dragon-flies (*Libellulæ*). Magnificent creatures they are, after having emerged from their very ugly fierce-looking water-loving pupæ. Indeed, they continue fierce, though not deserving the dread with which they are regarded by the village people, who call them horse-stingers, for they have no sting, and are terrible only to the insect race, whom they ruthlessly devour. See the intensely shining blue, long, pointed forms flitting about ; and in the track of a fisherman we may pick up the wings which the cruel man has pulled off before using the brilliant blue body for bait. We must take refuge in the assurance that an insect is not constructed to feel pain, and those wings are worth picking up to examine the wonderful web of nerves on which the transparent membrane is stretched, and the round spot which looks black, but which proves to be the deepest, darkest of blues. The eyes of the dragon-fly look large and fierce; they have immovable facets, so as to see all ways at once, and are one of the favourite marvels of the microscope.

This grand dark blue *Æshna varia* is the most frequent here, but there are also green ones, and orange without the dark spot; also the loveliest of all, the demoiselle, rather smaller, and of the most perfect turquoise-blue picked out with shining black. It is really the damoiseau who bears these sky-blue colours in full splendour; his lady is black, only sparsely banded with his blue. As we turn and take the upward course of the river, we must note the sedges, the friends of the emerging insect, who clings to their saw-like edges. They border the stream with their angular stems and saw-edged harsh leaves ; their roots are creeping and matted, and they are very useful in holding together the loose earth of banks. The species are innumerable on bog, moor, and mountain, but the ornamental one before our eyes is *Carex stricta*, which has three spikes of blossom, of rich black or very dark brown scales, from the uppermost of which protrude in contrast cream-coloured stamens, from the lower, threads of styles. Mixed with it is the handsome *Sparganium ram-osum*, or bur reed, often with balls of blossom, the uppermost a round puff of small anthers, the lower fruit bearing, and for all the world like that terrible weapon of old, the morning star.

If ever you heard a bird in a passion, here he is chatter, chatter, scold, scold, emphatically. It is Blethering Jock, as the Scottish shepherd-boys call that little sedge warbler, who bursts out of the reed bed, doing anything but warble. He is in fear for his nest, though quite needlessly; we could not get at it over the quaking bog, and if we wish to see the cradle suspended on the reeds that rock it, we must go to that delightful place, the South Kensington Museum. We may, however, see the scarlet-headed moor-hen, and the ridiculous little dab-chick lead forth their fleets, and all suddenly dive the very moment their little black eyes are aware of our approach; or the water-rat, or rather vole, swim across and disappear in a bank, or even a kingfisher dart across with a gleam of blue and russet.

However, we must turn from the river to chalky banks, and a disused chalkpit, in whose depths has been found a bee orchis, the real *Ophrys apifera*, lilac-winged, velvet-tailed of brown and yellow marbled together, just the colouring of a bee, though stingless. There is no security of finding it a second year in the same place, for it is very capricious as to blossoming. It will not bear transplantation, and in a place liable to marauders the best way to save its life is to gather it!

In the borders of the copse above we may find the butterfly orchis; why butterfly there is no knowing; honeysuckle orchis was a much more sensible name for the long thin-spurred and long-lipped, deliciously scented spike. It is not allowed to be an orchis any longer, but has become a *Habenaria bifolia*. Indeed, I once met with an all too scientific novel, in which the lover presents his lady with a *Habenaria* as a token. Did it by that name smell as sweet?

We pass a path overhung with hazels, and

showing below the little pearls and sweet-scented whorls of Woodruff (*Asperula odorata*), and under the stumps, and in the hedge banks, the tender and lovely wood-sorrels, otherwise *Oxalis acetosella*, ·with a coral scaly creeping stem, purple footstalks, purple backs to the drooping trefoil leaves, and delicate purple streaks in the slender graceful bud, and cuplike blossom, the most dainty and delicate of English flowers. It is disputed whether these complete trefoils are not the true shamrock; but it is not likely, though everywhere in Europe they are the Alleluia plant specially dedicated to Trinity Sunday.

All the Oxalis tribe, which is very numer·ous, is full of acid juice. Children who care for their palate more than their eyes bite the stems, and in some places a preserve is made of the leaves. I am glad there is not enough here to tempt any one.

There is the cuckoo—

In June
He altereth his tune,

and he is stammering with repeated cuck—cuck—cuck—cuck before he can bring out the final cuckoo. Some people think these are the imperfect efforts of the young cuckoos learning to sing; but they are hardly out of the nest so early. I suspect the hesitation to be caused by anger, for I have once seen a couple of quarrelsome cuckoos defying one another in broken language, or it may be from fright, when the bird is mobbed by the smaller fry, more probably because of its likeness to a hawk, than because of the misdeeds of its youth towards their offspring.

It has been proved that it carries in its mouth the egg, which it bestows upon the hedge-sparrow, or water-wagtail. I have watched one such awkward nursling alone in a nest in a heap of large flints, a gowk

K

in a dishwasher's nest, as it was announced
to us. We saw the little birds feeding it,
and one evening they were trying to entice
it out by holding a grub a little way off.
The next morning it was gone, so probably
they had succeeded. Another young cuckoo,
which was carried across the road, and placed
in a cage in an open window, was regularly
fed by its faithful foster-parents, who had
traced it thither. How curious it is that
though the American cuckoo has a nest of
her own, and brings up her family like a
respectable housewife, the cow bird acts the
fashionable mother like the English cuckoo.
The Indian cuckoo, we are told, sings, drops
her egg into alien nests, and is hunted ·like
her English sister.

We emerge from the wood to see fields
with ripples of wind passing over their full-
blossomed grass, making strange lights and
shades between the varied heads of brownish-

green, while ox-eyes and buttercups crop up
between. To the confusion of the poor corn-
crakes, early fields are beginning already,
and, it is hoped, may avoid the thunderstorms which are too apt to break up the
weather in the last fortnight of June. When
will it be cut ?

The swish of the scythe in the dewy
morning is seldom to be heard in these days.
It has given place to the squeak and cough
of the engine, and the long rows of women
in sunbonnets to the claws of the monster
haymaker. Haycocks we still have ; but
the pictures of children tumbling in delight
in the hay are, except on lawns on gala days,
a pleasing delusion. Farmers and farming
men consider children as their natural
enemies. A kind rector who used to
give a happy day in the hay to his school-
children, found that though the parish was
full of meadows, the most part had never

been in a hayfield in their lives. I have made nests in the hay in my time, and carried on a warfare from haycock to haycock, but under angry protest from our old farming man, who considered us to be spoiling *his* hay—how, I never could understand; but I believe that besides upsetting the neat haycock, we were supposed to tread out the fragrance.

And the hay-carrying is always a pleasant sight, picturesque even now, and delightful to man and beast, as the big horses enjoy themselves during the loading; and though one is sorry to lose the cocks that made such long shadows in the dewy sunrise of the dear, bright long days, still, anxiety is off our minds, and we are thankful.

Everybody goes after some club festival or other at Whitsuntide, so our Flower Service, a modern institution, has to be either on 'St. Barnaby bright,' or on Midsummer Day, when it is grand to see the altar steps heaped with nosegays of every kind, filling ten or eleven boxes for London hospitals, when tiny little children are led up to deposit their offerings in the great brass tray held down to them. The bouquet that lives most in my memory was entirely of red campion, seen through a lacework of the lovely delicate umbelliferous flower of the pig-nut. This was made by a farmer's daughters, whose brother had been in a London hospital, and tenderly remembered the flowers there. They used to make up some of their offerings as 'button-holes,' he having said that these were specially available.

Another hint is that bunches of grasses in blossom are greatly valued for their long duration, and they are often valued by nursing Sisterhoods used to decorate mortuaries.

The ' May Queen ' remembers

> The oat grass and the sword grass, and the bulrush
> in the pool,

with all Tennyson's wonderful exactness to the details of Nature.

The bulrush is not the grand reed maçe which we are apt to call by that name, and which is a later production, but the humble Rush (*Juncus conglomeratus*), one long single, leafless, pointed, bending, tapering spike, with a tuft of brown, six-stamened blossoms near the top, a delightful toy of childhood which makes it into green baskets and helmets, and learns plaiting upon it. And, again, its soft white pith is by our young folks twisted into the semblance of white roses, and set among ivy leaves.

It had a greater value once in the days of domestic manufactures, when duly peeled of its shining green coat, it served for the wicks of candles. Even at the beginning of the century, Miss Edgeworth conducts her Frank to see the making of these candles by successive dips of the pith-made wick into a caldron of properly melted and compounded mutton fat.

And till the days of the lucifer match and little fat solid nightlight did the rushlight survive, to beguile the night watches, enshrined in a tall, circular temple, about a quarter of a yard high, and pierced with numerous holes of about the size of a sixpence. There was a mysterious awe in the sight of the circle of light on the ceiling, surrounded by the lesser rounds, which gradually changed their places, till at last there was a dread sound of hissing and fizzing, and all was dark, as the slender rushlight burnt down, and was extinct in the pan of water ready to receive it. The little Woodrush, or *Luzula*, makes a dainty foil to the pink campion and its relative, the garden white pink, whereof I rejoice in a thick border that reminds me of the seashore, the blue-green foliage being the waves, the overflowing white flowers the foam. It is the earliest of the Pink kind— a delightful race, named from their pinked or indented edges, and giving their name to the lovely colour which the good little tracts of the early years of the century held as emblematic of vanity as the tulip or the peacock !

Dianthus caryophyllus, with two delicately curved styles, is the parent of all our garden pinks and carnations, white, red, and yellow, including that most deliciously scented of flowers, the deep crimson clove gillyflower. It warns me, however, by its very name, that it belongs to next month; but June must not pass over her Midsummer men, properly known as Orpine, a crimson-flowered plant with ten stamens, three styles, fleshy leaves, and stems, ranked with the starry stone-crops as *Sedum telephium*, though it grows not on rocks but on mossy banks. It is a plant of augury. I have known an old woman who had duly, on St. John's Eve, laid out nine pairs of Orpines, naming them after the couples thought to be courting. The pairs that kept together betokened a happy marriage, those that fell apart boded no good to the love affairs!

The jenneting-tree, under which some of Jane Taylor's little heroines sit, is really the June-eating apple-tree. Very funny work did old gardeners make of fine names of flowers and fruits. The *Quatre saisons* rose might very fairly become the Quarter Sessions rose; but the great pear known as the *Duchesse d'Angoulême* became on their lips 'Duchess Dangle'em,' and the list of plums in a catalogue was corrected by an old Cornish gardener from *drap d'or* into 'trapdoor,' the other being evidently to his mind a misprint.

The schoolmaster has destroyed much diversion in rural bills.   We never had the celebrated

		s.
Won Wooden Barrer as woodnt soot		10
Won Wooden Barrer as wood soot		10

but ' Jams ' (*i.e.* James) has sent us in a bill for a Sally Mander, and likewise for mending a three-legged Jonathan, which we concluded to be a trivet for hanging on a grate to hold a kettle.

The name Frederick was quite past our farming man, who entered it as Frikit; but most notable was a shoe bill in the penny club—

	s.	*d.*
1 Hideous Gurl boots	7	6
1 Hideous Gurl boots	5	6

Whether the adjective was intended to apply to the boots or to the girls was doubtful; but it proved that a family was meant of the name of Hedges.   As the cobbler no doubt pronounced hideous as ' hidjus,' he thought this the correct designation, though, as it happened, the damsels were the very reverse of hideous.

Wanderings in the garden are very delightful in the twilight, only after showers it is needful to be cautious not to tread on snails. We sometimes have said the snails must be giving a ball, there has been such a wonderful outbreak of them ; I have counted eighty on a very small circuit of gravel walk on a dewy evening. That was when we had a fine *Tritoma*, commonly called Red-hot Poker, elegantly, Flame Lily. Its mass of long narrow leaves afforded a capital harbour, to which we resorted when we wished for a snail race !

It really is amusing, and certainly not cruel, to put all the snails one can catch, in a row on a wall, or along a board, and see what they will do. One will

Draw in his head,
And go in his own little chamber to bed ;

others will set off to find fresh quarters, sometimes straight, sometimes turning to the right or left, spying about with their horns to explore the new country. The round eyes at the end of the horns are easily seen, with a nerve going up to them through the transparent skin.

The liveliest, as well as the prettiest, are the *Helix nemoralis*, whose mollusc has a delicate graceful head, with two slender feelers, and whose shell varies much from pale yellow to yellow, with a single coloured stripe of purple, stripes, and dark brown, edged round the coils with yellow.

The Common Snail (*Helix hortensis*) is quite worth looking at, when its brown and purple-marked thin shell is fresh. It makes a startling noise sometimes at night, a kind of music produced by crawling on glass windowpanes. Blackbirds and thrushes devour them in numbers. They may be seen with the unlucky mollusc on the beak in search of a stone to dash the shell against.

In the days when a merry cousinhood made shops of flowers in the garden, when lady-grass was our 'ribbon, beetroot our purple and pall, fuchsias our jewels, butter-cups and daisies our coins, a path which had been the thrushes' larder provided our crockery—alas, never whole!

The great edible Roman Snail (*Helix Pomatia*) was out of our reach. He never strays far from the Roman settlements, whither he was first imported, and has dwelt these fifteen hundred years! Once we had a basket sent us, and presently, after the string had been cut, the lid began to move, and a great horned head or two protruded, recalling the nursery rhyme of the ten tailors who went out to kill a snail—

> She put out her horns like a little Kerry cow,
> Run, tailors, run, or she'll kill you all now.

The little snails on the bents of grass on the downs (*Helix virgata*), white with a single purple line on the whorls, are sometimes strung by the children into necklaces. It is to be hoped the inmates are dead ; but they retire so far into their shells that it is always difficult to guess; and I have found a snail from Italy walking about the room awaked by the warmth.

A basket of snails is a welcome gift to the ducks, and one's gardening heart must be hardened against them when we behold tall white lilies, bereft of every leaf all the way up the stem, struggling to bloom with ragged petals, and their noble buds almost destroyed.

Circles of ashes only protect till the next shower of rain, and then out come those worse enemies still, the houseless snails. *Limax* is their Latin name, Slug their English.

The black one, who is dignified by the grand name of *Arion ater*, is really, if you look at him, rather handsome, with a gracefully-formed body and horns, and I have a kindness for that slug striped like a tabby cat; but the gray one is the most mischievous to our young plants. There is a still more unpleasant looking one—pale, fat, and with an orange-coloured edging to his foot (*Arion albus*), who lives under old neglected logs of wood.

It is very amusing to turn up one of these, especially if it have bark on it loosened with damp and decay. Tear off a piece and see the medley of odd creatures rolling or scampering off, the branching patterns traced within the bark by some kind of worm, the white grubs, the millepedes, centipedes, and the wood-lice. The centipede, happily not on so large a scale as his formidable French brother, has actually often fifty-five pairs of little legs, a pair in each of his articulations, and is not pleasant to encounter when eating a strawberry or peach. The Millepede (*Iulus*), in spite of his name, has really only twelve pairs of legs, and curls into a spiral. He it is whom we are most likely to find under the bark. Sure to be there is a comical creature of an oval shape, all in divisions, which curls itself up into a perfect ball, exactly like a pill when meddled with. *Armadillo vulgaris*, or Pill Wood-louse, is its correct title, but here we call it a Chiselbob, or sometimes a Cudworm. One of our cows was ill, and the old cowman pronounced that she had lost her cud—namely, the ball of hair licked from herself that she rolls in her throat while chewing meditatively. He proposed to restore it by administering one of these natural pills or cudworms. Whether he did so or not I cannot tell, but at any rate the poor cow died.

JULY

THE glory of the year has left the meadows
and the woods. The meadow grass is all
cut down, and before the end of the month
is reduced to stubble, if it may so be called.
Or if rain have hindered, the fields are a
woful sight, the tanned haycocks a great
deal too much tanned, in the midst of grass
a great deal too green, or else the old burs,
waving brown and uncut, hindering the
second growth. Clover, with its purple or
white heads, is slowly following, and so is
the most brilliant of the kind, sainfoin, with
its striped and shaded blossoms, and the
beauteous *Trifolium incarnatum*, which
makes such rich patches of deep red. It

L

figures in Curtis's *Botanical Magazine*, about
a century old, as a plant advisable to be introduced into gardens ; and when it made its
way into agriculture about fifty years ago,
the name was a sore puzzle to the labourers.
'Some calls it Polium and some Napoleon,'
we were told; and once came the startling
announcement, as it might be from the
Valley of Humiliation, 'If you please, sir,
there's a man a-treading down your Apollyon.'

These early haytimes belong to our
Southern counties.   In the North the Otter-
burn ballad is most descriptive in its opening—

> It fell about the Lammas tide,
> When moormen win their hay.

The woods are so overgrown with their
young shoots and trailers, that the by-
paths, not yet trimmed for sportsmen, are
nearly impassable ; and there are few flowers
left in them except the little *Lysimachia
nemorum*, whose English name of Yellow

Pimpernel is confusing. It is one of the many golden stars with which the ground is spangled all spring and summer long.

The beech woods alone keep a curious peculiar vegetation of their own, and allow nothing to grow upon their russet pavement except the lovely lily-like orchid *Epipactis grandiflora*, and the queer brown *Listera nidus avis*, or Bird's-nest Orchis; not that it is much like a bird's nest, except that it is brown and withered-looking, the colour of the beech leaves among which it grows—a parasite, like the only other plants the tyrant beech tree endures beneath its lordly shade; the two very strange-looking plants, *Monotropa hypopithys*, Yellow Bird's-nest, and *Lathræa squamaria*, or Toothwort. In spite of this likeness to a 'bloated tyrant,' it is impossible not to delight in the beech tree, with its smooth silvery bole and widespread canopy. Some single trees are perfectly magnificent in bulk and shade, especially some favoured ones in the New Forest; and an extensive beech wood, with long arcades, is a place to dream of. Mr. Keble used to call the Ampfield beeches Hursley Cathedral; and verily they are like 'the long-drawn aisle and fretted vault.' However, in the walk I am thinking of, there is only one big beech to be passed before crossing the road and going through a slip rail into a farm road across a wide space of heathery moorland. I believe, from the appearance of the ground, that William the Conqueror had little to ride through save this kind of land after the downs were once passed between him and Winchester; for from their edge to the coast all is of the same sort of soil, with gravelly slopes here and there, but for the most part peaty ground, a good deal like the side of a mountain, minus the part of the mountain itself.

Plantation and cultivation have done a good deal, but there is much of primitive ground, and the walk I propose shows some old scenes, such as Alfred may have looked upon, not greatly altered by semi-cultivation. This road leads between low hedges of gorse, as much out of blossom now as gorse ever can be; indeed, its perpetuity is beginning to be kept up by its dwarf brother, *Ulex nanus.* Stand still a moment and you will hear an odd popping like fairy artillery. It is the bursting open of the pods of the gorse, which is firing off its little black seeds. We never call it gorse here, nor even furze; the villagers would not know what was meant unless we said 'fuzz.'

In the silence we may detect a movement in the deep ruts which border our path. It may prove to be a delicate little brown-striped lizard, a creature which our poor people call an evvet (corrupted from eft, its hand-

some water brother), and regard with horror.
'I saw an evvet once,' the children will say
with bated breath, as if they had seen a tiger.
'She brought home a bundle of grass from
the wood,' said the mother of a girl who had
a gathering in her hand, 'and I think an
evvet may have bitten her.' Poor little
harmless striped creature!

The margin of our path between the ruts
and the furze is full of heath of all the three
sorts, though only here and there a spike of
the rich crimsoned purple of the *Erica
vulgaris* has begun to ring its bells, and the
choice blushing clusters of the bell-heather
(*E. tetralix*) are coming out amid soft cushions
of bent grass; stars of four-petalled Tormentilla, loosely stemmed spangles of lesser
stitchwort; while small ringlet butterflies, just
emerged, sit drying themselves on the stalks,
all gray, and yellow rings on the outer wing
when closed, but sky-blue when opened.

The dark shining green wings, with a red spot on them, belong to the Burnet moth. When he opens them, they are bright red, edged with green. Or here may be seen, hawking and darting about, the very large dragon-fly, banded with green, yellow, and blue, divided by black lines, and with large shining eyes. Sometimes his wife appears, very unlike him, and much more resembling an overgrown hornet.

A little further on, and we look over the gorse into green spaces full of bracken (*Pteris aquilegia*), undulating like the waves of the sea. We slice a stem in two, and dispute whether the dark marking is most like or most unlike a spread eagle, or King Charles in the oak.

Here is a splendid bush close to the path of wild honeysuckle (*Lonicera periclymenum*). It climbs up the holly bushes, the stem getting incorporated with the bark, and finally killing the holly ; but never mind, holly there is enough and to spare, and who would grudge the support to those fragrant streamers of crimson buds and creamy blossoms of that peculiar trumpet shape, the petal four cleft above, with one long lip below ? There is another sort of honey-suckle, plentiful enough here but called rare by the books, with less red in the blossom, and with leaves, not like this one, distinct and in opposite pairs, but grown together and forming a cup round the stem.   This is the *Lonicera caprifolium*, goats being sup-posed to devour it, so that in French it is *chèvrefeuille*.

Lonicera is so well sounding a name, that it is surprising to find that it is only after Lonica, a German botanist.

Lonicera was the infant's name in a poem of Crabbe's, and she was better off than one I have been told of who was christened

'Sarsaparilla,' because the parents had seen it in a book !

Further on we come out on really open heath, where it is not always easy to find a path, or to steer clear of prickles of gorse. The little *Stellaria minor* and the Tormentilla give a spangling of white and yellow, and what is this strange brown spike—like a large bird's-nest orchis ?   No, only in colouring and absence of branches.   This has not the queer orchid structure, but is a regular labiate plant with two long and two short stamens within its brownish-yellow or yellowish-brown petal. It is likewise a parasite, but on the roots of the gorse.   Go down to the bottom and you will find an odd scaly thing a good deal like a lily bulb, only all brown.   It is the greater Broomrape (*Orobanche major*), and it has a lesser brother (*Orobanche minor*) with a little attempt at pale purple in its flowers, for which you must look in clover fields, where it is welcome to nobody save the botanist.   For parasites are too tempting to Mrs. Malaprop, being too often 'parricides.' Farmers are always taking the Englishman's resource of writing to the newspaper against that other clover parasite, the Greater Dodder (*Cuscuta europæa*), which spreads a fatal network of red threads over the young clover plants. Though called greater, its heads of blossom are much smaller and not half so pretty as those of the other species (*Cuscuta epithymum*) which you may see here, not doing any harm, but straggling about like a tangle of crimson threads, with white balls at intervals, upon the gorse and heather, balls composed of tiny star-like blossoms and their blushing buds.

Then comes a dip in the ground, with a little stream that has to be crossed on very variable stepping-stones, or else by striding across between the bushy banks a little lower down.   Then turn to the right into a wood of scanty small oaks. But beneath them behold a mass of purple spires, a glorious forest of foxgloves, small and great, each lifting its mace of bells, purple outside, white within, but there ornamented with dark rings close together, and with four stamens, two long and two short, curiously bent, and their anthers with dark spots. Foxgloves may be of any size, from the splendid plant as tall as a man, whose lowermost flowers hang in rows of six, down to the poor half-starved stem with scarcely a dozen blossoms. Poppies they are sometimes called, because the flower when inflated can be made to pop between the hands. I confess to a sense of indignation when I see this senseless sport used towards one of the most beautiful ornaments of the year, in wanton disregard of its loveliness. They are biennial, so that where they are in large numbers one year, they will probably not show their flowers, but only their gray downy leaves the next.   There is little doubt that they are properly folks' gloves, the gloves of the 'good people,' to answer to the ' Irish lusmore,' or fairy cup.   On the mountains of Ireland and Scotland they are finer and more luxuriant.   By Loch Katrine, in the *Lady of the Lake*, grew—

> Nightshade and foxglove, side by side,
> Emblems of punishment and pride.

When one of Mrs. Hemans's sons asked Sir Walter what this meant, he made the characteristic answer that poets were apt to write a good many things which had no particular meaning (or something to that effect).   The pure white ones are more common in Scotland than here.   I had five in my garden last year, in each one of which the marks within the throat were different.

The trees grow more scantily, and there is a stretch of regular moorland, chiefly of bent grass, with nothing remarkable about the plants, as it is too late for the cream-coloured Violet (*Viola lactea*), which ought to be called the milk-and-water violet, and gives something of that effect as it grows in large quantities along the ditches by the roadsides in the New Forest. It has long narrow leaves, unlike those of other violets.

Here the ground sinks, and there is a region of bog below with a sluggish stream in the middle of it. Once there was an attempt to form a lake in the park above, but the water declined to stay in it and rushed away, forming this stream and marsh, dearer to the botanist than to the passenger. Long ago, standing on this high ground, we saw far away a white sheet which excited our curiosity; but we had walked a good way, there was no particular path, and time and courage failed us for the investigation. So we remained content in the belief that it was really a mass of the White Crowfoot

(*Ranunculus aquatilis* or *R. hederaceus*) covering the pool after the example of many more.

We never did contrive to reach the spot till the dry summer of the Jubilee enabled us to walk up the quaking bank of the streamlet; and then we found no water, no crowfoot, only a piteous sight—in the hollow where the last water had been, a whole mass of dead eels, and, as I think, carp, whose grandparents had probably been intended to stock the lake!

The bog is a famous study, when it is possible to walk about from one of its tufts of rushes to another. There may be found the delicate Bog Pimpernel (*Anagallis tenella*), white with pink streaks, the lovely blue Skull-cap (*Scutellaria major*), the two less rare kinds of *Drosera*, or sundew, that queer carnivorous plant, which only opens its white blossoms at sunrise and soon closes them, while it waits with viscid drops on the red hairs of its battledore-shaped leaves to entrap the runaway insects which yield it nourishment.

I have found in these parts meads of yellow asphodel. If the blest dwelt in them they must have had a taste for bogs ; but the plant is a delightful one with its stiff orange-coloured stem, its six-pointed star blossoms, and six hairy stamens with red anthers. I am afraid that draining has banished it from hence as well as its companions, marsh pennywort, butterwort, and the beauteous little ivy - leaved Bell - flower (*Campanula hederacea*). They all may be found in the New Forest, but the high farming of the prosperous days of agriculture has made havoc of many a rare plant.

We have explored the bog, and crossed it by a quaking path, after which we get into a great plantation of firs, old enough now to whisper as we stand still among them.   It is almost the only sound, though broken now and then by the harsh squeak of that bird of beautiful plumage, but unrefined form and nature, the jay.   Now and then, too, a graceful little squirrel races across, but these are as much persecuted as are the jays by the keepers, on the plea that they injure the young trees by biting off the bark ; and I am afraid this is a true indictment.

The shade here is very delightful, and I will not tease you to look at any more flowers, except the grand pillars of Viper's Bugloss (*Echium vulgare*), kings of their family, with their deep blue flowers backed by red buds, both like the tints of a mediæval illumination.   One straight stalk they shoot up, with their curving axils of flowers, one on each all the way up, always open and blue, above the bristly stems.

Our walk has been so long that there is

hardly time to look at the garden, in all the
glory of roses, old and new, the old, despised
of gardeners, by far the sweetest, and the
prettiest in growth. The buds of the moss-
rose are really unequalled. Tea-roses are
exquisite in form, but there is nothing to be
said for their scent, and to keep pace with
the new kinds is quite beyond me. La
Marque and Gloire de Dijon seem recent to
me, though the younger race think them as
ancient as the Rose de Meaux, the fairy-
like creature of my childhood.

The big white lilies are looking magnificent in every cottage garden, and the little
thorny Scotch roses, the red china ones, and
many another are creeping over the cottages,
though alas! the flame-coloured Austrian
briar, which used to be the glory of the
village, is dead. A tramp was overheard
saying to his mate, 'Now what is a rose
like?' He must have enlarged his experi-

ence before he had passed through the place !

Long ago, in that still pretty, well-gardened cottage, which stands sideways to the road and looks up the hill, we had an enthusiastic gardener, an amateur in that as in other things, but so good, so remarkably good—poor dear man !—that I must tell his history, since there is no one left who can be pained by it.   He was a baker by profession, and made excellent bread, besides certain fair-complexioned plain buns, which swelled to a huge size in a cup of tea, and had a fame of their own in the neighbouring town where in later times I have seen spurious articles sold by their names.   All he produced had that delicate nicety which belongs to the work of a conscientious man, who does everything with his own hands and on a small scale, a perfection never attained by machinery, which may prevent the very bad,

but never attains to the very good. His
was genuine 'home-made' bread, made with
real yeast of beer. Ordinary baker's bread
had, he said, a 'vinosity taste.'

His delight was, however, in his plants.
He had ingeniously contrived to glaze over
the great excrescence made by his oven at
the back of his cottage, and put shelves over
it, and in this primitive greenhouse he nursed
geraniums and myrtle, and occasionally sold
an extra one. He was also a real old-
fashioned herbalist, and had one or two
curious old books which I wish I could see
with eyes better able to judge than I had in
his time. He compounded drugs and gave
his attendance and his medicines freely
out of pure charity. It was really valuable
doctoring in many simple cases. Union
doctors were not. Parishes were supposed
to be attended by busy surgeons, but this
came to nothing. The lady in each parish

had to be doctor, and make the best of the remarkable complaints she heard of. I remember a great white jug, where 'Jesuits' bark' was soaked before quinine in powder was cheaply attainable for the ague, which was then common in the parish. But the cure my mother thought the greatest was of a man of whom it was reported that the doctor said his liver was no bigger than a pigeon's egg, and he might take what he pleased, so would she send an 'imposing draught'? My father really knew a good deal about medicine, and sent a dose of calomel, and the man recovered. For ague one prescription in the next village was, among many others, to have a bandage round the wrists, lined with gunpowder and set on fire. Or to be led to the top of a mound, and violently pushed down! As a remedy for fits, to wear a ring of beaten sixpences given by six young women who had married without changing their surname; or to wear suspended from the neck 'a hair from the cross on the back of a he-donkey.' Moreover, a gentleman's butler, feeling a lump or rising in his throat, swallowed shot to 'keep down his lights'; and 'chaney'—crushed porcelain—was a favourite remedy.

But our little baker's was real herbalist treatment with simples, and, as far as we knew, not empiric. By and by, during the illness of the good man who united the offices of clerk and schoolmaster, he fulfilled them *con amore*, and was appointed. 'My Lords' had not risen on the horizon; he could read, write, and cypher better than most men in the parish; and he was deeply in earnest. I believe there was no complaint of his discipline, though it was peculiar, and a row of naughty boys were set down to kneel at a bench with books before them, and hands tied behind. His copies too were remarkable.   One was, 'A blind man's wife needs no paint.' 'Proverbs, sir, Proverbs,' he answered, when asked where it came from.

He kept a pair of felt shoes for the church, and it was a sight to see him, only wanting a frock to look a perfect lay brother, gliding about with a soft brush to the woodwork, which has never been so well kept since his time ; and still more wonderful it was to see him when a dramatic passage of Scripture was being read, unconsciously acting it.   To this hour, the Gospel for the Sunday in Lent recalls him, raising his chin as in the Syro-Phenician woman's entreaty, stretching out his hand to repel her—finally looking satisfied, all unconsciously, in intense attention ; but resolution not to look at him was needful.

Alas ! it was an excitable brain, and over-tasked.   He had two sisters who lived with him, both partially insane though harmless ;

but he was often up half the night with one or other of them. Each, too, had a son (perhaps one was a stepson), and one of these was to assist in the business, but was pronounced 'Never to get beyond the A B C book of baking.' The other was a cobbler, but both preyed upon him ; his affairs became entangled, and things grew worse and worse. The village shopkeeper, the maker of the 'vinosity' bread, actually came in private to beg the clergyman to convey secretly from him means for the household, saying he had often known bad debtors, whom he himself had refused, go and get their bread from the good man's unfailing charity.

While the authorities were considering what could be done for the dear little man, came the first note of school inspection, very mild and entirely religious, by Archdeacon Allen. But the very idea was fatal. The good man told the curate that he could not stand it ; and knowing the distress he was in, he was assured that his school should not be examined ; but the very notion, coming on all the rest, developed the latent insanity. He was missed, and finally found in the river, to the lasting grief of those who had always loved and honoured him, through all his quaintness.

AUGUST

August is apt to come in with thunderstorms. Indeed, the weather is apt to begin
to be thundery at the solstice in June, and
St. Swithin's promise is by no means in-
fallible, whether for wet or fair weather. In
some counties, such as Gloucestershire, they
prefer a shower on his day, and call it christening the apples; but Hampshire surely has
the best right to the augury, and we hold that—

> If Swithun's day be fair and clear,
> It betides a happy year;
> If Swithun's day be dark with rain,
> Then will be dear all sorts of grain.

Only twice have I known the forty days to
pass off without rain!

Thunderstorms are seldom severe here. We say they go up the river, but whether this is only one of the many foolish utterances that a tempest evokes, I do not know. I only do know that when they are seen, large purple and lurid in the south-west, they generally come towards us, and that within the last few years they have often come from the south-east. As to their coming against the wind, as they are said to do, that only means that the small cyclone that brings them is blowing one way with us, while the other side of the circle is bringing them. I do not love them, though there is a terrible beauty in the grand clouds in far distance in magnificent mountainous curves, of dazzling glistening whiteness, relieved against the deep azure of the sky. I respect those that can exult in the brilliant flash and mighty voice, but individually there is something to me distressing in the uncertainty when or what may come next, and what awful effect it may have, and it is a great relief when the intervals between flash and clap grow measurably longer each time, the birds begin to sing again, the sun comes out, and all the drops become diamonds on the leaves, while the cloud goes off in deep soft purples on the horizon.

Only about three times have I known the huge hailstones fall such as we read of. Once, long ago, a breakfast-cup full of them was collected. The perfect ones were like nitre balls, about as big as marbles, transparent outside and white at the centre, such pretty things, that it was a pity they melted almost instantly. Those that fell on roofs ran together into jagged masses, and broke windows, as well as doing other mischief, quite showing how the providential hailstones on the flying foe fought for Joshua and Barak. Another night, storm did much harm in this way ; but the last, on the 8th June 1889, was the worst.

It occurred in the course of numerous such storms, which visited the whole country. The lawn was whitened, the great balls came rushing down the chimneys, and breaking their way through glass. When the gleam came afterwards, we found the people mourning over their allotments, where the potato haulm was broken, and the poor beans, just putting out their fragrant black and white blossoms, were absolutely ruined. The turnpike road was torn up to its very bones of flint, and did not recover itself till after the winter's vicissitudes had worked in the insufficient repairs.

One cottage was struck by lightning, but not much harm was done. Some years ago an oak upon the hill was struck, a long ribbon of bark being peeled off all the way down. I know another tree where the topmost bough was scathed in like manner; but the most remarkable effect I have seen was in Somersetshire, where a tree (ash, if I remember rightly) had had such a strip torn off some way down, when the lightning seemed to have leapt off to the poor sheep, and finally had torn a hole in the ground.

Large holly bushes, also a limb of a yew-tree, have been seen to wither up and die, without apparent cause, and I have been told this is the effect of lightning from the earth; but I do not know if there is any reason in this. Mr. Keble once told me of having seen lightning run along the ground as he was coming home from a distant part of his parish, and there is no doubt of its often doing so in mountainous countries. Thus it may destroy the roots of these trees.

After one of these thunderstorms, when walking home late in the evening, in passing just where a stream crossed the road, begin-

ning in a pond, and proceeding to a marsh—
the same, by the bye, where we afterwards
found the dead eels,—there were all over the
road an untold multitude of tiny frogs about
an inch long, Charley frogs as the people
call them. The road was quite darkened
with them. I suppose they had just emerged
from their comical tadpole state and were
on their way to disperse themselves over the
country.

A pond full of the black tadpoles or
polliwigs, with their round heads and transparent tails wriggling, is a very amusing
sight. One year a whole party of young
cousins each set up a bowl of tadpoles in the
hope of seeing them become frogs, but they
always died when they grew their first pair
of legs, or the others killed them.

The eldest of us secluded one of hers
from the rest when it had two legs, and two
more appeared, and the tail became thin,

but then it died, I believe for want of mud
and reeds in which to hide.

Frogs are very entertaining with their
sudden leaps and droll faces. I have known
and loved them in my younger days, and have
even taken interest in the solemn, slow-paced
toad. He is still a horror to the ignorant.
A whole circle of maids was once found
standing round the dairy, afraid to enter
because a toad was ensconced there, till a
little girl, under six years old, walked in and
carried it out in her hands.

There was a toad who lived for many
years under an apple tree, close to a wicket-
gate, in honour and seclusion, until an unlucky day when, the gate being left open, it
got between the gate and the post, and thus
died, honoured and regretted.

Except from unusually violent storms
beating out the corn, or from prolonged
soaking rain, the harvest is by August toler-

ably secure. To be beaten down earlier in the year, when there is time for bindweed to grow over the stems, is much more fatal.

The noble full-eared wheat is, some whitening, some reddening into a beautiful amber tint; the beards of the barley unite in silver waves in the sunlight as the wind goes over them; the graceful oats shake their tresses, and in a few places the humble rye looks like a poor imitation of wheat. The school begins to thin, and holidays are talked of.

Harvest is not quite the parish feast it used to be, when I have known a little maid who had spent some time prosperously in service, begin to weep so pitifully and incessantly at the thought of the delights she was losing, that she had to be restored to her home!

The whole families used to turn out together, to reap and bind, and it was considered 'lucky' if the child, just promoted to reaping, cut herself with the sickle. Even if the top of a finger was cut off, it was speedily joined on with a quid of tobacco, after the remarkable practice of surgery which prevailed before the days of Union doctors.

Those were trifles. On worked and feasted the family in its own portions till the last sheaf—beautiful thing—was loaded, and the gladsome shout proclaimed it. Then, still more delightful, the women and children turned out to lease (as they call gleaning), and might be seen plodding home loaded with thin little sheaves artistically tied up with plaited straws, and great bags of ears that had fallen without their stems. Piles of corn were heaped before the houses, but, alas! few housewives either glean or bake now. They depend entirely on the baker's cart.

The joy of harvest has not passed away, and there is less wildness, less temptation therewith, but much picturesqueness is gone. The reaping machine has taken the place of the family, and leaves rows to be gathered and bound up into sheaves, and built up in the rain-repelling arrangements, which happily have never been improved upon.

The flowers appropriated to harvest associations are the tiny Cornflower (*Centaurea cyanus*), with its centre of perfect purple florets, surrounded by the ornamental, imperfect, brilliant, blue ones, all enclosed in a tight, imbricated calyx. It is a favourite for many reasons, chief of all, for the sake of the well-known story of Queen Louisa of Prussia flying before the French with her little children, and on some delay, keeping them happy and good with showing them the blue flowers in the fields; whence this was the favourite flower of her son, the Emperor William I.

It is said to be common, but it is a rarity here. I only know of two fields where it has been, though its fellow, the common Knapweed (*Centaurea nigra*), goes on showing its purple head to the last of autumn; and I have passed in succession a number of plants, each with a 'dumbledore,' apparently half asleep, in the central blossom.

It is the great time for compound flowers. The yellow corn Marigold (*Chrysanthemum segetum*), though properly a summer flower, spreads its brilliant gold over the fields till the frost destroys it; for, unlike its white brother, the ox-eye, it is an annual. Farmers hate it, but it has acquired a popularity since the Queen noticed it, and recorded it in her Scottish Journal. The flowers last so long that it is very useful for decorations.

Those beautiful plants, the thistles, spring up wherever they have a chance. The Dwarfs (*Cnicus acaulis*), brown and purple, on the chalk downs, *C. arvensis* in fields, *C. palustris* in marshes, their scaled calyces bearing a sharp barb on every scale, their leaves daintily folded in and out, but with a thorn at every point, their stems all a-bristle, all expressing the Scottish national motto, *Nemo me impune lacessit.* The Milk-thistle (*Carduus marianus*) has leaves varied with white ; the Scottish Thistle (*Cnicus lanceolatus*) (as I believe) is the handsomest and thorniest of all.

There is the Cotton Thistle, a *Cnicus* also, less formidable; and the pretty, delicate Saw-wort (*Serratula*), not quite a thistle. They all have the exquisite wings or plumes intended to scatter their seeds. A patch of thistles on a downside emits a perfect snow-storm of down, caught up by the goldfinches of flashing wing.

Of all these plumed seeds the most beautiful is that of the *Tragopogon major*, or Goat's-beard, better known as the Go-to-bed-at-noon ; for its yellow blossoms, within their very long narrow sepals, never remain expanded after twelve o'clock, but are in time replaced by most perfect and exquisite stars, perfect pentagons of cobweb texture, but stiffer than those of the dandelion.

The matrimonial auguries of the dandelion clock—

Tinker, Tailor,
Soldier, Sailor,
Clergyman, Gentleman,
Apothecary, Thief!

are well known to all.

The mop-like globe of the dandelion are of these pentagonal stars—the whole of the compound flowers *Syngenesia*, as Linnæus named the class, being formed on the rule of five, and the anthers being united together round the pretty forked style. Some are all perfect flowers like the thistle; some are perfect in the centre, with rays of imperfect flowers like the daisy; some, like knap-weed, have large but empty florets as the border.

Dandelion is really Dent de Lion, Lion'stooth, exactly translating the Latin *Leontodon*. It is one of the worthiest of the large class, its serrated leaves being good for salads, and its root (hard to dig up) being as good as chicory to mix with coffee. The golden blossoms, which Jefferies says are of a more brilliant colour in spring than in autumn, are among the most glorious of the many earth stars, and dandelion chains, made by linking loops formed by inserting the small end of the hollow stem in the larger one, so that they can be carried to any length. The only drawback is the brown stain that the milky juice leaves on the hands, drawing down the wrath of elders who care for the dainty appearance of little girls' pinky paws. The lion's teeth are to be looked for in the form of the soft leaves.

Whether Hawkweed (*Hieracium*) was so called as being good for hawks, I cannot tell. At any rate, Mouse-ear Hawkweed (*Hier-*

acium pilosella) is really good for whooping-cough. It is a very pretty little plant, with sulphur blossoms of about the size of a sixpence, on short stems, the buds tipped with red, the whole plant covered with down, and with a creeping root. It is one of the gayest stitches in the embroidery of the down in company with the delicate white eyebright, the dwarf red-rattle, and the purple tufts of stainless thistle, hawkweed, hawk's-beard, wild lettuce, and the like, all very much alike in their yellow blossoms, brighten the hedges and fields. Ragweed, or *Senecio squalidus*, has a ray of strap-shaped barren florets, like the daisy and camomile. It is beloved of caterpillars, striped like tigers, black and yellow. The Scottish name for it is Stinking William, under the belief that the Duke of Cumberland introduced it, a story that I always thought a libel till I heard that fifteen new plants had sprung up round Paris from

the forage of the Germans.   It is odd that
the universal groundsel, though without a
ray, should also be *Senecio.*

We have wandered away from the corn-
flowers without mentioning the other typical
one, the poppy, our only scarlet beauty except the tiny pimpernel, the shepherd's
weather-glass, and its own near relation, the
Adonis, or pheasant's eye.   Adonis may very
well have ensanguined this with his blood,
though I believe that the crimson anemone
has also the honour, and this, by the bye, is
said in Italy to be patriot's blood!

The dear *Papaver Rhœas,* the common
Poppy, may be seen of any size from the
well-grown plant with flowers of the circum-
ference of an orange to the starveling that
would hardly cover a shilling.   Each of the
four petals is of a magnificent crimson, in
almost, not all, cases with an intensely dark
purple or black spot at the base, so as to

have a deep-dyed cross at its heart. The profuse anthers are purple, surrounding one large four-divided capsule or urn, with a beautiful lid or cap, ornamented with velvety rays from the centre. In time, after the fall of the petals, this cover is lifted up on little supports, to let out the numerous seeds. The petals are very slightly attached, and before blooming are enclosed by two sepals, sea-green, rough, and hairy, which gradually part over the crumpled crimson within, and fall off when the flower expands. A neglected field on a hillside shows like a red handkerchief dropped down, and it is impossible to bestow due blame on the careless husbandry that has bestowed on us such a gorgeous spectacle. Yellow Welsh Poppies (*Meconopsis cambrica*) are in these parts only the ornament of shrubberies, and the great white Opium Poppy, with its dark purple cross (*Papaver somniferum*), though found in English botanical books, though of course in a wild state, is probably only a stray from gardens, where, with *P. medicinum*, it grows harmlessly and beautifully, and takes every variety of tint of the scarlet and purple gradations.   We may have poppies of every size, from the great emperor of the race, five feet high, in robes of royal crimson, and flowers, more than a foot across when expanded, down to the slender white-edged Iceland poppy, all bright and glowing, all with the peculiar sleepy smell, reminding us of laudanum, and of all the various uses and abuses of the juice scraped from them in Indian fields, and formed into the cakes of opium.

The glory of colour has passed to the heaths and moors.   Here the heath is in its beauty, beginning with the low growing, grayish-leaved *Erica tetralix*, or Bell-heather, with delicately-tinted blushing blossoms, in a single head at the top of each stalk, generally shaded rose colour, sometimes white, and then reminding us of the betrothal flower of Frederick the Noble.

It never grows tall, while the *Erica cinerea*, the common Heath, whose leaf, by the bye, is not nearly so ash-coloured as that of *tetralix*, can mount up by its tough-branched, woody stem to a considerable height, and rears its deep purple or crimson bells in tall spires. Though not so large individually as the blossoms of the bell-heather, they make much more show, and give colour to the landscape. The eight stamens lie deep within the monopetalous stiff, chaffy bell which hangs on, turning purple after the seeds have ripened. The other two British heaths (*E. ciliaris* and *E. vagans*, Irish and Cornish) are both very handsome, and are, we are told, remnants of the days of very, very old, when mountain chains now disrupted were all one. Why the

Cornish heath should be called *vagans* is not clear, for though where planted in favourable soil it grows freely, it has never voluntarily wandered out of its own peninsula, but remains there, just as the big Roman snails never get beyond the precincts of the villas where they were first introduced.

My favourite of the heather kind has been separated as a genus, having a more open bell.   The *Calluna vulgaris*, or common Ling, has a paler, more lilac blossom, growing in graceful branching, ascending spires, which always puts me in mind of early English architecture by the peculiar elegance of its forms.   A wood, the upper part of which is partly of unprosperous oak scrub, partly of mountain ash, has an undercurrent of magnificent ling, which contrasts with the ruddy Midsummer shoot of the oak, and the scarlet fruit and feathery leaves of the rowan or mountain ash.   This wood is said to be a place where foxes are always lost, and at one time it was supposed that they were under the protection of a handsome witch-like old dame, dead many years back.

Whether the woman had any connection with the rowan, I do not know. It is really, little as it looks like it, a relation of the pear. *Pyrus aucuparia* is its name, and it has a marvellous history really worth putting together. To begin with, Thor is said to have jumped over a river by the help of a branch of it when on his way to quell the Frost Giants. Also the Amazons made spears of it, and Virgil held that it attracted blackbirds and thrushes. (I could say so of nightingales, night-jars, and glow-worms.)

This is for the sake of the fruit, in the case at least of the mavis and merle, and the bright red little berry-like fruits are used for baits by bird-catchers, whence its names of the Fowler's service tree, and *Le sorbier des oiseaux.* They are so soon devoured that they never survive to serve as harvest decorations. In some places they are valued by human beings as ingredients in pleasant drinks.

Its mystic powers are, however, most curious ; Rowan in Scotch, Roan or Ruon in Scandinavia, are by some connected with the word Rune, by others with the sea-goddess Ran, the raiser of storms and fisher for ship-wrecked mariners in her net. The Vikings always took care to have a piece of this tree in their long ships as a protection against her, and the belief continued—

> Rowan tree and red thread
> Haud the witches a' in dread.

Crosses made of the twigs, tied with red thread, were worn by Highlandmen sewn into their clothes, and not only by them, but the notion was universal. Dame Sludge sewed a piece into Flibbertigibbet's collar as a protection against Wayland Smith's sorceries. In Yorkshire, Mr. Atkinson was told there were thirteen witches in the town, but they could do no harm to one who had his rowan tree safe in his pocket. So—

> If your whipstick be made of ro'an,
> You may ride your nag through any town ;

or—

> Woe to the lad
> Without a rowan tree gad.

In Wales, the rowans stand in churchyards like yew trees in England, and this is probably connected with the idea commemorated in an old engraving of the Blessed Saviour's descent into Hades, where He holds a rowan-tree cross, while releasing a spirit in prison.

It is as if a bit of the Northern myth about Thor had been Christianised, yet it is strange that it should be in Celtic parts that the notion prevails. Endless instances might be collected ; indeed, some think that the true reading of the 'Aroint thee, witch,' of the sailor's wife in *Macbeth*, should be ' A roan-tree, witch.'

August is the month of the greatest beauty in gardens, perhaps because the fashionable world inhabits its country houses then, and expects the borders to be full, so that more attention has been paid to the later flowers. The roses still are numerous, though it seems to me that the real delicately pink, emphatically rose-coloured roses keep to their proper season of June and July, and that almost all the later ones are either white or deep crimson, with very few exceptions. Is it some delicate quality in the summer sunshine that evokes that charming tint ? The later pinks are in their glory, notably the dark crimson clove, of unapproachable scent, so are all the geranium kind, whether the many-tinted *Pelargonium*, or the glowing scarlet, or the lesser scarlets, whose blossom has been sacrificed to their foliage.

The *Clematis Jackmanni* hangs a purple pall over houses, or else its many varieties show themselves much enlarged in white or pale lilac, while the little mountain clematis forms snowy sheets where it has taken a hold.

The great pink or white convolvulus likewise becomes rampant where it has once made a home ; indeed, that purest and most delicate of white flowers, the *Convolvulus sepium*, or White Bindweed, makes every hedge-side or neglected laurel bush charming. Its spiral buds are specially lovely ; and it is really in its extreme purity the most perfect of all its widespread class, well-named ' Morning Glories.' Very delightful is the major, in his varieties of purple spoked with pink, crimson with white, or white with purple, and not less so.

' His brother a minor, a cornet in blue,' as said the one line that has stayed with me, of one of the many weak imitations of the *Butterfly's Ball* and the *Peacock at Home.* Then there is the small mauve (*C. mauritanicus*), and the queen of all, the great Indian *Ipomea*, which I have only once seen, but never can forget, very large, of the softest, purest, most indescribable azure-blue, with pink divisions.

SEPTEMBER has its associations, though to the womankind who sit at home it means the sound of popping in the fields around, and the destruction of the coveys of round plump birds, which they have seen run as babies along the ruts, or rise in a stream of flight in the rear of their parents.

The day used to mean a rising very early in the morning by the young and lively, to give their gentlemen their break-fast, and see them off with their ecstatic spaniels before the dew was off. The dogs knew the day as well as the men, and I have actually known two who, when the great day fell on a Sunday, rushed off on their own account without their master, though as a rule dogs know Sunday perfectly well.

Things are changed now in matters of sport, and the freshness of the morning has ceased to be esteemed. Often, too, the harvest is not sufficiently advanced for the doom of the partridge—pat-rich, as the country folk call it. They are all still busy in the fields, and the shout proclaiming the carrying of the last sheaf rings out in turn from farm to farm, though most of the picturesque observances of the harvest home are dying away before the tramp of the schoolmaster, and still more the squeal and hum of the machine.

Certain evenings dwell on one's mind, one in especial, when I stood among the trees, with the gold of the sunset gleaming behind the hill, and on the other side the round red harvest moon slowly rising, while

in the stillness the shout over the final carrying rang out, mellowed by distance, and
poor Madge Wildfire's death-song comes to
memory—

> Our work is over, over now,
> The gudeman wipes his weary brow,
> The last long wain wends slow away,
> And we are free to sport and play.
>
> The night comes on when sets the sun,
> And labour ends when day is done.
> When Autumn's gone and Winter's come,
> We hold our joyous harvest home.

Gleaning is not what it was, mowing
and raking leave fewer ears, and it is
chiefly the holiday of the elder women for
old sake's sake, rather than the actual gain;
and, indeed, some farmers do not permit it
at all. Pigs finish off the remnants, guarded
by a boy, to the regret of the schoolmaster,
who, if he be past his fourth standard, will
probably never get him back again, even
when he is out of work.

Old-fashioned farmers still give their harvest supper; but the new generation, without mutual hereditary interests between them and the labourers, disregard it. A general harvest feast for the entire parish has been tried; but to make it a success, there should be a thorough element of geniality and enjoyment in the entertainers. If they only do the thing as a duty, it will fall flat, and the company will look with regret to the ruder pleasures, unrestrained by the gentry. Even the steadiest do not like the evening to end too soon, and dancing and fireworks have their use in keeping up the occupations, especially when the squire's or clergyman's family possess members to whom it is all a personal delight.

The harvest feast in church is another thing. It is a modern invention, but is thoroughly enjoyed by the people, if they are encouraged to make their offerings in kind for the sick in hospitals. Very queer things come, and difficult to dispose of—enormous pumpkins, great pieces of honeycomb, apples enough to make the church smell like an apple-chamber, onions which have to be relegated to the porch, and big purple and white turnips, or long-tailed red carrots to be judgmatically disposed of. Sometimes it is the best way to have a week-day evening for these substantial offerings, which are afterwards sent to a hospital; and a Sunday when beauty is alone consulted, and the staple of the decorations can be the three sorts of corn, assisted by grasses stored since summer, together with dahlias, scarlet geraniums, the brilliant, waxy berries of the wild guelder-rose, and the grand dark sceptres of the reed maces, which everybody insists on calling bulrushes.

Loaves of home-made bread are sometimes brought, reminiscences of the time when some of the good old house-mothers used to present their clergyman with a loaf out of their 'leasing corn' as their tithe.

Another tithe, acting the other way, was that when a tenth child was born in a family, without any previous deaths, a spray of myrtle was fastened in its christening cap—there were such things then—and the parson was bound to send it to school.

Such a tithe child have I seen baptized, and in contradiction to those who say that a labourer cannot provide for his old age, it is worth recording that the father, though by no means a distinguished workman, but sober, steady, and with a helpful, thrifty wife, saved enough to provide himself a weekly amount in his old age, though he lived to be over eighty. There was some addition made from the alms; but even otherwise, he would hardly have come to the workhouse.

Another apple-faced family, where the children amount to sixteen, and without any special powers or cleverness, have from the first been absolutely punctual in payments, small and great, neatly dressed, not only without but within, as measurements for dresses have revealed, and their cottage a pattern of tidiness. The young men are mostly out in the world—two soldiers and one a sailor in the Royal Navy, whose pay comes in part to his home. The lads have bought a wheeled chair for an invalid sister, and though grateful for broth or niceties in a stress of sickness, they never beg.

Sensation represents the labourer as getting nine shillings a week with twelve small children. The nine shillings once was true; but whether in the land of monogamy there ever were twelve children all small together may be doubted! The hardest time in a peasant family is when there are five or six children, none able to earn anything, and school laws preventing the elder ones from acting as nurses at home, and letting the mother earn something. It is really the best thing for the family in the end; but it presses hard till the school age is past. Then one has to submit to the girl being a victim. to the baby, and the boy to the cows, which in spite of their calm, innocent natures become very demoralising to the small herdsman, who has nothing to do but lounge about, never to be found when his cows are where they ought not to be.

It is drink on one side of the house, muddle on the other, that cause real poverty, far more than large families, or even ill-health. Yet the sickly woman must be a heroine in spirit who keeps up incessantly the task of being her own efficient servant of all work, without relaxation, and without sal volatile or any other stimulant than the beneficent tea!

The last remnants of the harvest holidays are often spent on blackberries. The world has found out how handsome the despised bramble is in its place, with its pearly blossom and its long twining limbs, with their load of fruit, black, red, and green in the several stages, and the five-leafleted foliage, which assumes every tint in the scale between crimson and green.

I have a drawing of a spray of leaf, flower, and fruit excellently drawn and coloured by an invalid village girl. When she was laid low by some spine affection, a lady, to amuse her, gave her a paint-box and a flower-drawing to copy. She did it so well that she was encouraged to go on, and gradually developed a really surprising talent for drawing flowers from nature. She could not originate, but she copied the real blossom admirably, and generally with much taste, and by the help of a clever contrivance of her brother, she could make the lettering of the Old English texts, which she illuminated, wonderfully even and straight. One year she designed the Christmas card for the G. E. S., but her work was not quite certain enough to be absolutely reliable for orders. She did, however, prosper well over illuminated texts, cards, menu cards, and even stools. Having been previously wretched at being a burden to her family, her spirits rose when she became an assistance to them, and the content thus occasioned really seemed to prolong her life, till the years of influenza broke down her strength finally.

The stubble fields have their embroidery in the tiny original pansy, barely freaked with jet, and not purple with love's wound, the *Viola tricolor*. It blossoms all the year, summer and autumn more or less, and so do all its splendid garden varieties, of royal dark purple velvet, glowing yellow, copper-coloured, or strangely - eyed, like human countenances, or cats' faces, only all these gradually degenerate till they almost return to their tiny original type in the cornfield. Three faces under a hood, herb Trinity, are among their names; besides that maidens call them love-in-idleness, while their jocund looks win them the name of heart's-ease; and the French *pensée*, from their variety, was known to Ophelia: 'There's pansies, that's for thoughts.' The Germans regard them as the *Stiefmutter*, showing the mother-in-law predominant in purple velvet, her own two daughters gay in purple and yellow, the two poor little Cinderellas more soberly and scantily attired, squeezed in between. It is a curious instance of unbending system that Linnæus grouped these with the compound flowers, because like them they have five anthers meeting in a point round the style.

Another lover of stubble is the Shepherd's Needle, or Venus's Comb (*Scandix Pecten-Veneris*), whose long spiked capsules are much more visible than the insignificant, umbelliferous blossom. See, too, the neat little gray crosses of the Field Madder (*Sherardia arvensis*), a near relation of the *Galium*, white and yellow, that ramp about in hedgerows, all with multitudinous white and yellow blossoms. They are, at least the smoother kinds, our lady's-bedstraw, and might afford a springy couch; but their more scantily blossoming brother, all over tiny pricks, is well named Cleavers or Cliders (*Galium aparine*), for it is very hard to be rid of. The family culminates in the fragrant Woodruff (*Asperula odorata*), over long ago. All have

angular stems and leaves in whorls. There
are the pretty little *Linarias*, tiny snap-
dragons, or toad-flax; the *Linaria elatine*
and *spuria*—one with heart-shaped leaves,
the other with egg-shaped ones—creep about
the ground, and show their long spurs and
yellow and deep purple flowers nearly all
through the year. The ivy-leaved *Linaria
cymbalaria* adorns old walls almost everywhere with pendent bunches of leaves, and
pretty pale purple flowers, and the very handsome *L. vulgaris* raises tall spikes of yellow
and orange flowers in the hedge. All have
long spurs, and the peculiar flower, closing
like a box, especially seen in the grand
banner of old castle walls, the *Antirrhinum
majus* (Snap-dragon), with its scarlet body
and yellow lip, gay, according to Sir John
Lubbock, on purpose to attract the insects on
whom the fertilisation depends. It is amusing to see a great dumbledore enter, the lid

close on him, and then his velvet tail back out gradually. The papilionaceous flowers have no such convenient doorway, so the bees bore a hole through the wrappings of the keel, which contains their sheaf of stamens, with one loose from the rest to allow for the swelling of the germ into a pod. Darwin has an amusing account of inter-dependence, showing how the prosperity of a bean-field depends on the number of bumble bees which carry about the pollen, how the bees may be reduced by the field-mice which eat the honey in their bag-like cells, and, I think, how the field-mice are kept down by hawks and owls, and so that the unspar-ing gamekeeper does serious damage to the crops, which are withering into blackness now from the once fragrant black and white labiate blossoms.

The balance of the commissariat of nature is, as has often been observed, most marvellously adjusted, though man, for his own purposes, disturbs it. Yet the instincts intended to keep it up still survive. For instance, certainly in one instance, I believe in two, where the mischievous *Anarcharis*, the American Pond-weed, astray from aquariums, had begun to choke a pond, two swans, which had lived childless for years, began to lay eggs, and produced cygnets enough to keep in check this their favourite food.

Even the much abused wasp has its value in keeping down the flies. The said wasps are at their worst in the end of August and beginning of September, though there are those who think the commotion they cause by far the worst part of the wasp visitation. In point of fact, the wasp has no desire to sting except in self-defence, and therefore it is wiser to let her alone in her investigations, though when they happen to concern our own dinner and our own heads they are teasing, but infinitely less so than jumping about and making dabs at her, which may very justly exasperate her. In truth, the modern female ought to have a sympathy with her, as she and her sisters, like the working bees, ants, and hornets, are the useful spinsters of the community. The wasp, too, is a worthier character than the bee, though less valuable to us. She does not murder her drone, but lets him be serviceable at home, until the final doom, when all die together of frost, except the valiant queens. Instead of spitefully killing their daughters, and when withheld, bouncing forth with a huge bodyguard, whizzing behind them, these heroines go out alone in solitude to be the valiant founders of fresh colonies. So much honour do these lonely dames deserve, that I always feel a certain cruelty in the saying—

> To kill a wasp in May
> Is worth a load of hay,

though the cruelty is kindness to the fruit, to the meat, and to the many people; and I did not sympathise with an old farming-man who deferred his onslaught on a hornet's nest till there should be more to kill. This hornet's nest was just within the door of an outhouse, where each insect had to crawl over the beam of the doorway before entering. Here he took his stand, and stabbed each as it crossed the fatal beam, till all were gone save the queen, the larvæ, and a solitary loyal guardswoman who stung him as he slew her queen. And the chicken ate up the grubs, including some just ready to emerge, perfect hornets in shape, but all white. We kept the nest for a long time, but it was less beautiful than the solitary wasps', which are pendent spiral gray paper circular folds enclosing a few cells.

The swarming ants come out now. They are perhaps the best emblems of modern

society, for while the little black or brown
unwedded females toil for the general welfare, tend the infants, bring home loads,
and some at least store up corn, and serve as
the famous example to the sluggard, their
more perfect sisters perish in their vanity.
As the Spanish proverb says: 'The ant
found wings for her own destruction.'

Out they burst on a sunny day, 'just
come out,' all with pairs of silver gauze wings,
all over gravel-walks and lawns. I have
seen them very appropriately, though very
inconveniently, swarming thus over the whole
of a terraced garden prepared for an after-
noon tea. They take a short flight in the
air, soon descend, and if not eaten by birds,
some are captured by their own kind, who
bite off their wings, and bring them to
fulfil domestic duties underground. Others
are said to strike off their wings, and become
the mothers of new homes.

As Kingsley says, what would become of us if lions had the power of acting together, and devoting themselves to the common good that ants have ?   Taking them altogether, they seem to me the most wonderful things in creation, with their herds of aphides, whom they pasture, protect, and obtain food for, from their self-devotion and ingenuity.   The great horse-ants, who build tall cones of pine needles in the plantations, have their roads leading up to their home ; but we have none of those strange slave-holding soldier-ants who become demoralised and helpless from being constantly waited on by the poor little black slaves whom they capture.

Let us give one glance at the great spiders who have those cottony webs in the furze, and may be seen at the entrance of the funnel-like den in the centre, with their eight legs upon their cords, ready to make their prey sooner or later 'walk into their parlour.'

They do look wicked enough for Web-spinner, that miser who entrapped the poor widow, 'One Madgie de la Moth'; but I have a kindness for the geometrical spider who hangs up those delicate regular constructions to be gemmed with diamonds on these dewy mornings; also for the hunter-spider, who lived and kept his larder under the stigma of an iris; and for the nest of babies who lived in one common web in my creeping juniper, generally all in one lump; but they would start all over the threads if the family web were touched with a pin. And the Gossamer (*Gottes cymar*) that floats over the grass, all shining in the low sunshine, was once Freya's veil—afterwards the Blessed Virgin's—all the work of tiny spiders, leaping from one bent to another!

Whom have we here? An enormous caterpillar as thick as a finger, of a delicate apple-green colour, with a little brown and yellow horn upon his tail, and a short dash of purple and white on each side of all his rings, and occasionally he rears up his head and front legs in a position that causes him and his kind to bear the name of Sphinx. He has been living on privet leaves for some weeks past, and now is come out for his final wandering. I have in past times found a ring of school-children in terror round this dreadful animal, and one braver than the' rest about to dispose of it with his heavy boot. Now, they are more inclined to present it to their young ladies as a great curiosity. This it scarcely can be called, for it is the commonest sort of sphinx or hawk-moth caterpillar. The jessamine and elephant species are much greater prizes, to say nothing of the strange Death's-head, who adds to the terror of his appearance by squeaking, and whose larva lives on potato haulm. Did Raleigh introduce it?

If you keep the privet larva, in another day or two he will look sickly, and the beautiful green will assume a yellowish tinge. This is the beginning of his change. Give him a deep pot of fresh soft earth, and he will bury himself, but ere many days are past will rise half out of his grave in mahogany-coloured cerements, where his future proboscis may be detected curled up. Let him alone, and next spring a beautiful brown-shaded and pinky large moth will emerge, but generally at some impossible time, and escape unseen. Once, indeed, instead of a moth there escaped from the chrysalis a whole family of little white ichneumon flies, to my exceeding horror and disgust, though I have since come to believe that it does not make much difference to caterpillar felicity whether these creatures live within it, or it comes to its proper development. The larva of the puss moth, the prettiest caterpillar I ever saw, has two horns, whence, at a touch on the back, two pink fibres are protruded, which *may* be whip-lashes to drive away the parent ichneumon fly from laying eggs in it. Another very pretty caterpillar may be found now, beautiful pale green, but with black velvet 'revelations' between its rings as it crawls, or rolls up in a ring, with tufts like those on a toothbrush along its sides, and one pink one on its tail. Its proper name is the Tussock. When about to change, it weaves its tufts and any fragments of wood it can saw off into a round cocoon, fastened against a wall. It is a good sort to keep, for it can be seen as through a veil in the act of weaving, with its head going from side to side.

Moths, especially sphinxes, are seldom to be seen in the daytime; but one, the humming-bird sphinx, pertains to the delicious sunny days of September, when it is to be seen hovering over late roses, blue salvias, dahlias, or any other gorgeous autumn flower, inserting its long trunk, but never settling, and all the time quivering its wings so rapidly, like the little birds it is named from, thát there is no detecting what they are like.

Not so the great splendid Peacock and Red Admiral butterflies, which sit basking, opening and closing their beauteous wings in extreme enjoyment. Twice it has been my good fortune to see some sixty or seventy magnificent admirals all together. Once it was on a heap of apples, once on some rare foreign shrub, which had somewhat the odour of apples. Whatever attracted them, they made one of the most beautiful exhibitions I ever beheld.

Those apples were in Devonshire, where every one of the little low gnarled apple-trees in the orchard, so beautiful with blossom in the spring, begins the month with brilliant red, green, and yellow heaps below them.   The more beautiful to look at, the more acid and uneatable, so the orchards are safe *even* from the almost omnivorous village boy.   Formerly, when cider was a universal drink, and often part of the weekly wages, every farm and every estate had its cider-press—a great granite thing nearly as large as the round table of the drawing-room of the former half-century, with patterns tooled on the edge, four or five inches thick, and a hole in the middle for the screw on which it was made to revolve by leverage of man or horse.   A Hampshire man, who was taken to fetch home a horse from Devon, was delighted with the cider, which he supposed to be a treat for a stranger.   The several dialects of the counties were amazing to one another. ' My sön, yöu talks French,' was said to him.

Now cider is far less often home-brewed, the granite presses have been made garden decorations, and the apples are often exported, to be used in clearing the colours of all those aniline shades of mauve which are extracted from coal, and, we are told, were stored in the primeval vegetation by the sunshine.

The Devon saying is, that to eat a roasted apple at bedtime prevents ever having to send for the doctor. An apple, however, is never so delicious as when eaten raw with the teeth in the garden. Then were enjoyed the stubbord, excellent in its prime, but soon woolly, the Duke of Cornwall, of orange below and freckled longitudinally with red, the red-streaked Ribstone pippin, the deep crimson Quarendon, red even in its flesh. These all belong to the old woman's younger days of apple-eating, and as grafted trees are said to have the same tenure of life as their parent stock, are in danger of becoming as extinct as is the golden pippin, or as a huge cooking-apple, of which we once had two old trees, and which a farmer's wife called the Buntry Dew. She is believed to have meant Bonté de Dieu.

This is not a cider country ; but we have enough to be the delight of youth, the worry of schools, and to afford plenty of picturesque apple - gathering. Alternate years seem needed for really plentiful crops, and one beneficent mission of spring frosts is to cut off the blossom and rest the trees.

OCTOBER

wrote Sara Coleridge long ago in her rhymes for her children.   And as to the first line, one can only say, ' Pity 'tis, 'tis true,' if one is neither a sportsman nor a housewife.   For what a sight the live pheasant is if we come on him suddenly in the evening sunshine that lights all his coppery feathers with metallic lustre, while he turns his stately neck, and looks round with his eye in its setting of red, his long barred tail giving the dignity of a train.   So tame are the beautiful creatures, often reared under hens, that I have known them feed on chestnuts on one side of a tree, while I have been picking on the other, and it has seemed hard that their confidence should so be deceived when battues begin. However, it may be better to live to be shot than never to have lived at all! And though, when game laws are in peril, I own to some wonder that the sporting system should be so managed as to make them specially irritating to the peasant and tempting to the poacher, it must be owned that preserving incidentally saves wild plants from being exterminated by unscrupulous marauders. Daffodils, snowdrops, lilies of the valley, ferns, and even primroses, would not long exist if every wood could be overrun by those who have no mercy on roots, and care not for the future.

And before we leave the pheasant, I must record, for the benefit of the polite letter-writer, a note in which a lady-farmer returned thanks for the present of one, declaring that her 'gastronomical powers did it full justice, as it became small by degrees and beauti-fully less,' which is not the usual course with the appearance of a half-eaten bird!

As to the nuts, a great deal of charm has been attributed to nutting, but it must be in some place where the breaking of hazel boughs is immaterial, as perhaps it was in the old easy-going times. Now the wood-men do not hail a fine crop with delight, as they have hard work to guard their bushes from being torn down. The conventional picture of the boy in a nut-tree throwing to the girl below, depicts what is here at least impossible, for our hazels would hardly sup-port a boy of seven years old!

The cluster of nuts is a pretty thing, with the softly tinted nut sunk within the long calyx. By the bye, what part of the nut-bush is supposed to be of the same colour as hazel eyes? The filbert is still more graceful, with much longer sheaths as beards, whence the name—full-beard.

The Walnut (*Juglans regia*), the royal Jove's acorn, namely, comes from Persia. Walnut is really the foreign nut, the first syllable being like Welsh, the Teutonic for 'stranger,' as the Germans call Italy *Welschland*, and turkeys *Welschhahnen*. The French *dinde* is 'de Inde'—the most correct of the three names for that fowl, as the wild turkey is assuredly not Turkish, but American, and so shares the name with the Red Indian and with Indian corn.

> Hops and turkeys, carp and beer,
> Came to England all in one year.

So says good old Izaak Walton, on the authority of Sir R. Baker, who makes the year 1523. Others insert the word pickerel, a young pike, and some say 'Reformation,' but I believe the above to be the right version.

Q

Beer or ale was assuredly drunk by the oldest English, though they did not, like the Northmen, make ale a part of their names, as Olaf—which is really ale-giver.   Probably, however, the name of beer had · in some way gone out of use, and the new brew, flavoured by hops, assumed the name. *Humulus lupulus*, the hop, is common enough in all our hedges, though it is sometimes doubted whether it is only a stray run wild from those hop gardens which, in their prime, rival the vineyards of the South with their graceful foliage and pretty leafy catkins. It is only as wild that they grow in these parts, and merely as a visitor that I have seen the long alleys between the well-laden poles.   The universal holiday in hopping villages is scarcely yet over : that time when old and young turn out, and the peculiar fragrance inspires a restful feeling beneficial to the nerves.   A hop pillow was one of the remedies that did poor old George III. the most good under Dr. Willis's care. The influx of rough strangers from the slums is the only drawback to the glad season, and they, poor things, are so much the better for what is for once a wholesome festival time to them, that it can hardly be grudged to them. Indeed, in one case at least, it is made by the clergy a means of trying to convey some spiritual benefit to them, and they show themselves grateful.

The summer birds are departing. The swallows sit in long rows on roofs and telegraph wires, meditating departure, and perhaps instructing their broods. The other birds go more quietly, and seldom notify their intentions, though I have once met a flock of hen chaffinches on their way, but here in the South migration is not so universal as in the North. Many of these ladies remain for the winter, and so do the golden-crested wrens, who migrate from Yorkshire, but whom I have often seen popping about quickset hedges in the winter.

This is the month above all of the glory of autumn. St. Martin's or St. Luke's little summer, or the Indian summer, whichever we are pleased to call it, brings the brightest of sunshine, and the sun being low comparatively early, lights up everything with a side-long ray that is specially embellishing to the red trunks of pines, and the gray lichen-clad boles of oaks.

The leaves have begun to put on their final robes of glory. Even little Herb-robert (*Geranium robertianum*), while blossoming still, has put his much-divided leaves into the robes of a doctor of divinity. The way-faring-tree, once a gray woolly thing, is equally crimson. So are the docks, the *lythrums*, the purple loosestrife, and the willow herbs. In fact, the red purple flowers seem to have leaves also susceptible of the same dye. They would make a beautiful bouquet, if it were not hard to find perfect ones, as they drop off as soon as gathered, the flow of sap from the vessels of the stem having ceased.

The hedge - side is a charming study of colouring—in masses of yellow, amber, purple, crimson, all shades of pale brown, and green in every variety. The yellow is generally maple, whose pinnate leaves take sundry tints of gold and brown, while some remain green and still show the little red ex-crescences which are the work (I believe) of one of the many bedeguars. The amber is the autumn dress of the hawthorn, each of whose tiny winged leaves takes a uniform colour. Purple and crimson adorn the Cornel or Dogwood (*Cornus sanguineus*), a dull, in-significant bush in the summer, with a poor little white four-stamened flower in corymbs, but in autumn imperially robed in all varieties of purple, sometimes so dark as to be almost black, sometimes bright blood-red, meriting the specific name, and the twigs standing up into the sun, perfectly brilliant as the light shines through them. The bits of oak are of all shades between brown and green, the later shoots, lingering after Midsummer, showing red. The dog-roses contribute golden leaves and hips of shining scarlet, or duller rounder balls of the white field-rose, long bents stand up from the still green grass, the bramble boughs bear blossoms and show all tints on their leaves, of purple, red, and yellow, sometimes mixed ; and over all winds the *Clematis vitalba*, well-named Traveller's-joy, or Old Man's Beard, displaying those soft white woolly wigs that are formed by the silky wings of the seeds. A few thistles, knap-weeds in rich purple, golden-rod in yellow, and herb-roberts in

pink, still star the banks, and it is quite difficult to get along the lane for counting the
variations of beauty. Here and there we
have bushes of the *Euonymus europœus*, or
Spindle-wood, Skewer-wood, some still bright
lively green, without a berry, being the male
plants ; and alternately with them, others
with the foliage further gone, but with
the unusually beautiful fruit, the five-divided
capsule of a delicate, pure pink, most uncommon in seed-vessels, and which, opening,
discloses a brilliant orange-coated seed. The
wood is very hard, and was used for the
spindle in spinning days, also for skewers,
which an old woman said were made from a
tree that grows on purpose.

Thence, of course, the English names ;
the Latin is more puzzling, as it is said to
come from Euonyme, the mother of the
Furies, whether because of the fitness of
the wood for weapons, or because the fruit

is peculiarly unwholesome, there is no guessing.

Above and beyond, the woods repeat and amplify the glory. The elms begin by being spangled with golden leaves here and there, and gradually become towering masses of gold. The beeches are in every shade from green and flame colour on each tree. I shall never forget the year of after-glows which we were told to ascribe to the volcanoes in Java, when in the sunsets one especial tall, upright tree, stood up opposite to the sunset, as it were a pillar of fire. The oaks repeat every possible shade of brown and 'old gold'; the wild cherries— once piles of snow—are now pyramids of crimson, and the seas of bracken beneath are at first sight all a yellow field, but on examination they show golden-yellow rising above the mass, green, edged with gold, and a whole scale of tints, while the slender birches above become again silver trees loaded with gold. The wayfaring trees and guelder roses are in various shades of crimson.

Then there are the fungi. Under the fir trees rose the magnificent *Agaricus muscarius*, of tiger-like brilliance—for it is extremely poisonous to human creatures, but its beauty is a warning. The stem and gills of the purest white, the upper umbrella-like part, properly called then the *pileus* or hat, deep dark crimson, sometimes plain, but oftener spotted over with raised white dots, like pearl-headed pins in a velvet cushion, really the remnant of the veil. There, too, was the eminently wholesome and excellent *Cantharellus cibarius*, or *chanterelle*, apricot-coloured and apricot-scented, much admired by adventurous eaters of toadstools. Their entirely unquestionable friend the Mushroom (*Agaricus campestris*), white-covered and rosy-gilled, so charming in dewy meadows in September, is generally over, only leaving its green fairy rings.   There is another species, called the Horse-mushroom (*Agaricus arvensis*), large and handsome, but coarse-looking, growing under trees, good for catsup, and sometimes called unwholesome, but really only becoming so when decaying and eaten by slugs.

The   little   buff - coloured   Champignon (*Agaricus oreades*), which grows in rings on the downs, is also good to eat, and so is St. George's Mushroom (*Agaricus georgii*), which, as the name implies, comes early in the year. These strange, wonderful things seem created to absorb the moisture of decaying nature, to grow up quickly, and convert what would otherwise be deleterious into food for various beings, or else, themselves passing away, form soil where other vegetable growth can spring.   The bare, red-

brick wall or bare wall, or the rough bark
of a tree, soon is varied, at every joint
or corner, by the yellow or gray crust of
lichen, with invisible seeds at its edges.
On them soon follow tender tufts of velvet-
like moss, and by and by, if there be a
coign of vantage, the polypody, the chick-
weed, the pellitory; in some counties the
wall penny-wort, and by and by follow the
red Valerian, the snap-dragon, and wallflower.

The lichen has begun the work; the
mushroom is generally in moist places, and
is more developed, bearing spores containing the germs of reproduction. The Agarics
are the most developed — with their um-
brella shape — the true toadstool, appropriate to Puck. They come up in round
buttons, gradually open their heads into
what botanists call a *pileus* or hat, smooth
or sometimes warty above. A veil which
had enclosed them becomes divided, leav-

ing a fringe above upon the *pileus*, and a ring below on the stem.

Below, the covering is divided into converging rays or gills, between which are contained the spores. Other fungi carry on the whole work of ripening under their outer covering; others have their spores within tubes, looking sponge-like. The numbers are infinite. In one walk of little more than a mile I counted full twenty-two sorts.

The Puff-ball (*Lycoperdon*), whose spores are first hidden in a spongy consistency of cells which becomes black powder, shut up in a round white wall of skin, is averred to be eatable; but I had rather not try, and would leave it to its proper use of smoking out bees. The *Boletus* is no beauty — a great, thick, lumpy thing, liver-coloured, and with apparently yellow sponge consisting of tiny tubes beneath it. Break it; when, if the fleshy interior retains the original lemon tint, it is probably wholesome, and is the *Boletus edulis*, with reticulations on the bulbous stem. If the flesh begins turning blue, it is *Boletus luridus*, and poisonous. Slugs, black and gray, seem to find both equally to their taste. Then on stumps of trees are the graceful, large, vase-like white *Polyporus*, the edge turned over on the up-sloping gills, so as to form cups that might be a model. Also on trees, clusters of gray or white curved *Polyporus squamosus*, like the eatable nests of the Chinese swallow, and on the oak tree branches that peculiar jelly-like *Tremella aurantium*, of a bright orange colour, which the Germans have named St. Gundula's lamp, in honour of the holy maiden who was wont to go out with her lamp in early twilight morning to visit the sick. Probably it is luminous, as decaying wood often is.

Then there are delicate lilac mushrooms, and tiny, tiny red or yellow Agarics peeping up through the grass by the roadside (*A. coccineus*); also the purple, yellow, or white-branched *Clavaria*. The *Peziza coccinea*, or Fairy Bath, a cup of brilliant poppy-red, is to be found upon dry sticks, generally at the back of hedges. Cup lichens, tiny gray cups, are to be found everywhere, and now and then that greater prize, the kind tipped, as it were, with red sealing-wax.

Nowhere is the story of *Eyes and No Eyes* more entirely to be carried out than in a lane in this and the ensuing months, so amusing all the year round to Eyes, scarcely ever interesting to No Eyes.

The gardens go on showing their late summer glory, the scarlet geranium which, coming from a Southern hemisphere, still finds autumn congenial ; the heliotrope, gray, purple and delicious; the fuchsia, with its crimson calyx, veiling the purple fold of petals, far more beautiful in the original colouring and form than in the tortured freaks of gardeners; the dahlia, crimson, sulphur, purple, or white, pinked and quilled in the double state, which for once I prefer to the single, though that has of late been the fashion. Both these names, like the Kalmia, sound so friendly and natural that it is odd to realise that they are formed from those of Fuchs, Dahl, and Kalm, three of the twelve men whom Linnæus termed his Apostles, and sent exploring into tropical regions, which proved fatal to the health of some of them.

The great vegetable marrows, called in Kent Timnals, perhaps from a first grower, for there seems no other cause, are in their fullest magnificence, stretching their long limbs covered with huge vine-like leaves in the utmost luxuriance, and showing their fine-looking fruit in all patterns and gradations—the ripe yellow, the striped green in alternate divisions of light and dark, the small-growing green, and the large, star-like yellow flowers, and corkscrew tendrils, reminding us for one thing of Cinderella's coach, for another, of the fabled husbandman who regretted that handsome trees like oaks and handsome fruit like the gourd did not go together, till an acorn fell on his face, and he cried—

> Rubbing the place,
> How lucky this was not a pumpkin?

I think this was in a charming book of my childhood, which I rather believe belonged to the S.P.C.K., but unluckily long since out of print. It was all fables in verse, and contained some capital things, of which I remember some fragments : one beginning—

> An owl from out a hollow tree
> One afternoon was peeping;
> It was about half-after-three,
> His usual time for sleeping.

He proceeds to wish it were always dark, with no sunshine—

> No glaring flowers would then be here,
> So gaudy and perfumy;
> But day would just like night appear
> As beautiful and gloomy.

Of course a moraliser comes by, far less amusing.

The gourds of primitive nations, and the pumpkin pies which are to America what Michaelmas geese are to us, come to mind, though it is hinted that the original 'pumpkin pie' was only *faute de mieux*, and that the regulation dish takes a great deal of flavouring to make it go down.

We have had a really Scriptural experience of gourds. A marrow which appeared at dinner was extremely bitter, and absolutely

R

nauseating, recalling in a moment Elisha's young prophets. The plant from which it came was hard to distinguish from its wholesome companions.

Of Jonah's gourd, though that was probably no gourd at all, but a Palma Christi, it is impossible not to think when, after one fine starlight night, the glorious plant lies a piteous wreck of ruin, wrought not by worm, but by frost, whose first touch destroys these natives of warmer regions. The heliotropes are blackened, the dahlias become wet, disgusting rags, though if warmer days follow, their buds, having more inherent warmth than the leaves, go on opening their flowers, looking like ornaments on a withered and decayed beauty. The scarlet geraniums survive a little longer, so, apparently, do the perpetual roses; but the foundations of these blossoms are sapped, and they fall off when gathered. The garden is a doleful scene of damp and decay, and there is nothing for it but to take up the annuals and put in the bulbs in future hope.

But how splendid are the sunsets! The slant beams light up the red trunks of the pines, and add to the glory of the foliage. One elm, a peculiarly formed one, with branches sloping upwards, which is always tardier, both in putting forth and losing its leaves, than the rest, becomes a pillar of gold, or more than gold, against the blue sky. Its splendour was unspeakable that autumn of remarkable after-glow, said to be owing to the dust of the Japanese volcano, when the western sky was such a red or orange hue that the young moon, by contrast, looked almost green. In ordinary years, however, the pine trees stand up dark and grand against skies of pale brightness, shading from blue into daffodil, like a wondrous illimitable coast of Eldorado (for want of a better word), with a golden surf of waves rolling in, or with the lovely fleeces that we used to call Aslauga's golden hair, and looked on as like dear memories, the last lingering bright traces of a joyous day never to be recalled.   Yet it might be 'the promise of the morrow.'

NOVEMBER

NOVEMBER is the month most abused in the whole year. Scott tells us that—

> November's sky is chill and drear,
> November's leaf is red and sere,

—valuable lines to the cappers of verse in distress for the letter ' N.'

But, in very truth, November has many delightfully quiet, still soft days, when ' calm decay' has set in, and the leaves, lately coloured by October's frost, come gently floating down in the 'calm undressing' of the woods. If it be dry weather, it is really delightful to go crackling among them—

> To heap and toss them wild and free,
> Their fragrance breathe, and o'er them see
> Soft evening lustre shed.

Some of them are very handsome too, especially those of the sycamore, which come down yellow, marked all over with round black spots —I believe a sort of fungus. Their keys are shed likewise, and produce multitudes of little trees, of which, however, very few continue to grow after they are a few inches high.

The horse-chestnut has become brown as to its leaves, and where the beauteous spikes that made it a giant's nosegay once were, are its fruits, by no means equalling the blossoms in number, for each spike only produces at most three of the round prickly green balls, which, when split open, as they generally are by their fall from the tree, show themselves to be lined with a strong white coating, with a partition in the middle, containing the two nuts, flat on one side, rounded on the other, each in colour, markings, and polish like a well-rubbed mahogany table, and forming charming playthings, though their bright beauty very soon disappears. If opened when half ripe, the mixture of brown and white makes them like piebald horses, but the white is instantly discoloured on exposure to the air. Deer like them, but for human creatures the large yellowish flesh within is unwholesome. However, the tree, whether in flower or fruit, is the great bait to boys, as affording endless 'cock-shys'; and it is vain to try to persuade them that, however it may be with the fruit, it is mere wantonness to throw at the flowers, and destroy the leaves in their beauteous youth and greenery.

Another valued plaything of nursery days was the ripe French bean, which is of a pretty polished black, varied with mauve, and preserves its beauty much longer than the chestnut. It can be strung into necklaces, and shovelled about in bowls, and altogether affords a far more interesting toy than the far too perfect articles to be bought in toy-shops, and it has the great advantage that—barring being swallowed whole—it is perfectly harmless.

The real chestnut is coming down now from its handsome trees in its spiked coatings. The *t* in its name has no reference to the chest, but is a remnant of the Latin *castaneus*. It is no native, as indeed we still remember when we distinguish it as Spanish chestnut, and when it has reached its prime, the weight of its crown exposes it to be too often ruined by sudden winds. Here—it could not be as in Italy, where a chestnut tree, or even part of a tree, is a family estate, and bread is made of the ground nuts—those that ripen here are often wizen little things, chiefly consisting of rind; but the village child can devour most things, and the paths to the school are strewn with 'shucks' of those eaten without preliminary roasting till the lips become raw and sore, after which experience, the chestnuts are politely presented to the school-mistress. The chestnuts, whose roasting is a fireside delight, or which are sold at little brasiers in the streets, come from Spain and Italy. Beech masts, equally prickly outside, never attain to size within sufficient to attract any-thing but swine.

These animals, after being herded in the stubble, have another lively time of excursions under the oak trees, prolonging the diversions of their little Gurth till he is pretty well spoilt for the thraldom of school. 'A visitation of acorns,' says the anxious school-manager; for in favourable seasons everybody capable turns out to pick the smooth oval fruit as it slips out of its little rough saucer. It is well to pick it from pastures, for the acorn is not easy of digestion, and cows who have indulged in it freely in plentiful years have often died

thereof.   Pigs in styes have to be fed spar-
ingly on it, though, when turned out, they
eat of it in combination with other delicacies
of the season, and do themselves no harm.
We hear of ancient Britons eating acorns,
and it appears that England did not forget
the pleasing diet, for, when a *crèche* was first
commenced in the nearest town, the poor
babies proved to be fed on a mixture of
which crushed acorns were a portion, and the
mothers complained that the good milk there
administered spoilt their taste for their home
food.   In the New Forest there is a period
called Pannage time, when the cottagers
have a right, for six weeks, to turn out their
swine to enjoy the harvest under the trees.

'Hampshire hogs' thus sometimes have
begun upon hogs' food.   I do not know
whether the Hampshire man is more devoted
to his pig than the natives of other counties,
but it certainly fills an important place in the

family possessions, though not in the household, like 'the gintleman that pays the rint' in Ireland. Nor does it run about at large, high-backed and bristly—only sleeping in a little dark den, as in Devonshire of old. Scarcely a house is without a tidy pigstye, the resort of the ruminating master, pipe in mouth, in Sunday leisure. A woman dying of a long illness expressed her mournful regrets to her clergyman that she had never seen the present pig, adding that her husband said that, if he had known in time how much she wished it, he would have carried it upstairs, but now it was too big and heavy.

So the pig is the family pet and pride until the day when the parish executioner comes. If early, the tender-hearted little girls of the cottage hide their ears under the blankets; if late, their mother hurries them off to school, out of hearing of the prolonged dying wails of their favourite, while the boys either hurry up, or else linger about, with all the horrid curiosity that used to attend executions, to behold the last struggles, which, happily, under an experienced hand, are brief. Then follows the further process of singeing off the bristles over a straw fire; after which piggy is hung up by the heels, fair and white, and the family are regaled upon fry, etc., at dinner. I am not sure whether the story is one of the stock clerical ones, but our rector of seventy years ago told it as happening to himself, that, being told that his flock could not understand the long words in his sermons, he asked a labourer if he knew what was meant by predestination, and was answered: 'Well, sir, I believe it is something about the innards of a pig!'

Here in Hampshire the further destination of the bacon pig, after being cut up into joints and salted, is to be smoked in a chimney adapted for the purpose, but only from a wood fire, and we found it impossible to induce cottagers to abstain from coal. The smoking is done specially at the village shop, and in fact both the preparing of bacon and the curing of hams by special private recipes are among the good arts that importation has overpowered. Pork shows itself by its name to be less an insular institution than bacon, whose name is said to be not even Anglo-Saxon, but British ; and, though we here respect the pork well-roasted and furrowed with crackle, and the fair delicate salt pork leg, we hold that bacon is no bacon unless smoked.

It is not by any means still the only flesh food of the labourer, who used to have his Sunday piece, of which wife and family partook as far as was judged expedient, but chiefly ate the potatoes, that 'if not the rose, had been near the rose.' Now there is more use of tinned meats, and carts from butchers come round and carry on a small traffic, giving more variety, as well as other carts of cheap fish, around which I see an unfailing assembly of women. I have seen little children, boys especially, at a school-dinner cry at the unwonted spectacle of a slice of meat; but this is not the case now. At a mothers' meeting, when I have read aloud 'Ways and Means in a Devonshire Parish,' there have been remarks on home economies which proved that the hearers did not live on bread and potatoes alone; though I confess that the audience did not include those hopeless managers who consume whatever the husband allows them in the first days of the week, and at the end let their children run about begging of their neighbours scraps, which the kind-hearted women are always ready to afford.

If pigs are attracted below the oak trees, rooks are ready to hover above, to seize on the acorns, which they sometimes bury, probably for a winter store. They also fly away with walnuts speared upon their strong bills. They seldom or never build on oaks; it is elms that are their special delight. There is no bird whose language one would better like to understand than that of the rooks. All *corvidæ* seem to be unusually intelligent; and rooks, like other gregarious animals, seem to have a wonderful amount of social qualities, if not of political.

We have vainly tried to induce them to colonise our trees, but, being oaks, these failed to attract them. Their conversational notes over their nest-building are a delightful spring sound to those who have known it from infancy, and always justify the meaning of the riddle that declares them the wisest of birds. What a sight they are, walking about in spring sunshine in their intensely black glossy coats, so shining as to reflect the sun in glancing brightness, every now and

then one giving a little sapient croak, while
their sentinel sits aloft upon a tree ready to
give warning at sight of a man with a gun,
which he is perfectly able to distinguish from
a harmless stick!   Then watch one changing
his place.   The broad black wings lift him
by a flap or two, but, when about to alight, he
sails on with them outspread and motionless,
and the two claws held up, till near the ground
he puts them out, closes his wings, and begins
his walk, seldom a hop, as he searches for the
grubs of cockchafers and daddy long-legs.

A croak from the sentry will raise a black
cloud, to hurry away through the sky.   There
are detached colonies in almost every park
where elms grow, but in the winter the rooks
seem to have a season.   About the end of
October, or beginning of November, the different parties from various regions all collect
over some favourite wood and there roost,
after numerous gyrations in the air, and a

loud cawing and calling to one another. 'The rooks are come' is a joyful announcement to the old friends who know and love them ; and it is really a wonderful sight to watch them wheeling round and round, the more distant so far off as to be the merest black specks, coming nearer and nearer, while the incessant caws are heard in every degree of sound. After they have gradually settled in the trees, the firing of a gun raises a marvellous outcry, rush of wings, and renewed wheelings, till they subside again for the night. In February they separate to their regular haunting-places, and only the permanent inhabitants remain.

To some it has been given to behold a parliament of rooks, all upon some open space, generally of down, where, in curious resemblance of the human kind, they congregate, and, at least apparently, hold consultation. Sometimes a downcast, drooping criminal or two may be guarded in a corner till sentence is received, when the rest of the community fall on the unfortunates and despatch them. It is reported that condign punishment has been seen to follow stealing sticks from other people's nests, also that enterprising couples building in a new tree are banished and persecuted. Mr. Fowler reports a case of this kind; but I know of one which had a happier termination.

The trees within a cathedral close had been inhabited from time immemorial, but never those beyond its precincts, until a pair were daring enough to commence a nest on a new tree outside the close. At first the nest underwent the inevitable fate of being pulled to pieces by the old conservatives; but afterwards a council was held on the grass within the close, all the sable community attending, and their caws sounding like intelligence. Finally—this really is true—a patriarch with white feathers in his poll gave his opinion, and forthwith the new tree was adopted and filled with nests, while one of the old trees was deserted. Moreover, this ancient elm was blown down in an ensuing storm! The final incident is melancholy, but vouches, as it were, for the truth of the story. The white-marked senior, who was respected by all the town, fell a victim to one of those wretched beings who carry guns, and cannot see a curious bird without marking it down for slaughter.

Jackdaws are very amusing pets. They are birds of a strong power of attachment to human beings. There was one here which selected the boy who fetched the newspapers for his favourite, and accompanied him wherever he went, whether to the station or the houses where the papers were left. Afterwards Jack transferred his affections to a girl pupil-teacher. He tapped at her window in the morning, followed her about, sitting on the roof of the school, or peering in at the windows, or even coming on her shoulder when she changed books at the library!

This daw was not vicious; but sometimes a tame one will be the terror of children, and likewise a great thief. I have known one which, in the course of his perquisitions in a cottage, was accidentally shut up in a drawer, but obtained his release by calls of ' Mother!' in the voice of one of the children. He was also wont to pick up a pen, and, as it was said by his admirers, to use it on the adjacent paper. Jack is a very pretty bird, quaint with his gray head, quick blue eye, and trim black plumage, and seen most to advantage in old towers—as Vincent Bourne, translated by Cowper, says—

> A great frequenter of the Church,
> Where, Bishop-like, he finds a perch,
> And dormitory too,

—which unfortunately was too often true of the easy-going Episcopate of Cowper's day.

But he is a voracious creature, and will kill and eat young birds when he can. Indeed, at Exeter, he has been seen throwing poor little daws out of the tower and murdering them on the grass with vehement squawking. Let us hope, for the sake of daw nature, that the parents were defending them against the aggressors. Daws, or caddows, their old name, are said to have driven out the Cornish chough. They seem to like to consort together, but apparently have not the public spirit of the rooks.

But though this is a long chapter, I cannot leave the crow-kind without a tender reminiscence of the delight and terror of my younger days, our old Magpie. He was brought from the nest, and speedily grew up very handsome and extremely clever. His head was jetty black, his breast and part of his wings pure white, the long feathers of his wings metallic blue, his tail of the metallic green of a cock's feathers, and he kept himself spotlessly and brilliantly clean and fresh, even after the time when he established his release from his wicker-cage, by constantly undoing any complication which fastened the door. He also untied and overthrew his cup of water, and as the fragments were generally held up to him by the maids with an exclamation of 'Mag, you rascal!' he learnt to make the same observation in triumph, as soon as the smash was effected. One wing was clipped, and he was then free of the lawn and house, for he would come in at any open window on the ground-floor, and hop upstairs on predatory expeditions. He was to be seen on the window-sill with a thimble on the end of his beak, or any other small article easy of transportation, which he would bury in some of his hoards. Once, when a segment of wedding-cake had been left on the table, while we accompanied some visitors to the end of the garden, it was missing on our return. Mag's voice, however, was heard on the rail at the top of the attic stairs going through the triumphant performance with which he was wont to celebrate his most daring feats of mischief.

'Mag—poor Mag! Mag, you rascal! Master Collins! Harriet!' repeated squeaks like a wheelbarrow, then a fit of coughing, a loud laugh, and finally an original chatter and scream. On pursuing him, there was a grand treasure-trove—not only the cake reduced to crumbs, but candle-grease, a thimble, and various other purloined commodities.

There stood on the lawn a very tall old apple tree, loaded at the top with ivy. Close to this was a pink thorn, and just

below a large Portugal laurel.   The ivy was
Mag's chosen roosting-place, and about sunset he began to make his way up from the
ground, through the laurel and thorn.   He
could come down all at once, though he
could not fly upwards, and his pan of water
being kept below, he used to proclaim his
descent by wheelbarrow squeaks till the dish
was filled, when he bathed, and, if possible,
spread himself out, an absurd spectacle, in
the sunshine, to be dried.   There was, year
after year, a nut-hatch's nest about four feet
from the ground, in a hole in the trunk of the
apple tree, and to rob this nest was his desire.
The trunk was smooth and the hole inacces-
sible from below, so he used to take the trouble
of mounting his ladder again and creeping
down, branch by branch, to some long loose
trails of ivy which waved nearly over the nest,
and by which he tried to swing himself to the
hole ; but he uniformly slipped off, fell down,

and then stood on his dish, squeaking and chattering in fury.

He was a tyrant on the lawn, pecking the heels unprotected by boots, and never suffering certain polyanthuses to be touched. Only two persons were exempt from his attacks—his little master and one of the maids, on whose shoulder he would sit and drink tea out of her spoon. Once, when two girl visitors arrived, somewhat overdone with the long journey, and not able to rise early the next day, shrieks were heard from their room, and the wicked bird was found dancing about on their counterpane, and making vicious dabs at any finger or eye which emerged for a moment.

A friend presented us with a second magpie, which had long been in a cage, and had rubbed off his tail, whence he was known as Stumptail, or Stump, long after the next season of liberty had repaired the loss.

Even then he was never quite so handsome as old Mag, and he must have had less brain, for his head was flat instead of round, and he was not nearly so clever, though his moral character might be higher, for he was neither thievish nor spiteful, though sometimes there was a combat between the two birds when old Mag disinterred his hoards.

Stump took a violent attachment to one of our young lady visitors. He was at her window in early morning, looked in at her all day, and followed her about out of doors. When she went away, he took to village life—could be seen in the school playground in the midst of a circle of children, as if he were teaching a class, and strayed further and further, till at last some stranger threw a stone which killed him.

If I remember right, these wanderings did not begin till after the death of the beloved old Mag, which was strangely occasioned by his running under the feet of his young master, who was jumping off a step, and came down with his full weight on the poor bird's head.

There was an endeavour some thirty years later to revive the magpie delights, but the later one was by no means equal to the former beauties. It never kept itself smart and clean. One day I said to it : ' Oh, Mag, why don't you wash ? What a figure you are ! ' It obeyed me too literally, for its body was found floating on the top of a tub of hot water where some clothes had been put to soak.

November has two noted days. Of course we—

Remember, remember,
The Fifth of November,
The gunpowder treason and plot.
There can be no reason
Why gunpowder treason
Should ever be forgot.

Here we have nothing specially characteristic, only the bonfire, which, unluckily, in
dry seasons, often leads to the burning of a
great deal of furze.   There is no carrying
about of Guy, nor do the boys, as in Devonshire, sing—

> The Pope, the Pope !
> Up the ladder and down the rope.

A French traveller in England, in the
seventeenth century, records bonfires on St.
Brice's night, in memory of the massacre of
the Danes on the 13th of November.   Could
he have confused this with the Gunpowder
Plot, or did this absorb St. Brice ?

As boys will not be baulked of their
saturnalia, the authorities of Winchester have
wisely devised a sort of pageant and procession, ending with fireworks, and this keeps
them out of mischief.

One of the many Saints Clement—
probably the one who is mentioned in the

Epistle to the Philippians—has his feast on the 23rd of November. Legend declares that he was thrown into the sea with an anchor fastened to him. Thereby he became the patron of forgers of anchors, and thence of blacksmiths, who have never ceased to hold a festival on his day. It used to be a grand affair in London, and here it is still honoured by the smiths exploding gunpowder on their anvils. In a neighbouring village they have a dinner, at which a curious legend is read of Solomon inviting all the workmen of the Temple to a banquet, but omitting the blacksmiths till they proved their claim by showing the bolts and bars they had made, when they were admitted, but washed clean !

In *Great Expectations*, Joe Gargerry sings a song at his forge where every verse ends with ' Old Clem '—another survival ; but I never came in for more than the bangs upon the anvil !

DECEMBER

December sets in usually with mild weather, a prolongation of November fogs, sparing all the plants that survived the October frost, and even encouraging a few to blossom. Primroses put out a few short-stemmed flowers, which cockneys in the country think wonderful enough to write to the papers about. Now and then a branch of pear tree, if it have been nipped in the summer, attempts to blossom, but is considered 'unlucky.'

Chrysanthemums have just attained to their full beauty; they are at present the chief subjects of gardeners' transformations. The old yellow daisy-like flower has been persuaded into interminable shapes and shades, and the varieties have almost as long a list of names as the roses. Here they are white, and curled at the tips, forming perfect snowballs, or star-like and straggling, or delicate sulphur-coloured, or of every shade of crimson, sometimes yellow above and crimson beneath—pompon when small and compact, Japanese when large and straggling—or with curled points, and lately with a tendency—by way of variety—to give up the central strap-shaped petals and revert to the daisy-like eye of the original flower. In all plants capable of variations there is first an original wild perfect adaptation and grace; there is next a sort of civilised beauty; and there is lastly a gardener's freak worked up into exaggeration for the sake of exhibition. Still we will not quarrel with the flower available for church decoration, lasting long, both gathered and ungathered, and brightening us up far into the winter.

Preferable, however, are the Christmas roses which do not lend themselves to important diversities.   Indeed, what we regard as the flower is only the bracts.   The petals are odd little horned things, almost mixed up with the stamens.   They really are, by their Latin name, *Helleborus niger*, and belong to a poisonous race, whose name has none of the associations of the Christmas rose.

If it is an open winter, we have good hope of plenty of berries ; but as to the belief that their number foretells hard weather, it rather points back to the absence of killing frosts at their blossoming time in the spring, when the holly ought to be threaded over with tiny white four-petalled, four-stamened flowers, to give place to the bright coral berries which nothing equals.   ' Holly ' is really ' holy.'   The old people here used to call a bush without berries ' holm,' in contradistinction, and sometimes a fine branch is termed 'Christmas.' Southey made us remark how the prickly leaves cease as the tree reaches a height beyond the reach of cattle, breathing a wish that—

> So the calm temper of my age may be
> Like the high leaves upon the holly tree.

One of the most simple as well as deep poems in the *Lyra Innocentium* was prompted by the exclamation of a little girl, who, looking into the church before the decorations were put up, exclaimed in disappointment, ' No Christmas here!'—

> What if that little maiden's Lord,
>   That awful Child on Mary's knee,
> Even now take up the accusing word,
>   ' No Christmas here I see.
>
> ' Where are the fruits I yearly seek,
>   As holy seasons pass away ;
> Eyes turned from ill, lips pure and meek,
>   A heart that strives to pray ?

T

> 'Where are the glad and artless smiles,
>   Like clustering hollies, seen afar
> At eve along the o'ershadowed aisles,
>   With the first twilight star?'

Holly, even in berryless years, is to my mind better alone than with any sham imitations of berries, though a scarlet tie for the sprays may be effective and allowable. Variegated holly, especially where a few leaves are ivory-white, is a great assistance in brightening, but I do not love yellow-berried holly.

Cotoneaster, though the wreaths of white blossoms are pretty against the wall, and the little red berries still more so, does not catch the light enough to be effective on these dark days. Even the clusters of Eccremocarpus, though looking brilliant out of doors, do not *tell* in church.

Ivy (*Hedera helix*) is the legitimate companion and rival of holly—everywhere cheerful, even in decay, and putting out its green heads of blossom so late in the year that the black berries are only ripe in time to keep the store which the birds have not gathered into barns. These heads only begin to be put forth after the ivy has ceased to climb, and produces branches and leaves of an unbroken pointed egg-shape, entirely different from the deeply divided and wonderfully varying leaves with which it climbs. To collect the different forms of ivy leaves to be met with in a walk is one of the diversions I should recommend to those who are unlucky enough to think a country walk in autumn or winter dull.

A berry larger than the holly and as beautiful, but seldom plentiful enough to be of much use, belongs to the Butcher's-broom, or Kneeholm (*Ruscus aculeatus*) — a very curious plant, related, of all families in the world, to the asparagus. Only the little green flowers are divided into sexes on the same plant, and have no stems, lying flat on the dark green, pointed, spine-ended leaves, where the fertile ones leave a very handsome red berry. It grows wild upon heaths, and is rare, but probably was once more common than now. The so-called Alexandrian laurel which makes useful wreaths is also a *Ruscus*; but it blossoms at the end of its sprays, and does not ripen fruit in this climate. Some say it is really the bay or laurel of which the wreath of successful poets was composed, and it is certainly more convenient for the purpose than the fragrant bay.

The other peculiarly Christmas plant, Mistletoe (*Viscus albatus*), is banished from our churches on account of the associations, sometimes merely merry, but too often degenerating into vulgarity and rudeness, which make all the lads go about with a sprig of mistletoe in their hats. The tales

of Druid worship are, as we all know, inti-
mately connected with the mistletoe, especially with the oak-grown plant, probably from
its extreme rarity; for though it is frequent
upon ash and apple trees, it is hardly ever
found on oaks. The Druid solemnity of
cutting it down with a golden knife, and
catching it in a white cloth, is well known.
It used to be found on oaks at Norwood
when that was a wood, and being supposed
to be medicinal when so growing, was sometimes cut down for apothecaries in London.
But the men who meddled with it were said
always to fall lame or become blind of an
eye! Its French name, *gui*, is probably
Celtic.

Its place in Norse myths is equally noted.
It was the exception when Freya charmed
all minerals, plants, and animals from harm-
ing Baldur, and therefore Loki pointed with
it the arrow which he persuaded blind

Hodur to shoot at the white deity. Whether it was from some lingering connection with its being the means of Baldur's death is not known, but there was a Christian legend that it had been a fine tree till it furnished the wood of the Cross, in expiation of which it became the strange imperfect plant that it now seems. In some parts of France it is called *l'herbe à la Croix*, and it was thought to be a spell against evil spirits, as well as a cure for epilepsy and many other diseases.

Scarcely noticed in the early part of the year, when the apple trees are in full leaf, it comes into full prominence when they are stripped, hanging with its yellow-green clusters of branches from the limbs. The root is firmly embedded in the fibre of the tree; the stem is repeatedly forked, a thickened ring at each fork. The leaves are stemless, leathery, of the same uniform yellow - green, the flowers also stemless,

perched within the forks and monœcious—
the female ones giving place to a soft white
berry, which is said to missel or soil the toes
of the missel-thrush, thus naming both bird
and bush, though the derivation is not very
satisfactory.

It is not ornamental enough to be a loss
to our church decorations. I remember
many phases of them—the sticking, by the
clerk, of holly boughs into the holes made on
purpose in the ancient pews, and the gradual
interference of the young ladies, who came
timidly and felt it an exceeding honour and
privilege to be allowed to assist, while old
people doubted of the lawfulness and expedi-
ence of using flowers at all.

An honour and privilege it is still to work
for the house of God and beautify the place
of His sanctuary ; but now that it has become a matter of course, how many clerical
houses feel it a burthen and perplexity, while

among the workers there is danger of irreverence, and difficulties of temper, and clashing taste. Well, in this world, first it is a point to do the thing, next to do it in the right way.

St. Thomas's Day ushers in Christmas. ' Pray, sir,' asked a boy, 'did they give St. Thomas the shortest day because he was not a very good saint?' That St. Thomas is compensated in the Antipodes had not occurred to him.

Here, as in some other Hampshire villages, St. Thomas's Day is spent by all the poorer women in what they call 'gooding' —going from house to house to receive something towards the Christmas dinner. A shilling to each widow, and sixpence to each wife, is the traditional amount; but hardly any one keeps up the dole, since modern changes have come in, and neither squires, farmers, nor peasants are in the old semi - feudal connection. In most places some other form of Christmas gift has been substituted, though nowhere can those questions which are the pain of almsgiving be avoided—who is too well-off, and, on the other hand, who ought not to be helped for fear of fostering evil and deceit? The traditional dole, however, carried no stigma of beggary.

Another ordinance of St. Thomas's Feast was the arrival of certain musical gipsies. 'It's the Lees!' has been the answer when asking the cause of an outbreak of drumming and the like; but this likewise has nearly come to an end, and the genuine gipsy is not a very frequent creature. Moreover, he travels no longer in a picturesque, ramshackle tilted cart, where the red-kerchiefed mother and bright-eyed, brown-faced children look out as from a bower, but in a yellow van, with a stove-pipe protruding from it. And he often has quarters in a town for the winter.

One genuine family was here some years ago, of thorough gipsy blood. A woman was very ill, and a kind gentleman let them remain in his field and sent broth and wine. They were strictly honest, and even refused offers of help from other quarters, saying that they were fully provided for. The woman died, and they lamented her with loud cries like Easterns. They talked of putting up a stone to her, but have never done so. Her name was Gerania.

This gipsy music is not connected with carols. Those carols, in the old time, had a flavour of wild beauty about them. I remember standing in the shrubbery in the dark, with stars overhead, and snatches of song floating on the wind from every quarter, giving a sense of Christmas joy.

But they needed to be heard at a distance.   Near at hand the children, then utterly untrained in voice, sang like ballad-singers, generally—

> While shepherds watched their flocks by night ;

but sometimes that notable carol where Lazarus is described among the dogs—

> He had no strength to drive them off,
> And so—and so they licked his sores ;

and finally ' Divers ' (as he was always called) sits on a serpent's knee !

The shrill thin voices of the children were only ignorantly irreverent, but there were parties of boisterous lads or idle men as ignorant, more profane, and sometimes half - tipsy, and on the way to be entirely so.

The practice had to be reformed.   Picturesqueness is apt not to bear close inspection, and propriety and reverence must be enforced even through primness and a little hard-heartedness.   So now the children of a fit age are taught well-chosen carols, and go round under the surveillance of the master and mistress, and the money-box is divided at the end, and produces more than the chance pence thrown at haphazard and not at all after the change is exhausted ; and the children, who do not remember the old days of license, greatly delight in their rounds.

The elders are, or ought to be, in the choir, and have a regular festival supper ; and to the undesirable, it is really best to turn a deaf ear.

Christmas, unless the salt of life be there, grows sadder as we grow older, and it is one of the stock moralisings of the worldly sort to murmur at being expected to be merry by rule, to make presents, pay bills, and partake of indigestible fare.

The conventional Christmas of illustrated

papers and Christmas cards is only too apt
to foster this more outward phase of the
festival, of which the pudding wreathed with
holly is the symbol. To keep the day
primarily as the Birthday of the Lord,
rejoicing evermore, because He is close at
hand, is the only way to keep the rejoicing through life, and hinder the external
festivities from becoming hollow and weary.
So may the 'Outlook,' going beyond the
pleasures around and the delights of nature,
illuminate them all with a brighter light than
that which otherwise ever shone on sea or
land.

THE END

Printed by R. & R. CLARK, *Edinburgh.*

MESSRS. MACMILLAN & CO.'S PUBLICATIONS.

UNIFORM EDITION OF THE NOVELS AND TALES

OF

CHARLOTTE M. YONGE.

In Crown 8vo, Cloth extra, Illustrated, 3s. 6d. each.

MACMILLAN AND CO., LONDON.

MESSRS. MACMILLAN & CO.'S PUBLICATIONS.

BY THE SAME AUTHOR.

Crown 8vo, Cloth.

THE LIFE OF JOHN COLERIDGE PATTESON. 2 vols. 12s.

THE PUPILS OF ST. JOHN. Illustrated. 6s.

PIONEERS AND FOUNDERS; or Recent Workers in the Mission Field. 6s.

HISTORY OF CHRISTIAN NAMES. New Edition, revised. 7s. 6d.

THE VICTORIAN HALF-CENTURY. 1s. 6d. Sewed, 1s.

THE HERB OF THE FIELD. A New Edition, revised. 5s.

Globe 8vo.

A STOREHOUSE OF STORIES. 2 vols. 2s. 6d. each.

THE POPULATION OF AN OLD PEAR TREE; or Stories of Insect Life. From the French of E. VAN BRUYSSEL. Illustrated. 2s. 6d.

SCRIPTURE READINGS FOR SCHOOLS AND FAMILIES. 1s. 6d. each; also with Comments, 3s. 6d. each. First Series: GENESIS TO DEUTERONOMY. Second Series: JOSHUA TO SOLOMON. Third Series: KINGS AND THE PROPHETS. Fourth Series: THE GOSPEL TIMES. Fifth Series: APOSTOLIC TIMES.

Extra fcap. 8vo.

CAMEOS FROM ENGLISH HISTORY. 5s. each. Vol. I. FROM ROLLO TO EDWARD II. Vol. II. THE WARS IN FRANCE. Vol. III. THE WARS OF THE ROSES. Vol. IV. REFORMATION TIMES. Vol. V. ENGLAND AND SPAIN. Vol. VI. FORTY YEARS OF STUART RULE (1603–1643). Vol. VII. THE RE-BELLION AND RESTORATION (1642–1678).

18mo.

A BOOK OF WORTHIES: Gathered from the Old Histories and written Anew. 2s. 6d. net.

THE STORY OF THE CHRISTIANS AND MOORS IN SPAIN. 2s. 6d. net.

A BOOK OF GOLDEN DEEDS. 2s. 6d. net.
Abridged Edition. 1s.
Globe Readings Edition. Globe 8vo. 2s.

FRANCE. 1s. [*History Primers.*

HISTORY OF FRANCE. Maps. 3s. 6d. [*Historical Course.*

MACMILLAN AND CO., LONDON

MACMILLAN'S THREE - AND - SIXPENNY SERIES

OF

WORKS BY POPULAR AUTHORS.

In Crown 8vo.   Cloth extra.   Price 3s. 6d. each.

By Sir SAMUEL BAKER.

TRUE TALES FOR MY GRANDSONS.

By ROLF BOLDREWOOD.

SATURDAY REVIEW—"Mr. Boldrewood can tell what he knows with great point and vigour, and there is no better reading than the adventurous parts of his books."

PALL MALL GAZETTE—"The volumes are brimful of adventure, in which gold, gold-diggers, prospectors, claim-holders, take an active part."

ROBBERY UNDER ARMS.	THE SQUATTER'S DREAM.
THE MINER'S RIGHT.	A SYDNEY-SIDE SAXON.
A COLONIAL REFORMER.	NEVERMORE.

By FRANCES HODGSON BURNETT.

LOUISIANA; AND THAT LASS O' LOWRIE'S.

By HUGH CONWAY.

MORNING POST—"Life-like and full of individuality."

DAILY NEWS—"Throughout written with spirit, good feeling, and ability, and a certain dash of humour."

LIVING OR DEAD? | A FAMILY AFFAIR.

By Mrs. CRAIK.

(The Author of "JOHN HALIFAX, GENTLEMAN.")

OLIVE. With Illustrations by G. BOWERS.	TWO MARRIAGES.
THE OGILVIES. With Illustrations.	THE LAUREL BUSH.
AGATHA'S HUSBAND. With Illustrations.	MY MOTHER AND I. With Illustrations.
HEAD OF THE FAMILY. With Illustrations.	MISS TOMMY: A Mediæval Romance. Illustrated.
	KING ARTHUR : Not a Love Story.

SERMONS OUT OF CHURCH.

By F. MARION CRAWFORD.

SPECTATOR—"With the solitary exception of Mrs. Oliphant we have no living novelist more distinguished for variety of theme and range of imaginative outlook than Mr. Marion Crawford."

MR. ISAACS: A Tale of Modern India. Portrait of Author.	A TALE OF A LONELY PARISH.
DR. CLAUDIUS: A True Story.	PAUL PATOFF.
A ROMAN SINGER.	WITH THE IMMORTALS.
ZOROASTER.	GREIFENSTEIN.
MARZIO'S CRUCIFIX.	SANT' ILARIO.
	A CIGARETTE-MAKER'S ROMANCE.

By Sir HENRY CUNNINGHAM, K.C.I.E.

ST. JAMES'S GAZETTE—"Interesting as specimens of romance, the style of writing is so excellent—scholarly and at the same time easy and natural—that the volumes are worth reading on that account alone.   But there is also masterly description of persons, places, and things ; skilful analysis of character ; a constant play of wit and humour ; and a happy gift of instantaneous portraiture."

THE CŒRULEANS. | THE HERIOTS.

WHEAT AND TARES.

By CHARLES DICKENS.

THE PICKWICK PAPERS. With 50 Illustrations.
OLIVER TWIST. With 27 Illustrations.
NICHOLAS NICKLEBY. With 44 Illustrations.
MARTIN CHUZZLEWIT. With 41 Illustrations.
THE OLD CURIOSITY SHOP. With 97 Illustrations.
BARNABY RUDGE. With 76 Illustrations.

July 25.
August 26.

By LANOE FALCONER.

CECILIA DE NOEL.

By W. WARDE FOWLER.

A YEAR WITH THE BIRDS. Illustrated by BRYAN HOOK.
TALES OF THE BIRDS. Illustrated by BRYAN HOOK.

By the Rev. JOHN GILMORE.

STORM WARRIORS.

By THOMAS HARDY.

TIMES—"There is hardly a novelist, dead or living, who so skillfully harmonises the poetry of moral life with its penury. Just as Millet could in the figure of a solitary peasant toiling on a plain convey a world of pathetic meaning, so Mr. Hardy with his yeomen and villagers. Their occupations in his hands wear a pathetic dignity, which not even the encomiums of a Ruskin could heighten."

THE WOODLANDERS. | WESSEX TALES.

By BRET HARTE.

SPEAKER—"The best work of Mr. Bret Harte stands entirely alone . . . marked on every page by distinction and quality. . . . Strength and delicacy, spirit and tenderness, go together in his best work."

CRESSY.
THE HERITAGE OF DEDLOW MARSH.
A FIRST FAMILY OF TASAJARA.

By the Author of "Hogan, M.P."

HOGAN, M.P.

By THOMAS HUGHES.

TOM BROWN'S SCHOOLDAYS. With Illustrations by A. HUGHES and S. P. HALL.
TOM BROWN AT OXFORD. With Illustrations by S. P. HALL.
THE SCOURING OF THE WHITE HORSE, AND THE ASHEN FAGGOT. With Illustrations by RICHARD DOYLE.

By HENRY JAMES.

SATURDAY REVIEW—"He has the power of seeing with the artistic perception of the few, and of writing about what he has seen, so that the many can understand and feel with him."

WORLD—"His touch is so light, and his humour, while shrewd and keen, so free from bitterness."

A LONDON LIFE. | THE ASPERN PAPERS.
THE TRAGIC MUSE.

By ANNIE KEARY.

SPECTATOR—" In our opinion there have not been many novels published better worth reading. The literary workmanship is excellent, and all the windings of the stories are worked with patient fulness and a skill not often found."

CASTLE DALY.	JANET'S HOME.
A YORK AND A LANCASTER ROSE.	OLDBURY.
A DOUBTING HEART.	

By PATRICK KENNEDY.
LEGENDARY FICTIONS OF THE IRISH CELTS.

By CHARLES KINGSLEY.

WESTWARD HO!	LITERARY AND GENERAL LECTURES.
HYPATIA.	THE HERMITS.
YEAST.	GLAUCUS; OR, THE WONDERS OF THE SEA-SHORE. With Coloured Illustrations.
ALTON LOCKE.	
TWO YEARS AGO.	
HEREWARD THE WAKE.	
POEMS.	VILLAGE AND TOWN AND COUNTRY SERMONS.
THE HEROES.	
THE WATER BABIES.	THE WATER OF LIFE, AND OTHER SERMONS.
MADAM HOW AND LADY WHY.	
AT LAST.	SERMONS ON NATIONAL SUBJECTS, AND THE KING OF THE EARTH.
PROSE IDYLLS.	
PLAYS AND PURITANS, &c.	
THE ROMAN AND THE TEUTON.	SERMONS FOR THE TIMES.
SANITARY AND SOCIAL LECTURES AND ESSAYS.	GOOD NEWS OF GOD.
	THE GOSPEL OF THE PENTATEUCH, AND DAVID.
HISTORICAL LECTURES AND ESSAYS.	DISCIPLINE, AND OTHER SERMONS.
SCIENTIFIC LECTURES AND ESSAYS.	WESTMINSTER SERMONS.

ALL SAINTS' DAY, AND OTHER SERMONS.

By HENRY KINGSLEY.
TALES OF OLD TRAVEL.

By MARGARET LEE.
FAITHFUL AND UNFAITHFUL.

By AMY LEVY.
REUBEN SACHS.

By the EARL OF LYTTON.
THE RING OF AMASIS.

By MALCOLM M'LENNAN.
MUCKLE JOCK, AND OTHER STORIES OF PEASANT LIFE.

By LUCAS MALET.
MRS. LORIMER.

By A. B. MITFORD.
TALES OF OLD JAPAN. Illustrated.

By D. CHRISTIE MURRAY.

SPECTATOR—" Mr. Christie Murray has more power and genius for the delineation of English rustic life than any half-dozen of our surviving novelists put together."

SATURDAY REVIEW—" Few modern novelists can tell a story of English country life better than Mr. D. Christie Murray."

AUNT RACHEL.	SCHWARTZ.
JOHN VALE'S GUARDIAN.	THE WEAKER VESSEL.
HE FELL AMONG THIEVES.	By D. C. MURRAY and H. HERMAN.

By Mrs. OLIPHANT.

ACADEMY—" At her best she is, with one or two exceptions, the best of living English novelists."

SATURDAY REVIEW—" Has the charm of style, the literary quality and flavour that never fails to please."

A BELEAGUERED CITY.	KIRSTEEN.
JOYCE.	HESTER.
NEIGHBOURS ON THE GREEN.	HE THAT WILL NOT WHEN HE MAY.

By W. CLARK RUSSELL.

TIMES—" Mr. Clark Russell is one of those writers who have set themselves to revive the British sea story in all its glorious excitement. Mr. Russell has made a considerable reputation in this line. His plots are well conceived, and that of *Marooned* is no exception to this rule."

MAROONED. | A STRANGE ELOPEMENT.

By J. H. SHORTHOUSE.

ANTI-JACOBIN—" Powerful, striking, and fascinating romances."

JOHN INGLESANT.	THE LITTLE SCHOOLMASTER MARK.
SIR PERCIVAL.	THE COUNTESS EVE.

A TEACHER OF THE VIOLIN.

By Mrs. HUMPHRY WARD.

MISS BRETHERTON.

By MONTAGU WILLIAMS, Q.C.

LEAVES OF A LIFE. | LATER LEAVES.

By Miss CHARLOTTE M. YONGE.

THE HEIR OF REDCLYFFE.	LOVE AND LIFE.
HEARTSEASE.	UNKNOWN TO HISTORY.
HOPES AND FEARS.	STRAY PEARLS.
DYNEVOR TERRACE.	THE ARMOURER'S 'PRENTICES.
THE DAISY CHAIN.	THE TWO SIDES OF THE SHIELD.
THE TRIAL: MORE LINKS OF THE DAISY CHAIN.	NUTTIE'S FATHER.
	SCENES AND CHARACTERS.
PILLARS OF THE HOUSE. Vol. I.	CHANTRY HOUSE.
PILLARS OF THE HOUSE. Vol. II.	A MODERN TELEMACHUS.
THE YOUNG STEPMOTHER.	BYE-WORDS.
THE CLEVER WOMAN OF THE FAMILY.	BEECHCROFT AT ROCKSTONE.
	MORE BYWORDS.
THE THREE BRIDES.	A REPUTED CHANGELING.
MY YOUNG ALCIDES.	THE LITTLE DUKE.
THE CAGED LION.	THE LANCES OF LYNWOOD.
THE DOVE IN THE EAGLE'S NEST.	THE PRINCE AND THE PAGE.
THE CHAPLET OF PEARLS.	P's AND Q's AND LITTLE LUCY'S WONDERFUL GLOBE.
LADY HESTER, AND THE DANVERS PAPERS.	THE TWO PENNILESS PRINCESSES.
MAGNUM BONUM.	

By ARCHDEACON FARRAR.

SEEKERS AFTER GOD.	IN THE DAYS OF THY YOUTH.
ETERNAL HOPE.	SAINTLY WORKERS.
THE FALL OF MAN.	EPHPHATHA.
THE WITNESS OF HISTORY TO CHRIST.	MERCY AND JUDGMENT. *Aug.*
	SERMONS AND ADDRESSES
THE SILENCE AND VOICES OF GOD.	DELIVERED IN AMERICA. *Sept.*

By FREDERICK DENISON MAURICE.

SERMONS PREACHED IN LINCOLN'S INN CHAPEL. *In 6 vols.*

MACMILLAN & CO., BEDFORD STREET,
STRAND, LONDON.

20.7.92.

A CLASSIFIED
CATALOGUE OF BOOKS
IN GENERAL LITERATURE
PUBLISHED BY
MACMILLAN AND CO.
BEDFORD STREET, STRAND, LONDON, W.C.

For purely Educational Works see MACMILLAN AND CO.'s *Educational Catalogue*

AGRICULTURE.

(*See also* BOTANY; GARDENING.)

FRANKLAND (Prof. P. F.).—A HANDBOOK OF AGRICULTURAL CHEMICAL ANALYSIS. Cr. 8vo. 7s. 6d.

TANNER (Henry).—ELEMENTARY LESSONS IN THE SCIENCE OF AGRICULTURAL PRACTICE. Fcp. 8vo. 3s. 6d.
—— FIRST PRINCIPLES OF AGRICULTURE. 18mo. 1s.
—— THE PRINCIPLES OF AGRICULTURE. For Use in Elementary Schools. Ext. fcp. 8vo.—THE ALPHABET OF THE PRINCIPLES OF AGRICULTURE. 6d.—FURTHER STEPS IN THE PRINCIPLES OF AGRICULTURE. 1s.—ELEMENTARY SCHOOL READINGS ON THE PRINCIPLES OF AGRICULTURE FOR THE THIRD STAGE. 1s.

—— THE ABBOT'S FARM; or, Practice with Science. Cr. 8vo. 3s. 6d.

ANATOMY, Human. (*See* PHYSIOLOGY.)

ANTHROPOLOGY.

BROWN (J. Allen).—PALÆOLITHIC MAN IN NORTH-WEST MIDDLESEX. 8vo. 7s. 6d.

DAWKINS (Prof. W. Boyd).—EARLY MAN IN BRITAIN AND HIS PLACE IN THE TERTIARY PERIOD. Med. 8vo. 25s.

DAWSON (James). — AUSTRALIAN ABORIGINES. Small 4to. 14s.

FINCK (Henry T.).—ROMANTIC LOVE AND PERSONAL BEAUTY. 2 vols. Cr. 8vo. 18s.

FISON (L.) and HOWITT (A. W.).—KAMILAROI AND KURNAI GROUP. Group-Marriage and Relationship, and Marriage by Elopement. 8vo. 15s.

FRAZER (J. G.).—THE GOLDEN BOUGH: A Study in Comparative Religion. 2 vols. 8vo. 28s.

GALTON (Francis).—ENGLISH MEN OF SCIENCE: THEIR NATURE AND NURTURE. 8vo. 8s. 6d.
—— INQUIRIES INTO HUMAN FACULTY AND ITS DEVELOPMENT. 8vo. 16s.
—— RECORD OF FAMILY FACULTIES. Consisting of Tabular Forms and Directions for Entering Data. 4to. 2s. 6d.
—— LIFE-HISTORY ALBUM: Being a Personal Note-book, combining Diary, Photograph Album, a Register of Height, Weight, and other Anthropometrical Observations, and a Record of Illnesses. 4to. 3s. 6d.—Or with Cards of Wool for Testing Colour Vision. 4s. 6d.
—— NATURAL INHERITANCE. 8vo. 9s.

M'LENNAN (J. F.).—THE PATRIARCHAL THEORY. Edited and completed by DONALD M'LENNAN, M.A. 8vo. 14s.
—— STUDIES IN ANCIENT HISTORY. Comprising "Primitive Marriage." 8vo. 16s.

MONTELIUS—WOODS. — THE CIVILISATION OF SWEDEN IN HEATHEN TIMES. By Prof. OSCAR MONTELIUS. Translated by Rev. F. H. WOODS. Illustr. 8vo. 14s.

TURNER (Rev. Geo.).—SAMOA, A HUNDRED YEARS AGO AND LONG BEFORE. Cr. 8vo. 9s.

TYLOR (E. B.). — ANTHROPOLOGY. With Illustrations. Cr. 8vo. 7s. 6d.

WESTERMARCK (Dr. Edward).—THE HISTORY OF HUMAN MARRIAGE. With Preface by Dr. A. R. WALLACE. 8vo. 14s. net.

WILSON (Sir Daniel).—PREHISTORIC ANNALS OF SCOTLAND. Illustrated. 2 vols. 8vo. 36s.
—— PREHISTORIC MAN: Researches into the Origin of Civilisation in the Old and New World. Illustrated. 2 vols. 8vo. 36s.
—— THE RIGHT HAND: LEFT HANDEDNESS. Cr. 8vo. 4s. 6d.

ANTIQUITIES.

(*See also* ANTHROPOLOGY.)

ATKINSON (Rev. J. C.).—FORTY YEARS IN A MOORLAND PARISH. Ext. cr. 8vo. 8s. 6d. net.—*Illustrated Edition.* 12s. net.

BURN (Robert).—ROMAN LITERATURE IN RELATION TO ROMAN ART. With Illustrations. Ext. cr. 8vo. 14s.

DILETTANTI SOCIETY'S PUBLICATIONS.
ANTIQUITIES OF IONIA. Vols. I.—III. 2l. 2s. each, or 5l. 5s. the set, net.—Vol. IV. Folio, half morocco, 3l. 13s. 6d. net.
AN INVESTIGATION OF THE PRINCIPLES OF ATHENIAN ARCHITECTURE. By F. C. PENROSE. Illustrated. Folio. 7l. 7s. net.
SPECIMENS OF ANCIENT SCULPTURE: EGYPTIAN, ETRUSCAN, GREEK, AND ROMAN. Vol. II. Folio. 5l. 5s. net.

DYER (Louis).—STUDIES OF THE GODS IN GREECE AT CERTAIN SANCTUARIES RECENTLY EXCAVATED. Ext. cr. 8vo. 8s. 6d. net.

GARDNER (Percy).—SAMOS AND SAMIAN COINS: An Essay. 8vo. 7s. 6d.

GOW (J., Litt.D.).—A COMPANION TO SCHOOL CLASSICS. Illustrated. 3rd Ed. Cr. 8vo. 6s.

HARRISON (Miss Jane) and VERRALL (Mrs.).—MYTHOLOGY AND MONUMENTS OF ANCIENT ATHENS. Illustrated. Cr. 8vo. 16s.

ANTIQUITIES—*continued.*

LANCIANI (Prof. R.).—ANCIENT ROME IN THE LIGHT OF RECENT DISCOVERIES. 4to. 24s.

MAHAFFY (Prof. J. P.).—A PRIMER OF GREEK ANTIQUITIES. 18mo. 1s.
—— SOCIAL LIFE IN GREECE FROM HOMER TO MENANDER. 6th Edit. Cr. 8vo. 9s.
—— RAMBLES AND STUDIES IN GREECE. Illustrated. 3rd Edit. Cr. 8vo. 10s. 6d.
(*See also* HISTORY, p. 11.)

NEWTON (Sir C. T.).—ESSAYS ON ART AND ARCHÆOLOGY. 8vo. 12s. 6d.

SHUCHHARDT (Carl).—DR. SCHLIEMANN'S EXCAVATIONS AT TROY, TIRYNS, MYCENAE, ORCHOMENOS, ITHACA, IN THE LIGHT OF RECENT KNOWLEDGE. Trans. by EUGENIE SELLERS. Preface by WALTER LEAF, Litt.D. Illustrated. 8vo. 18s. net.

STRANGFORD. (*See* VOYAGES & TRAVELS.)

WALDSTEIN (C.).—CATALOGUE OF CASTS IN THE MUSEUM OF CLASSICAL ARCHÆOLOGY, CAMBRIDGE. Crown 8vo. 1s. 6d.—Large Paper Edition. Small 4to. 5s.

WHITE (Gilbert). (*See* NATURAL HISTORY.)

WILKINS (Prof. A. S.).—A PRIMER OF ROMAN ANTIQUITIES. 18mo. 1s.

ARCHÆOLOGY. (*See* ANTIQUITIES.)

ARCHITECTURE.

FREEMAN (Prof. E. A.).—HISTORY OF THE CATHEDRAL CHURCH OF WELLS. Cr. 8vo. 3s. 6d.
—— HISTORICAL AND ARCHITECTURAL SKETCHES, CHIEFLY ITALIAN. Illustrated by the Author. Cr. 8vo. 10s. 6d.

HULL (E.).—A TREATISE ON ORNAMENTAL AND BUILDING STONES OF GREAT BRITAIN AND FOREIGN COUNTRIES. 8vo. 12s.

MOORE (Prof. C. H.).—THE DEVELOPMENT AND CHARACTER OF GOTHIC ARCHITECTURE. Illustrated. Med. 8vo. 18s.

PENROSE (F. C.). (*See* ANTIQUITIES.)

STEVENSON (J. J.).—HOUSE ARCHITECTURE. With Illustrations. 2 vols. Roy. 8vo. 18s. each.—Vol. I. ARCHITECTURE; Vol. II. HOUSE PLANNING.

ART.
(*See also* MUSIC.)

ART AT HOME SERIES. Edited by W. J. LOFTIE, B.A. Cr. 8vo.
THE BEDROOM AND BOUDOIR. By Lady BARKER. 2s. 6d.
NEEDLEWORK. By ELIZABETH GLAISTER. Illustrated. 2s. 6d.
MUSIC IN THE HOUSE. By JOHN HULLAH. 4th edit. 2s. 6d.
THE LIBRARY. By ANDREW LANG, with a Chapter on English Illustrated Books, by AUSTIN DOBSON. 3s. 6d.
THE DINING-ROOM. By Mrs. LOFTIE. With Illustrations. 2nd Edit. 2s. 6d.
AMATEUR THEATRICALS. By WALTER H. POLLOCK and LADY POLLOCK. Illustrated by KATE GREENAWAY. 2s. 6d.

ATKINSON (J. B.).—AN ART TOUR TO NORTHERN CAPITALS OF EUROPE. 8vo. 12s.

BURN (Robert). (*See* ANTIQUITIES.)

CARR (J. Comyns).—PAPERS ON ART. Cr. 8vo. 8s. 6d.

COLLIER (Hon. John).—A PRIMER OF ART. 18mo. 1s.

COOK (E. T.).—A POPULAR HANDBOOK TO THE NATIONAL GALLERY. Including Notes collected from the Works of Mr. RUSKIN. 3rd Edit. Cr. 8vo, half morocco. 14s.—Large paper Edition, 250 copies. 2 vols. 8vo.

CRANE (Lucy).—LECTURES ON ART AND THE FORMATION OF TASTE. Cr. 8vo. 6s.

DELAMOTTE (Prof. P. H.).—A BEGINNER'S DRAWING-BOOK. Cr. 8vo. 3s. 6d.

ELLIS (Tristram).—SKETCHING FROM NATURE. Illustr. by H. STACY MARKS, R.A., and the Author. 2nd Edit. Cr. 8vo. 3s. 6d.

HAMERTON (P. G.).—THOUGHTS ABOUT ART. New Edit. Cr. 8vo. 8s. 6d.

HERKOMER (H.).—ETCHING AND MEZZOTINT ENGRAVING. 4to. 42s. net.

HOOPER (W. H.) and PHILLIPS (W. C.).—A MANUAL OF MARKS ON POTTERY AND PORCELAIN. 16mo. 4s. 6d.

HUNT (W.).—TALKS ABOUT ART. With a Letter from Sir J. E. MILLAIS, Bart., R.A. Cr. 8vo. 3s. 6d.

LECTURES ON ART. By REGD. STUART POOLE, Professor W. B. RICHMOND, E. J. POYNTER, R.A., J. T. MICKLETHWAITE, and WILLIAM MORRIS. Cr. 8vo. 4s. 6d.

NEWTON (Sir C. T.).—(*See* ANTIQUITIES.)

PALGRAVE (Prof. F. T.).—ESSAYS ON ART. Ext. fcp. 8vo. 6s.

PATER (W.).—THE RENAISSANCE: Studies in Art and Poetry. 4th Edit. Cr. 8vo. 10s. 6d.

PENNELL (Joseph).—PEN DRAWING AND PEN DRAUGHTSMEN. With 158 Illustrations. 4to. 3l. 13s. 6d. net.

PROPERT (J. Lumsden).—A HISTORY OF MINIATURE ART. Illustrated. Super roy. 4to. 3l. 13s. 6d.—Bound in vellum. 4l. 14s. 6d.

TURNER'S LIBER STUDIORUM: A DESCRIPTION AND A CATALOGUE. By W. G. RAWLINSON. Med. 8vo. 12s. 6d.

TYRWHITT (Rev. R. St. John).—OUR SKETCHING CLUB. 5th Edit. Cr. 8vo. 7s. 6d.

WYATT (Sir M. Digby).—FINE ART: A Sketch of its History, Theory, Practice, and Application to Industry. 8vo. 5s.

ASTRONOMY.

AIRY (Sir G. B.).—POPULAR ASTRONOMY. Illustrated. 7th Edit. Fcp. 8vo. 4s. 6d.
—— GRAVITATION. An Elementary Explanation of the Principal Perturbations in the Solar System. 2nd Edit. Cr. 8vo. 7s. 6d.

BLAKE (J. F.).—ASTRONOMICAL MYTHS. With Illustrations. Cr. 8vo. 9s.

CHEYNE (C. H. H.).—AN ELEMENTARY TREATISE ON THE PLANETARY THEORY. Cr. 8vo. 7s. 6d.

CLARK (L.) and SADLER (H.).—THE STAR GUIDE. Roy. 8vo. 5s.

CROSSLEY (E.), GLEDHILL (J.), and WILSON (J. M.).—A HANDBOOK OF DOUBLE STARS. 8vo. 21s.
—— CORRECTIONS TO THE HANDBOOK OF DOUBLE STARS. 8vo. 1s.

FORBES (Prof. George).—THE TRANSIT OF VENUS. Illustrated. Cr. 8vo. 3s. 6d.

GODFRAY (Hugh).—AN ELEMENTARY TREATISE ON THE LUNAR THEORY. 2nd Edit. Cr. 8vo. 5s. 6d.
—— A TREATISE ON ASTRONOMY, FOR THE USE OF COLLEGES AND SCHOOLS. 8vo. 12s. 6d.

LOCKYER (J. Norman, F.R.S.).—A PRIMER OF ASTRONOMY. Illustrated. 18mo. 1s.
—— ELEMENTARY LESSONS IN ASTRONOMY. Illustr. New Edition. Fcp. 8vo. 5s. 6d.
—— QUESTIONS ON THE SAME. By J. FORBES ROBERTSON. Fcp. 8vo. 1s. 6d.
—— THE CHEMISTRY OF THE SUN. Illustrated. 8vo. 14s.
—— THE METEORITIC HYPOTHESIS OF THE ORIGIN OF COSMICAL SYSTEMS. Illustrated. 8vo. 17s. net.
—— THE EVOLUTION OF THE HEAVENS AND THE EARTH. Illustrated. Cr. 8vo.
—— STAR-GAZING PAST AND PRESENT. Expanded from Notes with the assistance of G. M. SEABROKE. Roy. 8vo. 21s.

MILLER (R. Kalley).—THE ROMANCE OF ASTRONOMY. 2nd Edit. Cr. 8vo. 4s. 6d.

NEWCOMB (Prof. Simon).—POPULAR ASTRONOMY. Engravings and Maps. 8vo. 18s.

PENROSE (Francis).—ON A METHOD OF PREDICTING, BY GRAPHICAL CONSTRUCTION, OCCULTATIONS OF STARS BY THE MOON AND SOLAR ECLIPSES FOR ANY GIVEN PLACE. 4to. 12s.

RADCLIFFE (Charles B.).—BEHIND THE TIDES. 8vo. 4s. 6d.

ROSCOE—SCHUSTER. (See CHEMISTRY.)

ATLASES.
(See also GEOGRAPHY).

BARTHOLOMEW (J. G.).—ELEMENTARY SCHOOL ATLAS. 4to. 1s.
—— PHYSICAL AND POLITICAL SCHOOL ATLAS. 80 maps. 4to. 8s. 6d.; half mor. 10s. 6d.
—— LIBRARY REFERENCE ATLAS OF THE WORLD. With Index to 100,000 places. Folio. 52s. 6d. net.—Also in 7 parts. 5s. net; Geographical Index, 7s. 6d. net.

LABBERTON (R. H.).—NEW HISTORICAL ATLAS AND GENERAL HISTORY. 4to. 15s.

BIBLE. (See under THEOLOGY, p. 30.)

BIBLIOGRAPHY.

A BIBLIOGRAPHICAL CATALOGUE OF MACMILLAN AND CO.'S PUBLICATIONS, 1843—89. Med. 8vo. 10s. net.

MAYOR (Prof. John E. B.).—A BIBLIOGRAPHICAL CLUE TO LATIN LITERATURE. Cr. 8vo. 10s. 6d.

RYLAND (F.).—CHRONOLOGICAL OUTLINES OF ENGLISH LITERATURE. Cr. 8vo. 6s.

BIOGRAPHY.
(See also HISTORY.)

For other subjects of BIOGRAPHY, *see* ENGLISH MEN OF LETTERS, ENGLISH MEN OF ACTION, TWELVE ENGLISH STATESMEN.

ABBOTT (E. A.).—THE ANGLICAN CAREER OF CARDINAL NEWMAN. 2 vols. 8vo. 25s. net.

AGASSIZ (Louis): HIS LIFE AND CORRESPONDENCE. Edited by ELIZABETH CARY AGASSIZ. 2 vols. Cr. 8vo. 18s.

ALBEMARLE (Earl of).—FIFTY YEARS OF MY LIFE. 3rd Edit., revised. Cr. 8vo. 7s. 6d.

ALFRED THE GREAT. By THOMAS HUGHES. Cr. 8vo. 6s.

AMIEL (Henri Fréderic).—THE JOURNAL INTIME. Translated by Mrs. HUMPHRY WARD. 2nd Edit. Cr. 8vo. 6s.

ANDREWS (Dr. Thomas). (See PHYSICS.)

ARNAULD, ANGELIQUE. By FRANCES MARTIN. Cr. 8vo. 4s. 6d.

ARTEVELDE. JAMES AND PHILIP VAN ARTEVELDE. By W. J. ASHLEY. Cr. 8vo. 6s.

BACON (Francis): AN ACCOUNT OF HIS LIFE AND WORKS. By E. A. ABBOTT. 8vo. 14s.

BARNES. LIFE OF WILLIAM BARNES, POET AND PHILOLOGIST. By his Daughter, LUCY BAXTER ("Leader Scott"). Cr. 8vo. 7s. 6d.

BERLIOZ (Hector): AUTOBIOGRAPHY OF. Trns. by R. & E. HOLMES. 2 vols. Cr. 8vo. 21s.

BERNARD (St.). THE LIFE AND TIMES OF ST. BERNARD, ABBOT OF CLAIRVAUX. By J. C. MORISON, M.A. Cr. 8vo. 6s.

BLACKBURNE. LIFE OF THE RIGHT HON. FRANCIS BLACKBURNE, late Lord Chancellor of Ireland, by his Son, EDWARD BLACKBURNE. With Portrait. 8vo. 12s.

BLAKE. LIFE OF WILLIAM BLAKE. With Selections from his Poems, etc. Illustr. from Blake's own Works. By ALEXANDER GILCHRIST. 2 vols. Med. 8vo. 42s.

BOLEYN (Anne): A CHAPTER OF ENGLISH HISTORY, 1527—36. By PAUL FRIEDMANN. 2 vols. 8vo. 28s.

BROOKE (Sir Jas.), THE RAJA OF SARAWAK (Life of). By GERTRUDE L. JACOB. 2 vols. 8vo. 25s.

BURKE. By JOHN MORLEY. Globe 8vo. 5s.

CALVIN. (See SELECT BIOGRAPHY, p. 5.)

CARLYLE (Thomas). Edited by CHARLES E. NORTON. Cr. 8vo.
—— REMINISCENCES. 2 vols. 12s.
—— EARLY LETTERS, 1814—26. 2 vols. 18s.
—— LETTERS, 1826—36. 2 vols. 18s.
—— CORRESPONDENCE BETWEEN GOETHE AND CARLYLE. 9s.

CARSTARES (Wm.): A CHARACTER AND CAREER OF THE REVOLUTIONARY EPOCH (1649—1715). By R. H. STORY. 8vo. 12s.

CAVOUR. (See SELECT BIOGRAPHY, p. 5.)

CHATTERTON: A STORY OF THE YEAR 1770. By Prof. DAVID MASSON. Cr. 8vo. 5s.
—— A BIOGRAPHICAL STUDY. By Sir DANIEL WILSON. Cr. 8vo. 6s. 6d.

CLARK. MEMORIALS FROM JOURNALS AND LETTERS OF SAMUEL CLARK, M.A. Edited by his Wife. Cr. 8vo. 7s. 6d.

CLOUGH (A. H.). (See LITERATURE, p. 19.

COMBE. LIFE OF GEORGE COMBE. By CHARLES GIBBON. 2 vols. 8vo. 32s.

CROMWELL. (See SELECT BIOGRAPHY, p. 5.)

DAMIEN (Father): A JOURNEY FROM CASHMERE TO HIS HOME IN HAWAII. By EDWARD CLIFFORD. Portrait. Cr. 8vo. 2s. 6d.

DANTE: AND OTHER ESSAYS. By Dean CHURCH. Globe 8vo. 5s.

MACMILLAN (D.). MEMOIR OF DANIEL MACMILLAN. By THOMAS HUGHES, Q.C. With Portrait. Cr. 8vo. 4s. 6d.—Cheap Edition. Cr. 8vo, sewed. 1s.

MALTHUS AND HIS WORK. By JAMES BONAR. 8vo. 12s. 6d.

MARCUS AURELIUS. (See SELECT BIOGRAPHY, below.)

MATHEWS. THE LIFE OF CHARLES J. MATHEWS. Edited by CHARLES DICKENS. With Portraits. 2 vols. 8vo. 25s.

MAURICE. LIFE OF FREDERICK DENISON MAURICE. By his Son, FREDERICK MAURICE, Two Portraits. 2 vols. 8vo. 36s.—Popular Edit. (4th Thousand). 2 vols. Cr. 8vo. 16s.

MAXWELL. PROFESSOR CLERK MAXWELL, A LIFE OF. By Prof. L. CAMPBELL, M.A., and W. GARNETT, M.A. Cr. 8vo. 7s. 6d.

MAZZINI. (See SELECT BIOGRAPHY.)

MELBOURNE. MEMOIRS OF VISCOUNT MELBOURNE. By W. M. TORRENS. With Portrait. 2nd Edit. 2 vols. 8vo. 32s.

MILTON. THE LIFE OF JOHN MILTON. By Prof. DAVID MASSON. Vol. I., 21s.; Vol. III., 18s.; Vols. IV. and V., 32s.; Vol. VI., with Portrait, 21s. (See also p. 13.)

MILTON, JOHNSON'S LIFE OF. With Introduction and Notes by K. DEIGHTON. Globe 8vo. 1s. 9d.

NAPOLEON I., HISTORY OF. By P. LANFREY. 4 vols. Cr. 8vo. 30s.

NELSON. SOUTHEY'S LIFE OF NELSON. With Introduction and Notes by MICHAEL MACMILLAN, B.A. Globe 8vo. 3s. 6d.

NORTH (M.).—RECOLLECTIONS OF A HAPPY LIFE. Being the Autobiography of MARIANNE NORTH. Ed. by Mrs. J. A. SYMONDS. 2nd Edit. 2 vols. Ex. cr. 8vo. 17s. net.

OXFORD MOVEMENT, THE, 1833—45. By Dean CHURCH. Gl. 8vo. 5s.

PATTESON. LIFE AND LETTERS OF JOHN COLERIDGE PATTESON, D.D., MISSIONARY BISHOP. By C. M. YONGE. 2 vols. Cr. 8vo. 12s. (See also BOOKS FOR THE YOUNG, p. 38.)

PATTISON (M.).—MEMOIRS. Cr. 8vo. 8s. 6d.

PITT. (See SELECT BIOGRAPHY.)

POLLOCK (Sir Frdk., 2nd Bart.).—PERSONAL REMEMBRANCES. 2 vols. Cr. 8vo. 16s.

POOLE, THOS., AND HIS FRIENDS. By Mrs. SANDFORD. 2nd edit. Cr. 8vo. 6s.

ROBINSON (Matthew): AUTOBIOGRAPHY OF. Edited by J. E. B. MAYOR. Fcp. 8vo. 5s.

ROSSETTI (Dante Gabriel): A RECORD AND A STUDY. By W. SHARP. Cr. 8vo. 10s. 6d.

RUMFORD. (See COLLECTED WORKS, p. 22.)

SCHILLER, LIFE OF. By Prof. H. DÜNTZER. Trans. by P. E. PINKERTON. Cr. 8vo. 10s. 6d.

SHELBURNE. LIFE OF WILLIAM, EARL OF SHELBURNE. By Lord EDMOND FITZMAURICE. In 3 vols.—Vol. I. 8vo. 12s.—Vol. II. 8vo. 12s.—Vol. III. 8vo. 16s.

SIBSON. (See MEDICINE.)

SMETHAM (Jas.).: LETTERS OF. Ed. by SARAH SMETHAM and W. DAVIES. Portrait. Cr. 8vo. 7s. 6d. net.

SPINOZA: A STUDY OF. By JAMES MARTINEAU. LL.D. 2nd Edit. Cr. 8vo. 6s.

TAIT. THE LIFE OF ARCHIBALD CAMPBELL TAIT, ARCHBISHOP OF CANTERBURY. By the BISHOP OF ROCHESTER and Rev. W. BENHAM, B.D. 2 vols. Cr. 8vo. 10s. net.
—— CATHARINE AND CRAWFURD TAIT, WIFE AND SON OF ARCHIBALD CAMPBELL, ARCHBISHOP OF CANTERBURY: A Memoir. Ed. by Rev. W. BENHAM, B.D. Cr. 8vo. 6s.—Popular Edit., abridged. Cr. 8vo. 2s. 6d.

THRING (Edward): A MEMORY OF. By J. H. SKRINE. Cr. 8vo. 6s.

VICTOR EMMANUEL II., FIRST KING OF ITALY. By G. S. GODKIN. Cr. 8vo. 6s.

WARD. WILLIAM GEORGE WARD AND THE OXFORD MOVEMENT. By his Son, WILFRID WARD. With Portrait. 8vo. 14s.

WATSON. A RECORD OF ELLEN WATSON. By ANNA BUCKLAND. Cr. 8vo. 6s.

WHEWELL. DR. WILLIAM WHEWELL, late Master of Trinity College, Cambridge. An Account of his Writings, with Selections from his Literary and Scientific Correspondence By I. TODHUNTER, M.A. 2 vols. 8vo. 25s.

WILLIAMS (Montagu).—LEAVES OF A LIFE. Cr. 8vo. 3s. 6d.
—— LATER LEAVES. Being further Reminiscences. With Portrait. Cr. 8vo. 3s. 6d.

WILSON. MEMOIR OF PROF. GEORGE WILSON, M.D. By HIS SISTER. With Portrait. 2nd Edit. Cr. 8vo. 6s.

WORDSWORTH. DOVE COTTAGE, WORDSWORTH'S HOME, 1800—8. Gl. 8vo, swd. 1s.

Select Biography.

FARRAR (Archdeacon).—SEEKERS AFTER GOD. Cr. 8vo. 3s. 6d.

FAWCETT (Mrs. H.). — SOME EMINENT WOMEN OF OUR TIMES. Cr. 8vo. 2s. 6d.

GUIZOT.—GREAT CHRISTIANS OF FRANCE: ST. LOUIS AND CALVIN. Cr. 8vo. 6s.

HARRISON (Frederic).—THE NEW CALENDAR OF GREAT MEN. Ex. cr. 8vo. 7s. 6d. net.

MARRIOTT (J. A. R.).—THE MAKERS OF MODERN ITALY: MAZZINI, CAVOUR, GARIBALDI. Cr. 8vo. 1s. 6d.

MARTINEAU (Harriet). — BIOGRAPHICAL SKETCHES, 1852—75. Cr. 8vo. 6s.

NEW HOUSE OF COMMONS, JULY, 1892. Reprinted from the *Times*. 16mo. 1s.

SMITH (Goldwin).—THREE ENGLISH STATESMEN: CROMWELL, PYM, PITT. Cr. 8vo. 5s.

WINKWORTH (Catharine). — CHRISTIAN SINGERS OF GERMANY. Cr. 8vo. 4s. 6d.

YONGE (Charlotte M.).—THE PUPILS OF ST. JOHN. Illustrated. Cr. 8vo. 6s.
—— PIONEERS AND FOUNDERS; or, Recent Workers in the Mission Field. Cr. 8vo. 6s.
—— A BOOK OF WORTHIES. 18mo. 2s. 6d. net.
—— A BOOK OF GOLDEN DEEDS. 18mo. 2s. 6d. net.—*Globe Readings Edition.* Gl. 8vo. 2s.—*Abridged Edition.* Pott 8vo. 1s.

BIOLOGY.

(See also BOTANY; NATURAL HISTORY; PHYSIOLOGY; ZOOLOGY.)

BALFOUR (F. M.).—COMPARATIVE EMBRYOLOGY. Illustrated. 2 vols. 8vo. Vol. I. 18s. Vol. II. 21s.

BIOLOGY—*continued.*

BALL (W. P.).—ARE THE EFFECTS OF USE AND DISUSE INHERITED? Cr. 8vo. 3*s.* 6*d.*

BASTIAN (H. Charlton).—THE BEGINNINGS OF LIFE. 2 vols. Crown 8vo. 28*s.*
—— EVOLUTION AND THE ORIGIN OF LIFE. Cr. 8vo. 6*s.* 6*d*:

BATESON (W.).—MATERIALS FOR THE STUDY OF VARIATION IN ANIMALS. Part I. DISCONTINUOUS VARIATION. Illustr. 8vo.

BERNARD (H. M.).—THE APODIDAE. Cr. 8vo. 7*s.* 6*d.*

BIRKS (T. R.).— MODERN PHYSICAL FATALISM, AND THE DOCTRINE OF EVOLUTION. Including an Examination of Mr. Herbert Spencer's "First Principles." Cr. 8vo. 6*s.*

EIMER (G. H. T.).—ORGANIC EVOLUTION AS THE RESULT OF THE INHERITANCE OF ACQUIRED CHARACTERS ACCORDING TO THE LAWS OF ORGANIC GROWTH. Translated by J. T. CUNNINGHAM, M.A. 8vo. 12*s.* 6*d.*

FISKE (John).—OUTLINES OF COSMIC PHILOSOPHY, BASED ON THE DOCTRINE OF EVOLUTION. 2 vols. 8vo. 25*s.*
—— MAN'S DESTINY VIEWED IN THE LIGHT OF HIS ORIGIN. Cr. 8vo. 3*s.* 6*d.*

FOSTER (Prof. M.) and BALFOUR (F. M.). —THE ELEMENTS OF EMBRYOLOGY. Ed. A. SEDGWICK, and WALTER HEAPE. Illus. 3rd Edit., revised and enlarged. Cr. 8vo. 10*s.* 6*d.*

HUXLEY (T. H.) and MARTIN (H. N.).— (*See under* ZOOLOGY, p. 40.)

KLEIN (Dr. E.).—MICRO-ORGANISMS AND DISEASE. With 121 Engravings. 3rd Edit. Cr. 8vo. 6*s.*

LANKESTER (Prof. E. Ray).—COMPARATIVE LONGEVITY IN MAN AND THE LOWER ANIMALS. Cr. 8vo. 4*s.* 6*d.*

LUBBOCK (Sir John, Bart.).— SCIENTIFIC LECTURES. Illustrated. 2nd Edit. 8vo. 8*s.* 6*d.*

PARKER (T. Jeffery).—LESSONS IN ELEMENTARY BIOLOGY. Illustr. Cr. 8vo. 10*s.* 6*d.*

ROMANES (G. J.).—SCIENTIFIC EVIDENCES OF ORGANIC EVOLUTION. Cr. 8vo. 2*s.* 6*d.*

VARIGNY (H. de).—EXPERIMENTAL EVOLUTION. Cr. 8vo. [*In the Press.*

WALLACE (Alfred R.).—DARWINISM: An Exposition of the Theory of Natural Selection. Illustrated. 3rd Edit. Cr. 8vo. 9*s.*
—— CONTRIBUTIONS TO THE THEORY OF NATURAL SELECTION, AND TROPICAL NATURE: and other Essays. New Ed. Cr. 8vo. 6*s.*
—— THE GEOGRAPHICAL DISTRIBUTION OF ANIMALS. Illustrated. 2 vols. 8vo. 42*s.*
—— ISLAND LIFE. Illustr. Ext. Cr. 8vo. 6*s.*

BIRDS. (*See* ZOOLOGY; ORNITHOLOGY.)

BOOK-KEEPING.

THORNTON (J.).—FIRST LESSONS IN BOOK-KEEPING. New Edition. Cr. 8vo. 2*s.* 6*d.*
—— KEY. Oblong 4to. 10*s.* 6*d.*
—— PRIMER OF BOOK-KEEPING. 18mo. 1*s.*
—— KEY. Demy 8vo. 2*s.* 6*d.*
—— EXERCISES IN BOOK-KEEPING. 18mo. 1*s.*

BOTANY.

See also AGRICULTURE; GARDENING.)

ALLEN (Grant). — ON THE COLOURS OF FLOWERS. Illustrated. Cr. 8vo. 3*s.* 6*d.*

BALFOUR (Prof. J. B.) and WARD (Prof. H. M.). — A GENERAL TEXT-BOOK OF BOTANY. 8vo. [*In preparation.*

BETTANY (G. T.).—FIRST LESSONS IN PRACTICAL BOTANY. 18mo. 1*s.*

BOWER (Prof. F. O.).—A COURSE OF PRACTICAL INSTRUCTION IN BOTANY. Cr. 8vo. 10*s.* 6*d.*—Abridged Edition. [*In preparation.*

CHURCH (Prof. A. H.) and SCOTT (D. H.). —MANUAL OF VEGETABLE PHYSIOLOGY. Illustrated. Crown 8vo. [*In preparation.*

GOODALE (Prof. G. L.).—PHYSIOLOGICAL BOTANY.—1. OUTLINES OF THE HISTOLOGY OF PHÆNOGAMOUS PLANTS; 2. VEGETABLE PHYSIOLOGY. 8vo. 10*s.* 6*d.*

GRAY (Prof. Asa).—STRUCTURAL BOTANY; or, Organography on the Basis of Morphology. 8vo. 10*s.* 6*d.*
—— THE SCIENTIFIC PAPERS OF ASA GRAY. Selected by C. S. SARGENT. 2 vols. 8vo. 21*s.*

HANBURY (Daniel). — SCIENCE PAPERS, CHIEFLY PHARMACOLOGICAL AND BOTANICAL. Med. 8vo. 14*s.*

HARTIG (Dr. Robert).—TEXT-BOOK OF THE DISEASES OF TREES. Transl. by Prof. WM. SOMERVILLE, B.Sc. With Introduction by Prof. H. MARSHALL WARD. 8vo.

HOOKER (Sir Joseph D.).—THE STUDENT'S FLORA OF THE BRITISH ISLANDS. 3rd Edit. Globe 8vo. 10*s.* 6*d.*
—— A PRIMER OF BOTANY. 18mo. 1*s.*

LASLETT (Thomas).—TIMBER AND TIMBER TREES, NATIVE AND FOREIGN. Cr. 8vo. 8*s.* 6*d.*

LUBBOCK (Sir John, Bart.).—ON BRITISH WILD FLOWERS CONSIDERED IN RELATION TO INSECTS. Illustrated. Cr. 8vo. 4*s.* 6*d.*
—— FLOWERS, FRUITS, AND LEAVES. With Illustrations. Cr. 8vo. 4*s.* 6*d.*

MÜLLER—THOMPSON.—THE FERTILISATION OF FLOWERS. By Prof. H. MÜLLER. Transl. by D'ARCY W. THOMPSON. Preface by CHARLES DARWIN, F.R.S. 8vo. 21*s.*

OLIVER (Prof. Daniel).—LESSONS IN ELEMENTARY BOTANY. Illustr. Fcp. 8vo. 4*s.* 6*d.*
—— FIRST BOOK OF INDIAN BOTANY. Illustrated. Ext. fcp. 8vo. 6*s.* 6*d.*

ORCHIDS: BEING THE REPORT ON THE ORCHID CONFERENCE HELD AT SOUTH KENSINGTON, 1885. 8vo. 2*s.* net.

PETTIGREW (J. Bell).—THE PHYSIOLOGY OF THE CIRCULATION IN PLANTS, IN THE LOWER ANIMALS, AND IN MAN. 8vo. 12*s.*

SMITH (J.).—ECONOMIC PLANTS, DICTIONARY OF POPULAR NAMES OF; THEIR HISTORY, PRODUCTS, AND USES. 8vo. 14*s.*

SMITH (W. G.).—DISEASES OF FIELD AND GARDEN CROPS, CHIEFLY SUCH AS ARE CAUSED BY FUNGI. Illust. Fcp. 8vo. 4*s.* 6*d.*

STEWART (S. A.) and CORRY (T. H.).— A FLORA OF THE NORTH-EAST OF IRELAND. Cr. 8vo. 5*s.* 6*d.*

WARD (Prof. H. M.).—TIMBER AND SOME OF ITS DISEASES. Illustrated. Cr. 8vo. 6*s.*

YONGE (C. M.).—THE HERB OF THE FIELD. New Edition, revised. Cr. 8vo. 5*s.*

BREWING AND WINE.

PASTEUR—FAULKNER. — STUDIES ON FERMENTATION: THE DISEASES OF BEER, THEIR CAUSES, AND THE MEANS OF PREVENTING THEM. By L. PASTEUR. Translated by FRANK FAULKNER. 8vo. 21s.

THUDICHUM (J. L. W.) and (DUPRÉ (A.). —TREATISE ON THE ORIGIN, NATURE, AND VARIETIES OF WINE. Med. 8vo. 25s.

CHEMISTRY.

(See also METALLURGY.)

BRODIE (Sir Benjamin). —IDEAL CHEMISTRY. Cr. 8vo. 2s.

COHEN (J. B.). — THE OWENS COLLEGE COURSE OF PRACTICAL ORGANIC CHEMISTRY. Fcp. 8vo. 2s. 6d.

COOKE (Prof. J. P., jun.). —PRINCIPLES OF CHEMICAL PHILOSOPHY. New Ed. 8vo. 19s.

DOBBIN (L.) and WALKER (Jas.). —CHEMICAL THEORY FOR BEGINNERS. 18mo. 2s. 6d.

FLEISCHER (Emil). —A SYSTEM OF VOLUMETRIC ANALYSIS. Transl. with Additions, by M. M. P. MUIR, F.R.S.E. Cr. 8vo. 7s. 6d.

FRANKLAND (Prof. P. F.). *(See* AGRICULTURE.)

GLADSTONE (J. H.) and TRIBE (A.). — THE CHEMISTRY OF THE SECONDARY BATTERIES OF PLANTÉ AND FAURE. Cr. 8vo. 2s. 6d.

HARTLEY (Prof. W. N.). —A COURSE OF QUANTITATIVE ANALYSIS FOR STUDENTS. Globe 8vo. 5s.

HEMPEL (Dr. W.). — METHODS OF GAS ANALYSIS. Translated by L. M. DENNIS. Cr. 8vo. 7s. 6d.

HOFMANN (Prof. A. W.). —THE LIFE WORK OF LIEBIG IN EXPERIMENTAL AND PHILOSOPHIC CHEMISTRY. 8vo. 5s.

JONES (Francis). —THE OWENS COLLEGE JUNIOR COURSE OF PRACTICAL CHEMISTRY. Illustrated. Fcp. 8vo. 2s. 6d.

—— QUESTIONS ON CHEMISTRY. Fcp. 8vo. 3s.

LANDAUER (J.). — BLOWPIPE ANALYSIS. Translated by J. TAYLOR. Gl. 8vo. 4s. 6d.

LOCKYER (J. Norman, F.R.S.). — THE CHEMISTRY OF THE SUN. Illustr. 8vo. 14s.

LUPTON (S.). — CHEMICAL ARITHMETIC. With 1200 Problems. Fcp. 8vo. 4s. 6d.

MANSFIELD (C. B.). —A THEORY OF SALTS. Cr. 8vo. 14s.

MELDOLA (Prof. R.). —THE CHEMISTRY OF PHOTOGRAPHY. Illustrated. Cr. 8vo. 6s.

MEYER (E. von). —HISTORY OF CHEMISTRY FROM EARLIEST TIMES TO THE PRESENT DAY. Trans. G. McGOWAN. 8vo. 14s. net.

MIXTER (Prof. W. G.). —AN ELEMENTARY TEXT-BOOK OF CHEMISTRY. Cr. 8vo. 7s. 6d.

MUIR (M. M. P.). —PRACTICAL CHEMISTRY FOR MEDICAL STUDENTS (First M. B. Course). Fcp. 8vo. 1s. 6d.

MUIR (M. M. P.) and WILSON (D. M.). —ELEMENTS OF THERMAL CHEMISTRY. 12s. 6d.

OSTWALD (Prof.). —OUTLINES OF GENERAL CHEMISTRY. Trans. Dr. J. WALKER. 10s. net.

RAMSAY (Prof. William). —EXPERIMENTAL PROOFS OF CHEMICAL THEORY FOR BEGINNERS. 18mo. 2s. 6d.

REMSEN (Prof. Ira). —THE ELEMENTS OF CHEMISTRY. Fcp. 8vo. 2s. 6d.

—— AN INTRODUCTION TO THE STUDY OF CHEMISTRY (INORGANIC CHEMISTRY). Cr. 8vo. 6s. 6d.

—— A TEXT-BOOK OF INORGANIC CHEMISTRY. 8vo. 16s.

—— COMPOUNDS OF CARBON ; or, An Introduction to the Study of Organic Chemistry. Cr. 8vo. 6s. 6d.

ROSCOE (Sir Henry E., F.R.S.). —A PRIMER OF CHEMISTRY. Illustrated. 18mo. 1s.

—— LESSONS IN ELEMENTARY CHEMISTRY, INORGANIC AND ORGANIC. Fcp. 8vo. 4s. 6d.

ROSCOE (Sir H. E.) and SCHORLEMMER (Prof. C.). —A COMPLETE TREATISE ON INORGANIC AND ORGANIC CHEMISTRY. Illustr. 8vo.—Vols. I. and II. INORGANIC CHEMISTRY: Vol. I. THE NON-METALLIC ELEMENTS, 2nd Edit., 21s. Vol. II. Parts I. and II. METALS, 18s. each.—Vol. III. ORGANIC CHEMISTRY: THE CHEMISTRY OF THE HYDRO-CARBONS AND THEIR DERIVATIVES. Parts I. II. IV. and VI. 21s. ; Parts III. and V. 18s. each.

ROSCOE (Sir H. E.) and SCHUSTER (A.). —SPECTRUM ANALYSIS. By Sir HENRY E. ROSCOE. 4th Edit., revised by the Author and A. SCHUSTER, F.R.S. With Coloured Plates. 8vo. 21s.

THORPE (Prof. T. E.) and TATE (W.). —A SERIES OF CHEMICAL PROBLEMS. With KEY. Fcp. 8vo. 2s.

THORPE (Prof. T. E.) and RÜCKER (Prof. A. W.). —A TREATISE ON CHEMICAL PHYSICS. Illustrated. 8vo. [*In preparation.*

WURTZ (Ad.). —A HISTORY OF CHEMICAL THEORY. Transl. by H. WATTS. Cr. 8vo. 6s.

CHRISTIAN CHURCH, History of the
(*See under* THEOLOGY, p. 31.)

CHURCH OF ENGLAND, The.
(*See under* THEOLOGY, p. 32.)

COLLECTED WORKS.
(*See under* LITERATURE, p. 19.)

COMPARATIVE ANATOMY.
(*See under* ZOOLOGY, p. 39.)

COOKERY.
(*See under* DOMESTIC ECONOMY, p. 8.)

DEVOTIONAL BOOKS.
(*See under* THEOLOGY, p. 32.)

DICTIONARIES AND GLOSSARIES.

AUTENRIETH (Dr. G.). —AN HOMERIC DICTIONARY. Translated from the German, by R. P. KEEP, Ph.D. Cr. 8vo. 6s.

BARTLETT (J.). —FAMILIAR QUOTATIONS.

—— A SHAKESPEARE GLOSSARY. Cr. 8vo. 12s. 6d.

GROVE (Sir George). —A DICTIONARY OF MUSIC AND MUSICIANS. (*See* MUSIC.)

HOLE (Rev. C.). —A BRIEF BIOGRAPHICAL DICTIONARY. 2nd Edit. 18mo. 4s. 6d.

MASSON (Gustave). —A COMPENDIOUS DICTIONARY OF THE FRENCH LANGUAGE. Cr. 8vo. 3s. 6d.

PALGRAVE (R. H. I.). —A DICTIONARY OF POLITICAL ECONOMY. (*See* POLITICAL ECONOMY.)

DICTIONARIES—*continued.*

WHITNEY (Prof. W. D.).—A COMPENDIOUS GERMAN AND ENGLISH DICTIONARY. Cr. 8vo. 5s.—German-English Part separately. 3s. 6d.

WRIGHT (W. Aldis).—THE BIBLE WORD-BOOK. 2nd Edit. Cr. 8vo. 7s. 6d.

YONGE (Charlotte M.).—HISTORY OF CHRISTIAN NAMES. Cr. 8vo. 7s. 6d.

DOMESTIC ECONOMY.
Cookery—Nursing—Needlework.

Cookery.

BARKER (Lady).—FIRST LESSONS IN THE PRINCIPLES OF COOKING. 3rd Ed. 18mo. 1s.

FREDERICK (Mrs.).—HINTS TO HOUSE-WIVES ON SEVERAL POINTS, PARTICULARLY ON THE PREPARATION OF ECONOMICAL AND TASTEFUL DISHES. Cr. 8vo. 1s.

MIDDLE-CLASS COOKERY BOOK, THE. Compiled for the Manchester School of Cookery. Fcp. 8vo. 1s. 6d.

TEGETMEIER (W. B.).—HOUSEHOLD MANAGEMENT AND COOKERY. 18mo. 1s.

WRIGHT (Miss Guthrie). — THE SCHOOL COOKERY-BOOK. 18mo. 1s.

Nursing.

CRAVEN (Mrs. Dacre).—A GUIDE TO DISTRICT NURSES. Cr. 8vo. 2s. 6d.

FOTHERGILL (Dr. J. M.).—FOOD FOR THE INVALID, THE CONVALESCENT, THE DYSPEPTIC, AND THE GOUTY. Cr. 8vo. 3s. 6d.

JEX-BLAKE (Dr. Sophia).—THE CARE OF INFANTS. 18mo. 1s.

RATHBONE (Wm.).—THE HISTORY AND PROGRESS OF DISTRICT NURSING, FROM 1859 TO THE PRESENT DATE. Cr. 8vo. 2s. 6d.

RECOLLECTIONS OF A NURSE. By E. D. Cr. 8vo. 2s.

STEPHEN (Caroline E.).—THE SERVICE OF THE POOR. Cr. 8vo. 6s. 6d.

Needlework.

GLAISTER (Elizabeth).—NEEDLEWORK. Cr. 8vo. 2s. 6d.

GRAND'HOMME. — CUTTING OUT AND DRESSMAKING. From the French of Mdlle. E. GRAND'HOMME. 18mo. 1s.

GRENFELL (Mrs.)—DRESSMAKING. 18mo. 1s.

DRAMA, The.
(*See under* LITERATURE, p. 14.)

ELECTRICITY.
(*See under* PHYSICS, p. 26.)

EDUCATION.

ARNOLD (Matthew).—HIGHER SCHOOLS AND UNIVERSITIES IN GERMANY. Cr. 8vo. 6s.
—— REPORTS ON ELEMENTARY SCHOOLS, 1852-82. Ed. by Lord SANDFORD. 8vo. 3s. 6d.
—— A FRENCH ETON: OR MIDDLE CLASS EDUCATION AND THE STATE. Cr. 8vo. 6s.

BLAKISTON (J. R.).—THE TEACHER: HINTS ON SCHOOL MANAGEMENT. Cr. 8vo. 2s. 6d.

CALDERWOOD (Prof. H.).—ON TEACHING. 4th Edit. Ext. fcp. 8vo. 2s. 6d.

COMBE (George).—EDUCATION: ITS PRINCIPLES AND PRACTICE AS DEVELOPED BY GEORGE COMBE. Ed. by W. JOLLY. 8vo. 15s.

CRAIK (Henry).—THE STATE IN ITS RELATION TO EDUCATION. Cr. 8vo. 3s. 6d.

FEARON (D. R.).—SCHOOL INSPECTION 6th Edit. Cr. 8vo. 2s. 6d.

FITCH (J. G.). — NOTES ON AMERICAN SCHOOLS AND TRAINING COLLEGES. Reprinted by permission. Globe 8vo. 2s. 6d.

GLADSTONE (J. H.).—SPELLING REFORM FROM AN EDUCATIONAL POINT OF VIEW. 3rd Edit. Cr. 8vo. 1s. 6d.

HERTEL (Dr.).—OVERPRESSURE IN HIGH SCHOOLS IN DENMARK. With Introduction by Sir J. CRICHTON-BROWNE. Cr. 8vo. 3s. 6d.

KINGSLEY (Charles).—HEALTH AND EDUCATION. Cr. 8vo. 6s.

LUBBOCK (Sir John, Bart.).—POLITICAL AND EDUCATIONAL ADDRESSES. 8vo. 8s. 6d.

MAURICE (F. D.).—LEARNING AND WORKING. Cr. 8vo. 4s. 6d.

RECORD OF TECHNICAL AND SECONDARY EDUCATION. Crown 8vo. Sewed, 2s. net. No. I. Nov. 1891.

THRING (Rev. Edward).—EDUCATION AND SCHOOL. 2nd Edit. Cr. 8vo. 6s.

ENGINEERING.

ALEXANDER (T.) and THOMSON (A. W.) —ELEMENTARY APPLIED MECHANICS. Part II. TRANSVERSE STRESS. Cr. 8vo. 10s. 6d.

CHALMERS (J. B.).—GRAPHICAL DETERMINATION OF FORCES IN ENGINEERING STRUCTURES. Illustrated. 8vo. 24s.

COTTERILL (Prof. J. H.).—APPLIED MECHANICS: An Elementary General Introduction to the Theory of Structures and Machines. 3rd Edit. 8vo. 18s.

COTTERILL (Prof. J. H.) and SLADE (J. H.).—LESSONS IN APPLIED MECHANICS. Fcp. 8vo. 5s. 6d.

KENNEDY (Prof. A. B. W.).—THE MECHANICS OF MACHINERY. Cr. 8vo. 12s. 6d.

PEABODY (Prof. C. H.).—THERMODYNAMICS OF THE STEAM ENGINE AND OTHER HEAT-ENGINES. 8vo. 21s.

SHANN (G.).—AN ELEMENTARY TREATISE ON HEAT IN RELATION TO STEAM AND THE STEAM-ENGINE. Illustrated. Cr. 8vo. 4s. 6d.

WHITHAM (Prof. J. M.).—STEAM-ENGINE DESIGN. For the use of Mechanical Engineers, Students, and Draughtsmen. Illustrated. 8vo. 25s.

WOODWARD (C. M.).—A HISTORY OF THE ST. LOUIS BRIDGE. 4to. 2l. 2s. net.

YOUNG (E. W.).—SIMPLE PRACTICAL METHODS OF CALCULATING STRAINS ON GIRDERS, ARCHES, AND TRUSSES. 8vo. 7s. 6d.

ENGLISH CITIZEN SERIES.
(*See* POLITICS.)

ENGLISH MEN OF ACTION.
(*See* BIOGRAPHY.)

ENGLISH MEN OF LETTERS.
(*See* BIOGRAPHY.)

ENGLISH STATESMEN, Twelve.
(*See* BIOGRAPHY.)

ENGRAVING. (*See* ART.)

ESSAYS. (*See under* LITERATURE, p. 19.)

ETCHING. (*See* ART.)

ETHICS. (*See under* PHILOSOPHY, p. 25.)

FATHERS, The.
See under THEOLOGY, p. 32.)

FICTION, Prose.
(*See under* LITERATURE, p. 17.)

GARDENING.
(*See also* AGRICULTURE; BOTANY.)

BLOMFIELD (R.) and THOMAS (F. I.).—THE FORMAL GARDEN IN ENGLAND. Illustrated. Ex. cr. 8vo. 7s. 6d. net.—Large Paper Edition. 8vo. 21s. net.

BRIGHT (H. A.).—THE ENGLISH FLOWER GARDEN. Cr. 8vo. 3s. 6d.
—— A YEAR IN A LANCASHIRE GARDEN. Cr. 8vo. 3s. 6d.

HOBDAY (E.). — VILLA GARDENING. A Handbook for Amateur and Practical Gardeners. Ext. cr. 8vo. 6s.

HOPE (Frances J.).—NOTES'AND THOUGHTS ON GARDENS AND WOODLANDS. Cr. 8vo. 6s.

GEOGRAPHY.
(*See also* ATLASES.)

BLANFORD (H. F.).—ELEMENTARY GEOGRAPHY OF INDIA, BURMA, AND CEYLON. Globe 8vo. 2s. 6d.

CLARKE (C. B.).—A GEOGRAPHICAL READER AND COMPANION TO THE ATLAS. Cr. 8vo. 2s.
—— A CLASS-BOOK OF GEOGRAPHY. With 18 Coloured Maps. Fcp. 8vo. 3s.; swd., 2s. 6d.

DAWSON (G. M.) and SUTHERLAND (A.). ELEMENTARY GEOGRAPHY OF THE BRITISH COLONIES. Globe 8vo. 3s.

ELDERTON (W. A.).—MAPS AND MAP DRAWING. Pott 8vo. 1s.

GEIKIE (Sir Archibald).—THE TEACHING OF GEOGRAPHY. A Practical Handbook for the use of Teachers. Globe 8vo. 2s.
—— GEOGRAPHY OF THE BRITISH ISLES. 18mo. 1s.

GREEN (J. R. and A. S.).—A SHORT GEOGRAPHY OF THE BRITISH ISLANDS. Fcp. 8vo. 3s. 6d.

GROVE (Sir George).—A PRIMER OF GEOGRAPHY. Maps. 18mo. 1s.

KIEPERT (H.).—MANUAL OF ANCIENT GEOGRAPHY. Cr. 8vo. 5s.

MILL (H. R.).—ELEMENTARY CLASS-BOOK OF GENERAL GEOGRAPHY. Cr. 8vo. 3s. 6d.

SIME (James).—GEOGRAPHY OF EUROPE. With Illustrations. Globe 8vo. 3s.

STRACHEY (Lieut.-Gen. R.).—LECTURES ON GEOGRAPHY. Cr. 8vo. 4s. 6d.

TOZER (H. F.).—A PRIMER OF CLASSICAL GEOGRAPHY. 18mo. 1s.

GEOLOGY AND MINERALOGY.

BLANFORD (W. T.). — GEOLOGY AND ZOOLOGY OF ABYSSINIA. 8vo. 21s.

COAL: ITS HISTORY AND ITS USES. By Profs. GREEN, MIALL, THORPE, RÜCKER, and MARSHALL. 8vo. 12s. 6d.

DAWSON (Sir J. W.).—THE GEOLOGY OF NOVA SCOTIA, NEW BRUNSWICK, AND PRINCE EDWARD ISLAND; or, Acadian Geology. 4th Edit. 8vo. 21s.

GEIKIE (Sir Archibald).—A PRIMER OF GEOLOGY. Illustrated. 18mo. 1s.
—— CLASS-BOOK OF GEOLOGY. Illustrated. Cr. 8vo. 4s. 6d.
—— OUTLINES OF FIELD GEOLOGY. With numerous Illustrations. Gl. 8vo. 3s. 6d.

GEIKIE (Sir A.).—GEOLOGICAL SKETCHES AT HOME AND ABROAD. Illus. 8vo. 10s. 6d.
—— TEXT-BOOK OF GEOLOGY. Illustrated. 2nd Edit. 7th Thousand. Med. 8vo. 28s.
—— THE SCENERY OF SCOTLAND. Viewed in connection with its Physical Geology. 2nd Edit. Cr. 8vo. 12s. 6d.

HULL (E.).—A TREATISE ON ORNAMENTAL AND BUILDING STONES OF GREAT BRITAIN AND FOREIGN COUNTRIES. 8vo. 12s.

PENNINGTON (Rooke).—NOTES ON THE BARROWS AND BONE CAVES OF DERBYSHIRE. 8vo. 6s.

RENDU—WILLS.—THE THEORY OF THE GLACIERS OF SAVOY. By M. LE CHANOINE RENDU. Trans. by A. WILLS, Q.C. 8vo. 7s. 6d.

ROSENBUSCH—IDDINGS.—MICROSCOPICAL PHYSIOGRAPHY OF THE ROCK-MAKING MINERALS. By Prof. H. ROSENBUSCH. Transl. by J. P. IDDINGS. Illustr. 8vo. 24s.

WILLIAMS (G. H.).—ELEMENTS OF CRYSTALLOGRAPHY. Cr. 8vo. 6s.

GLOBE LIBRARY. (*See* LITERATURE, p. 20.)

GLOSSARIES. (*See* DICTIONARIES.)

GOLDEN TREASURY SERIES.
(*See* LITERATURE, p. 20.)

GRAMMAR. (*See* PHILOLOGY.)

HEALTH. (*See* HYGIENE.)

HEAT. (*See under* PHYSICS, p. 27.)

HISTOLOGY. (*See* PHYSIOLOGY.)

HISTORY.
(*See also* BIOGRAPHY.)

ANNALS OF OUR TIME. A Diurnal of Events, Social and Political, Home and Foreign. By JOSEPH IRVING. 8vo.—Vol. I. June 20th, 1837, to Feb. 28th, 1871, 18s.; Vol. II. Feb. 24th, 1871, to June 24th, 1887, 18s. Also Vol. II. in 3 parts: Part I. Feb. 24th, 1871, to March 19th, 1874, 4s. 6d.; Part II. March 20th, 1874, to July 22nd, 1878, 4s. 6d.; Part III. July 23rd, 1878, to June 24th, 1887, 9s. Vol. III. By H. H. FYFE. Part I. June 25th, 1887, to Dec. 30th, 1890. 4s. 6d.; sewed, 3s. 6d. Part II. 1891, 1s. 6d.; sewed, 1s.

ARNOLD (T.).—THE SECOND PUNIC WAR. By THOMAS ARNOLD, D.D. Ed. by W. T. ARNOLD, M.A. With 8 Maps. Cr. 8vo. 5s.

ARNOLD (W. T.).—A HISTORY OF THE EARLY ROMAN EMPIRE. Cr. 8vo. [*In prep.*

BEESLY (Mrs.).—STORIES FROM THE HISTORY OF ROME. Fcp. 8vo. 2s. 6d.

BLACKIE (Prof. John Stuart).—WHAT DOES HISTORY TEACH? Globe 8vo. 2s. 6d.

BRYCE (James, M.P.).—THE HOLY ROMAN EMPIRE. 8th Edit. Cr. 8vo. 7s. 6d.— *Library Edition.* 8vo. 14s.

BUCKLEY (Arabella).—HISTORY OF ENGLAND FOR BEGINNERS. Globe 8vo. 3s.

BURKE (Edmund). (*See* POLITICS.)

BURY (J. B.).—A HISTORY OF THE LATER ROMAN EMPIRE FROM ARCADIUS TO IRENE, A.D. 390—800. 2 vols. 8vo. 32s.

CASSEL (Dr. D.).—MANUAL OF JEWISH HISTORY AND LITERATURE. Translated by Mrs. HENRY LUCAS. Fcp. 8vo. 2s. 6d.

COX (G. V.).—RECOLLECTIONS OF OXFORD. 2nd Edit. Cr. 8vo. 6s.

HISTORY—*continued*.

ENGLISH STATESMEN, TWELVE. (*See* BIOGRAPHY.)

FISKE (John).—THE CRITICAL PERIOD IN AMERICAN HISTORY, 1783—89. Ext. cr. 8vo. 10s. 6d.
—— THE BEGINNINGS OF NEW ENGLAND; or, The Puritan Theocracy in its Relations to Civil and Religious Liberty. Cr. 8vo. 7s. 6d.
—— THE AMERICAN REVOLUTION. 2 vols. Cr. 8vo. 18s.
—— THE DISCOVERY OF AMERICA. 2 vols. Cr. 8vo. 18s.

FRAMJI (Dosabhai).—HISTORY OF THE PARSIS, INCLUDING THEIR MANNERS, CUSTOMS, RELIGION, AND PRESENT POSITION. With Illustrations. 2 vols. Med. 8vo. 36s.

FREEMAN (Prof. E. A.).—HISTORY OF THE CATHEDRAL CHURCH OF WELLS. Cr. 8vo. 3s. 6d.
—— OLD ENGLISH HISTORY. With 3 Coloured Maps. 9th Edit., revised. Ext. fcp. 8vo. 6s.
—— HISTORICAL ESSAYS. First Series. 4th Edit. 8vo. 10s. 6d.
—— —— Second Series. 3rd Edit., with Additional Essays. 8vo. 10s. 6d.
—— —— Third Series. 8vo. 12s.
—— —— Fourth Series. 8vo. 12s. 6d.
—— THE GROWTH OF THE ENGLISH CONSTITUTION FROM THE EARLIEST TIMES. 5th Edit. Cr. 8vo. 5s.
—— COMPARATIVE POLITICS. Lectures at the Royal Institution. To which is added "The Unity of History." 8vo. 14s.
—— SUBJECT AND NEIGHBOUR LANDS OF VENICE. Illustrated. Cr. 8vo. 10s. 6d.
—— ENGLISH TOWNS AND DISTRICTS. A Series of Addresses and Essays. 8vo. 14s.
—— THE OFFICE OF THE HISTORICAL PROFESSOR. Cr. 8vo. 2s.
—— DISESTABLISHMENT AND DISENDOWMENT; WHAT ARE THEY? Cr. 8vo. 2s.
—— GREATER GREECE AND GREATER BRITAIN: GEORGE WASHINGTON THE EXPANDER OF ENGLAND. With an Appendix on IMPERIAL FEDERATION. Cr. 8vo. 3s. 6d.
—— THE METHODS OF HISTORICAL STUDY. Eight Lectures at Oxford. 8vo. 10s. 6d.
—— THE CHIEF PERIODS OF EUROPEAN HISTORY. With Essay on "Greek Cities under Roman Rule." 8vo. 10s. 6d.
—— FOUR OXFORD LECTURES, 1887; FIFTY YEARS OF EUROPEAN HISTORY; TEUTONIC CONQUEST IN GAUL AND BRITAIN. 8vo. 5s.

FRIEDMANN (Paul). (*See* BIOGRAPHY.)

GIBBINS (H. de B.).—HISTORY OF COMMERCE IN EUROPE. Globe 8vo. 3s. 6d.

GREEN (John Richard).—A SHORT HISTORY OF THE ENGLISH PEOPLE. New Edit., revised. 159th Thousand. Cr. 8vo. 8s. 6d.—Also in Parts, with Analysis. 3s. each.—Part I. 607—1265; II. 1204—1553; III. 1540—1689; IV. 1660—1873.—*Illustrated Edition*, in Parts. Super roy. 8vo. 1s. each net.—Part I. Oct. 1891.
—— HISTORY OF THE ENGLISH PEOPLE. In 4 vols. 8vo. 16s. each.
—— THE MAKING OF ENGLAND. 8vo. 16s.
—— THE CONQUEST OF ENGLAND. With Maps and Portrait. 8vo. 18s.
—— READINGS IN ENGLISH HISTORY. In 3 Parts. Fcp. 8vo. 1s. 6d. each.

GREEN (Alice S.).—THE ENGLISH TOWN IN THE 15TH CENTURY. 2 vols. 8vo.

GUEST (Dr. E.).—ORIGINES CELTICÆ. Maps. 2 vols. 8vo. 32s.

GUEST (M. J.).—LECTURES ON THE HISTORY OF ENGLAND. Cr. 8vo. 6s.

HISTORY PRIMERS. Edited by JOHN RICHARD GREEN. 18mo. 1s. each.
EUROPE. By E. A. FREEMAN, M.A.
GREECE. By C. A. FYFFE, M.A.
ROME. By Bishop CREIGHTON.
FRANCE. By CHARLOTTE M. YONGE.

HISTORICAL COURSE FOR SCHOOLS. Ed. by EDW. A. FREEMAN, D.C.L. 18mo.
GENERAL SKETCH OF EUROPEAN HISTORY. By E. A. FREEMAN. Maps. 3s. 6d.
HISTORY OF ENGLAND. By EDITH THOMPSON. Coloured Maps. 2s. 6d.
HISTORY OF SCOTLAND. By MARGARET MACARTHUR. 2s.
HISTORY OF ITALY. By the Rev. W. HUNT, M.A. With Coloured Maps. 3s. 6d.
HISTORY OF GERMANY. By JAMES SIME, M.A. 3s.
HISTORY OF AMERICA. By J. A. DOYLE. With Maps. 4s. 6d.
HISTORY OF EUROPEAN COLONIES. By E. J. PAYNE, M.A. Maps. 4s. 6d.
HISTORY OF FRANCE. By CHARLOTTE M. YONGE. Maps. 3s. 6d.

HOLE (Rev. C.).—GENEALOGICAL STEMMA OF THE KINGS OF ENGLAND AND FRANCE. On a Sheet. 1s.

INGRAM (T. Dunbar).—A HISTORY OF THE LEGISLATIVE UNION OF GREAT BRITAIN AND IRELAND. 8vo. 10s. 6d.
—— TWO CHAPTERS OF IRISH HISTORY: 1. The Irish Parliament of James II.; 2. The Alleged Violation of the Treaty of Limerick. 8vo. 6s.

JEBB (Prof. R. C.).—MODERN GREECE. Two Lectures. Crown 8vo. 5s.

JENNINGS (A. C.).—CHRONOLOGICAL TABLES OF ANCIENT HISTORY. 8vo. 5s.

KEARY (Annie).—THE NATIONS AROUND. Cr. 8vo. 4s. 6d.

KINGSLEY (Charles).—THE ROMAN AND THE TEUTON. Cr. 8vo. 3s. 6d.
—— HISTORICAL LECTURES AND ESSAYS. Cr. 8vo. 3s. 6d.

LABBERTON (R. H.). (*See* ATLASES.)

LEGGE (Alfred O.).—THE GROWTH OF THE TEMPORAL POWER OF THE PAPACY. Cr. 8vo. 8s. 6d.

LETHBRIDGE (Sir Roper).—A SHORT MANUAL OF THE HISTORY OF INDIA. Cr. 8vo. 5s.
—— THE WORLD'S HISTORY. Cr. 8vo, swd. 1s.
—— EASY INTRODUCTION TO THE HISTORY OF INDIA. Cr. 8vo, sewed. 1s. 6d.
—— HISTORY OF ENGLAND. Cr. 8vo, swd. 1s. 6d.
—— EASY INTRODUCTION TO THE HISTORY AND GEOGRAPHY OF BENGAL. Cr. 8vo. 1s. 6d.

LYTE (H. C. Maxwell).—A HISTORY OF ETON COLLEGE, 1440—1884. Illustrated. 8vo. 21s.
—— A HISTORY OF THE UNIVERSITY OF OXFORD, FROM THE EARLIEST TIMES TO THE YEAR 1530. 8vo. 16s.

MAHAFFY (Prof. J. P.).—SOCIAL LIFE IN GREECE, FROM HOMER TO MENANDER. 6th Edit. Cr. 8vo. 9s.

MAHAFFY (Prof. J. P.).—GREEK LIFE AND THOUGHT, FROM THE AGE OF ALEXANDER TO THE ROMAN CONQUEST. Cr. 8vo. 12s. 6d.
—— THE GREEK WORLD UNDER ROMAN SWAY, FROM POLYBIUS TO PLUTARCH. Cr. 8vo. 10s. 6d.
—— PROBLEMS IN GREEK HISTORY. Crown 8vo. 7s. 6d.

MARRIOTT (J. A. R.). (See SELECT BIOGRAPHY, p. 5.)

MICHELET (M.).—A SUMMARY OF MODERN HISTORY. Translated by M. C. M. SIMPSON. Globe 8vo. 4s. 6d.

MULLINGER (J. B.).—CAMBRIDGE CHARACTERISTICS IN THE SEVENTEENTH CENTURY. Cr. 8vo. 4s. 6d.

NORGATE (Kate).—ENGLAND UNDER THE ANGEVIN KINGS. In 2 vols. 8vo. 32s.

OLIPHANT (Mrs. M. O. W.).—THE MAKERS OF FLORENCE: DANTE, GIOTTO, SAVONAROLA, AND THEIR CITY. Illustr. Cr. 8vo. 10s. 6d.—Edition de Luxe. 8vo. 21s. net.
—— THE MAKERS OF VENICE: DOGES, CONQUERORS, PAINTERS, AND MEN OF LETTERS. Illustrated. Cr. 8vo. 10s. 6d.
—— ROYAL EDINBURGH: HER SAINTS, KINGS, PROPHETS, AND POETS. Illustrated by G. REID, R.S.A. Cr. 8vo. 10s. 6d.
—— JERUSALEM, ITS HISTORY AND HOPE. Illust. 8vo. 21s.—Large Paper Edit. 50s. net.

OTTÉ (E. C.).—SCANDINAVIAN HISTORY. With Maps. Globe 8vo. 6s.

PALGRAVE (Sir F.).—HISTORY OF NORMANDY AND OF ENGLAND. 4 vols. 8vo. 4l. 4s.

PARKMAN (Francis). — MONTCALM AND WOLFE. Library Edition. Illustrated with Portraits and Maps. 2 vols. 8vo. 12s. 6d. each.
—— THE COLLECTED WORKS OF FRANCIS PARKMAN. Popular Edition. In 10 vols. Cr. 8vo. 7s. 6d. each; or complete, 3l. 13s. 6d.—PIONEERS OF FRANCE IN THE NEW WORLD, 1 vol.; THE JESUITS IN NORTH AMERICA, 1 vol.; LA SALLE AND THE DISCOVERY OF THE GREAT WEST, 1 vol.; THE OREGON TRAIL, 1 vol., THE OLD RÉGIME IN CANADA UNDER LOUIS XIV., 1 vol.; COUNT FRONTENAC AND NEW FRANCE UNDER LOUIS XIV., 1 vol.; MONTCALM AND WOLFE, 2 vols.; THE CONSPIRACY OF PONTIAC, 2 vols.
—— A HALF CENTURY OF CONFLICT. 2 vols. 8vo. 25s.

POOLE (R. L.).—A HISTORY OF THE HUGUENOTS OF THE DISPERSION AT THE RECALL OF THE EDICT OF NANTES. Cr. 8vo. 6s.

ROGERS (Prof. J. E. Thorold).—HISTORICAL GLEANINGS. Cr. 8vo.—1st Series. 4s. 6d.—2nd Series. 6s.

SAYCE (Prof. A. H.).—THE ANCIENT EMPIRES OF THE EAST. Cr. 8vo. 6s.

SEELEY (Prof. J. R.). — LECTURES AND ESSAYS. 8vo. 10s. 6d.
—— THE EXPANSION OF ENGLAND. Two Courses of Lectures. Cr. 8vo. 4s. 6d.
—— OUR COLONIAL EXPANSION. Extracts from the above. Cr. 8vo. 1s.

SEWELL (E. M.) and YONGE (C. M.).—EUROPEAN HISTORY, NARRATED IN A SERIES OF HISTORICAL SELECTIONS FROM THE BEST AUTHORITIES. 2 vols. 3rd Edit. Cr. 8vo. 6s. each.

SHUCKBURGH (E. S.).—A SCHOOL HISTORY OF ROME. Cr. 8vo. [In preparation

STEPHEN (Sir J. Fitzjames, Bart.).—THE STORY OF NUNCOMAR AND THE IMPEACHMENT OF SIR ELIJAH IMPEY. 2 vols. Cr. 8vo. 15s.

TAIT (C. W. A.).—ANALYSIS OF ENGLISH HISTORY, BASED ON GREEN'S "SHORT HISTORY OF THE ENGLISH PEOPLE." Cr. 8vo. 4s. 6d.

TOUT (T. F.).—ANALYSIS OF ENGLISH HISTORY. 18mo. 1s.

TREVELYAN (Sir Geo. Otto).—CAWNPORE. Cr. 8vo. 6s.

WHEELER (J. Talboys).—PRIMER OF INDIAN HISTORY, ASIATIC AND EUROPEAN. 18mo. 1s.
—— COLLEGE HISTORY OF INDIA, ASIATIC AND EUROPEAN. Cr. 8vo. 3s.; swd. 2s. 6d.
—— A SHORT HISTORY OF INDIA. With Maps. Cr. 8vo. 12s.
—— INDIA UNDER BRITISH RULE. 8vo. 12s. 6d.

WOOD (Rev. E. G.).—THE REGAL POWER OF THE CHURCH. 8vo. 4s. 6d.

YONGE (Charlotte).—CAMEOS FROM ENGLISH HISTORY. Ext. fcp. 8vo. 5s. each.—Vol. 1. FROM ROLLO TO EDWARD II.; Vol. 2. THE WARS IN FRANCE; Vol. 3. THE WARS OF THE ROSES; Vol. 4. REFORMATION TIMES; Vol. 5. ENGLAND AND SPAIN; Vol. 6. FORTY YEARS OF STEWART RULE (1603—43); Vol. 7. THE REBELLION AND RESTORATION (1642—1678).
—— THE VICTORIAN HALF-CENTURY. Cr. 8vo. 1s. 6d.; sewed, 1s.
—— THE STORY OF THE CHRISTIANS AND MOORS IN SPAIN. 18mo. 4s. 6d.

HORTICULTURE. (See GARDENING.)

HYGIENE.

BERNERS (J.)—FIRST LESSONS ON HEALTH. 18mo. 1s.

BLYTH (A. Wynter).—A MANUAL OF PUBLIC HEALTH. 8vo. 17s. net.

BROWNE (J. H. Balfour).—WATER SUPPLY. Cr. 8vo. 2s. 6d.

CORFIELD (Dr. W. H.).—THE TREATMENT AND UTILISATION OF SEWAGE. 3rd Edit. Revised by the Author, and by LOUIS C. PARKES, M.D. 8vo. 16s.

GOODFELLOW (J.).—THE DIETETIC VALUE OF BREAD. Cr. 8vo. 6s.

KINGSLEY (Charles).—SANITARY AND SOCIAL LECTURES. Cr. 8vo. 3s. 6d.
—— HEALTH AND EDUCATION. Cr. 8vo. 6s.

REYNOLDS (Prof. Osborne).—SEWER GAS, AND HOW TO KEEP IT OUT OF HOUSES. 3rd Edit. Cr. 8vo. 1s. 6d.

RICHARDSON (Dr. B. W.).—HYGEIA: A CITY OF HEALTH. Cr. 8vo. 1s.
—— THE FUTURE OF SANITARY SCIENCE. Cr. 8vo. 1s.
—— ON ALCOHOL. Cr. 8vo. 1s.

HYMNOLOGY.
(See under THEOLOGY, p. 33.)

ILLUSTRATED BOOKS.

BALCH (Elizabeth). — GLIMPSES OF OLD ENGLISH HOMES. Gl. 4to. 14s.

BLAKE. (*See* BIOGRAPHY.)

BOUGHTON (G. H.) and ABBEY (E. A.). (*See* VOYAGES AND TRAVELS.)

CHRISTMAS CAROL (A). Printed in Colours, with Illuminated Borders. 4to. 21s.

DAYS WITH SIR ROGER DE COVERLEY. From the *Spectator*. Illustrated by HUGH THOMSON. Cr. 8vo. 6s.

DELL (E. C.).—PICTURES FROM SHELLEY. Engraved by J. D. COOPER. Folio. 21s. net.

ENGLISH ILLUSTRATED MAGAZINE, THE. (*See* PERIODICALS.)
—— Proof Impressions of Engravings originally published in *The English Illustrated Magazine*. 1884. In Portfolio 4to. 21s.

GASKELL (Mrs.).—CRANFORD. Illustrated by HUGH THOMSON. Cr. 8vo. 6s.—Also with uncut edges paper label. 6s.

GOLDSMITH (Oliver). — THE VICAR OF WAKEFIELD. New Edition, with 182 Illustrations by HUGH THOMSON. Preface by AUSTIN DOBSON. Cr. 8vo. 6s.—Also with Uncut Edges, paper label. 6s.

GREEN (John Richard). — ILLUSTRATED EDITION OF THE SHORT HISTORY OF THE ENGLISH PEOPLE. In Parts. Sup. roy. 8vo. 1s. each net. Part I. Oct. 1891. Vol. I., 12s. net.

GRIMM. (*See* BOOKS FOR THE YOUNG.)

HALLWARD (R. F.).—FLOWERS OF PARADISE. Music, Verse, Design, Illustration. 6s.

HAMERTON (P. G.).—MAN IN ART. With Etchings and Photogravures.

IRVING (Washington).—OLD CHRISTMAS. From the Sketch Book. Illustr. by RANDOLPH CALDECOTT. Gilt edges. Cr. 8vo. 6s.—Also with uncut edges, paper label. 6s.
—— BRACEBRIDGE HALL. Illustr. by RANDOLPH CALDECOTT. Gilt edges. Cr. 8vo. 6s.—Also with uncut edges, paper label. 6s.
—— OLD CHRISTMAS AND BRACEBRIDGE HALL. *Edition de Luxe.* Roy. 8vo. 21s.

KINGSLEY (Charles).—THE WATER BABIES. (*See* BOOKS FOR THE YOUNG.)
—— THE HEROES. (*See* BOOKS for the YOUNG.)
—— GLAUCUS. (*See* NATURAL HISTORY.)

LANG (Andrew).—THE LIBRARY. With a Chapter on Modern Illustrated Books, by AUSTIN DOBSON. Cr. 8vo. 3s. 6d.

LYTE (H. C. Maxwell). (*See* HISTORY.)

MAHAFFY (Rev. Prof. J. P.) and ROGERS (J. E.). (*See* VOYAGES AND TRAVELS.)

MEREDITH (L. A.).—BUSH FRIENDS IN TASMANIA. Native Flowers, Fruits, and Insects, with Prose and Verse Descriptions. Folio. 52s. 6d. net.

OLD SONGS. With Drawings by E. A. ABBEY and A. PARSONS. 4to, mor. gilt. 31s. 6d.

PROPERT (J. L.). (*See* ART.)

STUART, RELICS OF THE ROYAL HOUSE OF. Illustrated by 40 Plates in Colours drawn from Relics of the Stuarts by WILLIAM GIBB. With an Introduction by JOHN SKELTON, C.B., LL.D., and Descriptive Notes by W. ST. JOHN HOPE. Folio, half morocco, gilt edges. 10l. 10s. net.

TENNYSON (Hon. Hallam).—JACK AND THE BEAN-STALK. English Hexameters. Illustrated by R. CALDECOTT. Fcp. 4to. 3s. 6d.

TRISTRAM (W. O.).—COACHING DAYS AND COACHING WAYS. Illust. H. RAILTON and HUGH THOMSON. Ext. cr. 4to. 31s. 6d.

TURNER'S LIBER STUDIORUM: A DESCRIPTION AND A CATALOGUE. By W. G. RAWLINSON. Med. 8vo. 12s. 6d.

WALTON and COTTON—LOWELL.—THE COMPLETE ANGLER. With Introduction by JAS. RUSSELL LOWELL. 2 vols. Ext. cr. 8vo. 52s. 6d. net.

LANGUAGE. (*See* PHILOLOGY.)

LAW.

BERNARD (M.).—FOUR LECTURES ON SUBJECTS CONNECTED WITH DIPLOMACY. 8vo. 9s.

BIGELOW (M. M.).—HISTORY OF PROCEDURE IN ENGLAND FROM THE NORMAN CONQUEST, 1066-1204. 8vo. 16s.

BOUTMY (E.). — STUDIES IN CONSTITUTIONAL LAW. Transl. by Mrs. DICEY. Preface by Prof. A. V. DICEY. Cr. 8vo. 6s.
—— THE ENGLISH CONSTITUTION. Transl. by Mrs. EADEN. Introduction by Sir F. POLLOCK, Bart. Cr. 8vo. 6s.

CHERRY (R. R.). — LECTURES ON THE GROWTH OF CRIMINAL LAW IN ANCIENT COMMUNITIES. 8vo. 5s. net.

DICEY (Prof. A. V.).—LECTURES INTRODUCTORY TO THE STUDY OF THE LAW OF THE CONSTITUTION. 3rd Edit. 8vo. 12s. 6d.

ENGLISH CITIZEN SERIES, THE. (*See* POLITICS.)

HOLLAND (Prof. T. E.).—THE TREATY RELATIONS OF RUSSIA AND TURKEY, FROM 1774 TO 1853. Cr. 8vo. 2s.

HOLMES (O. W., jun.). — THE COMMON LAW. 8vo. 12s.

LIGHTWOOD (J. M.).—THE NATURE OF POSITIVE LAW. 8vo. 12s. 6d.

MAITLAND (F. W.).—PLEAS OF THE CROWN FOR THE COUNTY OF GLOUCESTER, A.D. 1221. 8vo. 7s. 6d.
—— JUSTICE AND POLICE. Cr. 8vo. 3s. 6d.

MONAHAN (James H.).—THE METHOD OF LAW. Cr. 8vo. 6s.

PATERSON (James).—COMMENTARIES ON THE LIBERTY OF THE SUBJECT, AND THE LAWS OF ENGLAND RELATING TO THE SECURITY OF THE PERSON. 2 vols. Cr. 8vo. 21s.
—— THE LIBERTY OF THE PRESS, SPEECH, AND PUBLIC WORSHIP. Cr. 8vo. 12s.

PHILLIMORE (John G.).—PRIVATE LAW AMONG THE ROMANS. 8vo. 6s.

POLLOCK (Sir F., Bart.).—ESSAYS IN JURISPRUDENCE AND ETHICS. 8vo. 10s. 6d.
—— THE LAND LAWS. Cr. 8vo. 3s. 6d.
—— LEADING CASES DONE INTO ENGLISH. Cr. 8vo. 3s. 6d.

RICHEY (Alex. G.).—THE IRISH LAND LAWS. Cr. 8vo. 3s. 6d.

SELBORNE (Earl of).—JUDICIAL PROCEDURE IN THE PRIVY COUNCIL. 8vo. 1s. net.

STEPHEN (Sir J. Fitzjames, Bart.).—A DI-
GEST OF THE LAW OF EVIDENCE. Cr. 8vo. 6s.
—— A DIGEST OF THE CRIMINAL LAW:
CRIMES AND PUNISHMENTS. 4th Ed. 8vo. 16s.
—— A DIGEST OF THE LAW OF CRIMINAL
PROCEDURE IN INDICTABLE OFFENCES. By
Sir J. F., Bart., and HERBERT STEPHEN,
LL.M. 8vo. 12s. 6d.
—— A HISTORY OF THE CRIMINAL LAW OF
ENGLAND. 3 vols. 8vo. 48s.
—— A GENERAL VIEW OF THE CRIMINAL
LAW OF ENGLAND. 2nd Edit. 8vo. 14s.

STEPHEN (J. K.).—INTERNATIONAL LAW
AND INTERNATIONAL RELATIONS. Cr.
8vo. 6s.

WILLIAMS (S. E.).—FORENSIC FACTS AND
FALLACIES. Globe 8vo. 4s. 6d.

LETTERS. (*See under* LITERATURE, p. 19.)

LIFE-BOAT.

GILMORE (Rev. John).—STORM WARRIORS;
or, Life-Boat Work on the Goodwin Sands.
Cr. 8vo. 3s. 6d.

LEWIS (Richard).—HISTORY OF THE LIFE-
BOAT AND ITS WORK. Cr. 8vo. 5s.

LIGHT. (*See under* PHYSICS, p. 27.)

LITERATURE.

*History and Criticism of—Commentaries,
etc.—Poetry and the Drama—Poetical Collections and Selections—Prose Fiction—Collected Works, Essays, Lectures, Letters,
Miscellaneous Works.*

History and Criticism of.

(*See also* ESSAYS, p. 19.)

ARNOLD (M.). (*See* ESSAYS. p. 19.)

BROOKE (Stopford A.).—A PRIMER OF ENG-
LISH LITERATURE. 18mo. 1s. — Large
Paper Edition. 8vo. 7s. 6d.
—— A HISTORY OF EARLY ENGLISH LITERA-
TURE. 2 vols. 8vo.

CLASSICAL WRITERS. Edited by JOHN
RICHARD GREEN. Fcp. 8vo. 1s. 6d. each.
DEMOSTHENES. By Prof. BUTCHER, M.A.
EURIPIDES. By Prof. MAHAFFY.
LIVY. By the Rev. W. W. CAPES, M.A.
MILTON. By STOPFORD A. BROOKE.
SOPHOCLES. By Prof. L. CAMPBELL, M.A.
TACITUS. By Messrs. CHURCH and BRODRIBB.
VERGIL. By Prof. NETTLESHIP, M.A.

ENGLISH MEN OF LETTERS. (*See*
BIOGRAPHY.)

HISTORY OF ENGLISH LITERATURE.
In 4 vols. Cr. 8vo.
EARLY ENGLISH LITERATURE. By STOP-
FORD BROOKE, M.A. [*In preparation.*
ELIZABETHAN LITERATURE (1560—1665).
By GEORGE SAINTSBURY. 7s. 6d.
EIGHTEENTH CENTURY LITERATURE (1660
—1780). By EDMUND GOSSE, M.A. 7s. 6d.
THE MODERN PERIOD. By Prof. DOWDEN.
[*In preparation.*

JEBB (Prof. R. C.).—A PRIMER OF GREEK
LITERATURE. 18mo. 1s.
—— THE ATTIC ORATORS, FROM ANTIPHON
TO ISAEOS. 2 vols 8vo. 25s.

JOHNSON'S LIVES OF THE POETS.
MILTON, DRYDEN, POPE, ADDISON, SWIFT,
AND GRAY. With Macaulay's "Life of
Johnson" Ed. by M. ARNOLD. Cr. 8vo. 4s. 6d.

KINGSLEY (Charles). — LITERARY AND
GENERAL LECTURES. Cr. 8vo. 3s. 6d.

MAHAFFY (Prof. J. P.).—A HISTORY OF
CLASSICAL GREEK LITERATURE. 2 vols.
Cr. 8vo.—Vol. 1. THE POETS. With an
Appendix on Homer by Prof. SAYCE. In 2
Parts.—Vol. 2. THE PROSE WRITERS. In 2
Parts. 4s. 6d. each.

MORLEY (John). (*See* COLLECTED WORKS,
p. 22.)

NICHOL (Prof. J.) and McCORMICK (Prof
(W. S.).—A SHORT HISTORY OF ENGLISH
LITERATURE. Globe 8vo. [*In preparation.*

OLIPHANT (Mrs. M. O. W.).—THE LITE-
RARY HISTORY OF ENGLAND IN THE END
OF THE 18TH AND BEGINNING OF THE 19TH
CENTURY. 3 vols. 8vo. 21s.

RYLAND (F.).—CHRONOLOGICAL OUTLINES
OF ENGLISH LITERATURE. Cr. 8vo. 6s.

WARD (Prof. A. W.).—A HISTORY OF ENG-
LISH DRAMATIC LITERATURE, TO THE
DEATH OF QUEEN ANNE. 2 vols. 8vo. 32s.

WILKINS (Prof. A. S.).—A PRIMER OF RO-
MAN LITERATURE. 18mo. 1s.

Commentaries, etc.

BROWNING.
A PRIMER ON BROWNING. By MARY WILSON.
Cr. 8vo. 2s. 6d.

DANTE.
READINGS ON THE PURGATORIO OF DANTE.
Chiefly based on the Commentary of Ben-
venuto da Imola. By the Hon. W. W.
VERNON, M.A. With an Introduction by
Dean CHURCH. 2 vols. Cr. 8vo. 24s.

HOMER.
HOMERIC DICTIONARY. (*See* DICTIONARIES.)
THE PROBLEM OF THE HOMERIC POEMS.
By Prof. W. D. GEDDES. 8vo. 14s.
HOMERIC SYNCHRONISM. An Inquiry into
the Time and Place of Homer. By the
Rt. Hon. W. E. GLADSTONE. Cr. 8vo. 6s.
PRIMER OF HOMER. By the same. 18mo. 1s.
LANDMARKS OF HOMERIC STUDY, TOGETHER
WITH AN ESSAY ON THE POINTS OF CON-
TACT BETWEEN THE ASSYRIAN TABLETS
AND THE HOMERIC TEXT. By the same.
Cr. 8vo. 2s. 6d.
COMPANION TO THE ILIAD FOR ENGLISH
READERS. By W. LEAF, Litt.D. Crown
8vo. 7s. 6d.

HORACE.
STUDIES, LITERARY AND HISTORICAL, IN
THE ODES OF HORACE. By A. W. VER-
RALL, Litt.D. 8vo. 8s. 6d.

SHAKESPEARE.
SHAKESPEARE GLOSSARY. See DICTIONARIES.
A PRIMER OF SHAKSPERE. By Prof. DOW-
DEN. 18mo. 1s.
A SHAKESPEARIAN GRAMMAR. By Rev.
E. A. ABBOTT. Ext. fcp. 8vo. 6s.
SHAKESPEAREANA GENEALOGICA. By G. R.
FRENCH. 8vo. 15s.
A SELECTION FROM THE LIVES IN NORTH'S
PLUTARCH WHICH ILLUSTRATE SHAKES-
PEARE'S PLAYS. Edited by Rev. W. W.
SKEAT, M.A. Cr. 8vo. 6s.
SHORT STUDIES OF SHAKESPEARE'S PLOTS.
By Prof. CYRIL RANSOME. Cr. 8vo. 3s. 6d.
CALIBAN: A Critique on "The Tempest"
and "A Midsummer Night's Dream." By
Sir DANIEL WILSON. 8vo. 10s. 6d.

TENNYSON.
> A COMPANION TO "IN MEMORIAM." By ELIZABETH R. CHAPMAN. Globe 8vo. 2*s.*

WORDSWORTH.
> WORDSWORTHIANA: A Selection of Papers read to the Wordsworth Society. Edited by W. KNIGHT. Cr. 8vo. 7*s.* 6*d.*

Poetry and the Drama.

ALDRICH (T. Bailey).—THE SISTERS' TRAGEDY: with other Poems, Lyrical and Dramatic. Fcp. 8vo. 3*s.* 6*d.* net.

AN ANCIENT CITY: AND OTHER POEMS. Ext. fcp. 8vo. 6*s.*

ANDERSON (A.).—BALLADS AND SONNETS. Cr. 8vo. 5*s.*

ARNOLD (Matthew). — THE COMPLETE POETICAL WORKS. New Edition. 3 vols. Cr. 8vo. 7*s.* 6*d.* each.
> Vol. 1. EARLY POEMS, NARRATIVE POEMS AND SONNETS.
> Vol. 2. LYRIC AND ELEGIAC POEMS.
> Vol. 3. DRAMATIC AND LATER POEMS.
—— COMPLETE POETICAL WORKS. 1 vol. Cr. 8vo. 7*s.* 6*d.*
—— SELECTED POEMS. 18mo. 4*s.* 6*d.*

AUSTIN (Alfred).—POETICAL WORKS. New Collected Edition. 6 vols. Cr. 8vo. 5*s.* each.
> Vol. 1. THE TOWER OF BABEL.
> Vol. 2. SAVONAROLA, etc.
> Vol. 3. PRINCE LUCIFER.
> Vol. 4. THE HUMAN TRAGEDY.
> Vol. 5. LYRICAL POEMS.
> Vol. 6. NARRATIVE POEMS.
—— SOLILOQUIES IN SONG. Cr. 8vo. 6*s.*
—— AT THE GATE OF THE CONVENT: and other Poems. Cr. 8vo. 6*s.*
—— MADONNA'S CHILD. Cr. 4to. 3*s.* 6*d.*
—— ROME OR DEATH. Cr. 4to. 9*s.*
—— THE GOLDEN AGE. Cr. 8vo. 5*s.*
—— THE SEASON. Cr. 8vo. 5*s.*
—— LOVE'S WIDOWHOOD: and other Poems. Cr. 8vo. 6*s.*
—— ENGLISH LYRICS. Cr. 8vo. 3*s.* 6*d.*

BETSY LEE: A FO'C'S'LE YARN. Ext. fcp. 8vo. 3*s.* 6*d.*

BLACKIE (John Stuart).—MESSIS VITAE: Gleanings of Song from a Happy Life. Cr. 8vo. 4*s.* 6*d.*
—— THE WISE MEN OF GREECE. In a Series of Dramatic Dialogues. Cr. 8vo. 9*s.*
—— GOETHE'S FAUST. Translated into English Verse. 2nd Edit. Cr. 8vo. 9*s.*

BLAKE. (*See* BIOGRAPHY.)

BROOKE (Stopford A.).—RIQUET OF THE TUFT: A Love Drama. Ext. cr. 8vo. 6*s.*
—— POEMS. Globe 8vo. 6*s.*

BROWN (T. E.).—THE MANX WITCH: and other Poems. Cr. 8vo. 7*s.* 6*d.*

BURGON (Dean).—POEMS. Ex. fcp. 8vo. 4*s.* 6*d.*

BURNS. THE POETICAL WORKS. With a Biographical Memoir by ALEXANDER SMITH. In 2 vols. Fcp. 8vo. 10*s.* (*See also* GLOBE LIBRARY, p. 20.)

BUTLER (Samuel).—HUDIBRAS. Edit. by ALFRED MILNES. Fcp. 8vo.—Part I. 3*s.* 6*d.*; Parts II. and III. 4*s.* 6*d.*

BYRON. (*See* GOLDEN TREASURY SERIES, p. 20.)

CALDERON.—SELECT PLAYS. Edited by NORMAN MACCOLL. Cr. 8vo. 14*s.*

CAUTLEY (G. S.).—A CENTURY OF EMBLEMS. With Illustrations by Lady MARION ALFORD. Small 4to. 10*s.* 6*d.*

CLOUGH (A. H.).—POEMS. Cr. 8vo. 7*s.* 6*d.*

COLERIDGE: POETICAL AND DRAMATIC WORKS. 4 vols. Fcp. 8vo. 31*s.* 6*d.*—Also an Edition on Large Paper, 2*l.* 12*s.* 6*d.*

COLQUHOUN.—RHYMES AND CHIMES. By F. S. COLQUHOUN (*née* F. S. FULLER MAITLAND). Ext. fcp. 8vo. 2*s.* 6*d.*

COWPER. (*See* GLOBE LIBRARY, p. 20; GOLDEN TREASURY SERIES, p. 20.)

CRAIK (Mrs.).—POEMS. Ext. fcp. 8vo. 6*s.*

DOYLE (Sir F. H.).—THE RETURN OF THE GUARDS: and other Poems. Cr. 8vo. 7*s.* 6*d.*

DRYDEN. (*See* GLOBE LIBRARY, p. 20.)

EMERSON. (*See* COLLECTED WORKS, p. 20.)

EVANS (Sebastian). — BROTHER FABIAN'S MANUSCRIPT: and other Poems. Fcp. 8vo. 6*s.*
—— IN THE STUDIO: A Decade of Poems. Ext. fcp. 8vo. 5*s.*

FITZ GERALD (Caroline).—VENETIA VICTRIX: and other Poems. Ext. fcp. 8vo. 3*s.* 6*d.*

FITZGERALD (Edward).—THE RUBÁIYÁT OF OMAR KHÁYYÁM. Ext. cr. 8vo. 10*s.* 6*d.*

FO'C'SLE YARNS, including "Betsy Lee," and other Poems. Cr. 8vo. 7*s.* 6*d.*

FRASER-TYTLER. — SONGS IN MINOR KEYS. By C. C. FRASER-TYTLER (Mrs. EDWARD LIDDELL). 2nd Edit. 18mo. 6*s.*

FURNIVALL (F. J.).—LE MORTE ARTHUR. Edited from the Harleian MSS. 2252, in the British Museum. Fcp. 8vo. 7*s.* 6*d.*

GARNETT (R.).—IDYLLS AND EPIGRAMS. Chiefly from the Greek Anthology. Fcp. 8vo. 2*s.* 6*d.*

GOETHE.—FAUST. (*See* BLACKIE.)
—— REYNARD THE FOX. Transl. into English Verse by A. D. AINSLIE. Cr. 8vo. 7*s.* 6*d.*

GOLDSMITH.—THE TRAVELLER AND THE DESERTED VILLAGE. With Introduction and Notes, by ARTHUR BARRETT, B.A. 1*s.* 9*d.*; sewed, 1*s.* 6*d.*—THE TRAVELLER (separately), sewed, 1*s.*—By J. W. HALES. Cr. 8vo. 6*d.* (*See also* GLOBE LIBRARY, p. 20.)

GRAHAM (David).—KING JAMES I. An Historical Tragedy. Globe 8vo. 7*s.*

GRAY.—POEMS. With Introduction and Notes, by J. BRADSHAW, LL.D. Gl. 8vo. 1*s.* 9*d.*, sewed, 1*s.* 6*d.* (*See also* COLLECTED WORKS, p. 21.)

HALLWARD. (*See* ILLUSTRATED BOOKS.)

HAYES (A.).—THE MARCH OF MAN: and other Poems. Fcp. 8vo. 3*s.* 6*d.* net.

HERRICK. (*See* GOLDEN TREASURY SERIES, p. 20.)

HOPKINS (Ellice).—AUTUMN SWALLOWS. A Book of Lyrics. Ext. fcp. 8vo. 6*s.*

HOSKEN (J. D.).—PHAON AND SAPPHO, AND NIMROD. Fcp. 8vo. 5*s.*

JONES (H. A.).—SAINTS AND SINNERS. Ext. fcp. 8vo. 3s. 6d.

KEATS. (*See* GOLDEN TREASURY SERIES, p. 20.)

KINGSLEY (Charles).—POEMS. Cr. 8vo. 3s. 6d.—*Pocket Edition.* 18mo. 1s. 6d.—*Eversley Edition.* 2 vols. Cr. 8vo. 10s.

LAMB. (*See* COLLECTED WORKS, p. 21.)

LANDOR. (*See* GOLDEN TREASURY SERIES, p. 20.)

LONGFELLOW. (*See* GOLDEN TREASURY SERIES, p. 20.)

LOWELL (Jas. Russell).—COMPLETE POETICAL WORKS. 18mo. 4s. 6d.
—— With Introduction by THOMAS HUGHES, and Portrait. Cr. 8vo. 7s. 6d.
—— HEARTSEASE AND RUE. Cr. 8vo. 5s. (*See also* COLLECTED WORKS, p. 21.)

LUCAS (F.).—SKETCHES OF RURAL LIFE. Poems. Globe 8vo. 5s.

MEREDITH (George). — A READING OF EARTH. Ext. fcp. 8vo. 5s.
—— POEMS AND LYRICS OF THE JOY OF EARTH. Ext. fcp. 8vo. 6s.
—— BALLADS AND POEMS OF TRAGIC LIFE. Cr. 8vo. 6s.
—— MODERN LOVE. Ex. fcap. 8vo. 5s.

MILTON.—POETICAL WORKS. Edited, with Introductions and Notes, by Prof. DAVID MASSON, M.A. 3 vols. 8vo. 2l. 2s.—[Uniform with the Cambridge Shakespeare.]
—— —— Edited by Prof. MASSON. 3 vols. Fcp. 8vo. 15s.
—— —— *Globe Edition.* Edited by Prof. MASSON. Globe 8vo. 3s. 6d.
—— PARADISE LOST, BOOKS 1 and 2. Edited by MICHAEL MACMILLAN, B.A. 1s. 9d.; sewed, 1s. 6d.—BOOKS 1 and 2 (separately), 1s. 3d. each; sewed, 1s. each.
—— L'ALLEGRO, IL PENSEROSO, LYCIDAS, ARCADES, SONNETS, ETC. Edited by WM. BELL, M.A. 1s. 9d.; sewed, 1s. 6d.
—— COMUS. By the same. 1s. 3d.; swd. 1s.
—— SAMSON AGONISTES. Edited by H. M. PERCIVAL, M.A. 2s.; sewed, 1s. 9d.

MOULTON (Louise Chandler). — IN THE GARDEN OF DREAMS: Lyrics and Sonnets. Cr. 8vo. 6s.

MUDIE (C. E.).—STRAY LEAVES: Poems. 4th Edit. Ext. fcp. 8vo. 3s. 6d.

MYERS (E.).—THE PURITANS: A Poem. Ext. fcp. 8vo. 2s. 6d.
—— POEMS. Ext. fcp. 8vo. 4s. 6d.
—— THE DEFENCE OF ROME: and other Poems. Ext. fcp. 8vo. 5s.
—— THE JUDGMENT OF PROMETHEUS: and other Poems. Ext. fcp. 8vo. 3s. 6d.

MYERS (F. W. H.).—THE RENEWAL OF YOUTH: and other Poems. Cr. 8vo. 7s. 6d.
—— ST. PAUL: A Poem. Ext. fcp. 8vo. 2s. 6d.

NORTON (Hon. Mrs.).—THE LADY OF LA GARAYE. 9th Edit. Fcp. 8vo. 4s. 6d.

PALGRAVE (Prof. F. T.).—ORIGINAL HYMNS. 3rd Edit. 18mo. 1s. 6d.
—— LYRICAL POEMS. Ext. fcp. 8vo. 6s.
—— VISIONS OF ENGLAND. Cr. 8vo. 7s. 6d.

PALGRAVE (W. G.).—A VISION OF LIFE: SEMBLANCE AND REALITY. Cr. 8vo. 7s. net.

PEEL (Edmund).—ECHOES FROM HOREB: and other Poems. Cr. 8vo. 3s. 6d

POPE. (*See* GLOBE LIBRARY, p. 20.)

RAWNSLEY (H. D.).—POEMS, BALLADS, AND BUCOLICS. Fcp. 8vo. 5s.

ROSCOE (W. C.).—POEMS. Edit. by E. M Roscoe. Cr. 8vo. 7s. net.

ROSSETTI (Christina).—POEMS. New Collected Edition. Globe 8vo. 7s. 6d.
—— A PAGEANT: and other Poems. Ext. fcp. 8vo. 6s.

SCOTT.—THE LAY OF THE LAST MINSTREL, and THE LADY OF THE LAKE. Edited by Prof. F. T. PALGRAVE. 1s.
—— THE LAY OF THE LAST MINSTREL. By G. H. STUART, M.A., and E. H. ELLIOT, B.A. Globe 8vo. 2s.; sewed, 1s. 9d.—Canto I. 9d.—Cantos I.—III. and IV.—VI. 1s. 3d. each; sewed, 1s. each.
—— MARMION. Edited by MICHAEL MACMILLAN, B.A. 3s.; sewed, 2s. 6d.
—— MARMION, and THE LORD OF THE ISLES. By Prof. F. T. PALGRAVE. 1s.
—— THE LADY OF THE LAKE. By G. H. STUART, M.A. Gl. 8vo. 2s. 6d.; swd. 2s.
—— ROKEBY. By MICHAEL MACMILLAN, B.A. 3s.; sewed, 2s. 6d.

(*See also* GLOBE LIBRARY, p. 20.)

SHAIRP (John Campbell).—GLEN DESSERAY: and other Poems, Lyrical and Elegiac. Ed. by F. T. PALGRAVE. Cr. 8vo. 6s.

SHAKESPEARE.—THE WORKS OF WILLIAM SHAKESPEARE. *Cambridge Edition.* New and Revised Edition, by W. ALDIS WRIGHT, M.A. 9 vols. 8vo. 10s. 6d. each.—Quarterly Vols. Vol. I. Jan. 1891.
—— —— *Victoria Edition.* In 3 vols.—COMEDIES; HISTORIES; TRAGEDIES. Cr. 8vo. 6s. each.
—— THE TEMPEST. With Introduction and Notes, by K. DEIGHTON. Gl. 8vo. 1s. 9d.; sewed, 1s. 6d.
—— MUCH ADO ABOUT NOTHING. 2s.; sewed, 1s. 9d.
—— A MIDSUMMER NIGHT'S DREAM. 1s. 9d.; sewed, 1s. 6d.
—— THE MERCHANT OF VENICE. 1s. 9d.; sewed, 1s. 6d.
—— AS YOU LIKE IT. 1s. 9d.; sewed, 1s. 6d.
—— TWELFTH NIGHT. 1s. 9d.; sewed, 1s. 6d.
—— THE WINTER'S TALE. 2s.; sewed, 1s. 9d.
—— KING JOHN. 1s. 9d.; sewed, 1s. 6d.
—— RICHARD II. 1s. 9d.; sewed, 1s. 6d.
—— HENRY V. 1s. 9d.; sewed, 1s. 6d.
—— RICHARD III. By C. H. TAWNEY, M.A. 2s. 6d.; sewed, 2s.
—— CORIOLANUS. By K. DEIGHTON. 2s. 6d.; sewed, 2s.
—— JULIUS CÆSAR. 1s. 9d.; sewed, 1s. 6d.
—— MACBETH. 1s. 9d.; sewed, 1s. 6d.
—— HAMLET. 2s. 6d.; sewed, 2s.
—— KING LEAR. 1s. 9d.; sewed, 1s. 6d.
—— OTHELLO. 2s.; sewed, 1s. 9d.
—— ANTONY AND CLEOPATRA. 2s. 6d.; swd. 2s.
—— CYMBELINE. 2s. 6d.; sewed, 2s.

(*See also* GLOBE LIBRARY, p. 20; GOLDEN TREASURY SERIES, p. 20.)

SHELLEY.—COMPLETE POETICAL WORKS. Edited by Prof. DOWDEN. Portrait. Cr. 8vo. 7s. 6d. (*See* GOLDEN TREASURY SERIES, p. 20.)

LITERATURE.
Poetry and the Drama—*continued.*

SMITH (C. Barnard).—POEMS. Fcp. 8vo. 5*s.*

SMITH (Horace).—POEMS. Globe 8vo. 5*s.*

SPENSER. (*See* GLOBE LIBRARY, p. 20.)

STEPHENS (J. B.).—CONVICT ONCE: and other Poems. Cr. 8vo. 7*s.* 6*d.*

STRETTELL (Alma).—SPANISH AND ITALIAN FOLK SONGS. Illustr. Roy.16mo. 12*s.*6*d.*

SYMONS (Arthur). — DAYS AND NIGHTS. Globe 8vo. 6*s.*

TENNYSON (Lord).—COMPLETE WORKS. New and Enlarged Edition, with Portrait. Cr. 8vo. 7*s.* 6*d.*—*School Edition.* In Four Parts. Cr. 8vo. 2*s.* 6*d.* each.
—— POETICAL WORKS. *Pocket Edition.* 18mo, morocco, gilt edges. 7*s.* 6*d.* net.
—— WORKS. *Library Edition.* In 8 vols. Globe 8vo. 5*s.* each. [Each volume may be had separately.]—POEMS, 2 vols.—IDYLLS OF THE KING.—THE PRINCESS, and MAUD.—ENOCH ARDEN, and IN MEMORIAM.—BALLADS, and other Poems.—QUEEN MARY, and HAROLD.—BECKET, and other Plays.
—— WORKS. *Ext. fcp. 8vo. Edition,* on Handmade Paper. In 7 vols. (supplied in sets only). 3*l.* 13*s.* 6*d.*—EARLY POEMS.—LUCRETIUS, and other Poems.—IDYLLS OF THE KING.—THE PRINCESS, and MAUD.—ENOCH ARDEN, and IN MEMORIAM.—QUEEN MARY, and HAROLD.—BALLADS, and other Poems.
—— WORKS. *Miniature Edition,* in 16 vols., viz. THE POETICAL WORKS. 12 vols. in a box. 25*s.*—THE DRAMATIC WORKS. 4 vols. in a box. 10*s.* 6*d.*
—— *The Original Editions.* Fcp. 8vo.
POEMS. 6*s.*
MAUD: and other Poems. 3*s.* 6*d.*
THE PRINCESS. 3*s.* 6*d.*
THE HOLY GRAIL: and other Poems. 4*s.*6*d.*
BALLADS: and other Poems. 5*s.*
HAROLD: A Drama. 6*s.*
QUEEN MARY: A Drama. 6*s.*
THE CUP, and THE FALCON. 5*s.*
BECKET. 6*s.*
TIRESIAS: and other Poems. 6*s.*
LOCKSLEY HALL SIXTY YEARS AFTER, etc. 6*s.*
DEMETER: and other Poems. 6*s.*
THE FORESTERS: ROBIN HOOD AND MAID MARIAN. 6*s.*
—— *The Royal Edition.* 1 vol. 8vo. 16*s.*
—— THE TENNYSON BIRTHDAY BOOK. Edit. by EMILY SHAKESPEAR. 18mo. 2*s.* 6*d.*
—— THE BROOK. With 20 Illustrations by A. WOODRUFF. 32mo. 2*s.* 6*d.*
—— SONGS FROM TENNYSON'S WRITINGS. Square 8vo. 2*s.* 6*d.*
—— SELECTIONS FROM TENNYSON. With Introduction and Notes, by F. J. ROWE, M.A., and W. T. WEBB, M.A. Globe 8vo. 3*s.* 6*d.*
—— ENOCH ARDEN. By W. T. WEBB, M.A. Globe 8vo. 2*s.*
—— AYLMER'S FIELD. By W. T. WEBB, M.A. Globe 8vo. 2*s.*
—— THE COMING OF ARTHUR, and THE PASSING OF ARTHUR. By F. J. ROWE. Gl. 8vo. 2*s.*
—— THE PRINCESS. By P. M. WALLACE, M.A. Globe 8vo. 3*s.* 6*d.*
—— GARETH AND LYNETTE. By G. C. MACAULAY, M.A.   [*In the Press.*
—— TENNYSON FOR THE YOUNG. By Canon AINGER. 18mo. 1*s.* net.—Large Paper, uncut, 3*s.* 6*d.*; gilt edges, 4*s.* 6*d.*

TENNYSON (Frederick).—THE ISLES OF GREECE: SAPPHO AND ALCAEUS. Cr. 8vo. 7*s.* 6*d.*
—— DAPHNE: and other Poems. Cr.8vo. 7*s.*6*d.*

TENNYSON (Hon. Hallam). (*See* ILLUSTRATED BOOKS.)

TRUMAN (Jos.).—AFTER-THOUGHTS: Poems. Cr. 8vo. 3*s.* 6*d.*

TURNER (Charles Tennyson).—COLLECTED SONNETS, OLD AND NEW. Ext.fcp.8vo. 7*s.*6*d.*

TYRWHITT (R. St. John).—FREE FIELD. Lyrics, chiefly Descriptive. Gl. 8vo. 3*s.* 6*d.*
—— BATTLE AND AFTER, CONCERNING SERGEANT THOMAS ATKINS, GRENADIER GUARDS: and other Verses. Gl. 8vo. 3*s.*6*d.*

WARD (Samuel).—LYRICAL RECREATIONS. Fcp. 8vo. 6*s.*

WATSON (W.).—POEMS. Fcap. 8vo. 5*s.*

WHITTIER.—COMPLETE POETICAL WORKS OF JOHN GREENLEAF WHITTIER. With Portrait. 18mo. 4*s.* 6*d.* (*See also* COLLECTED WORKS.)

WILLS (W. G.).—MELCHIOR. Cr. 8vo. 9*s.*

WOOD (Andrew Goldie).—THE ISLES OF THE BLEST: and other Poems. Globe 8vo. 5*s.*

WOOLNER (Thomas). — MY BEAUTIFUL LADY. 3rd Edit. Fcp. 8vo. 5*s.*
—— PYGMALION. Cr. 8vo. 7*s.* 6*d.*
—— SILENUS. Cr. 8vo. 6*s.*

WORDSWORTH. — COMPLETE POETICAL WORKS. Copyright Edition. -With an Introduction by JOHN MORLEY, and Portrait. Cr. 8vo. 7*s.* 6*d.*
—— THE RECLUSE. Fcp.8vo. 2*s.* 6*d.*—Large Paper Edition. 8vo. 10*s.* 6*d.*
(*See also* GOLDEN TREASURY SERIES, p. 20.)

Poetical Collections and Selections.

(*See also* GOLDEN TREASURY SERIES, p. 20; BOOKS FOR THE YOUNG, p. 38.)

HALES (Prof. J. W.).—LONGER ENGLISH POEMS. With Notes, Philological and Explanatory, and an Introduction on the Teaching of English. Ext. fcp. 8vo. 4*s.* 6*d.*

MACDONALD (George).—ENGLAND'S ANTIPHON. Cr. 8vo. 4*s.* 6*d.*

MARTIN (F.). (*See* BOOKS FOR THE YOUNG, p. 38.)

MASSON (R. O. and D.).—THREE CENTURIES OF ENGLISH POETRY. Being Selections from Chaucer to Herrick. Globe 8vo. 3*s.* 6*d.*

PALGRAVE (Prof. F. T.).—THE GOLDEN TREASURY OF THE BEST SONGS AND LYRICAL POEMS IN THE ENGLISH LANGUAGE. Large Type. Cr. 8vo. 10*s.* 6*d.* (*See also* GOLDEN TREASURY SERIES, p. 20; BOOKS FOR THE YOUNG, p. 38.)

WARD (T. H.).—ENGLISH POETS. Selections, with Critical Introductions by various Writers, and a General Introduction by MATTHEW ARNOLD. Edited by T. H. WARD, M.A. 4 vols. 2nd Edit. Cr. 8vo. 7*s.* 6*d.* each.— Vol. I. CHAUCER TO DONNE; II. BEN JONSON TO DRYDEN; III. ADDISON TO BLAKE; IV. WORDSWORTH TO ROSSETTI.

WOODS (M. A.).—A First Poetry Book. Fcp. 8vo. 2s. 6d.
—— A Second Poetry Book. 2 Parts. Fcp. 8vo. 2s. 6d. each.—Complete, 4s. 6d.
—— A Third Poetry Book. Fcp. 8vo. 4s. 6d.
WORDS FROM THE POETS. With a Vignette and Frontispiece. 12th Edit. 18mo. 1s.

Prose Fiction.

BIKELAS (D.).—Loukis Laras; or, The Reminiscences of a Chiote Merchant during the Greek War of Independence. Translated by J. Gennadius. Cr. 8vo. 7s. 6d.
BJÖRNSON (B.).—Synnöve Solbakken. Translated by Julie Sutter. Cr. 8vo. 6s.
BOLDREWOOD (Rolf).—*Uniform Edition.* Cr. 8vo. 3s. 6d. each.
  Robbery Under Arms: A Story of Life and Adventure in the Bush and in the Goldfields of Australia.
  The Miner's Right.
  The Squatter's Dream.
  A Sydney-Side Saxon.
  A Colonial Reformer.
  Nevermore.
BURNETT (F. H.).—Haworth's. Gl. 8vo. 2s.
—— Louisiana, and That Lass o' Lowrie's. Illustrated. Cr. 8vo. 3s. 6d.
CARMARTHEN (Marchioness of). — A Lover of the Beautiful. Cr. 8vo. 6s.
CONWAY (Hugh). — A Family Affair. Cr. 8vo. 3s. 6d.
—— Living or Dead. Cr. 8vo. 3s. 6d.
CORBETT (Julian).—The Fall of Asgard: A Tale of St. Olaf's Day. 2 vols. Gl. 8vo. 12s.
—— For God and Gold. Cr. 8vo. 6s.
—— Kophetua the Thirteenth. 2 vols. Globe 8vo. 12s.
CRAIK (Mrs.).—*Uniform Edition.* Cr. 8vo. 3s. 6d. each.
  Olive.
  The Ogilvies. Also Globe 8vo, 2s.
  Agatha's Husband. Also Globe 8vo, 2s.
  The Head of the Family.
  Two Marriages. Also Globe 8vo, 2s.
  The Laurel Bush.
  My Mother and I.
  Miss Tommy: A Mediæval Romance.
  King Arthur: Not a Love Story.
CRAWFORD (F. Marion).—*Uniform Edition.* Cr. 8vo. 3s. 6d. each.
  Mr. Isaacs: A Tale of Modern India.
  Dr. Claudius.
  A Roman Singer.
  Zoroaster.
  A Tale of a Lonely Parish.
  Marzio's Crucifix.
  Paul Patoff.
  With the Immortals.
  Greifenstein.
  Sant' Ilario.
  A Cigarette Maker's Romance.
—— Khaled: A Tale of Arabia. Cr. 8vo. 6s.
—— The Witch of Prague. Cr. 8vo. 6s.
—— The Three Fates. Cr. 8vo. 6s.
—— Don Orsino.
—— Children of the King.
CUNNINGHAM (Sir H. S.).—The Cœruleans: A Vacation Idyll. Cr. 8vo. 3s. 6d.
—— The Heriots. Cr. 8vo. 3s. 6d.
—— Wheat and Tares. Cr. 8vo. 3s. 6d.

DAGONET THE JESTER. Cr. 8vo. 4s. 6d.
DAHN (Felix).—Felicitas. Translated by M. A. C. E. Cr. 8vo. 4s. 6d.
DAY (Rev. Lal Behari).—Bengal Peasant Life. Cr. 8vo. 6s.
—— Folk Tales of Bengal. Cr. 8vo. 4s. 6d.
DEFOE (D.). (*See* Globe Library, p. 20: Golden Treasury Series, p. 20.)
DEMOCRACY: An American Novel. Cr. 8vo. 4s. 6d.
DICKENS (Charles). — *Uniform Edition.* Cr. 8vo. 3s. 6d. each.
  The Pickwick Papers.
  Oliver Twist.
  Nicholas Nickleby.
  Martin Chuzzlewit.
  The Old Curiosity Shop.
  Barnaby Rudge.
  Dombey and Son.
  Christmas Books.   [*Nov.* 1892.
  Sketches by Boz.   [*Dec.* 1892.
  American Notes, and Pictures from Italy.   [*Jan.* 1893.
—— The Posthumous Papers of the Pickwick Club. Illust. Edit. by C. Dickens, Jun. 2 vols. Ext. cr. 8vo. 21s.
DILLWYN (E. A.).—Jill. Cr. 8vo. 6s.
—— Jill and Jack. 2 vols. Globe 8vo. 12s.
DUNSMUIR (Amy).—Vida: Study of a Girl. 3rd Edit. Cr. 8vo. 6s.
EBERS (Dr. George).—The Burgomaster's Wife. Transl. by C. Bell. Cr. 8vo. 4s. 6d.
—— Only a Word. Translated by Clara Bell. Cr. 8vo. 4s. 6d.
"ESTELLE RUSSELL" (The Author of).—Harmonia. 3 vols. Cr. 8vo. 31s. 6d.
FALCONER (Lanoe).—Cecilia de Noel. Cr. 8vo. 3s. 6d.
FLEMING (G.).—A Nile Novel. Gl. 8vo. 2s.
—— Mirage: A Novel. Globe 8vo. 2s.
—— The Head of Medusa. Globe 8vo. 2s.
—— Vestigia. Globe 8vo. 2s.
FRATERNITY: A Romance. 2 vols. Cr. 8vo. 21s.
"FRIENDS IN COUNCIL" (The Author of).—Realmah. Cr. 8vo. 6s.
GRAHAM (John W.).—Neæra: A Tale of Ancient Rome. Cr. 8vo. 6s.
HARBOUR BAR, THE. Cr. 8vo. 6s.
HARDY (Arthur Sherburne).—But yet a Woman: A Novel. Cr. 8vo. 4s. 6d.
—— The Wind of Destiny. 2 vols. Gl. 8vo. 12s.
HARDY (Thomas). — The Woodlanders. Cr. 8vo. 3s. 6d.
—— Wessex Tales. Cr. 8vo. 3s. 6d.
HARTE (Bret).—Cressy. Cr. 8vo. 3s. 6d.
—— The Heritage of Dedlow Marsh: and other Tales. Cr. 8vo. 3s. 6d.
—— A First Family of Tasajara. Cr. 8vo. 3s. 6d.
"HOGAN, M.P." (The Author of).—Hogan, M.P. Cr. 8vo. 3s. 6d. Globe 8vo. 2s.
—— The Hon. Miss Ferrard. Gl. 8vo. 2s.
—— Flitters, Tatters, and the Counsellor, etc. Globe 8vo. 2s.
—— Christy Carew. Globe 8vo. 2s.
—— Ismay's Children. Globe 8vo. 2s.

2

LITERATURE.
Prose Fiction—*continued.*

HOPPUS (Mary).—A GREAT TREASON: A Story of the War of Independence. 2 vols. Cr. 8vo. 9s.

HUGHES (Thomas).—TOM BROWN'S SCHOOL DAYS. By AN OLD BOY.—Golden Treasury Edition. 4s. 6d.—Uniform Edition. 3s. 6d.—People's Edition. 2s.—People's Sixpenny Edition. Illustr. Med. 4to. 6d.—Uniform with Sixpenny Kingsley. Med. 8vo. 6d.

—— TOM BROWN AT OXFORD. Cr. 8vo. 3s. 6d.

—— THE SCOURING OF THE WHITE HORSE, and THE ASHEN FAGGOT. Cr. 8vo. 3s. 6d.

IRVING (Washington). (*See* ILLUSTRATED BOOKS, p. 12.)

JACKSON (Helen).—RAMONA. Gl. 8vo. 2s.

JAMES (Henry).—THE EUROPEANS: A Novel. Cr. 8vo. 6s.; 18mo, 2s.

—— DAISY MILLER: and other Stories. Cr. 8vo. 6s.; Globe 8vo, 2s.

—— THE AMERICAN. Cr. 8vo. 6s.—18mo. 2 vols. 4s.

—— RODERICK HUDSON. Cr. 8vo. 6s.; Gl. 8vo, 2s.; 18mo, 2 vols. 4s.

—— THE MADONNA OF THE FUTURE: and other Tales. Cr. 8vo. 6s.; Globe 8vo, 2s.

—— WASHINGTON SQUARE, THE PENSION BEAUREPAS. Globe 8vo. 2s.

—— THE PORTRAIT OF A LADY. Cr. 8vo. 6s. 18mo, 3 vols. 6s.

—— STORIES REVIVED. In Two Series. Cr. 8vo. 6s. each.

—— THE BOSTONIANS. Cr. 8vo. 6s.

—— NOVELS AND TALES. Pocket Edition. 18mo. 2s. each volume.
CONFIDENCE. 1 vol.
THE SIEGE OF LONDON; MADAME DE MAUVES. 1 vol.
AN INTERNATIONAL EPISODE; THE PENSION BEAUREPAS; THE POINT OF VIEW. 1 vol.
DAISY MILLER, a Study; FOUR MEETINGS; LONGSTAFF'S MARRIAGE; BENVOLIO. 1 vol.
THE MADONNA OF THE FUTURE; A BUNDLE OF LETTERS; THE DIARY OF A MAN OF FIFTY; EUGENE PICKERING. 1 vol.

—— TALES OF THREE CITIES. Cr. 8vo. 4s. 6d.

—— THE PRINCESS CASAMASSIMA. Cr. 8vo. 6s.; Globe 8vo, 2s.

—— THE REVERBERATOR. Cr. 8vo. 6s.

—— THE ASPERN PAPERS; LOUISA PALLANT; THE MODERN WARNING. Cr. 8vo. 3s. 6d.

—— A LONDON LIFE. Cr. 8vo. 3s. 6d.

—— THE TRAGIC MUSE. Cr. 8vo. 3s. 6d.

—— THE LESSON OF THE MASTER, AND OTHER STORIES. Cr. 8vo. 6s.

KEARY (Annie).—JANET'S HOME. Cr. 8vo. 3s. 6d.

—— CLEMENCY FRANKLYN. Globe 8vo. 2s.

—— OLDBURY. Cr. 8vo. 3s. 6d.

—— A YORK AND A LANCASTER ROSE. Cr 8vo. 3s. 6d.

—— CASTLE DALY. Cr. 8vo. 3s. 6d.

—— A DOUBTING HEART. Cr. 8vo. 3s. 6d

KENNEDY (P.).—LEGENDARY FICTIONS OF THE IRISH CELTS. Cr. 8vo. 3s. 6d.

KINGSLEY (Charles).—*Eversley Edition.* 13 vols. Globe 8vo. 5s. each.—WESTWARD HO! 2 vols.—TWO YEARS AGO. 2 vols.—HYPATIA. 2 vols.—YEAST. 1 vol.—ALTON LOCKE. 2 vols.—HEREWARD THE WAKE. 2 vols.

—— *Complete Edition.* Cr. 8vo. 3s. 6d. each.—WESTWARD HO! With a Portrait.—HYPATIA.—YEAST.—ALTON LOCKE.—TWO YEARS AGO.—HEREWARD THE WAKE.

—— *Sixpenny Edition.* Med. 8vo. 6d. each. — WESTWARD HO! — HYPATIA. — YEAST.—ALTON LOCKE.—TWO YEARS AGO. —HEREWARD THE WAKE.

KIPLING (Rudyard).—PLAIN TALES FROM THE HILLS. Cr. 8vo. 6s.

—— THE LIGHT THAT FAILED. Cr. 8vo. 6s.

—— LIFE'S HANDICAP: Being Stories of mine own People. Cr. 8vo. 6s.

LAFARGUE (Philip).—THE NEW JUDGMENT OF PARIS. 2 vols. Globe 8vo. 12s.

LEE (Margaret).—FAITHFUL AND UNFAITHFUL. Cr. 8vo. 3s. 6d.

LEVY (A.).—REUBEN SACHS. Cr. 8vo. 3s. 6d.

LITTLE PILGRIM IN THE UNSEEN, A. 24th Thousand. Cr. 8vo. 2s. 6d.

"LITTLE PILGRIM IN THE UNSEEN, A" (Author of).—THE LAND OF DARKNESS. Cr. 8vo. 5s.

LYTTON (Earl of).—THE RING OF AMASIS: A Romance. Cr. 8vo. 3s. 6d.

McLENNAN (Malcolm).—MUCKLE JOCK; and other Stories of Peasant Life in the North. Cr. 8vo. 3s. 6d.

MACQUOID (K. S.).—PATTY. Gl. 8vo. 2s.

MADOC (Fayr).—THE STORY OF MELICENT. Cr. 8vo. 4s. 6d.

MALET (Lucas).—MRS. LORIMER: A Sketch in Black and White. Cr. 8vo. 3s. 6d.

MALORY (Sir Thos.). (*See* GLOBE LIBRARY, p. 20.)

MINTO (W.).—THE MEDIATION OF RALPH HARDELOT. 3 vols. Cr. 8vo. 31s. 6d.

MITFORD (A. B.).—TALES OF OLD JAPAN. With Illustrations. Cr. 8vo. 3s. 6d.

MIZ MAZE (THE); OR, THE WINKWORTH PUZZLE. A Story in Letters by Nine Authors. Cr. 8vo. 4s. 6d.

MURRAY (D. Christie). — AUNT RACHEL. Cr. 8vo. 3s. 6d.

—— SCHWARTZ. Cr. 8vo. 3s. 6d.

—— THE WEAKER VESSEL. Cr. 8vo. 3s. 6d.

—— JOHN VALE'S GUARDIAN. Cr. 8vo. 3s. 6d.

MURRAY (D. Christie) and HERMAN (H.). —HE FELL AMONG THIEVES. Cr. 8vo. 3s. 6d.

NEW ANTIGONE, THE: A ROMANCE. Cr. 8vo. 3s. 6d.

NOEL (Lady Augusta).—HITHERSEA MERE. 3 vols. Cr. 8vo. 31s. 6d.

NORRIS (W. E.).—MY FRIEND JIM. Globe 8vo. 2s.

—— CHRIS. Globe 8vo. 2s.

NORTON (Hon. Mrs.).—OLD SIR DOUGLAS. Cr. 8vo. 6s.

OLIPHANT (Mrs. M. O. W.).—A SON OF THE SOIL. Globe 8vo. 2s.
—— THE CURATE IN CHARGE. Globe 8vo. 2s.
—— YOUNG MUSGRAVE. Globe 8vo. 2s.
—— HE THAT WILL NOT WHEN HE MAY. Cr. 8vo. 3s. 6d.—Globe 8vo. 2s.
—— SIR TOM. Globe 8vo. 2s.
—— HESTER. Cr. 8vo. 3s. 6d.
—— THE WIZARD'S SON. Globe 8vo. 2s.
—— THE COUNTRY GENTLEMAN AND HIS FAMILY. Globe 8vo. 2s.
—— THE SECOND SON. Globe 8vo. 2s.
—— NEIGHBOURS ON THE GREEN. Cr. 8vo. 3s. 6d.
—— JOYCE. Cr. 8vo. 3s. 6d.
—— A BELEAGUERED CITY. Cr. 8vo. 3s. 6d.
—— KIRSTEEN. Cr. 8vo. 3s. 6d.
—— THE RAILWAY MAN AND HIS CHILDREN. Cr. 8vo. 3s. 6d.
—— THE MARRIAGE OF ELINOR Cr. 8vo. 3s. 6d.
—— THE HEIR-PRESUMPTIVE AND THE HEIR-APPARENT. 3 vols. Cr. 8vo. [Oct. 1892
PALMER (Lady Sophia).—MRS. PENICOTT'S LODGER: and other Stories. Cr. 8vo. 2s. 6d.
PARRY (Gambier).—THE STORY OF DICK. Cr. 8vo. 6s.
PATER (Walter).—MARIUS THE EPICUREAN: HIS SENSATIONS AND IDEAS. 3rd Edit. 2 vols. 8vo. 12s.
ROSS (Percy).—A MISGUIDIT LASSIE. Cr. 8vo. 4s. 6d.
ROY (J.).—HELEN TREVERYAN: OR, THE RULING RACE 3 vols. Cr. 8vo. 31s. 6d.
RUSSELL (W. Clark).—MAROONED. Cr. 8vo. 3s. 6d.
—— A STRANGE ELOPEMENT. Cr. 8vo. 3s. 6d.
ST. JOHNSTON (A.). — A SOUTH SEA LOVER: A Romance. Cr. 8vo. 6s.
SHORTHOUSE (J. Henry).—*Uniform Edition*. Cr. 8vo. 3s. 6d. each.
JOHN INGLESANT: A Romance.
SIR PERCIVAL: A Story of the Past and of the Present.
THE LITTLE SCHOOLMASTER MARK: A Spiritual Romance.
THE COUNTESS EVE.
A TEACHER OF THE VIOLIN: and other Tales.
—— BLANCHE, LADY FALAISE. Cr. 8vo. 6s.
SLIP IN THE FENS, A. Globe 8vo. 2s.
THEODOLI (Marchesa)—UNDER PRESSURE. 3 vols 31s. 6d.
TIM. Cr. 8vo. 6s.
TOURGÉNIEF.—VIRGIN SOIL. Translated by ASHTON W. DILKE. Cr. 8vo. 6s.
VELEY (Margaret).—A GARDEN OF MEMORIES; MRS. AUSTIN; LIZZIE'S BARGAIN. Three Stories. 2 vols. Globe 8vo. 12s.
VICTOR (H.).—MARIAM: OR TWENTY-ONE DAYS. Cr. 8vo. 6s.
VOICES CRYING IN THE WILDERNESS: A NOVEL. Cr. 8vo. 7s. 6d.
WARD (Mrs. T. Humphry).—MISS BRETHERTON. Cr. 8vo. 3s. 6d.
WORTHEY (Mrs.).—THE NEW CONTINENT: A Novel. 2 vols. Globe 8vo. 12s.
YONGE (Charlotte M.).—*Uniform Edition*. Cr. 8vo. 3s. 6d. each.
THE HEIR OF REDCLYFFE.
HEARTSEASE. | HOPES AND FEARS.
DYNEVOR TERRACE. | THE DAISY CHAIN.
THE TRIAL: More Links of the Daisy Chain.

YONGE (Charlotte M.).—*Uniform Edition*. Cr. 8vo. 3s. 6d. each.
PILLARS OF THE HOUSE. Vol. I.
PILLARS OF THE HOUSE. Vol. II.
THE YOUNG STEPMOTHER.
CLEVER WOMAN OF THE FAMILY.
THE THREE BRIDES.
MY YOUNG ALCIDES. | THE CAGED LION.
THE DOVE IN THE EAGLE'S NEST.
. THE CHAPLET OF PEARLS.
LADY HESTER, and THE DANVERS PAPERS.
MAGNUM BONUM. | LOVE AND LIFE.
UNKNOWN TO HISTORY. | STRAY PEARLS.
THE ARMOURER'S PRENTICES.
THE TWO SIDES OF THE SHIELD.
NUTTIE'S FATHER.
SCENES AND CHARACTERS.
CHANTRY HOUSE.
A MODERN TELEMACHUS. | BYE WORDS.
BEECHCROFT AT ROCKSTONE.
MORE BYWORDS. | A REPUTED CHANGELING.
THE LITTLE DUKE, RICHARD THE FEARLESS.
THE LANCES OF LYNWOOD.
THE PRINCE AND THE PAGE.
P'S AND Q'S: LITTLE LUCY'S WONDERFUL GLOBE.
THE TWO PENNILESS PRINCESSES.
THAT STICK.

Collected Works; Essays; Lectures; Letters; Miscellaneous Works.

AN AUTHOR'S LOVE. Being the Unpublished Letters of PROSPER MÉRIMÉE'S "Inconnue." 2 vols. Ext. cr. 8vo. 12s.
ARNOLD (Matthew).—ESSAYS IN CRITICISM. 6th Edit. Cr. 8vo. 9s.
—— ESSAYS IN CRITICISM. Second Series. Cr. 8vo. 7s. 6d.
—— DISCOURSES IN AMERICA. Cr. 8vo. 4s. 6d.
BACON. With Introduction and Notes, by F. G. SELBY, M.A. Gl. 8vo. 3s.; swd. 2s. 6d. (*See also* GOLDEN TREASURY SERIES, p. 20.)
BLACKIE (J. S.).—LAY SERMONS. Cr. 8vo. 6s.
BRIDGES (John A.).—IDYLLS OF A LOST VILLAGE. Cr. 8vo. 7s. 6d.
BRIMLEY (George).—ESSAYS. Globe 8vo. 5s.
BUNYAN (John).—THE PILGRIM'S PROGRESS FROM THIS WORLD TO THAT WHICH IS TO COME. 18mo. 2s. 6d. net.
BUTCHER (Prof. S. H.)—SOME ASPECTS OF THE GREEK GENIUS. Cr. 8vo. 7s. 6d. net.
CARLYLE (Thomas). (*See* BIOGRAPHY.)
CHURCH (Dean).—MISCELLANEOUS WRITINGS. Collected Edition. 6 vols. Globe 8vo. 5s. each.—Vol. I. MISCELLANEOUS ESSAYS.—II. DANTE: AND OTHER ESSAYS.—III. ST. ANSELM.—IV. SPENSER.—V. BACON.—VI. THE OXFORD MOVEMENT, 1833—45.
CLIFFORD (Prof. W. K.). LECTURES AND ESSAYS. Edited by LESLIE STEPHEN and Sir F. POLLOCK. Cr. 8vo. 8s. 6d.
CLOUGH (A. H.).—PROSE REMAINS. With a Selection from his Letters, and a Memoir by HIS WIFE. Cr. 8vo. 7s. 6d.
COLLINS (J. Churton).—THE STUDY OF ENGLISH LITERATURE. Cr. 8vo. 4s. 6d.
CRAIK (Mrs.). — CONCERNING MEN: and other Papers. Cr. 8vo. 4s. 6d.
—— ABOUT MONEY: and other Things. Cr. 8vo. 6s.
—— SERMONS OUT OF CHURCH. Cr. 8vo. 3s. 6d.

LITERATURE.

Collected Works; Essays; Lectures; Letters; Miscellaneous Works—*contd.*

DE VERE (Aubrey).—ESSAYS CHIEFLY ON POETRY. 2 vols. Globe 8vo. 12*s.*
—— ESSAYS, CHIEFLY LITERARY AND ETHICAL. Globe 8vo. 6*s.*

DICKENS.—LETTERS OF CHARLES DICKENS Ed. by GEORGINA HOGARTH and MARY DICKENS. Cr. 8vo.

DRYDEN, ESSAYS OF. Edited by Prof. C. D. YONGE. Fcp. 8vo. 2*s.* 6*d.* (*See also* GLOBE LIBRARY, p. 20.)

DUFF (Rt. Hon. Sir M. E. Grant).—MISCELLANIES, Political and Literary. 8vo. 10*s.* 6*d.*

EMERSON (Ralph Waldo).—THE COLLECTED WORKS. 6 vols. Globe 8vo. 5*s.* each.—I. MISCELLANIES. With an Introductory Essay by JOHN MORLEY.—II. ESSAYS.—III. POEMS.—IV. ENGLISH TRAITS; REPRESENTATIVE MEN.—V. CONDUCT OF LIFE; SOCIETY AND SOLITUDE.—VI. LETTERS; SOCIAL AIMS, ETC.

FITZGERALD (Edward): LETTERS AND LITERARY REMAINS OF. Ed. by W. ALDIS WRIGHT, M.A. 3 vols. Cr. 8vo. 31*s.* 6*d.*

GLOBE LIBRARY. Gl. 8vo. 3*s.* 6*d.* each :
BURNS.—COMPLETE POETICAL WORKS AND LETTERS. Edited, with Life and Glossarial Index, by ALEXANDER SMITH.
COWPER.—POETICAL WORKS. Edited by the Rev. W. BENHAM, B.D.
DEFOE.—THE ADVENTURES OF ROBINSON CRUSOE. Introduction by H. KINGSLEY.
DRYDEN.—POETICAL WORKS. A Revised Text and Notes. By W. D. CHRISTIE, M.A.
GOLDSMITH. — MISCELLANEOUS WORKS. Edited by Prof. MASSON.
HORACE.—WORKS. Rendered into English Prose by JAMES LONSDALE and S. LEE.
MALORY.—LE MORTE D'ARTHUR. Sir Thos. Malory's Book of King Arthur and of his Noble Knights of the Round Table. The Edition of Caxton, revised for modern use. By Sir E. STRACHEY, Bart.
MILTON.—POETICAL WORKS. Edited, with Introductions, by Prof. MASSON.
POPE.—POETICAL WORKS. Edited, with Memoir and Notes, by Prof. WARD.
SCOTT.—POETICAL WORKS. With Essay by Prof. PALGRAVE.
SHAKESPEARE.—COMPLETE WORKS. Edit. by W. G. CLARK and W. ALDIS WRIGHT. *India Paper Edition.* Cr. 8vo, cloth extra, gilt edges. 10*s.* 6*d.* net.
SPENSER.—COMPLETE WORKS Edited by R. MORRIS. Memoir by J. W. HALES, M.A.
VIRGIL.—WORKS. Rendered into English Prose by JAMES LONSDALE and S. LEE.

GOLDEN TREASURY SERIES.—Uniformly printed in 18mo, with Vignette Titles by Sir J. E. MILLAIS, Sir NOEL PATON, T. WOOLNER, W. HOLMAN HUNT, ARTHUR HUGHES, etc. 4*s.* 6*d.* each.—Also a re-issue in fortnightly vols. 2*s.* 6*d.* net, from June, 1891.
THE GOLDEN TREASURY OF THE BEST SONGS AND LYRICAL POEMS IN THE ENGLISH LANGUAGE. Selected and arranged, with Notes, by Prof. F. T. PALGRAVE.—Large Paper Edition. 8vo. 10*s.* 6*d.* net.
THE CHILDREN'S GARLAND FROM THE BEST POETS. Selected by COVENTRY PATMORE.

GOLDEN TREASURY SERIES—*contd.*

BUNYAN.—THE PILGRIM'S PROGRESS FROM THIS WORLD TO THAT WHICH IS TO COME.—Large Paper Edition. 8vo. 10*s.* 6*d.* net.
BACON.—ESSAYS, and COLOURS OF GOOD AND EVIL. With Notes and Glossarial Index by W. ALDIS WRIGHT, M.A.—Large Paper Edition. 8vo. 10*s.* 6*d.* net.
THE BOOK OF PRAISE. From the Best English Hymn Writers. Selected by ROUNDELL, EARL OF SELBORNE.
SHELLEY.—POEMS. Edited by STOPFORD A. BROOKE.—Large Paper Edit. 12*s.* 6*d.*
THE FAIRY BOOK: THE BEST POPULAR FAIRY STORIES. Selected by Mrs. CRAIK, Author of "John Halifax, Gentleman."
WORDSWORTH.—POEMS. Chosen and Edited by M. ARNOLD.—Large Paper Edition. 9*s.*
PLATO.—THE TRIAL AND DEATH OF SOCRATES. Being the Euthyphron, Apology, Crito and Phaedo of Plato. Trans. F. J. CHURCH.
THE JEST BOOK. The Choicest Anecdotes and Sayings. Arranged by MARK LEMON.
HERRICK.—CHRYSOMELA. Edited by Prof. F. T. PALGRAVE.
THE BALLAD BOOK. A Selection of the Choicest British Ballads. Edited by WILLIAM ALLINGHAM.
THE SUNDAY BOOK OF POETRY FOR THE YOUNG. Selected by C. F. ALEXANDER.
A BOOK OF GOLDEN DEEDS. By C. M. YONGE.
A BOOK OF WORTHIES. By C. M. YONGE.
KEATS.—THE POETICAL WORKS. Edited by Prof. F. T. PALGRAVE.
PLATO.—THE REPUBLIC. Translated by J. LL. DAVIES, M.A., and D. J. VAUGHAN.—Large Paper Edition. 8vo. 10*s.* 6*d.* net.
ADDISON.—ESSAYS. Chosen and Edited by JOHN RICHARD GREEN.
DEUTSCHE LYRIK. The Golden Treasury of the best German Lyrical Poems. Selected by Dr. BUCHHEIM.
SIR THOMAS BROWNE.—RELIGIO MEDICI, LETTER TO A FRIEND, &c., AND CHRISTIAN MORALS. Ed. W. A. GREENHILL.
LAMB.—TALES FROM SHAKSPEARE. Edited by Rev. ALFRED AINGER, M.A.
THE SONG BOOK. Words and Tunes selected and arranged by JOHN HULLAH.
SCOTTISH SONG. Compiled by MARY CARLYLE AITKEN.
LA LYRE FRANÇAISE. Selected and arranged, with Notes, by G. MASSON.
BALLADEN UND ROMANZEN. Being a Selection of the best German Ballads and Romances. Edited, with Introduction and Notes, by Dr. BUCHHEIM.
A BOOK OF GOLDEN THOUGHTS. By HENRY ATTWELL.
MATTHEW ARNOLD.—SELECTED POEMS.
BYRON.—POETRY. Chosen and arranged by M. ARNOLD.—Large Paper Edit. 9*s.*
COWPER.—SELECTIONS FROM POEMS. With an Introduction by Mrs. OLIPHANT.
—— LETTERS. Edited, with Introduction, by Rev. W. BENHAM.
DEFOE.—THE ADVENTURES OF ROBINSON CRUSOE. Edited by J. W. CLARK, M.A.
BALTHASAR GRACIAN'S ART OF WORLDLY WISDOM. Trans. J. JACOBS. [*In the Press.*
HARE.—GUESSES AT TRUTH. By Two Brothers.
HUGHES.—TOM BROWN'S SCHOOL DAYS.
LANDOR.—SELECTIONS. Ed. by S. COLVIN.

GOLDEN TREASURY SERIES—*contd.*

LONGFELLOW.—POEMS OF PLACES: ENGLAND AND WALES. Edited by H. W. LONGFELLOW. 2 vols.

— BALLADS, LYRICS, AND SONNETS.

MOHAMMAD.—SPEECHES AND TABLE-TALK. Translated by STANLEY LANE-POOLE.

NEWCASTLE.—THE CAVALIER AND HIS LADY. Selections from the Works of the First Duke and Duchess of Newcastle. With an Introductory Essay by E. JENKINS.

PLATO.—THE PHAEDRUS, LYSIS, AND PROTAGORAS. Translated by J. WRIGHT.

SHAKESPEARE.—SONGS AND SONNETS. Ed. with Notes, by Prof. F. T. PALGRAVE.

TENNYSON.—LYRICAL POEMS. Selected and Annotated by Prof. F. T. PALGRAVE.—Large Paper Edition. 9s.

— IN MEMORIAM. Large Paper Edit. 9s.

THEOCRITUS.—BION, AND MOSCHUS. Rendered into English Prose by ANDREW LANG.—Large Paper Edition. 9s.

CHARLOTTE M. YONGE.—THE STORY OF THE CHRISTIANS AND MOORS IN SPAIN.

GOLDSMITH, ESSAYS OF. Edited by C. D. YONGE, M.A. Fcp. 8vo. 2s. 6d. (*See also* GLOBE LIBRARY, p. 20; ILLUSTRATED BOOKS, p. 12.)

GRAY (Thomas).—WORKS. Edited by EDMUND GOSSE. In 4 vols. Globe 8vo. 20s.—Vol. I. POEMS, JOURNALS, AND ESSAYS.—II. LETTERS.—III. LETTERS.—IV. NOTES ON ARISTOPHANES AND PLATO.

HAMERTON (P. G.).—THE INTELLECTUAL LIFE. Cr. 8vo. 10s. 6d.

—— HUMAN INTERCOURSE. Cr. 8vo. 8s. 6d.

—— FRENCH AND ENGLISH: A Comparison. Cr. 8vo. 10s. 6d.

HARRISON (Frederic).—THE CHOICE OF BOOKS. Gl. 8vo. 6s.—Large Paper Ed. 15s.

HARWOOD (George).—FROM WITHIN. Cr. 8vo. 6s.

HELPS (Sir Arthur).—ESSAYS WRITTEN IN THE INTERVALS OF BUSINESS. With Introduction and Notes, by F. J. ROWE, M.A., and W. T. WEBB, M.A. 1s. 9d.; swd. 1s. 6d.

HOBART (Lord).—ESSAYS AND MISCELLANEOUS WRITINGS. With Biographical Sketch. Ed. Lady HOBART. 2 vols. 8vo. 25s.

HUTTON (R. H.).—ESSAYS ON SOME OF THE MODERN GUIDES OF ENGLISH THOUGHT IN MATTERS OF FAITH. Globe 8vo. 6s.

—— ESSAYS. 2 vols. Gl. 8vo. 6s. each. - Vol. I. Literary; II. Theological.

HUXLEY (Prof. T. H.).—LAY SERMONS, ADDRESSES, AND REVIEWS. 8vo. 7s. 6d.

—— CRITIQUES AND ADDRESSES. 8vo. 10s. 6d.

—— AMERICAN ADDRESSES, WITH A LECTURE ON THE STUDY OF BIOLOGY. 8vo. 6s. 6d.

—— SCIENCE AND CULTURE, AND OTHER ESSAYS. 8vo. 10s. 6d.

—— INTRODUCTORY SCIENCE PRIMER. 18mo. 1s.

—— ESSAYS UPON SOME CONTROVERTED QUESTIONS. 8vo. 14s.

JAMES (Henry).—FRENCH POETS AND NOVELISTS. New Edition. Cr. 8vo. 4s. 6d.

—— PORTRAITS OF PLACES. Cr. 8vo. 7s. 6d.

—— PARTIAL PORTRAITS. Cr. 8vo. 6s.

KEATS.—LETTERS. Edited by SIDNEY COLVIN. Globe 8vo. 6s.

KINGSLEY (Charles).—COMPLETE EDITION OF THE WORKS OF CHARLES KINGSLEY. Cr. 8vo. 3s. 6d. each.

WESTWARD HO! With a Portrait.

HYPATIA.

YEAST.

ALTON LOCKE.

TWO YEARS AGO.

HEREWARD THE WAKE.

POEMS.

THE HEROES; or, Greek Fairy Tales for my Children.

THE WATER BABIES: A Fairy Tale for a Land Baby.

MADAM HOW AND LADY WHY; or, First Lesson in Earth-Lore for Children.

AT LAST: A Christmas in the West Indies.

PROSE IDYLLS.

PLAYS AND PURITANS.

THE ROMAN AND THE TEUTON. With Preface by Professor MAX MÜLLER.

SANITARY AND SOCIAL LECTURES.

HISTORICAL LECTURES AND ESSAYS.

SCIENTIFIC LECTURES AND ESSAYS.

LITERARY AND GENERAL LECTURES.

THE HERMITS.

GLAUCUS; or, The Wonders of the Sea-Shore. With Coloured Illustrations.

VILLAGE AND TOWN AND COUNTRY SERMONS.

THE WATER OF LIFE, AND OTHER SERMONS.

SERMONS ON NATIONAL SUBJECTS: AND THE KING OF THE EARTH.

SERMONS FOR THE TIMES.

GOOD NEWS OF GOD.

THE GOSPEL OF THE PENTATEUCH: AND DAVID.

DISCIPLINE, AND OTHER SERMONS.

WESTMINSTER SERMONS.

ALL SAINTS' DAY, AND OTHER SERMONS.

LAMB (Charles).—COLLECTED WORKS. Ed., with Introduction and Notes, by the Rev. ALFRED AINGER, M.A. Globe 8vo. 5s. each volume.—I. ESSAYS OF ELIA.—II. PLAYS, POEMS, AND MISCELLANEOUS ESSAYS.—III. MRS. LEICESTER'S SCHOOL; THE ADVENTURES OF ULYSSES; AND OTHER ESSAYS.—IV. TALES FROM SHAKESPEARE.—V. and VI. LETTERS. Newly arranged, with additions.

—— TALES FROM SHAKESPEARE. 18mo. 4s. 6d.

LANKESTER (Prof. E. Ray).—THE ADVANCEMENT OF SCIENCE. Occasional Essays and Addresses. 8vo. 10s. 6d.

LIGHTFOOT (Bishop).—ESSAYS. 2 vols. I. DISSERTATIONS ON THE APOSTOLIC AGE. II. MISCELLANEOUS. 8vo.

LODGE (Prof. Oliver).—THE PIONEERS OF SCIENCE. Illustrated. Ext. cr. 8vo.

LOWELL (Jas. Russell).—COMPLETE WORKS. 10 vols. Cr. 8vo. 6s. each.—Vols. I.—IV. LITERARY ESSAYS.—V. POLITICAL ESSAYS.—VI. LITERARY AND POLITICAL ADDRESSES. VII.—X. POETICAL WORKS.

—— POLITICAL ESSAYS. Ext. cr. 8vo. 7s. 6d.

—— LATEST LITERARY ESSAYS. Cr. 8vo. 6s.

LUBBOCK (Rt. Hon. Sir John, Bart.).—SCIENTIFIC LECTURES. Illustrated. 2nd Edit. revised. 8vo. 8s. 6d.

—— POLITICAL AND EDUCATIONAL ADDRESSES. 8vo. 8s. 6d.

—— FIFTY YEARS OF SCIENCE: Address to the British Association, 1881. 5th Edit. Cr. 8vo. 2s. 6d.

LITERATURE.
Collected Works; Essays; Lectures; Letters; Miscellaneous Works—*contd.*

LUBBOCK (Rt. Hon Sir John, Bart.).—THE PLEASURES OF LIFE. New Edition. 60th Thousand. Gl.8vo. Part I. 1s.6d.; swd. 1s.—*Library Edition.* 3s. 6d.—Part II. 1s. 6d.; sewed, 1s.—*Library Edition.* 3s. 6d.—Complete in 1 vol. 2s. 6d.

MACMILLAN (Rev. Hugh).—ROMAN MOSAICS; or, Studies in Rome and its Neighbourhood. Globe 8vo. 6s.

MAHAFFY (Prof. J. P.).—THE PRINCIPLES OF THE ART OF CONVERSATION. Cr.8vo. 4s.6d.

MASSON (David).—WORDSWORTH, SHELLEY, KEATS: and other Essays. Cr. 8vo. 5s.

MAURICE (F. D.).—THE FRIENDSHIP OF BOOKS: and other Lectures. Cr. 8vo. 4s. 6d.

MORLEY (John).—WORKS. Collected Edit. In 11 vols. Globe 8vo. 5s. each.—VOLTAIRE. 1 vol.—ROUSSEAU. 2 vols.—DIDEROT AND THE ENCYLOPÆDISTS. 2 vols.—ON COMPROMISE. 1 vol.—MISCELLANIES. 3 vols.—BURKE. 1 vol.—STUDIES IN LITERATURE. 1 vol.

MYERS (F. W. H.).—ESSAYS. 2 vols. Cr. 8vo. 4s. 6d. each.—I. CLASSICAL; II. MODERN.

NADAL (E. S.).—ESSAYS AT HOME AND ELSEWHERE. Cr. 8vo. 6s.

OLIPHANT (T. L. Kington).—THE DUKE AND THE SCHOLAR: and other Essays. 8vo. 7s.6d.

OWENS COLLEGE ESSAYS AND ADDRESSES. By Professors and Lecturers of the College. 8vo. 14s.

PATER (W.).—THE RENAISSANCE; Studies in Art and Poetry. 4th Ed. Cr. 8vo. 10s. 6d.
—— IMAGINARY PORTRAITS. Cr. 8vo. 6s.
—— APPRECIATIONS. With an Essay on "Style." 2nd Edit. Cr. 8vo. 8s. 6d.
—— MARIUS THE EPICUREAN. 2 vols. Cr. 8vo. 12s.

PICTON (J. A.).—THE MYSTERY OF MATTER: and other Essays. Cr. 8vo. 6s.

POLLOCK (Sir F., Bart.).—OXFORD LECTURES: and other Discourses. 8vo. 9s.

POOLE (M. E.).—PICTURES OF COTTAGE LIFE IN THE WEST OF ENGLAND. 2nd Ed. Cr. 8vo. 3s. 6d.

POTTER (Louisa).—LANCASHIRE MEMORIES. Cr. 8vo. 6s.

PRICKARD (A. O.).—ARISTOTLE ON THE ART OF POETRY. Cr. 8vo. 3s. 6d.

RUMFORD.—COMPLETE WORKS OF COUNT RUMFORD. Memoir by G. ELLIS. Portrait. 5 vols. 8vo. 4l. 14s. 6d.

SCIENCE LECTURES AT SOUTH KENSINGTON. Illustr. 2 vols. Cr. 8vo. 6s. each.

SMALLEY (George W.).—LONDON LETTERS AND SOME OTHERS. 2 vols. 8vo. 32s.

STEPHEN (Sir James F., Bart.).—HORAE SABBATICAE. Two Series. Gl 8vo. 5s. each.

THRING (Edward).—THOUGHTS ON LIFE SCIENCE. 2nd Edit. Cr. 8vo. 7s. 6d.

WESTCOTT (Bishop). (*See* THEOLOGY, p. 36.)

WILSON (Dr. George).—RELIGIO CHEMICI. Cr. 8vo. 8s. 6d.
—— THE FIVE GATEWAYS OF KNOWLEDGE. 9th Edit. Ext. fcp. 8vo. 2s. 6d.

WHITTIER (John Greenleaf). THE COMPLETE WORKS. 7 vols. Cr. 8vo. 6s. each.—Vol. I. NARRATIVE AND LEGENDARY POEMS. —II. POEMS OF NATURE; POEMS SUBJECTIVE AND REMINISCENT; RELIGIOUS POEMS. —III. ANTI-SLAVERY POEMS; SONGS OF LABOUR AND REFORM.—IV. PERSONAL POEMS; OCCASIONAL POEMS; THE TENT ON THE BEACH; with the Poems of ELIZABETH H. WHITTIER, and an Appendix containing Early and Uncollected Verses.—V. MARGARET SMITH'S JOURNAL; TALES AND SKETCHES.—VI. OLD PORTRAITS AND MODERN SKETCHES; PERSONAL SKETCHES AND TRIBUTES; HISTORICAL PAPERS.—VII. THE CONFLICT WITH SLAVERY, POLITICS, AND REFORM; THE INNER LIFE, CRITICISM.

LOGIC. (*See under* PHILOSOPHY, p. 26.)

MAGAZINES. (*See* PERIODICALS).

MAGNETISM. (*See under* PHYSICS, p. 26.)

MATHEMATICS, History of.

BALL (W. W. R.).—A SHORT ACCOUNT OF THE HISTORY OF MATHEMATICS. Cr. 8vo. 10s. 6d.
—— MATHEMATICAL RECREATIONS AND PROBLEMS. Cr. 8vo. 7s. net.

MEDICINE.
(*See also* DOMESTIC ECONOMY; NURSING; HYGIENE; PHYSIOLOGY.)

ACLAND (Sir H. W.).—THE ARMY MEDICAL SCHOOL: Address at Netley Hospital. 1s.

ALLBUTT (Dr. T. Clifford).—ON THE USE OF THE OPHTHALMOSCOPE. 8vo. 15s.

ANDERSON (Dr. McCall).—LECTURES ON CLINICAL MEDICINE. Illustr. 8vo. 10s. 6d.

BALLANCE (C. A.) and EDMUNDS (Dr. W.). LIGATION IN CONTINUITY. Illustr. Roy. 8vo. 30s. net.

BARWELL (Richard, F.R.C.S.). — THE CAUSES AND TREATMENT OF LATERAL CURVATURE OF THE SPINE. Cr. 8vo. 5s.
—— ON ANEURISM, ESPECIALLY OF THE THORAX AND ROOT OF THE NECK. 3s. 6d.

BASTIAN (H. Charlton).—ON PARALYSIS FROM BRAIN DISEASE IN ITS COMMON FORMS. Cr. 8vo. 10s. 6d.

BICKERTON (T. H.).—ON COLOUR BLINDNESS. Cr. 8vo.

BRAIN: A JOURNAL OF NEUROLOGY. Edited for the Neurological Society of London, by A. DE WATTEVILLE. Quarterly. 8vo. 3s.6d. (Part I. in Jan. 1878.) Vols. I. to XII. 8vo. 15s. each. [Cloth covers for binding, 1s. each.]

BRUNTON (Dr. T. Lauder). — A TEXT-BOOK OF PHARMACOLOGY, THERAPEUTICS, AND MATERIA MEDICA. 3rd Edit. Med. 8vo. 21s.—Or in 2 vols. 22s. 6d.—SUPPLEMENT, 1s.
—— DISORDERS OF DIGESTION: THEIR CONSEQUENCES AND TREATMENT. 8vo. 10s. 6d.
—— PHARMACOLOGY AND THERAPEUTICS; or, Medicine Past and Present. Cr. 8vo. 6s.
—— TABLES OF MATERIA MEDICA: A Companion to the Materia Medica Museum. 8vo. 5s.
—— AN INTRODUCTION TO MODERN THERAPEUTICS. Croonian Lectures on the Relationship between Chemical Structure and Physiological Action. 8vo. 3s. 6d net.

BUCKNILL (Dr.).—THE CARE OF THE INSANE. Cr. 8vo. 3s. 6d.

CARTER (R. Brudenell, F.C.S.).—A PRACTICAL TREATISE ON DISEASES OF THE EYE. 8vo. 16s.

—— EYESIGHT, GOOD AND BAD. Cr. 8vo. 6s.

—— MODERN OPERATIONS FOR CATARACT. 8vo. 6s.

CHRISTIE (J.).—CHOLERA EPIDEMICS IN EAST AFRICA. 8vo. 15s.

COWELL (George).—LECTURES ON CATARACT: ITS CAUSES, VARIETIES, AND TREATMENT. Cr. 8vo. 4s. 6d.

FLÜCKIGER (F. A.) and HANBURY (D.).—PHARMACOGRAPHIA. A History of the Principal Drugs of Vegetable Origin met with in Great Britain and India. 8vo. 21s.

FOTHERGILL (Dr. J. Milner).—THE PRACTITIONER'S HANDBOOK OF TREATMENT; or, The Principles of Therapeutics. 8vo. 16s.

—— THE ANTAGONISM OF THERAPEUTIC AGENTS, AND WHAT IT TEACHES. Cr. 8vo. 6s.

—— FOOD FOR THE INVALID, THE CONVALESCENT, THE DYSPEPTIC, AND THE GOUTY. 2nd Edit. Cr. 8vo. 3s. 6d.

FOX (Dr. Wilson). — ON THE ARTIFICIAL PRODUCTION OF TUBERCLE IN THE LOWER ANIMALS. With Plates. 4to. 5s. 6d.

—— ON THE TREATMENT OF HYPERPYREXIA, AS ILLUSTRATED IN ACUTE ARTICULAR RHEUMATISM BY MEANS OF THE EXTERNAL APPLICATION OF COLD. 8vo. 2s. 6d.

GRIFFITHS (W. H.).—LESSONS ON PRESCRIPTIONS AND THE ART OF PRESCRIBING. New Edition. 18mo. 3s. 6d.

HAMILTON (Prof. D. J.).—ON THE PATHOLOGY OF BRONCHITIS, CATARRHAL PNEUMONIA, TUBERCLE, AND ALLIED LESIONS OF THE HUMAN LUNG. 8vo. 8s. 6d.

—— A TEXT-BOOK OF PATHOLOGY, SYSTEMATIC AND PRACTICAL. Illustrated. Vol. I. 8vo. 25s.

HANBURY (Daniel). — SCIENCE PAPERS, CHIEFLY PHARMACOLOGICAL AND BOTANICAL. Med. 8vo. 14s.

KLEIN (Dr. E.).—MICRO-ORGANISMS AND DISEASE. An Introduction into the Study of Specific Micro-Organisms. Cr. 8vo. 6s.

—— THE BACTERIA IN ASIATIC CHOLERA. Cr. 8vo. 5s.

LEPROSY INVESTIGATION COMMITTEE, JOURNAL OF THE. Edited by P. S. ABRAHAM, M.A. Nos. 2—4. 2s. 6d. each net.

LINDSAY (Dr. J. A.). — THE CLIMATIC TREATMENT OF CONSUMPTION. Cr. 8vo. 5s.

MACLAGAN (Dr. T.).—THE GERM THEORY. 8vo. 10s. 6d.

MACLEAN (Surgeon-General W. C.).—DISEASES OF TROPICAL CLIMATES. Cr. 8vo. 10s. 6d.

MACNAMARA (C.).—A HISTORY OF ASIATIC CHOLERA. Cr. 8vo. 10s. 6d.

—— ASIATIC CHOLERA, HISTORY UP TO JULY 15, 1892: CAUSES AND TREATMENT. 8vo. 2s. 6d.

MERCIER (Dr. C.).—THE NERVOUS SYSTEM AND THE MIND. 8vo. 12s. 6d.

PIFFARD (H. G.).—AN ELEMENTARY TREATISE ON DISEASES OF THE SKIN. 8vo. 16s.

PRACTITIONER, THE: A MONTHLY JOURNAL OF THERAPEUTICS AND PUBLIC HEALTH. Edited by T. LAUDER BRUNTON, F.R.S., etc.; DONALD MACALISTER, M.A., M.D., and J. MITCHELL BRUCE, M.D. 1s. 6d. monthly. Vols. I.—XLVI. Half-yearly vols. 10s. 6d. each. [Cloth covers for binding, 1s. each.]

REYNOLDS (J. R.).—A SYSTEM OF MEDICINE. Edited by J. RUSSELL REYNOLDS, M.D., In 5 vols. Vols. I.—III. and V. 8vo. 25s. each.—Vol. IV. 21s.

RICHARDSON (Dr. B. W.).—DISEASES OF MODERN LIFE. Cr. 8vo.

—— THE FIELD OF DISEASE. A Book f Preventive Medicine. 8vo. 25s.

SEATON (Dr. Edward C.).—A HANDBOOK OF VACCINATION. Ext. fcp. 8vo. 8s. 6d.

SEILER (Dr. Carl). — MICRO-PHOTOGRAPHS IN HISTOLOGY, NORMAL AND PATHOLOGICAL. 4to. 31s. 6d.

SIBSON (Dr. Francis).—COLLECTED WORKS. Edited by W. M. ORD, M.D. Illustrated. 4 vols. 8vo. 3l. 3s.

SPENDER (J. Kent).—THERAPEUTIC MEANS FOR THE RELIEF OF PAIN. 8vo. 8s. 6d.

SURGERY (THE INTERNATIONAL ENCYCLOPAEDIA OF). A Systematic Treatise on the Theory and Practice of Surgery by Authors of various Nations. Edited by JOHN ASHHURST, jun., M.D. 6 vols. Roy. 8vo. 31s. 6d. each.

THORNE (Dr. Thorne).—DIPHTHERIA. Cr. 8vo. 8s. 6d.

WHITE (Dr. W. Hale).—A TEXT-BOOK OF GENERAL THERAPEUTICS. Cr. 8vo. 8s. 6d.

ZIEGLER (Ernst).—A TEXT-BOOK OF PATHOLOGICAL ANATOMY AND PATHOGENESIS. Translated and Edited by DONALD MACALISTER, M.A., M.D. Illustrated. 8vo.—Part I. GENERAL PATHOLOGICAL ANATOMY. 12s. 6d.—Part II. SPECIAL PATHOLOGICAL ANATOMY. Sections I.—VIII. and IX.—XII. 8vo. 12s. 6d. each.

METALLURGY.
(*See also* CHEMISTRY.)

HIORNS (Arthur H.).—A TEXT-BOOK OF ELEMENTARY METALLURGY. Gl. 8vo. 4s.

—— PRACTICAL METALLURGY AND ASSAYING. Illustrated. 2nd Edit. Globe 8vo. 6s.

—— IRON AND STEEL MANUFACTURE. Illustrated. Globe 8vo. 3s. 6d.

—— MIXED METALS OR METALLIC ALLOYS. Globe 8vo. 6s.

PHILLIPS (J. A.).—A TREATISE ON ORE DEPOSITS. Illustrated. Med. 8vo. 25s.

METAPHYSICS.
(*See under* PHILOSOPHY, p. 25.)

MILITARY ART AND HISTORY.

ACLAND (Sir H. W.). (*See* MEDICINE.)

AITKEN (Sir W.).—THE GROWTH OF THE RECRUIT AND YOUNG SOLDIER. Cr. 8vo. 8s. 6d.

MILITARY HISTORY—*continued.*

CUNYNGHAME (Gen. Sir A. T.).—MY COMMAND IN SOUTH AFRICA, 1874—78. 8vo. 12s. 6d.

DILKE (Sir C.) and WILKINSON (S.).—IMPERIAL DEFENCE. Cr. 8vo. 3s. 6d.

HOZIER (Lieut.-Col. H. M.).—THE SEVEN WEEKS' WAR. 3rd Edit. Cr. 8vo. 6s.

—— THE INVASIONS OF ENGLAND. 2 vols. 8vo. 28s.

MARTEL (Chas.).—MILITARY ITALY. With Map. 8vo. 12s. 6d.

MAURICE (Lt.-Col.).—WAR. 8vo. 5s. net.

—— THE NATIONAL DEFENCES. Cr. 8vo.

MERCUR (Prof. J.).—ELEMENTS OF THE ART OF WAR. 8vo. 17s.

SCRATCHLEY — KINLOCH COOKE. — AUSTRALIAN DEFENCES AND NEW GUINEA. Compiled from the Papers of the late Major-General Sir PETER SCRATCHLEY, R.E., by C. KINLOCH COOKE. 8vo. 14s.

THROUGH THE RANKS TO A COMMISSION. New Edition. Cr. 8vo. 2s. 6d.

WILKINSON (S.). — THE BRAIN OF AN ARMY. A Popular Account of the German General Staff. Cr. 8vo. 2s. 6d.

WINGATE (Major F. R.).—MAHDIISM AND THE EGYPTIAN SUDAN. An Account of the Rise and Progress of Mahdiism, and of Subsequent Events in the Sudan to the Present Time. With 17 Maps. 8vo. 30s. net.

WOLSELEY (General Viscount).—THE SOLDIER'S POCKET-BOOK FOR FIELD SERVICE. 5th Edit. 16mo, roan. 5s.

—— FIELD POCKET-BOOK FOR THE AUXILIARY FORCES. 16mo. 1s. 6d.

MINERALOGY. (*See* GEOLOGY.)

MISCELLANEOUS WORKS.
(*See under* LITERATURE, p. 19.)

MUSIC.

FAY (Amy).—MUSIC-STUDY IN GERMANY. Preface by Sir GEO. GROVE. Cr. 8vo. 4s. 6d.

GROVE (Sir George).—A DICTIONARY OF MUSIC AND MUSICIANS, A.D. 1450—1889. Edited by Sir GEORGE GROVE, D.C.L. In 4 vols. 8vo. 21s. each. With Illustrations in Music Type and Woodcut.—Also published in Parts. Parts I.—XIV., XIX.—XXII. 3s. 6d. each; XV. XVI. 7s.; XVII. XVIII. 7s.; XXIII.—XXV., Appendix. Edited by J. A. FULLER MAITLAND, M.A. 9s. [Cloth cases for binding the volumes, 1s. each.]

—— A COMPLETE INDEX TO THE ABOVE. By Mrs. E. WODEHOUSE. 8vo. 7s. 6d.

HULLAH (John).—MUSIC IN THE HOUSE. 4th Edit. Cr. 8vo. 2s. 6d.

TAYLOR (Franklin).—A PRIMER OF PIANOFORTE PLAYING. 18mo. 1s.

TAYLOR (Sedley).—SOUND AND MUSIC. 2nd Edit. Ext. cr. 8vo. 8s. 6d.

—— A SYSTEM OF SIGHT-SINGING FROM THE ESTABLISHED MUSICAL NOTATION. 8vo. 5s. net.

—— RECORD OF THE CAMBRIDGE CENTENARY OF W. A. MOZART. Cr. 8vo. 2s. 6d. net.

NATURAL HISTORY.

ATKINSON (J. C.). (*See* ANTIQUITIES, p. 1.)

BAKER (Sir Samuel W.). (*See* SPORT, p. 30.)

BLANFORD (W. T.).—GEOLOGY AND ZOOLOGY OF ABYSSINIA. 8vo. 21s.

FOWLER (W. W.).—TALES OF THE BIRDS. Illustrated. Cr. 8vo. 3s. 6d.

—— A YEAR WITH THE BIRDS. Illustrated. Cr. 8vo. 3s. 6d.

KINGSLEY (Charles).—MADAM HOW AND LADY WHY; or, First Lessons in Earth-Lore for Children. Cr. 8vo. 3s. 6d.

—— GLAUCUS; or, The Wonders of the Sea-Shore. With Coloured Illustrations. Cr. 8vo. 3s. 6d.—*Presentation Edition.* Cr. 8vo, extra cloth. 7s. 6d.

KLEIN (E.).—ETIOLOGY AND PATHOLOGY OF GROUSE DISEASE. 8vo. 7s. net.

WALLACE (Alfred Russel).—THE MALAY ARCHIPELAGO: The Land of the Orang Utang and the Bird of Paradise. Maps and Illustrations. Ext. cr. 8vo. 6s. (*See also* BIOLOGY.)

WATERTON (Charles).—WANDERINGS IN SOUTH AMERICA, THE NORTH-WEST OF THE UNITED STATES, AND THE ANTILLES. Edited by Rev. J. G. WOOD. Illustrated. Cr. 8vo. 6s.—People's Edition. 4to. 6d.

WHITE (Gilbert).—NATURAL HISTORY AND ANTIQUITIES OF SELBORNE. Ed. by FRANK BUCKLAND. With a Chapter on Antiquities by the EARL OF SELBORNE. Cr. 8vo. 6s.

NATURAL PHILOSOPHY. (*See* PHYSICS.)

NAVAL SCIENCE.

KELVIN (Lord).—POPULAR LECTURES AND ADDRESSES.—Vol. III. NAVIGATION. Cr. 8vo. 7s. 6d.

ROBINSON (Rev. J. L.).—MARINE SURVEYING, AN ELEMENTARY TREATISE ON. For Younger Naval Officers. Illust. Cr. 8vo. 7s. 6d.

SHORTLAND (Admiral).—NAUTICAL SURVEYING. 8vo. 21s.

NOVELS. (*See* PROSE FICTION, p. 17.)

NURSING.
(*See under* DOMESTIC ECONOMY, p. 8.)

OPTICS (or LIGHT). (*See* PHYSICS, p. 27.)

PAINTING. (*See* ART, p. 2.)

PATHOLOGY. (*See* MEDICINE, p. 22.)

PERIODICALS.

AMERICAN JOURNAL OF PHILOLOGY, THE. (*See* PHILOLOGY.)

BRAIN. (*See* MEDICINE.)

ECONOMIC JOURNAL, THE. (*See* POLITICAL ECONOMY.)

ECONOMICS, THE QUARTERLY JOURNAL OF. (*See* POLITICAL ECONOMY.)

ENGLISH ILLUSTRATED MAGAZINE, THE. — Profusely Illustrated. Published Monthly. No. I. October, 1883. 6d.—Vol. I. 1884. 7s. 6d.—Vols. II.-VIII. Super royal 8vo, extra cloth, coloured edges. 8s. each. [Cloth Covers for binding Volumes, 1s. each. Reading Case, 1s. net.]

NATURAL SCIENCE: A MONTHLY REVIEW OF SCIENTIFIC PROGRESS. 8vo. 1s. net. No. 1. March 1892.

NATURE: A WEEKLY ILLUSTRATED JOURNAL OF SCIENCE. Published every Thursday. Price 6*d.* Monthly Parts, 2*s.* and 2*s.* 6*d.*; Current Half-yearly vols., 15*s.* each. Vols. I.—XLIII. [Cases for binding vols. 1*s.* 6*d.* each.]

HELLENIC STUDIES, THE JOURNAL OF. Pub. Half-Yearly from 1880. 8vo. 30*s.*; or each Part, 15*s.* Vol. XII. Part I. 15*s.* net.
 The Journal will be sold at a reduced price to Libraries wishing to subscribe, but official application must in each case be made to the Council. Information on this point, and upon the conditions of Membership, may be obtained on application to the Hon. Sec., Mr. George Macmillan, 29, Bedford Street, Covent Garden.

LEPROSY INVESTIGATION COMMITTEE, JOURNAL OF. (*See* MEDICINE.)

MACMILLAN'S MAGAZINE. Published Monthly. 1*s.*—Vols. I.-LXV. 7*s.* 6*d.* each. [Cloth covers for binding, 1*s.* each.]

PHILOLOGY, THE JOURNAL OF. (*See* PHILOLOGY.)

PRACTITIONER, THE. (*See* MEDICINE.)

RECORD OF TECHNICAL AND SECONDARY EDUCATION. (*See* EDUCATION, p. 8.)

PHILOLOGY.

AMERICAN JOURNAL OF PHILOLOGY, THE. Edited by Prof. BASIL L. GILDERSLEEVE. 4*s.* 6*d.* each No. (quarterly).

AMERICAN PHILOLOGICAL ASSOCIATION, TRANSACTIONS OF. Vols. I.—XX. 8*s.* 6*d.* per vol. net, except Vols. XV. and XX., which are 10*s.* 6*d.* net.

CORNELL UNIVERSITY STUDIES IN CLASSICAL PHILOLOGY. Edited by I. FLAGG, W. G. HALE, and B. I. WHEELER. I. THE *C U M*-CONSTRUCTIONS: their History and Functions. Part I. Critical. 1*s.* 8*d.* net. Part II. Constructive. By W. G. HALE. 3*s.* 4*d.* net.—II. ANALOGY AND THE SCOPE OF ITS APPLICATION IN LANGUAGE. By B. I. WHEELER. 1*s.* 3*d.* net.

GILES (P.).—A SHORT MANUAL OF PHILOLOGY FOR CLASSICAL STUDENTS. Cr. 8vo.

JOURNAL OF SACRED AND CLASSICAL PHILOLOGY. 4 vols. 8vo. 12*s.* 6*d.* each.

JOURNAL OF PHILOLOGY. New Series. Edited by W. A. WRIGHT, M.A., I. BYWATER, M.A., and H. JACKSON, M.A. 4*s.* 6*d.* each No. (half-yearly).

KELLNER (Dr. L.). — HISTORICAL OUTLINES OF ENGLISH SYNTAX. Ex. fcp. 8vo.

MORRIS (Rev. Richard, LL.D.).—PRIMER OF ENGLISH GRAMMAR. 18mo. 1*s.*
—— ELEMENTARY LESSONS IN HISTORICAL ENGLISH GRAMMAR. 18mo. 2*s.* 6*d.*
—— HISTORICAL OUTLINES OF ENGLISH ACCIDENCE. Extra fcp. 8vo. 6*s.*

MORRIS (R.) and BOWEN (H. C.).—ENGLISH GRAMMAR EXERCISES. 18mo. 1*s.*

OLIPHANT (T. L. Kington). — THE OLD AND MIDDLE ENGLISH. Globe 8vo. 9*s.*
—— THE NEW ENGLISH. 2 vols. Cr. 8vo. 21*s.*

PEILE (John). —A PRIMER OF PHILOLOGY. 18mo. 1*s.*

PELLISSIER (E.).—FRENCH ROOTS AND THEIR FAMILIES. Globe 8vo. 6*s.*

TAYLOR (Isaac).—WORDS AND PLACES. 9th Edit. Maps. Globe 8vo. 6*s.*
—— ETRUSCAN RESEARCHES. 8vo. 14*s.*
—— GREEKS AND GOTHS: A Study of the Runes. 8vo. 9*s.*

WETHERELL (J.).—EXERCISES ON MORRIS'S PRIMER OF ENGLISH GRAMMAR. 18mo. 1*s.*

YONGE (C. M.).—HISTORY OF CHRISTIAN NAMES. New Edit., revised. Cr. 8vo. 7*s.* 6*d.*

PHILOSOPHY.

Ethics and Metaphysics—Logic—Psychology.

Ethics and Metaphysics.

BIRKS (Thomas Rawson).—FIRST PRINCIPLES OF MORAL SCIENCE. Cr. 8vo. 8*s.* 6*d.*
—— MODERN UTILITARIANISM; or, The Systems of Paley, Bentham, and Mill Examined and Compared. Cr. 8vo. 6*s.* 6*d.*
—— MODERN PHYSICAL FATALISM, AND THE DOCTRINE OF EVOLUTION. Including an Examination of Mr. Herbert Spencer's "First Principles." Cr. 8vo. 6*s.*

CALDERWOOD (Prof. H.).—A HANDBOOK OF MORAL PHILOSOPHY. Cr. 8vo. 6*s.*

FISKE (John).—OUTLINES OF COSMIC PHILOSOPHY, BASED ON THE DOCTRINE OF EVOLUTION. 2 vols. 8vo. 25*s.*

FOWLER (Rev. Thomas). — PROGRESSIVE MORALITY: An Essay in Ethics. Cr. 8vo. 5*s.*

HARPER (Father Thomas).—THE METAPHYSICS OF THE SCHOOL. In 5 vols.—Vols. I. and II. 8vo. 18*s.* each.—Vol. III. Part I. 12*s.*

KANT.—KANT'S CRITICAL PHILOSOPHY FOR ENGLISH READERS. By J. P. MAHAFFY, D.D., and J. H. BERNARD, B.D. 2 vols. Cr. 8vo.—Vol. I. THE KRITIK OF PURE REASON EXPLAINED AND DEFENDED. 7*s.* 6*d.*—Vol. II. THE PROLEGOMENA. Translated, with Notes and Appendices. 6*s.*
—— KRITIK OF JUDGMENT. Translated by J. H. BERNARD, D.D. 8vo. 10*s.* net.

KANT—MAX MÜLLER. — CRITIQUE OF PURE REASON BY IMMANUEL KANT. Translated by F. MAX MÜLLER. With Introduction by LUDWIG NOIRÉ. 2 vols. 8vo. 16*s.* each (sold separately).—Vol. I. HISTORICAL INTRODUCTION, by LUDWIG NOIRÉ, etc.—Vol. II. CRITIQUE OF PURE REASON.

MAURICE (F. D.).—MORAL AND METAPHYSICAL PHILOSOPHY. 2 vols. 8vo. 16*s.*

McCOSH (Rev. Dr. James).—THE METHOD OF THE DIVINE GOVERNMENT, PHYSICAL AND MORAL. 8vo. 10*s.* 6*d.*
—— THE SUPERNATURAL IN RELATION TO THE NATURAL. Cr. 8vo. 7*s.* 6*d.*
—— INTUITIONS OF THE MIND. 8vo. 10*s.* 6*d.*
—— AN EXAMINATION OF MR. J. S. MILL'S PHILOSOPHY. 8vo. 10*s.* 6*d.*
—— CHRISTIANITY AND POSITIVISM. Lectures on Natural Theology and Apologetics. Cr. 8vo. 7*s.* 6*d.*
—— THE SCOTTISH PHILOSOPHY FROM HUTCHESON TO HAMILTON, BIOGRAPHICAL, EXPOSITORY, CRITICAL. Roy. 8vo. 16*s.*
—— REALISTIC PHILOSOPHY DEFENDED IN A PHILOSOPHIC SERIES. 2 vols.—Vol. I. EXPOSITORY. Vol. II. HISTORICAL AND CRITICAL. Cr. 8vo. 14*s.*

PHILOSOPHY.
Ethics and Metaphysics—*continued.*

McCOSH (Rev. Dr. J.).—FIRST AND FUNDAMENTAL TRUTHS. Being a Treatise on Metaphysics. 8vo. 9s.
—— THE PREVAILING TYPES OF PHILOSOPHY: CAN THEY LOGICALLY REACH REALITY? 8vo. 3s. 6d.

MASSON (Prof. David).—RECENT BRITISH PHILOSOPHY. 3rd Edit. Cr. 8vo. 6s.

SIDGWICK (Prof. Henry).—THE METHODS OF ETHICS. 4th Edit., revised. 8vo. 14s.
—— A SUPPLEMENT TO THE SECOND EDITION. Containing all the important Additions and Alterations in the Fourth Edition. 8vo. 6s.
—— OUTLINES OF THE HISTORY OF ETHICS FOR ENGLISH READERS. Cr. 8vo. 3s. 6d.

THORNTON (W. T.). — OLD-FASHIONED ETHICS AND COMMON-SENSE METAPHYSICS. 8vo. 10s. 6d.

Logic.

BOOLE (George). — THE MATHEMATICAL ANALYSIS OF LOGIC. 8vo. sewed. 5s.

CARROLL (Lewis).—THE GAME OF LOGIC. Cr. 8vo. 3s. net.

JEVONS (W. Stanley).—A PRIMER OF LOGIC. 18mo. 1s.
—— ELEMENTARY LESSONS IN LOGIC, DEDUCTIVE AND INDUCTIVE. 18mo. 3s. 6d.
—— STUDIES IN DEDUCTIVE LOGIC. 2nd Edit. Cr. 8vo. 6s.
—— THE PRINCIPLES OF SCIENCE: Treatise on Logic and Scientific Method. Cr. 8vo. 12s. 6d.
—— PURE LOGIC: and other Minor Works. Edited by R. ADAMSON, M.A., and HARRIET A. JEVONS. 8vo. 10s. 6d.

KEYNES (J. N.).—STUDIES AND EXERCISES IN FORMAL LOGIC. 2nd Edit. Cr. 8vo. 10s. 6d.

McCOSH (Rev. Dr.).—THE LAWS OF DISCURSIVE THOUGHT. A Text-Book of Formal Logic. Cr. 8vo. 5s.

RAY (Prof. P. K.).—A TEXT-BOOK OF DEDUCTIVE LOGIC. 4th Edit. Globe 8vo. 4s. 6d.

VENN (Rev. John).—THE LOGIC OF CHANCE. 2nd Edit. Cr. 8vo. 10s. 6d.
—— SYMBOLIC LOGIC. Cr. 8vo. 10s. 6d.
—— THE PRINCIPLES OF EMPIRICAL OR INDUCTIVE LOGIC. 8vo. 18s.

Psychology.

BALDWIN (Prof. J. M.).—HANDBOOK OF PSYCHOLOGY: Senses and Intellect. 8vo. 12s. 6d.
—— FEELING AND WILL. 8vo. 12s. 6d.

CALDERWOOD (Prof. H.). — THE RELATIONS OF MIND AND BRAIN. 3rd Ed. 8vo. 8s.

CLIFFORD (W. K.).—SEEING AND THINKING. Cr. 8vo. 3s. 6d.

HÖFFDING (Prof. H.).—OUTLINES OF PSYCHOLOGY. Translated by M. E. LOWNDES. Cr. 8vo. 6s.

JAMES (Prof. William).—THE PRINCIPLES OF PSYCHOLOGY. 2 vols. Demy 8vo. 25s. net.
—— TEXT-BOOK OF PSYCHOLOGY. Cr. 8vo. 7s. net.

JARDINE (Rev. Robert).—THE ELEMENTS OF THE PSYCHOLOGY OF COGNITION. 3rd Edit. Cr. 8vo. 6s. 6d.

McCOSH (Rev. Dr.).—PSYCHOLOGY. Cr. 8vo. I. THE COGNITIVE POWERS. 6s. 6d.—II. THE MOTIVE POWERS. 6s. 6d.
—— THE EMOTIONS. 8vo. 9s.

MAUDSLEY (Dr. Henry).—THE PHYSIOLOGY OF MIND. Cr. 8vo. 10s. 6d.
—— THE PATHOLOGY OF MIND. 8vo. 18s.
—— BODY AND MIND. Cr. 8vo. 6s. 6d.

MURPHY (J. J.).—HABIT AND INTELLIGENCE. 2nd Edit. Illustrated. 8vo. 16s.

PHOTOGRAPHY.

MELDOLA (Prof. R.).—THE CHEMISTRY OF PHOTOGRAPHY. Cr. 8vo. 6s.

PHYSICS OR NATURAL PHILOSOPHY.
General—Electricity and Magnetism—, Heat, Light, and Sound.

General.

ANDREWS (Dr. Thomas): THE SCIENTIFIC PAPERS OF THE LATE. With a Memoir by Profs. TAIT and CRUM BROWN. 8vo. 18s.

DANIELL (A.).—A TEXT-BOOK OF THE PRINCIPLES OF PHYSICS. Illustrated. 2nd Edit. Med. 8vo. 21s.

EVERETT (Prof. J. D.).—THE C. G. S. SYSTEM OF UNITS, WITH TABLES OF PHYSICAL CONSTANTS. New Edit. Globe 8vo. 5s.

FESSENDEN (C.).—ELEMENTS OF PHYSICS. Fcp. 8vo. 3s.

FISHER (Rev. Osmond).—PHYSICS OF THE EARTH'S CRUST. 2nd Edit. 8vo. 12s.

GUILLEMIN (Amédée).—THE FORCES OF NATURE. A Popular Introduction to the Study of Physical Phenomena. 455 Woodcuts. Roy. 8vo. 21s.

HEAVISIDE (O.)—SCIENTIFIC PAPERS. 8vo.
[In the Press.

KELVIN (Lord).—POPULAR LECTURES AND ADDRESSES.—Vol. I. CONSTITUTION OF MATTER. Cr. 8vo. 7s. 6d.

KEMPE (A. B.).—HOW TO DRAW A STRAIGHT LINE. Cr. 8vo. 1s. 6d.

LOEWY (B.).—QUESTIONS AND EXAMPLES IN EXPERIMENTAL PHYSICS, SOUND, LIGHT, HEAT, ELECTRICITY, AND MAGNETISM. Fcp. 8vo. 2s.
—— A GRADUATED COURSE OF NATURAL SCIENCE. Part I. Gl. 8vo. 2s.—Part II. 2s. 6d.

MOLLOY (Rev. G.).—GLEANINGS IN SCIENCE: A Series of Popular Lectures on Scientific Subjects. 8vo. 7s. 6d.

STEWART (Prof. Balfour). — A PRIMER OF PHYSICS. Illustrated. 18mo. 1s.
—— LESSONS IN ELEMENTARY PHYSICS. Illustrated. Fcp. 8vo. 4s. 6d.
—— QUESTIONS. By T. H. CORE. 18mo. 2s.

STEWART (Prof. Balfour) and GEE (W. W. Haldane).—LESSONS IN ELEMENTARY PRACTICAL PHYSICS. Illustrated.—GENERAL PHYSICAL PROCESSES. Cr. 8vo. 6s.

TAIT (Prof. P. G.).—LECTURES ON SOME RECENT ADVANCES IN PHYSICAL SCIENCE. 3rd Edit. Cr. 8vo. 9s.

Electricity and Magnetism.

CUMMING (Linnæus).—AN INTRODUCTION TO ELECTRICITY. Cr. 8vo. 8s. 6d.

DAY (R. E.).—ELECTRIC LIGHT ARITHMETIC. 18mo. 2s.

GRAY (Prof. Andrew).—THE THEORY AND PRACTICE OF ABSOLUTE MEASUREMENTS IN ELECTRICITY AND MAGNETISM. 2 vols. Cr. 8vo. Vol. I. 12s. 6d.

GRAY (Prof. Andrew).—ABSOLUTE MEASUREMENTS IN ELECTRICITY AND MAGNETISM. Fcp. 8vo. 5s. 6d.

GUILLEMIN (A.).—ELECTRICITY AND MAGNETISM. A Popular Treatise. Translated and Edited by Prof. SILVANUS P. THOMPSON. Super Roy. 8vo. 31s. 6d.

KELVIN (Lord). — PAPERS ON ELECTROSTATICS AND MAGNETISM. 8vo. 18s.

LODGE (Prof. Oliver).—MODERN VIEWS OF ELECTRICITY. Cr. 8vo. 6s. 6d.

MENDENHALL (T. C.).—A CENTURY OF ELECTRICITY. Cr. 8vo. 4s. 6d.

STEWART (Prof. Balfour) and GEE (W. W. Haldane).—LESSONS IN ELEMENTARY PRACTICAL PHYSICS. Cr. 8vo. Illustrated.—ELECTRICITY AND MAGNETISM. 7s. 6d.
—— PRACTICAL PHYSICS FOR SCHOOLS. Gl. 8vo.—ELECTRICITY AND MAGNETISM. 2s.6d.

THOMPSON (Prof. Silvanus P.). — ELEMENTARY LESSONS IN ELECTRICITY AND MAGNETISM. Illustrated. Fcp. 8vo. 4s. 6d.

TURNER (H. H.).—EXAMPLES ON HEAT AND ELECTRICITY. Cr. 8vo. 2s. 6d.

Heat, Light, and Sound.

AIRY (Sir G. B.).—ON SOUND AND ATMOSPHERIC VIBRATIONS. Cr. 8vo. 9s.

CARNOT--THURSTON.--REFLECTIONS ON THE MOTIVE POWER OF HEAT, AND ON MACHINES FITTED TO DEVELOP THAT POWER. From the French of N. L. S. CARNOT. Edited by R. H. THURSTON, LL.D. Cr. 8vo. s. 6d.

JOHNSON (Amy).—SUNSHINE. Illustrated. Cr. 8vo. 6s.

JONES (Prof. D. E.).—HEAT, LIGHT, AND SOUND. Globe 8vo. 2s. 6d.
—— LESSONS IN HEAT AND LIGHT. Globe 8vo. 3s. 6d.

MAYER (Prof. A. M.).—SOUND. A Series of Simple Experiments. Illustr. Cr. 8vo. 3s.6d.

MAYER (Prof. A. M.) and BARNARD (C.)—LIGHT. A Series of Simple Experiments. Illustrated. Cr. 8vo. 2s. 6d.

PARKINSON (S.).—A TREATISE ON OPTICS. 4th Edit., revised. Cr. 8vo. 10s. 6d.

PEABODY (Prof. C. H.).—THERMODYNAMICS OF THE STEAM ENGINE AND OTHER HEATENGINES. 8vo. 21s.

PERRY (Prof. J.).—STEAM: An Elementary Treatise. 18mo. 4s. 6d.

PRESTON (T.).—THE THEORY OF LIGHT. Illustrated. 8vo. 15s. net.
—— THE THEORY OF HEAT. 8vo.

RAYLEIGH (Lord).—THEORY OF SOUND. 8vo. Vol. I. 12s. 6d.—Vol. II. 12s. 6d.

SHANN (G.).—AN ELEMENTARY TREATISE ON HEAT IN RELATION TO STEAM AND THE STEAM-ENGINE. Illustr. Cr. 8vo. 4s. 6d.

SPOTTISWOODE (W.).—POLARISATION OF LIGHT. Illustrated. Cr. 8vo. 3s. 6d.

STEWART (Prof. Balfour) and GEE (W. W. Haldane).—LESSONS IN ELEMENTARY PRACTICAL PHYSICS. Cr. 8vo. Illustrated.—OPTICS, HEAT, AND SOUND.
—— PRACTICAL PHYSICS FOR SCHOOLS. Gl. 8vo.—HEAT, LIGHT, AND SOUND.

STOKES (Sir George G.).--ON LIGHT. The Burnett Lectures. Cr. 8vo. 7s. 6d.

STONE (W. H.).—ELEMENTARY LESSONS ON SOUND. Illustrated. Fcp. 8vo. 3s. 6d.

TAIT (Prof. P. G.).—HEAT. With Illustrations. Cr. 8vo. 6s.

TAYLOR (Sedley).—SOUND AND MUSIC. 2nd Edit. Ext. cr. 8vo. 8s. 6d.

TURNER (H. H.). (See ELECTRICITY.)

WRIGHT (Lewis).—LIGHT. A Course of Experimental Optics. Illust. Cr. 8vo. 7s. 6d.

PHYSIOGRAPHY and METEOROLOGY.

ARATUS.—THE SKIES AND WEATHER FORECASTS OF ARATUS. Translated by E. POSTE, M.A. Cr. 8vo. 3s. 6d.

BLANFORD (H. F.).—THE RUDIMENTS OF PHYSICAL GEOGRAPHY FOR THE USE OF INDIAN SCHOOLS. Illustr. Cr. 8vo. 2s. 6d.
—— A PRACTICAL GUIDE TO THE CLIMATES AND WEATHER OF INDIA, CEYLON AND BURMAH, AND THE STORMS OF INDIAN SEAS. 8vo. 12s 6d.

FERREL (Prof. W.).—A POPULAR TREATISE ON THE WINDS. 8vo. 18s.

FISHER (Rev. Osmond).—PHYSICS OF THE EARTH'S CRUST. 2nd Edit. 8vo. 12s.

GALTON (Francis).—METEOROGRAPHICA; or, Methods of Mapping the Weather. 4to. 9s.

GEIKIE (Sir Archibald).—A PRIMER OF PHYSICAL GEOGRAPHY. Illustrated. 18mo. 1s.
—— ELEMENTARY LESSONS IN PHYSICAL GEOGRAPHY. Illustrated. Fcp. 8vo. 4s. 6d.
—— QUESTIONS ON THE SAME. 1s. 6d.

HUXLEY (Prof. T. H.).—PHYSIOGRAPHY. Illustrated. Cr. 8vo. 6s.

LOCKYER (J. Norman).—OUTLINES OF PHYSIOGRAPHY: THE MOVEMENTS OF THE EARTH. Illustrated. Cr. 8vo, swd. 1s. 6d.

MELDOLA (Prof. R.) and WHITE (Wm.).—REPORT ON THE EAST ANGLIAN EARTHQUAKE OF APRIL 22ND, 1884. 8vo. 3s. 6d.

PHYSIOLOGY.

FEARNLEY (W.).—A MANUAL OF ELEMENTARY PRACTICAL HISTOLOGY. Cr. 8vo. 7s. 6d.

FOSTER (Prof. Michael).—A TEXT-BOOK OF PHYSIOLOGY. Illustrated. 5th Edit. 8vo.—Part I. Book I. BLOOD: THE TISSUES OF MOVEMENT, THE VASCULAR MECHANISM. 10s. 6d.—Part II. Book II. THE TISSUES OF CHEMICAL ACTION, WITH THEIR RESPECTIVE MECHANISMS: NUTRITION. 10s. 6d.—Part III. Book III. THE CENTRAL NERVOUS SYSTEM. 7s. 6d.—Part IV. Book III. THE SENSES, AND SOME SPECIAL MUSCULAR MECHANISMS.—BOOK IV. THE TISSUES AND MECHANISMS OF REPRODUCTION. 10s. 6d.
—— A PRIMER OF PHYSIOLOGY. 18mo. 1s.

FOSTER (Prof. M.) and LANGLEY (J. N.).—A COURSE OF ELEMENTARY PRACTICAL PHYSIOLOGY AND HISTOLOGY. Cr. 8vo. 7s. 6d.

GAMGEE (Arthur).—A TEXT-BOOK OF THE PHYSIOLOGICAL CHEMISTRY OF THE ANIMAL BODY. Vol. I. 8vo. 18s. Vol. II.

HUMPHRY (Prof. Sir G. M.).—THE HUMAN FOOT AND THE HUMAN HAND. Illustrated. Fcp. 8vo. 4s. 6d.

PHYSIOLOGY—*continued.*

HUXLEY (Prof. Thos. H.).—LESSONS IN ELEMENTARY PHYSIOLOGY. Fcp. 8vo. 4s. 6d.
—— QUESTIONS. By T. ALCOCK. 18mo. 1s. 6d.

MIVART (St. George).—LESSONS IN ELEMENTARY ANATOMY. Fcp. 8vo. 6s. 6d.

PETTIGREW (J. Bell).—THE PHYSIOLOGY OF THE CIRCULATION IN PLANTS IN THE LOWER ANIMALS AND IN MAN. 8vo. 12s.

SEILER (Dr. Carl).—MICRO-PHOTOGRAPHS IN HISTOLOGY, NORMAL AND PATHOLOGICAL. 4to. 31s. 6d.

POETRY. (*See under* LITERATURE, p. 14.)

POLITICAL ECONOMY.

BASTABLE (Prof. C. F.).—PUBLIC FINANCE. 12s. 6d. net.

BÖHM-BAWERK (Prof.).—CAPITAL AND INTEREST. Trans. by W. SMART. 8vo. 12s. net.
—— THE POSITIVE THEORY OF CAPITAL. By the same Translator. 12s. net.

BOISSEVAIN (G. M.).—THE MONETARY QUESTION. 8vo, sewed. 3s. net.

BONAR (James).—MALTHUS AND HIS WORK. 8vo. 12s. 6d.

CAIRNES (J. E.).—SOME LEADING PRINCIPLES OF POLITICAL ECONOMY NEWLY EXPOUNDED. 8vo. 14s.
—— THE CHARACTER AND LOGICAL METHOD OF POLITICAL ECONOMY. Cr. 8vo. 6s.

CLARKE (C. B.). — SPECULATIONS FROM POLITICAL ECONOMY. Cr. 8vo. 3s. 6d.

DICTIONARY OF POLITICAL ECONOMY, A. By various Writers. Ed. R. H. I. PALGRAVE. 3s. 6d. net. (Part I. July, 1891.)

ECONOMIC JOURNAL, THE. — THE JOURNAL OF THE BRITISH ECONOMIC ASSOCIATION. Edit. by Prof. F. Y. EDGEWORTH. Published Quarterly. 8vo. 5s. (Part I. April, 1891.) Vol. I. 21s. [Cloth Covers for binding Volumes, 1s. 6d. each.]

ECONOMICS: THE QUARTERLY JOURNAL OF. Vol. II. Parts II. III. IV. 2s. 6d. each. —Vol. III. 4 parts. 2s. 6d. each.—Vol. IV. 4 parts. 2s. 6d. each.—Vol. V. 4 parts. 2s. 6d. each.—Vol. VI. 4 parts. 2s. 6d. each.

FAWCETT (Henry).—MANUAL OF POLITICAL ECONOMY. 7th Edit. Cr. 8vo. 12s.
—— AN EXPLANATORY DIGEST OF THE ABOVE. By C. A. WATERS. Cr. 8vo. 2s. 6d.
—— FREE TRADE AND PROTECTION. 6th Edit. Cr. 8vo. 3s. 6d.

FAWCETT (Mrs. H.).—POLITICAL ECONOMY FOR BEGINNERS, WITH QUESTIONS. 7th Edit. 18mo. 2s. 6d.

FIRST LESSONS IN BUSINESS MATTERS. By A BANKER'S DAUGHTER. 2nd Edit. 18mo. 1s.

GILMAN (N. P.). — PROFIT-SHARING BETWEEN EMPLOYER AND EMPLOYEE. Cr. 8vo. 7s. 6d.

GOSCHEN (Rt. Hon. George J.).—REPORTS AND SPEECHES ON LOCAL TAXATION. 8vo. 5s.

GUIDE TO THE UNPROTECTED: IN EVERY-DAY MATTERS RELATING TO PROPERTY AND INCOME. Ext. fcp. 8vo. 3s. 6d.

GUNTON (George).—WEALTH AND PROGRESS. Cr. 8vo. 6s.

HORTON (Hon. S. Dana).—THE SILVER POUND AND ENGLAND'S MONETARY POLICY SINCE THE RESTORATION. 8vo. 14s.

HOWELL (George).—THE CONFLICTS OF CAPITAL AND LABOUR. Cr. 8vo. 7s. 6d.

JEVONS (W. Stanley).—A PRIMER OF POLITICAL ECONOMY. 18mo. 1s.
—— THE THEORY OF POLITICAL ECONOMY. 3rd Ed. 8vo. 10s. 6d.
—— INVESTIGATIONS IN CURRENCY AND FINANCE. Edit. by H. S. FOXWELL. 8vo. 21s.

KEYNES (J. N.).—THE SCOPE AND METHOD OF POLITICAL ECONOMY. Cr. 8vo. 7s. net.

MACDONELL (John).—THE LAND QUESTION. 8vo. 10s. 6d.

MARSHALL (Prof. Alfred).—PRINCIPLES OF ECONOMICS. 2 vols. 8vo. Vol. I. 12s. 6d. net.
—— ELEMENTS OF ECONOMICS OF INDUSTRY. Crown 8vo. 3s. 6d.

MARTIN (Frederick). — THE HISTORY OF LLOYD'S, AND OF MARINE INSURANCE IN GREAT BRITAIN. 8vo. 14s.

PRICE (L. L. F. R.).—INDUSTRIAL PEACE: ITS ADVANTAGES, METHODS, AND DIFFICULTIES. Med. 8vo. 6s.

SIDGWICK (Prof. Henry).—THE PRINCIPLES OF POLITICAL ECONOMY. 2nd Edit. 8vo. 16s.

SMART (W.).—AN INTRODUCTION TO THE THEORY OF VALUE. Cr. 8vo. 3s. net.

WALKER (Francis A.).—FIRST LESSONS IN POLITICAL ECONOMY. Cr. 8vo. 5s.
—— A BRIEF TEXT-BOOK OF POLITICAL ECONOMY. Cr. 8vo. 6s. 6d.
—— POLITICAL ECONOMY. 8vo. 12s. 6d.
—— THE WAGES QUESTION. Ext. cr. 8vo. 8s. 6d. net.
—— MONEY. New Edit. Ext. cr. 8vo. 8s. 6d. net.
—— MONEY IN ITS RELATION TO TRADE AND INDUSTRY. Cr. 8vo. 7s. 6d.
—— LAND AND ITS RENT. Fcp. 8vo. 3s. 6d.

WALLACE (A. R.).—BAD TIMES: An Essay. Cr. 8vo. 2s. 6d.

WICKSTEED (Ph. H.).—THE ALPHABET OF ECONOMIC SCIENCE.—I. ELEMENTS OF THE THEORY OF VALUE OR WORTH. Gl. 8vo. 2s. 6d.

POLITICS.

(*See also* HISTORY, p. 9.)

ADAMS (Sir F. O.) and CUNNINGHAM (C.)—THE SWISS CONFEDERATION. 8vo. 14s.

BAKER (Sir Samuel W.).—THE EGYPTIAN QUESTION. 8vo, sewed. 2s.

BATH (Marquis of).—OBSERVATIONS ON BULGARIAN AFFAIRS. Cr. 8vo. 3s. 6d.

BRIGHT (John).—SPEECHES ON QUESTIONS OF PUBLIC POLICY. Edit. by J. E. THOROLD ROGERS. With Portrait. 2 vols. 8vo. 25s.
—*Popular Edition.* Ext. fcp. 8vo. 3s. 6d.
—— PUBLIC ADDRESSES. Edited by J. E. T. ROGERS. 8vo. 14s.

BRYCE (Jas., M.P.).—THE AMERICAN COMMONWEALTH. 2 vols. Ext. cr. 8vo. 25s.

BUCKLAND (Anna).—OUR NATIONAL INSTITUTIONS. 18mo. 1s.

BURKE (Edmund).—LETTERS, TRACTS, AND SPEECHES ON IRISH AFFAIRS. Edited by MATTHEW ARNOLD, with Preface. Cr. 8vo. 6s.
—— REFLECTIONS ON THE FRENCH REVOLUTION. Ed. by F. G. SELBY. Globe 8vo. 5s.

CAIRNES (J. E.).—POLITICAL ESSAYS. 8vo. 10s. 6d.
—— THE SLAVE POWER. 8vo. 10s. 6d.

COBDEN (Richard).—SPEECHES ON QUESTIONS OF PUBLIC POLICY. Ed. by J. BRIGHT and J. E. THOROLD ROGERS. Gl. 8vo. 3s. 6d.

DICEY (Prof. A. V.).—LETTERS ON UNIONIST DELUSIONS. Cr. 8vo. 2s. 6d.

DILKE (Rt. Hon. Sir Charles W.).—GREATER BRITAIN. 9th Edit. Cr. 8vo. 6s.
—— PROBLEMS OF GREATER BRITAIN. Maps. 3rd Edit. Ext. cr. 8vo. 12s. 6d.

DONISTHORPE (Wordsworth). — INDIVIDUALISM: A System of Politics. 8vo. 14s

DUFF (Rt. Hon. Sir M. E. Grant).—MISCELLANIES, POLITICAL AND LITERARY. 8vo. 10s. 6d.

ENGLISH CITIZEN, THE.—His Rights and Responsibilities. Ed. by HENRY CRAIK, C.B. Cr. 8vo. 3s. 6d. each.
THE PUNISHMENT AND PREVENTION OF CRIME. By Col. Sir EDMUND DU CANE.
LOCAL GOVERNMENT. By M. D. CHALMERS.
COLONIES AND DEPENDENCIES: Part I. INDIA. By J. S. COTTON, M.A.—II. THE COLONIES. By E. J. PAYNE.
THE STATE IN ITS RELATION TO EDUCATION. By HENRY CRAIK, C.B.
THE STATE AND THE CHURCH. By Hon. ARTHUR ELLIOTT, M.P.
THE STATE IN ITS RELATION TO TRADE. By Sir T. H. FARRER, Bart.
THE POOR LAW. By the Rev. T. W. FOWLE.
THE STATE IN RELATION TO LABOUR. By W. STANLEY JEVONS.
JUSTICE AND POLICE. By F. W. MAITLAND.
THE NATIONAL DEFENCES. By Colonel MAURICE, R.A. [In the Press.
THE LAND LAWS. By Sir F. POLLOCK, Bart. 2nd Edit.
CENTRAL GOVERNMENT. By H. D. TRAILL.
THE ELECTORATE AND THE LEGISLATURE. By SPENCER WALPOLE.
FOREIGN RELATIONS. By S. WALPOLE.
THE NATIONAL BUDGET; NATIONAL DEBT; TAXES AND RATES. By A. J. WILSON.

FAWCETT (Henry). — SPEECHES ON SOME CURRENT POLITICAL QUESTIONS. 8vo. 10s. 6d.
—— FREE TRADE AND PROTECTION. 6th Edit. Cr. 8vo. 3s. 6d.

FAWCETT (Henry and Mrs. H.).—ESSAYS AND LECTURES ON POLITICAL AND SOCIAL SUBJECTS. 8vo. 10s. 6d.

FISKE (John).—AMERICAN POLITICAL IDEAS VIEWED FROM THE STAND-POINT OF UNIVERSAL HISTORY. Cr. 8vo. 4s.
—— CIVIL GOVERNMENT IN THE UNITED STATES CONSIDERED WITH SOME REFERENCE TO ITS ORIGIN. Cr. 8vo. 6s. 6d.

FREEMAN (Prof. E. A.).—DISESTABLISHMENT AND DISENDOWMENT. WHAT ARE THEY? 4th Edit. Cr. 8vo. 1s.
—— COMPARATIVE POLITICS and THE UNITY OF HISTORY. 8vo. 14s.
—— THE GROWTH OF THE ENGLISH CONSTITUTION. 5th Edit. Cr. 8vo. 5s.

HARWOOD (George).—DISESTABLISHMENT; or, a Defence of the Principle of a National Church. 8vo. 12s.
—— THE COMING DEMOCRACY. Cr. 8vo. 6s.

HILL (Florence D.).—CHILDREN OF THE STATE. Ed. by FANNY FOWKE. Cr. 8vo. 6s.

HILL (Octavia).—OUR COMMON LAND, AND OTHER ESSAYS. Ext. fcp. 8vo. 3s. 6d.

HOLLAND (Prof. T. E.).—THE TREATY RELATIONS OF RUSSIA AND TURKEY, FROM 1774 TO 1853. Cr. 8vo. 2s.

JENKS (Prof. Edward).—THE GOVERNMENT OF VICTORIA (AUSTRALIA). 8vo. 14s.

JEPHSON (H.).—THE PLATFORM: ITS RISE AND PROGRESS. 2 vols. 8vo. 21s.

LOWELL (J. R.). (See COLLECTED WORKS.)

LUBBOCK (Sir J.). (See COLLECTED WORKS.)

MACDONELL (John).—THE LAND QUESTION. 8vo. 10s. 6d.

PALGRAVE (Reginald F. D.).—THE HOUSE OF COMMONS: Illustrations of its History and Practice. Cr. 8vo. 2s. 6d.

PALGRAVE (W. Gifford). — ESSAYS ON EASTERN QUESTIONS. 8vo. 10s. 6d.

PARKIN (G. R.).—IMPERIAL FEDERATION. Cr. 8vo. 4s. 6d.

POLLOCK (Sir F., Bart.).—INTRODUCTION TO THE HISTORY OF THE SCIENCE OF POLITICS. Cr. 8vo. 2s. 6d.
—— LEADING CASES DONE INTO ENGLISH. Crown 8vo. 3s. 6d.

PRACTICAL POLITICS. 8vo. 6s.

ROGERS (Prof. J. E. T.).—COBDEN AND POLITICAL OPINION. 8vo. 10s. 6d.

ROUTLEDGE (Jas.).—POPULAR PROGRESS IN ENGLAND. 8vo. 16s.

RUSSELL (Sir Charles).—NEW VIEWS ON IRELAND. Cr. 8vo. 2s. 6d.
—— THE PARNELL COMMISSION: THE OPENING SPEECH FOR THE DEFENCE. 8vo. 10s. 6d.
—Popular Edition. Sewed. 2s

SIDGWICK (Prof. Henry).—THE ELEMENTS OF POLITICS. 8vo. 14s. net.

SMITH (Goldwin).—CANADA AND THE CANADIAN QUESTION. 8vo. 8s. net.

STATESMAN'S YEAR-BOOK, THE. (See STATISTICS.)

STATHAM (R.). — BLACKS, BOERS, AND BRITISH. Cr. 8vo. 6s.

THORNTON (W. T.).—A PLEA FOR PEASANT PROPRIETORS. New Edit. Cr. 8vo. 7s. 6d.
—— INDIAN PUBLIC WORKS, AND COGNATE INDIAN TOPICS. Cr. 8vo. 8s. 6d.

TRENCH (Capt. F.).—THE RUSSO-INDIAN QUESTION. Cr. 8vo. 7s. 6d.

WALLACE (Sir Donald M.).—EGYPT AND THE EGYPTIAN QUESTION. 8vo. 14s.

PSYCHOLOGY.
(See under PHILOSOPHY, p. 26.)

SCULPTURE. (See ART.)

SOCIAL ECONOMY.

BOOTH (C.).—A PICTURE OF PAUPERISM. Cr. 8vo. 5s.—Cheap Edit. 8vo. Swd., 6d.

FAWCETT (H. and Mrs. H.). (See POLITICS.)

HILL (Octavia).—HOMES OF THE LONDON POOR. Cr. 8vo, sewed. 1s.

HUXLEY (Prof. T. H.).—SOCIAL DISEASES AND WORSE REMEDIES: Letters to the "Times." Cr. 8vo. sewed. 1s. net.

JEVONS (W. Stanley).—METHODS OF SOCIAL REFORM. 8vo. 10s. 6d.

STANLEY (Hon. Maude). — CLUBS FOR WORKING GIRLS. Cr. 8vo. 3s. 6d.

SOUND. (*See under* PHYSICS, p. 27.)

SPORT.

BAKER (Sir Samuel W.).—WILD BEASTS AND THEIR WAYS: REMINISCENCES OF EUROPE, ASIA, AFRICA, AMERICA, FROM 1845—88. Illustrated. Ext. cr. 8vo. 12s. 6d.

CHASSERESSE (D.).—SPORTING SKETCHES. Illustrated. Cr. 8vo. 3s. 6d.

EDWARDS-MOSS (Sir J. E., Bart).—A SEASON IN SUTHERLAND. Cr. 8vo. 1s. 6d.

STATISTICS.

STATESMAN'S YEAR-BOOK, THE. Statistical and Historical Annual of the States of the World for the Year 1892. Revised after Official Returns. Ed. by J. SCOTT KELTIE. Cr. 8vo. 10s. 6d.

SURGERY. (*See* MEDICINE.)

SWIMMING.

LEAHY (Sergeant).—THE ART OF SWIMMING IN THE ETON STYLE. Cr. 8vo. 2s.

THEOLOGY.

The Bible—History of the Christian Church—The Church of England—Devotional Books—The Fathers—Hymnology—Sermons, Lectures, Addresses, and Theological Essays.

The Bible.

History of the Bible—

THE ENGLISH BIBLE; An External and Critical History of the various English Translations of Scripture. By Prof. JOHN EADIE. 2 vols. 8vo. 28s.

THE BIBLE IN THE CHURCH. By Right Rev. Bp. WESTCOTT. 10th edit. 18mo. 4s. 6d.

Biblical History—

BIBLE LESSONS. By Rev. E. A. ABBOTT. Cr. 8vo. 4s. 6d.

SIDE-LIGHTS UPON BIBLE HISTORY. By Mrs. SYDNEY BUXTON. Cr. 8vo. 5s.

STORIES FROM THE BIBLE. By Rev. A. J. CHURCH. Illust. Cr. 8vo. 2 parts. 3s. 6d. each.

BIBLE READINGS SELECTED FROM THE PENTATEUCH AND THE BOOK OF JOSHUA. By Rev. J. A. CROSS. Gl. 8vo. 2s. 6d.

THE CHILDREN'S TREASURY OF BIBLE STORIES. By Mrs. H. GASKOIN. 18mo. 1s. each.—Part I. Old Testament; II. New Testament; III. The Apostles.

A CLASS-BOOK OF OLD TESTAMENT HISTORY. By Rev. Dr. MACLEAR. 18mo. 4s. 6d.

A CLASS-BOOK OF NEW TESTAMENT HISTORY. By the same. 18mo. 5s. 6d.

A SHILLING BOOK OF OLD TESTAMENT HISTORY. By the same. 18mo. 1s.

A SHILLING BOOK OF NEW TESTAMENT HISTORY. By the same. 18mo. 1s.

The Old Testament—

SCRIPTURE READINGS FOR SCHOOLS AND FAMILIES. By C. M. YONGE. Globe 8vo. 1s. 6d. each: also with comments, 3s. 6d. each. — GENESIS TO DEUTERONOMY.—JOSHUA TO SOLOMON.—KINGS AND THE PROPHETS.—THE GOSPEL TIMES.—APOSTOLIC TIMES.

THE PATRIARCHS AND LAWGIVERS OF THE OLD TESTAMENT. By F. D. MAURICE. 7th Edit. Cr. 8vo. 4s. 6d.

THE PROPHETS AND KINGS OF THE OLD TESTAMENT. By the same. Cr. 8vo. 6s.

THE CANON OF THE OLD TESTAMENT. By Prof. H. E. RYLE. Cr. 8vo. 6s.

The Pentateuch—

AN HISTORICO-CRITICAL INQUIRY INTO THE ORIGIN AND COMPOSITION OF THE HEXATEUCH (PENTATEUCH AND BOOK OF JOSHUA). By Prof. A. KUENEN. Trans. by P. H. WICKSTEED, M.A. 8vo. 14s.

The Psalms—

THE PSALMS CHRONOLOGICALLY ARRANGED. By FOUR FRIENDS. Cr. 8vo. 5s. net.

GOLDEN TREASURY PSALTER. Student's Edition of the above. 18mo. 3s. 6d.

THE PSALMS. With Introduction and Notes. By A. C. JENNINGS, M.A., and W. H. LOWE, M.A. 2 vols. Cr. 8vo. 10s. 6d. each.

INTRODUCTION TO THE STUDY AND USE OF THE PSALMS. By Rev. J. F. THRUPP. 2nd Edit. 2 vols. 8vo. 21s.

Isaiah—

ISAIAH XL.—LXVI. With the Shorter Prophecies allied to it. Edited by MATTHEW ARNOLD. Cr. 8vo. 5s.

ISAIAH OF JERUSALEM. In the Authorised English Version, with Introduction and Notes. By the same. Cr. 8vo. 4s. 6d.

A BIBLE-READING FOR SCHOOLS. The Great Prophecy of Israel's Restoration (Isaiah xl.—lxvi.). Arranged and Edited for Young Learners. By the same. 18mo. 1s.

COMMENTARY ON THE BOOK OF ISAIAH: Critical, Historical, and Prophetical; including a Revised English Translation. By T. R. BIRKS. 2nd Edit. 8vo. 12s. 6d.

THE BOOK OF ISAIAH CHRONOLOGICALLY ARRANGED. By T. K. CHEYNE. Cr. 8vo. 7s. 6d.

Zechariah—

THE HEBREW STUDENT'S COMMENTARY ON ZECHARIAH, Hebrew and LXX. By W. H. LOWE, M.A. 8vo. 10s. 6d.

The New Testament—

THE NEW TESTAMENT. Essay on the Right Estimation of MS. Evidence in the Text of the New Testament. By T. R. BIRKS. Cr. 8vo. 3s. 6d.

THE MESSAGES OF THE BOOKS. Discourses and Notes on the Books of the New Testament. By Archd. FARRAR. 8vo. 14s.

THE CLASSICAL ELEMENT IN THE NEW TESTAMENT. Considered as a Proof of its Genuineness, with an Appendix on the Oldest Authorities used in the Formation of the Canon. By C. H. HOOLE. 8vo. 10s. 6d.

ON A FRESH REVISION OF THE ENGLISH NEW TESTAMENT. With an Appendix on the last Petition of the Lord's Prayer. By Bishop LIGHTFOOT. Cr. 8vo. 7s. 6d.

THE UNITY OF THE NEW TESTAMENT. By F. D. MAURICE. 2 vols. Cr. 8vo. 12s.

A COMPANION TO THE GREEK TESTAMENT AND THE ENGLISH VERSION. By PHILIP SCHAFF, D.D. Cr. 8vo. 12s.

A GENERAL SURVEY OF THE HISTORY OF THE CANON OF THE NEW TESTAMENT DURING THE FIRST FOUR CENTURIES. By Bishop WESTCOTT. Cr. 8vo. 10s. 6d.

THE NEW TESTAMENT IN THE ORIGINAL GREEK. The Text revised by Bishop WESTCOTT, D.D., and Prof. F. J. A. HORT, D.D. 2 vols. Cr. 8vo. 10s. 6d. each.—Vol. I. Text.—Vol. II. Introduction and Appendix.

SCHOOL EDITION OF THE ABOVE. 18mo, 4s. 6d.; 18mo, roan, 5s. 6d.; morocco, gilt edges, 6s. 6d.

The Gospels—
THE COMMON TRADITION OF THE SYNOPTIC GOSPELS. In the Text of the Revised Version. By Rev. E. A. ABBOTT and W. G. RUSHBROOKE. Cr. 8vo. 3s. 6d.

SYNOPTICON: An Exposition of the Common Matter of the Synoptic Gospels. By W. G. RUSHBROOKE. Printed in Colours. In Six Parts, and Appendix. 4to.—Part I. 3s. 6d.—Parts II. and III. 7s.—Parts IV. V. and VI., with Indices, 10s. 6d.—Appendices, 10s. 6d.—Complete in 1 vol. 35s.

INTRODUCTION TO THE STUDY OF THE FOUR GOSPELS. By Bp. WESTCOTT. Cr. 8vo. 10s. 6d.

THE COMPOSITION OF THE FOUR GOSPELS. By Rev. ARTHUR WRIGHT. Cr. 8vo. 5s.

Gospel of St. Matthew—
THE GREEK TEXT, with Introduction and Notes by Rev. A. SLOMAN. Fcp. 8vo. 2s. 6d.

CHOICE NOTES ON ST. MATTHEW. Drawn from Old and New Sources. Cr. 8vo. 4s. 6d. (St. Matthew and St. Mark in 1 vol. 9s.)

Gospel of St. Mark—
SCHOOL READINGS IN THE GREEK TESTAMENT. Being the Outlines of the Life of our Lord as given by St. Mark, with additions from the Text of the other Evangelists. Edited, with Notes and Vocabulary, by Rev. A. CALVERT, M.A. Fcp. 8vo. 2s. 6d.

CHOICE NOTES ON ST. MARK. Drawn from Old and New Sources. Cr. 8vo. 4s. 6d. (St. Matthew and St. Mark in 1 vol. 9s.)

Gospel of St. Luke—
GREEK TEXT, with Introduction and Notes by Rev. J. BOND, M.A. Fcp. 8vo. 2s. 6d.

CHOICE NOTES ON ST. LUKE. Drawn from Old and New Sources. Cr. 8vo. 4s. 6d.

THE GOSPEL OF THE KINGDOM OF HEAVEN. A Course of Lectures on the Gospel of St. Luke. By F. D. MAURICE. Cr. 8vo. 6s.

Gospel of St. John—
THE GOSPEL OF ST. JOHN. By F. D. MAURICE. 8th Ed. Cr. 8vo. 6s.

CHOICE NOTES ON ST. JOHN. Drawn from Old and New Sources. Cr. 8vo. 4s. 6d.

The Acts of the Apostles—
GREEK TEXT, with Notes by T. E. PAGE, M.A. Fcp. 8vo. 3s. 6d.

THE CHURCH OF THE FIRST DAYS: THE CHURCH OF JERUSALEM, THE CHURCH OF THE GENTILES, THE CHURCH OF THE WORLD. Lectures on the Acts of the Apostles. By Very Rev. C. J. VAUGHAN. Cr. 8vo. 10s. 6d.

The Epistles of St. Paul—
THE EPISTLE TO THE ROMANS. The Greek Text, with English Notes. By the Very Rev. C. J. VAUGHAN. 7th Edit. Cr. 8vo. 7s. 6d.

THE EPISTLES TO THE CORINTHIANS. Greek Text, with Commentary. By Rev. W. KAY. 8vo. 9s.

THE EPISTLE TO THE GALATIANS. A Revised Text, with Introduction, Notes, and Dissertations. By Bishop LIGHTFOOT. 10th Edit. 8vo. 12s.

THE EPISTLE TO THE PHILIPPIANS. A Revised Text, with Introduction, Notes, and Dissertations. By the same. 8vo. 12s.

The Epistles of St. Paul—
THE EPISTLE TO THE PHILIPPIANS. With Translation, Paraphrase, and Notes for English Readers. By the Very Rev. C. J. VAUGHAN. Cr. 8vo. 5s.

THE EPISTLES TO THE COLOSSIANS AND TO PHILEMON. A Revised Text, with Introductions, etc. By Bishop LIGHTFOOT. 9th Edit. 8vo. 12s.

THE EPISTLES TO THE EPHESIANS, THE COLOSSIANS, AND PHILEMON. With Introduction and Notes. By Rev. J. Ll. DAVIES. 2nd Edit. 8vo. 7s. 6d.

THE FIRST EPISTLE TO THE THESSALONIANS. By Very Rev. C. J. VAUGHAN. 8vo, sewed. 1s. 6d.

THE EPISTLES TO THE THESSALONIANS. Commentary on the Greek Text. By Prof. JOHN EADIE. 8vo. 12s.

The Epistle of St. James—
THE GREEK TEXT, with Introduction and Notes. By Rev. JOSEPH MAYOR. 8vo.

The Epistles of St. John—
THE EPISTLES OF ST. JOHN. By F. D. MAURICE. 4th Edit. Cr. 8vo. 6s.

— The Greek Text, with Notes, by Bishop WESTCOTT. 3rd Edit. 8vo. 12s. 6d

The Epistle to the Hebrews—
GREEK AND ENGLISH. Edited by Rev. FREDERIC RENDALL. Cr. 8vo. 6s.

ENGLISH TEXT, with Commentary. By the same. Cr. 8vo. 7s. 6d.

THE GREEK TEXT, with Notes, by Very Rev. C. J. VAUGHAN. Cr. 8vo. 7s. 6d.

THE GREEK TEXT, with Notes and Essays, by Bishop WESTCOTT. 8vo. 14s.

Revelation—
LECTURES ON THE APOCALYPSE. By F. D. MAURICE. 2nd Edit. Cr. 8vo. 6s.

THE REVELATION OF ST. JOHN. By Rev. Prof. W. MILLIGAN. Cr. 8vo. 7s. 6d.

LECTURES ON THE APOCALYPSE. By the same. Crown 8vo. 5s.

LECTURES ON THE REVELATION OF ST. JOHN. By Very Rev. C. J. VAUGHAN. 5th Edit. Cr. 8vo. 10s. 6d.

THE BIBLE WORD-BOOK. By W. ALDIS WRIGHT. 2nd Edit. Cr. 8vo. 7s. 6d.

History of the Christian Church.

CHURCH (Dean).—THE OXFORD MOVEMENT, 1833—45. Gl. 8vo. 5s.

CUNNINGHAM (Rev. John).—THE GROWTH OF THE CHURCH IN ITS ORGANISATION AND INSTITUTIONS. 8vo. 9s.

CUNNINGHAM (Rev. William). — THE CHURCHES OF ASIA: A Methodical Sketch of the Second Century. Cr. 8vo. 6s.

DALE (A. W. W.).—THE SYNOD OF ELVIRA, AND CHRISTIAN LIFE IN THE FOURTH CENTURY. Cr. 8vo. 10s. 6d.

HARDWICK (Archdeacon).—A HISTORY OF THE CHRISTIAN CHURCH: MIDDLE AGE. Edited by Bp. STUBBS. Cr. 8vo. 10s. 6d.

—— A HISTORY OF THE CHRISTIAN CHURCH DURING THE REFORMATION. 9th Edit., revised by Bishop STUBBS. Cr. 8vo. 10s. 6d.

THEOLOGY.

History of the Christian Church—*contd.*

HORT (Dr. F. J. A.).—TWO DISSERTATIONS. I. ON ΜΟΝΟΓΕΝΗΣ ΘΕΟΣ IN SCRIPTURE AND TRADITION. II. ON THE "CONSTANTINOPOLITAN" CREED AND OTHER EASTERN CREEDS OF THE FOURTH CENTURY. 8vo. 7s. 6d.

KILLEN (W. D.).—ECCLESIASTICAL HISTORY OF IRELAND, FROM THE EARLIEST DATE TO THE PRESENT TIME. 2 vols. 8vo. 25s.

SIMPSON (Rev. W.).—AN EPITOME OF THE HISTORY OF THE CHRISTIAN CHURCH. 7th Edit. Fcp. 8vo. 3s. 6d.

VAUGHAN (Very Rev. C. J.).—THE CHURCH OF THE FIRST DAYS: THE CHURCH OF JERUSALEM, THE CHURCH OF THE GENTILES, THE CHURCH OF THE WORLD. Cr. 8vo. 10s. 6d.

WARD (W.).—WILLIAM GEORGE WARD AND THE OXFORD MOVEMENT. 8vo. 14s.

The Church of England.

Catechism of—

A CLASS-BOOK OF THE CATECHISM OF THE CHURCH OF ENGLAND. By Rev. Canon MACLEAR. 18mo. 1s. 6d.

A FIRST CLASS-BOOK OF THE CATECHISM OF THE CHURCH OF ENGLAND. By the same. 18mo. 6d.

THE ORDER OF CONFIRMATION. With Prayers and Devotions. By the same. 32mo. 6d.

Collects—

COLLECTS OF THE CHURCH OF ENGLAND. With a Coloured Floral Design to each Collect. Cr. 8vo. 12s.

Disestablishment—

DISESTABLISHMENT AND DISENDOWMENT. WHAT ARE THEY? By Prof. E. A. FREEMAN. 4th Edit. Cr. 8vo. 1s.

DISESTABLISHMENT; or, A Defence of the Principle of a National Church. By GEO. HARWOOD. 8vo. 12s.

A DEFENCE OF THE CHURCH OF ENGLAND AGAINST DISESTABLISHMENT. By ROUNDELL, EARL OF SELBORNE. Cr. 8vo. 2s. 6d.

ANCIENT FACTS AND FICTIONS CONCERNING CHURCHES AND TITHES. By the same. 2nd Edit. Cr. 8vo. 7s. 6d.

Dissent in its Relation to—

DISSENT IN ITS RELATION TO THE CHURCH OF ENGLAND. By Rev. G. H. CURTEIS. Bampton Lectures for 1871. Cr. 8vo. 7s. 6d.

Holy Communion—

THE COMMUNION SERVICE FROM THE BOOK OF COMMON PRAYER. With Select Readings from the Writings of the Rev. F. D. MAURICE. Edited by Bishop COLENSO. 6th Edit. 16mo. 2s. 6d.

BEFORE THE TABLE: An Inquiry, Historical and Theological, into the Meaning of the Consecration Rubric in the Communion Service of the Church of England. By Very Rev. J. S. HOWSON. 8vo. 7s. 6d.

FIRST COMMUNION. With Prayers and Devotions for the newly Confirmed. By Rev. Canon MACLEAR. 32mo. 6d.

A MANUAL OF INSTRUCTION FOR CONFIRMATION AND FIRST COMMUNION. With Prayers and Devotions. By the same. 32mo. 2s.

Liturgy—

AN INTRODUCTION TO THE CREEDS. By Rev. Canon MACLEAR. 18mo. 3s. 6d.

AN INTRODUCTION TO THE THIRTY-NINE ARTICLES. By same. 18mo. [*In the Press.*

A HISTORY OF THE BOOK OF COMMON PRAYER. By Rev. F. PROCTER. 18th Edit. Cr. 8vo. 10s. 6d.

AN ELEMENTAY INTRODUCTION TO THE BOOK OF COMMON PRAYER. By Rev. F. PROCTER and Rev. Canon MACLEAR. 18mo. 2s. 6d.

TWELVE DISCOURSES ON SUBJECTS CONNECTED WITH THE LITURGY AND WORSHIP OF THE CHURCH OF ENGLAND. By Very Rev. C. J. VAUGHAN. Fcp. 8vo. 6s.

A COMPANION TO THE LECTIONARY. By Rev. W. BENHAM, B.D. Cr. 8vo. 4s. 6d.

———

JUDGMENT IN THE CASE OF READ AND OTHERS *v.* THE LORD BISHOP OF LINCOLN. Nov. 21, 1890. By his Grace the ARCHBISHOP OF CANTERBURY. 8vo. 1s. 6d. net.

Devotional Books.

EASTLAKE (Lady).—FELLOWSHIP: LETTERS ADDRESSED TO MY SISTER-MOURNERS. Cr. 8vo. 2s. 6d.

IMITATIO CHRISTI. Libri IV. Printed in Borders after Holbein, Dürer, and other old Masters, containing Dances of Death, Acts of Mercy, Emblems, etc. Cr. 8vo. 7s. 6d.

KINGSLEY (Charles).—OUT OF THE DEEP WORDS FOR THE SORROWFUL. From the Writings of CHARLES KINGSLEY. Ext. fcp. 8vo. 3s. 6d.

—— DAILY THOUGHTS. Selected from the Writings of CHARLES KINGSLEY. By His WIFE. Cr. 8vo. 6s.

—— FROM DEATH TO LIFE. Fragments of Teaching to a Village Congregation. Edit. by His WIFE. Fcp. 8vo. 2s. 6d.

MACLEAR (Rev. Canon).—A MANUAL OF INSTRUCTION FOR CONFIRMATION AND FIRST COMMUNION, WITH PRAYERS AND DEVOTIONS. 32mo. 2s.

—— THE HOUR OF SORROW; or, The Office for the Burial of the Dead. 32mo. 2s.

MAURICE (F. D.).—LESSONS OF HOPE. Readings from the Works of F. D. MAURICE. Selected by Rev. J. LL. DAVIES, M.A. Cr. 8vo. 5s.

RAYS OF SUNLIGHT FOR DARK DAYS. With a Preface by Very Rev. C. J. VAUGHAN. D.D. New Edition. 18mo. 3s. 6d.

SERVICE (Rev. J.).—PRAYERS FOR PUBLIC WORSHIP. Cr. 8vo. 4s. 6d.

THE WORSHIP OF GOD, AND FELLOWSHIP AMONG MEN. By Prof. MAURICE and others. Fcp. 8vo. 3s. 6d.

WELBY-GREGORY (Hon. Lady).—LINKS AND CLUES. 2nd Edit. Cr. 8vo. 6s.

WESTCOTT (Rt. Rev. Bishop).—THOUGHTS ON REVELATION AND LIFE. Selections from the Writings of Bishop WESTCOTT. Edited by Rev. S. PHILLIPS. Cr. 8vo. 6s.

WILBRAHAM (Francis M.).—IN THE SERE AND YELLOW LEAF: THOUGHTS AND RECOLLECTIONS FOR OLD AND YOUNG. Globe 8vo. 3s. 6d.

The Fathers.

DONALDSON (Prof. James).—THE APOSTOLIC FATHERS. A Critical Account of their Genuine Writings, and of their Doctrines. 2nd Edit. Cr. 8vo. 7s. 6d.

Works of the Greek and Latin Fathers:
THE APOSTOLIC FATHERS. Revised Texts, with Introductions, Notes, Dissertations, and Translations. By Bishop LIGHTFOOT. —Part I. ST. CLEMENT OF ROME. 2 vols. 8vo. 32s.—Part II. ST. IGNATIUS TO ST. POLYCARP. 3 vols. 2nd Edit. 8vo. 48s.
THE APOSTOLIC FATHERS. Abridged Edit. With Short Introductions, Greek Text, and English Translation. By same. 8vo. 16s.
THE EPISTLE OF ST. BARNABAS. Its Date and Authorship. With Greek Text, Latin Version, Translation and Commentary. By Rev. W. CUNNINGHAM. Cr. 8vo. 7s. 6d.

Hymnology.

BROOKE (S. A.).—CHRISTIAN HYMNS. Gl. 8vo. 2s. 6d. net.--CHRISTIAN HYMNS AND SERVICE BOOK OF BEDFORD CHAPEL, BLOOMSBURY. Gl. 8vo. 3s. 6d. net.—SERVICE BOOK Gl. 8vo. 1s. net.

PALGRAVE (Prof. F. T.). — ORIGINAL HYMNS. 3rd Edit. 18mo. 1s. 6d.

SELBORNE (Roundell, Earl of).—THE BOOK OF PRAISE. 18mo. 2s. 6d. net.
—— A HYMNAL. Chiefly from " The Book of Praise."—A. Royal 32mo, limp. 6d.—B. 18mo, larger type. 1s.—C. Fine paper. 1s. 6d. —With Music, Selected, Harmonised, and Composed by JOHN HULLAH. 18mo. 3s. 6d.

WOODS (Miss M. A.).—HYMNS FOR SCHOOL WORSHIP. 18mo. 1s. 6d.

Sermons, Lectures, Addresses, and Theological Essays.

ABBOT (F. E.).—SCIENTIFIC THEISM. Cr. 8vo. 7s. 6d.
—— THE WAY OUT OF AGNOSTICISM ; or, The Philosophy of Free Religion. Cr. 8vo. 4s. 6d.

ABBOTT (Rev. E. A.).—CAMBRIDGE SERMONS. 8vo. 6s.
—— OXFORD SERMONS. 8vo. 7s. 6d.
—— PHILOMYTHUS. A discussion of Cardinal Newman's Essay on Ecclesiastical Miracles. Cr. 8vo. 3s. 6d.
—— NEWMANIANISM. Cr. 8vo. 1s. net.

AINGER (Canon).—SERMONS PREACHED IN THE TEMPLE CHURCH. Ext. fcp. 8vo. 6s.

ALEXANDER (W., Bishop of Derry and Raphoe).—THE LEADING IDEAS OF THE GOSPELS. New Edit. Cr. 8vo. 6s.

BAINES (Rev. Edward).—SERMONS. Preface and Memoir by Bishop BARRY. Cr. 8vo. 6s.

BATHER (Archdeacon).—ON SOME MINISTERIAL DUTIES, CATECHISING, PREACHING, Etc. Edited, with a Preface, by Very Rev. C. J. VAUGHAN, D.D. Fcp. 8vo. 4s. 6d.

BERNARD (Canon).—THE CENTRAL TEACHING OF CHRIST. Cr. 8vo. [*In the Press.*

BETHUNE-BAKER (J. F.).—THE INFLUENCE OF CHRISTIANITY ON WAR. 8vo. 5s.
—— THE STERNNESS OF CHRIST'S TEACHING, AND ITS RELATION TO THE LAW OF FORGIVENESS. Cr. 8vo. 2s. 6d.

BINNIE (Rev. W.).—SERMONS. Cr. 8vo. 6s.

BIRKS (Thomas Rawson).—THE DIFFICULTIES OF BELIEF IN CONNECTION WITH THE CREATION AND THE FALL, REDEMPTION, AND JUDGMENT. 2nd Edit. Cr. 8vo. 5s.
—— JUSTIFICATION AND IMPUTED RIGHTEOUSNESS. A Review. Cr. 8vo. 6s.
—— SUPERNATURAL REVELATION ; or, First Principles of Moral Theology. 8vo. 8s.

BROOKE S. A.).—SHORT SERMONS. Crown 8vo. 6s.

BROOKS (Bishop Phillips).—THE CANDLE OF THE LORD : and other Sermons. Cr. 8vo. 6s.
—— SERMONS PREACHED IN ENGLISH CHURCHES. Cr. 8vo. 6s.
—— TWENTY SERMONS. Cr. 8vo. 6s.
—— TOLERANCE. Cr. 8vo. 2s. 6d.
—— THE LIGHT OF THE WORLD. Cr. 8vo. 3s. 6d.

BRUNTON (T. Lauder).—THE BIBLE AND SCIENCE. Illustrated. Cr. 8vo. 10s. 6d.

BUTLER (Archer).—SERMONS, DOCTRINAL AND PRACTICAL. 11th Edit. 8vo. 8s.
—— SECOND SERIES OF SERMONS. 8vo. 7s.
—— LETTERS ON ROMANISM. 8vo. 10s. 6d.

BUTLER (Rev. Geo.).—SERMONS PREACHED IN CHELTENHAM COLL. CHAPEL. 8vo. 7s. 6d.

CAMPBELL (Dr. John M'Leod).—THE NATURE OF THE ATONEMENT. Cr. 8vo. 6s.
—— REMINISCENCES AND REFLECTIONS. Edited by his Son, DONALD CAMPBELL, M.A. Cr. 8vo. 7s. 6d.
—— THOUGHTS ON REVELATION. Cr. 8vo. 5s.
—— RESPONSIBILITY FOR THE GIFT OF ETERNAL LIFE. Compiled from Sermons preached 1829—31. Cr. 8vo. 5s.

CANTERBURY (Edward White, Archbishop of).—BOY-LIFE : ITS TRIAL, ITS STRENGTH, ITS FULNESS. Sundays in Wellington College, 1859—73. Cr. 8vo. 6s.
—— THE SEVEN GIFTS. Primary Visitation Address. Cr. 8vo. 6s.
—— CHRIST AND HIS TIMES. Second Visitation Address. Cr. 8vo. 6s.
—— A PASTORAL LETTER TO THE DIOCESE OF CANTERBURY, 1890. 8vo, sewed. 1d.

CARPENTER (W. Boyd, Bishop of Ripon).— TRUTH IN TALE. Addresses, chiefly to Children. Cr. 8vo. 4s. 6d.
—— THE PERMANENT ELEMENTS OF RELIGION. 2nd Edit. Cr. 8vo. 6s.

CAZENOVE (J. Gibson).—CONCERNING THE BEING AND ATTRIBUTES OF GOD. 8vo. 5s.

CHURCH (Dean).—HUMAN LIFE AND ITS CONDITIONS. Cr. 8vo. 6s.
—— THE GIFTS OF CIVILISATION : and other Sermons and Letters. Cr. 8vo. 7s. 6d.
—— DISCIPLINE OF THE CHRISTIAN CHARACTER ; and other Sermons. Cr. 8vo. 4s. 6d.
—— ADVENT SERMONS, 1885. Cr. 8vo. 4s. 6d.
—— VILLAGE SERMONS. Cr. 8vo. 6s.
—— CATHEDRAL AND UNIVERSITY SERMONS.

CLERGYMAN'S SELF-EXAMINATION CONCERNING THE APOSTLES' CREED. Ext. fcp. 8vo. 1s. 6d.

CONGREVE (Rev. John). — HIGH HOPES AND PLEADINGS FOR A REASONABLE FAITH, NOBLER THOUGHTS, AND LARGER CHARITY. Cr. 8vo. 5s.

THEOLOGY.
Sermons, Lectures, Addresses, and Theological Essays—*continued.*

COOKE (Josiah P., jun.).—RELIGION AND CHEMISTRY. Cr. 8vo. 7s. 6d.

COTTON (Bishop).—SERMONS PREACHED TO ENGLISH CONGREGATIONS IN INDIA. Cr. 8vo. 7s. 6d.

CUNNINGHAM (Rev. W.). — CHRISTIAN CIVILISATION, WITH SPECIAL REFERENCE TO INDIA. Cr. 8vo. 5s.

CURTEIS (Rev. G. H.).—THE SCIENTIFIC OBSTACLES TO CHRISTIAN BELIEF. The Boyle Lectures, 1884. Cr. 8vo. 6s.

DAVIES (Rev. J. Llewelyn).—THE GOSPEL AND MODERN LIFE. Ext. fcp. 8vo. 6s.
—— SOCIAL QUESTIONS FROM THE POINT OF VIEW OF CHRISTIAN THEOLOGY. Cr.8vo. 6s.
—— WARNINGS AGAINST SUPERSTITION. Ext. fcp. 8vo. 2s. 6d.
—— THE CHRISTIAN CALLING. Ext.fp.8vo, 6s.
—— ORDER AND GROWTH AS INVOLVED IN THE SPIRITUAL CONSTITUTION OF HUMAN SOCIETY. Cr. 8vo. 3s. 6d.
—— BAPTISM, CONFIRMATION, AND THE LORD'S SUPPER. Addresses. 18mo. 1s.

DIGGLE (Rev. J. W.).—GODLINESS AND MANLINESS. Cr. 8vo. 6s.

DRUMMOND (Prof. Jas.).—INTRODUCTION TO THE STUDY OF THEOLOGY. Cr. 8vo. 5s.

DU BOSE (W. P.).—THE SOTERIOLOGY OF THE NEW TESTAMENT. By W. P. Du Bose. Cr. 8vo. 7s. 6d.

ECCE HOMO: A SURVEY OF THE LIFE AND WORK OF JESUS CHRIST. Globe 8vo. 6s.

ELLERTON (Rev. John).—THE HOLIEST MANHOOD, AND ITS LESSONS FOR BUSY LIVES. Cr. 8vo. 6s.

FAITH AND CONDUCT: AN ESSAY ON VERIFIABLE RELIGION. Cr. 8vo. 7s. 6d.

FARRAR (Ven. Archdeacon).—WORKS. *Uniform Edition.* Cr. 8vo. 3s. 6d. each. Monthly from December, 1891.

   SEEKERS AFTER GOD.
   ETERNAL HOPE. Westminster Abbey Sermons.
   THE FALL OF MAN: and other Sermons.
   THE WITNESS OF HISTORY TO CHRIST. Hulsean Lectures, 1870.
   THE SILENCE AND VOICES OF GOD. Sermons.
   IN THE DAYS OF THY YOUTH. Marlborough College Sermons.
   SAINTLY WORKERS. Five Lenten Lectures.
   EPHPHATHA; or, The Amelioration of the MERCY AND JUDGMENT. [World.
   SERMONS AND ADDRESSES DELIVERED IN AMERICA.
—— THE HISTORY OF INTERPRETATION. Bampton Lectures, 1885. 8vo. 16s.

FISKE (John).—MAN'S DESTINY VIEWED IN THE LIGHT OF HIS ORIGIN. Cr. 8vo. 3s. 6d.

FORBES (Rev. Granville).—THE VOICE OF GOD IN THE PSALMS. Cr. 8vo. 6s. 6d.

FOWLE (Rev. T. W.).—A NEW ANALOGY BETWEEN REVEALED RELIGION AND THE COURSE AND CONSTITUTION OF NATURE. Cr. 8vo. 6s.

FRASER (Bishop).—SERMONS. Edited by JOHN W. DIGGLE. 2 vols. Cr. 8vo. 6s. each.

HAMILTON (John).—ON TRUTH AND ERROR. Cr. 8vo. 5s.
—— ARTHUR'S SEAT; or, The Church of the Banned. Cr. 8vo. 6s.
—— ABOVE AND AROUND: Thoughts on God and Man. 12mo. 2s. 6d.

HARDWICK (Archdeacon).—CHRIST AND OTHER MASTERS. 6th Edit. Cr. 8vo. 10s.6d.

HARE (Julius Charles).—THE MISSION OF THE COMFORTER. New Edition. Edited by Dean PLUMPTRE. Cr. 8vo. 7s. 6d.
—— THE VICTORY OF FAITH. Edited by Dean PLUMPTRE. With Notices by Prof. MAURICE and Dean STANLEY. Cr. 8vo. 6s.6d.

HARPER (Father Thomas).—THE METAPHYSICS OF THE SCHOOL. Vols. I. and II. 8vo. 18s. each.—Vol. III. Part I. 12s.

HARRIS (Rev. G. C.).—SERMONS. With a Memoir by C. M. YONGE. Ext. fcp. 8vo. 6s.

HUTTON (R. H.). (*See* p. 21.)

ILLINGWORTH (Rev. J. R.).—SERMONS PREACHED IN A COLLEGE CHAPEL. Cr.8vo. 5s.

JACOB (Rev. J. A.).—BUILDING IN SILENCE: and other Sermons. Ext. fcp. 8vo. 6s.

JAMES (Rev. Herbert). — THE COUNTRY CLERGYMAN AND HIS WORK. Cr. 8vo. 6s.

JEANS (Rev. G. E.).—HAILEYBURY CHAPEL: and other Sermons. Fcp. 8vo. 3s. 6d.

JELLETT (Rev. Dr.).—THE ELDER SON: and other Sermons. Cr. 8vo. 6s.
—— THE EFFICACY OF PRAYER. Cr 8vo. 5s.

KELLOGG (Rev. S. H.).—THE LIGHT OF ASIA AND THE LIGHT OF THE WORLD. Cr. 8vo. 7s. 6d.

KINGSLEY (Charles). (*See* COLLECTED WORKS, p. 21.)

KIRKPATRICK (Prof.).—THE DIVINE LIBRARY OF THE OLD TESTAMENT. Cr. 8vo. 3s. net.
—— WARBURTONIAN LECTURES ON THE MINOR PROPHETS. Cr. 8vo.

KYNASTON (Rev. Herbert, D.D.).—CHELTENHAM COLLEGE SERMONS. Cr. 8vo. 6s.

LEGGE (A. O.).—THE GROWTH OF THE TEMPORAL POWER OF THE PAPACY. Cr.8vo. 8s.6d.

LIGHTFOOT (Bishop).—LEADERS IN THE NORTHERN CHURCH: Sermons. Cr. 8vo. 6s.
—— ORDINATION ADDRESSES AND COUNSELS TO CLERGY. Cr. 8vo. 6s.
—— CAMBRIDGE SERMONS. Cr. 8vo. 6s.
—— SERMONS PREACHED IN ST. PAUL'S CATHEDRAL. Cr. 8vo. 6s.
—— SERMONS ON SPECIAL OCCASIONS. 8vo. 6s.
—— A CHARGE DELIVERED TO THE CLERGY OF THE DIOCESE OF DURHAM, 1886. 8vo. 2s.
—— ESSAYS ON THE WORK ENTITLED "SUPERNATURAL RELIGION." 8vo. 10s. 6d.
—— ON A FRESH REVISION OF THE ENGLISH NEW TESTAMENT. Cr. 8vo. 7s. 6d.
—— ESSAYS 2 vols. 8vo. I. DISSERTATIONS ON THE APOSTOLIC AGE. II. MISCELLANEOUS. [*In the Press.*

MACLAREN (Rev. A.).—SERMONS PREACHED AT MANCHESTER. 11th Ed. Fcp. 8vo. 4s. 6d.
—— SECOND SERIES. 7th Ed. Fcp. 8vo 4s. 6d.
—— THIRD SERIES. 6th Ed. Fcp. 8vo. 4s.6d.
—— WEEK-DAY EVENING ADDRESSES. 4th Edit. Fcp. 8vo. 2s. 6d.
—— THE SECRET OF POWER: and other Sermons. Fcp. 8vo. 4s. 6d.

MACMILLAN (Rev. Hugh).—BIBLE TEACHINGS IN NATURE. 15th Edit. Globe 8vo. 6s.
—— THE TRUE VINE; or, The Analogies of our Lord's Allegory. 5th Edit. Gl. 8vo. 6s.
—— THE MINISTRY OF NATURE. 8th Edit. Globe 8vo. 6s.
—— THE SABBATH OF THE FIELDS. 6th Edit. Globe 8vo. 6s.
—— THE MARRIAGE IN CANA. Globe 8vo. 6s.
—— TWO WORLDS ARE OURS. Gl. 8vo. 6s.
—— THE OLIVE LEAF. Globe 8vo. 6s.
—— THE GATE BEAUTIFUL: and other Bible Teachings for the Young. Cr. 8vo. 3s. 6d.

MAHAFFY (Prof. J. P.).—THE DECAY OF MODERN PREACHING. Cr. 8vo. 3s. 6d.

MATURIN (Rev. W.).—THE BLESSEDNESS OF THE DEAD IN CHRIST. Cr. 8vo. 7s. 6d.

MAURICE (Frederick Denison).—THE KINGDOM OF CHRIST. 3rd Ed. 2 vols. Cr. 8vo. 12s.
—— EXPOSITORY SERMONS ON THE PRAYER-BOOK, AND THE LORD'S PRAYER. Cr. 8vo. 6s.
—— SERMONS PREACHED IN COUNTRY CHURCHES. 2nd Edit. Cr. 8vo. 6s.
—— THE CONSCIENCE: Lectures on Casuistry. 3rd Edit. Cr. 8vo. 4s. 6d.
—— DIALOGUES ON FAMILY WORSHIP. Cr. 8vo. 4s. 6d.
—— THE DOCTRINE OF SACRIFICE DEDUCED FROM THE SCRIPTURES. 2nd Edit. Cr. 8vo. 6s.
—— THE RELIGIONS OF THE WORLD. 6th Edit. Cr. 8vo. 4s. 6d.
—— ON THE SABBATH DAY; THE CHARACTER OF THE WARRIOR; AND ON THE INTERPRETATION OF HISTORY. Fcp. 8vo. 2s. 6d.
—— LEARNING AND WORKING. Cr. 8vo. 4s. 6d.
—— THE LORD'S PRAYER, THE CREED, AND THE COMMANDMENTS. 18mo. 1s.
—— THEOLOGICAL ESSAYS. Cr. 8vo. 6s.
—— SERMONS PREACHED IN LINCOLN'S INN CHAPEL. 6 vols. Cr. 8vo. 3s. 6d. each.

MILLIGAN (Rev. Prof. W.).—THE RESURRECTION OF OUR LORD. 2nd Edit. Cr. 8vo. 5s.
—— THE ASCENSION AND HEAVENLY PRIESTHOOD OF OUR LORD. Cr. 8vo. 7s. 6d.

MOORHOUSE (J., Bishop of Manchester).—JACOB: Three Sermons. Ext. fcp. 8vo. 3s. 6d.
—— THE TEACHING OF CHRIST: its Conditions, Secret, and Results. Cr. 8vo. 3s. net.

MYLNE (L. G., Bishop of Bombay). —SERMONS PREACHED IN ST. THOMAS'S CATHEDRAL, BOMBAY. Cr. 8vo. 6s.

NATURAL RELIGION. By the Author of "Ecce Homo." 3rd Edit. Globe 8vo. 6s.

PATTISON (Mark).—SERMONS. Cr. 8vo. 6s.

PAUL OF TARSUS. 8vo. 10s. 6d.

PHILOCHRISTUS: MEMOIRS OF A DISCIPLE OF THE LORD. 3rd. Edit. 8vo. 12s.

PLUMPTRE (Dean).—MOVEMENTS IN RELIGIOUS THOUGHT. Fcp. 8vo. 3s. 6d.

POTTER (R.).—THE RELATION OF ETHICS TO RELIGION. Cr. 8vo. 2s. 6d.

REASONABLE FAITH: A SHORT ESSAY By "Three Friends." Cr. 8vo. 1s.

REICHEL (C. P., Bishop of Meath).—THE LORD'S PRAYER. Cr. 8vo. 7s. 6d.
—— CATHEDRAL AND UNIVERSITY SERMONS. Cr. 8vo. 6s.

RENDALL (Rev. F.).—THE THEOLOGY OF THE HEBREW CHRISTIANS. Cr. 8vo. 5s.

REYNOLDS (H. R.).—NOTES OF THE CHRISTIAN LIFE. Cr. 8vo. 7s. 6d.

ROBINSON (Prebendary H. G.).—MAN IN THE IMAGE OF GOD: and other Sermons. Cr. 8vo. 7s. 6d.

RUSSELL (Dean).—THE LIGHT THAT LIGHTETH EVERY MAN: Sermons. With an Introduction by Dean PLUMPTRE, D D. Cr. 8vo. 6s.

RYLE (Rev. Prof. H.).—THE EARLY NARRATIVES OF GENESIS. Cr. 8vo. [In the Press.

SALMON (Rev. George, D.D.).—NON-MIRACULOUS CHRISTIANITY: and other Sermons. 2nd Edit. Cr. 8vo. 6s.
—— GNOSTICISM AND AGNOSTICISM: and other Sermons. Cr. 8vo. 7s. 6d.

SANDFORD (Rt. Rev. C. W., Bishop of Gibraltar).—COUNSEL TO ENGLISH CHURCHMEN ABROAD. Cr. 8vo.

SCOTCH SERMONS, 1880. By Principal CAIRD and others. 3rd Edit. 8vo. 10s. 6d.

SERVICE (Rev. J.).—SERMONS. Cr. 8vo. 6s.

SHIRLEY (W. N.).—ELIJAH: Four University Sermons. Fcp. 8vo. 2s. 6d.

SMITH (Rev. Travers).—MAN'S KNOWLEDGE OF MAN AND OF GOD. Cr. 8vo. 6s.

SMITH (W. Saumarez).—THE BLOOD OF THE NEW COVENANT: An Essay. Cr. 8vo. 2s. 6d.

STANLEY (Dean).—THE NATIONAL THANKSGIVING. Sermons Preached in Westminster Abbey. 2nd Edit. Cr. 8vo. 2s. 6d.
—— ADDRESSES AND SERMONS delivered in America, 1878. Cr. 8vo. 6s.

STEWART (Prof. Balfour) and TAIT (Prof. P. G.).—THE UNSEEN UNIVERSE, OR PHYSICAL SPECULATIONS ON A FUTURE STATE. 15th Edit. Cr. 8vo. 6s.
—— PARADOXICAL PHILOSOPHY: A Sequel to the above. Cr. 8vo. 7s. 6d.

STUBBS (Rev. C. W.).—FOR CHRIST AND CITY. Sermons and Addresses. Cr. 8vo. 6s.

TAIT (Archbp.).—THE PRESENT CONDITION OF THE CHURCH OF ENGLAND. Primary Visitation Charge. 3rd Edit. 8vo. 3s. 6d.
—— DUTIES OF THE CHURCH OF ENGLAND. Second Visitation Addresses. 8vo. 4s. 6d.
—— THE CHURCH OF THE FUTURE. Quadrennial Visitation Charges. Cr. 8vo. 3s. 6d.

TAYLOR (Isaac).—THE RESTORATION OF BELIEF. Cr. 8vo. 8s. 6d.

TEMPLE (Frederick, Bishop of London).—SERMONS PREACHED IN THE CHAPEL OF RUGBY SCHOOL. SECOND SERIES. Ext. fcp. 8vo. 6s.
—— THIRD SERIES. 4th Edit. Ext. fcp. 8vo. 6s.
—— THE RELATIONS BETWEEN RELIGION AND SCIENCE. Bampton Lectures, 1884. 7th and Cheaper Edition. Cr. 8vo. 6s.

TRENCH (Archbishop). — THE HULSEAN LECTURES FOR 1845—6. 8vo. 7s. 6d.

TULLOCH (Principal).—THE CHRIST OF THE GOSPELS AND THE CHRIST OF MODERN CRITICISM. Ext. fcp. 8vo. 4s. 6d.

VAUGHAN (C. J., Dean of Landaff).—MEMORIALS OF HARROW SUNDAYS. 8vo. 10s. 6d.
—— EPIPHANY, LENT, AND EASTER. 8vo. 10s. 6d.
—— HEROES OF FAITH. 2nd Edit. Cr. 8vo. 6s.

THEOLOGY.
Sermons, Lectures, Addresses, and Theological Essays—*continued.*

VAUGHAN (Dr. C. J.).—LIFE'S WORK AND GOD'S DISCIPLINE. Ext. fcp. 8vo. 2s. 6d.

—— THE WHOLESOME WORDS OF JESUS CHRIST. 2nd Edit. Fcp. 8vo. 3s. 6d.

—— FOES OF FAITH. 2nd Edit. Fcp. 8vo. 3s. 6d.

—— CHRIST SATISFYING THE INSTINCTS OF HUMANITY. 2nd Edit. Ext. fcp. 8vo. 3s. 6d.

—— COUNSELS FOR YOUNG STUDENTS. Fcp. 8vo. 2s. 6d.

—— THE TWO GREAT TEMPTATIONS. 2nd Edit. Fcp. 8vo. 3s. 6d.

—— ADDRESSES FOR YOUNG CLERGYMEN. Ext. fcp. 8vo. 4s. 6d.

—— "MY SON, GIVE ME THINE HEART." Ext. fcp. 8vo. 5s.

—— REST AWHILE. Addresses to Toilers in the Ministry. Ext. fcp. 8vo. 5s.

—— TEMPLE SERMONS. Cr. 8vo. 10s. 6d.

—— AUTHORISED OR REVISED? Sermons. Cr. 8vo. 7s. 6d.

—— LESSONS OF THE CROSS AND PASSION; WORDS FROM THE CROSS; THE REIGN OF SIN; THE LORD'S PRAYER. Four Courses of Lent Lectures. Cr. 8vo. 10s. 6d.

—— UNIVERSITY SERMONS, NEW AND OLD. Cr. 8vo. 10s. 6d.

—— THE PRAYERS OF JESUS CHRIST. Globe 8vo. 3s. 6d.

—— DONCASTER SERMONS; LESSONS OF LIFE AND GODLINESS; WORDS FROM THE GOSPELS. Cr. 8vo. 10s. 6d.

—— NOTES FOR LECTURES ON CONFIRMATION. 14th Edit. Fcp. 8vo. 1s. 6d.

VAUGHAN (Rev. D. J.).—THE PRESENT TRIAL OF FAITH. Cr. 8vo. 9s.

VAUGHAN (Rev. E. T.)—SOME REASONS OF OUR CHRISTIAN HOPE. Hulsean Lectures for 1875. Cr. 8vo. 6s. 6d.

VAUGHAN (Rev. Robert).—STONES FROM THE QUARRY. Sermons. Cr. 8vo. 5s.

VENN (Rev. John).—ON SOME CHARACTERISTICS OF BELIEF, SCIENTIFIC, AND RELIGIOUS. Hulsean Lectures, 1869. 8vo. 6s. 6d.

WARINGTON (G.).—THE WEEK OF CREATION. Cr. 8vo. 4s. 6d.

WELLDON (Rev. J. E. C.).—THE SPIRITUAL LIFE: and other Sermons. Cr. 8vo. 6s.

WESTCOTT (Rt. Rev. B. F., Bishop of Durham).—ON THE RELIGIOUS OFFICE OF THE UNIVERSITIES. Sermons. Cr. 8vo. 4s. 6d.

—— GIFTS FOR MINISTRY. Addresses to Candidates for Ordination. Cr. 8vo. 1s. 6d.

—— THE VICTORY OF THE CROSS. Sermons Preached in 1888. Cr. 8vo. 3s. 6d.

—— FROM STRENGTH TO STRENGTH. Three Sermons (In Memoriam J. B. D.). Cr. 8vo. 2s.

—— THE REVELATION OF THE RISEN LORD. 4th Edit. Cr. 8vo. 6s.

—— THE HISTORIC FAITH. Cr. 8vo. 6s.

—— THE GOSPEL OF THE RESURRECTION. 6th Edit. Cr. 8vo. 6s.

—— THE REVELATION OF THE FATHER. Cr. 8vo. 6s.

—— CHRISTUS CONSUMMATOR. Cr. 8vo. 6s.

—— SOME THOUGHTS FROM THE ORDINAL. Cr. 8vo. 1s. 6d.

—— SOCIAL ASPECTS OF CHRISTIANITY. Cr. 8vo. 6s.

—— LECTURES ON GOSPEL LIFE. Crown 8vo. [*In the Press.*

WESTCOTT (Rt. Rev. B. F.).—ESSAYS IN THE HISTORY OF RELIGIOUS THOUGHT IN THE WEST. Globe 8vo. 6s.

WICKHAM (Rev. E. C.).—WELLINGTON COLLEGE SERMONS. Cr. 8vo. 6s.

WILKINS (Prof. A. S.).—THE LIGHT OF THE WORLD: An Essay. 2nd Ed. Cr. 8vo. 3s. 6d.

WILSON (J. M., Archdeacon of Manchester).—SERMONS PREACHED IN CLIFTON COLLEGE CHAPEL. 2nd Series, 1888—90. Cr. 8vo. 6s.

—— ESSAYS AND ADDRESSES. Cr. 8vo. 4s. 6d.

—— SOME CONTRIBUTIONS TO THE RELIGIOUS THOUGHT OF OUR TIME. Cr. 8vo. 6s.

WOOD (Rev. E. G.).—THE REGAL POWER OF THE CHURCH. 8vo. 4s. 6d.

THERAPEUTICS. (*See* MEDICINE, p. 22.)

TRANSLATIONS.

From the Greek—From the Italian—From the Latin—Into Latin and Greek Verse.

From the Greek.

AESCHYLUS.—THE SUPPLICES. With Translation, by T. G. TUCKER, Litt.D. 8vo. 10s. 6d.

—— THE SEVEN AGAINST THEBES. With Translation, by A. W. VERRALL, Litt. D. 8vo. 7s. 6d.

—— EUMENIDES. With Verse Translation, by BERNARD DRAKE, M.A. 8vo. 5s.

ARATUS. (*See* PHYSIOGRAPHY, p. 27.)

ARISTOPHANES.—THE BIRDS. Trans. into English Verse, by B. H. KENNEDY. 8vo. 6s.

ARISTOTLE ON FALLACIES; OR, THE SOPHISTICI ELENCHI. With Translation, by E. POSTE M.A. 8vo. 8s. 6d.

ARISTOTLE.—THE FIRST BOOK OF THE METAPHYSICS OF ARISTOTLE. By a Cambridge Graduate. 8vo. 5s.

—— THE POLITICS. By J. E. C. WELLDON, M.A. 10s. 6d.

—— THE RHETORIC. By same. Cr. 8vo. 7s. 6d.

—— THE NICOMACHEAN ETHICS. By same. [*In the Press.*

—— ON THE CONSTITUTION OF ATHENS. By E. POSTE. Cr. 8vo. 3s. 6d.

BION. (*See* THEOCRITUS.)

HERODOTUS.—THE HISTORY. By G. C. MACAULAY, M.A. 2 vols. Cr. 8vo. 18s.

HOMER.—THE ODYSSEY DONE INTO ENGLISH PROSE, by S. H. BUTCHER, M.A., and A. LANG, M.A. Cr. 8vo. 6s.

—— THE ODYSSEY. Books I.—XII. Transl. into English Verse by EARL OF CARNARVON. Cr. 8vo. 7s. 6d.

—— THE ILIAD DONE INTO ENGLISH PROSE, by ANDREW LANG, WALTER LEAF, and ERNEST MYERS. Cr. 8vo. 12s. 6d.

MELEAGER.—FIFTY POEMS. Translated into English Verse by WALTER HEADLAM. Fcp. 4to. 7s. 6d.

MOSCHUS. (*See* THEOCRITUS).

PINDAR.—THE EXTANT ODES. By ERNEST MYERS. Cr. 8vo. 5s.

PLATO.—TIMÆUS. With Translation, by R. D. ARCHER-HIND, M.A. 8vo. 16s. (*See also* GOLDEN TREASURY SERIES, p. 20.)

POLYBIUS.—THE HISTORIES. By E. S. SHUCKBURGH. Cr. 8vo. 24s.

SOPHOCLES.—ŒDIPUS THE KING. Translated into English Verse by E. D. A. MORSHEAD, M.A. Fcp. 8vo. 3s. 6d.

THEOCRITUS, BION, AND MOSCHUS. By A. LANG, M.A. 18mo. 4s. 6d.—Large Paper Edition. 8vo. 9s.

XENOPHON. — THE COMPLETE WORKS. By H. G. DAKYNS, M.A. Cr. 8vo.—Vol. I. THE ANABASIS AND BOOKS I. AND II. OF THE HELLENICA. 10s. 6d.
[Vol. II. in the Press.

From the Italian.

DANTE.—THE PURGATORY. With Transl. and Notes, by A. J. BUTLER. Cr. 8vo. 12s.6d.
—— THE PARADISE. By the same. 2nd Edit. Cr. 8vo. 12s. 6d.
—— THE HELL. By the same. Cr. 8vo. 12s.6d.
—— DE MONARCHIA. By F. J. CHURCH. 8vo. 4s. 6d.
—— THE DIVINE COMEDY. By C. E. NORTON. I. HELL. II. PURGATORY. III. PARADISE. Cr. 8vo. 6s. each.

From the Latin.

CICERO.—THE LIFE AND LETTERS OF MARCUS TULLIUS CICERO. By the Rev. G. E. JEANS, M.A. 2nd Edit. Cr. 8vo. 10s. 6d.
—— THE ACADEMICS. By J.S. REID. 8vo. 5s.6d.

HORACE: THE WORKS OF. By J. LONSDALE, M.A., and S. LEE, M.A. Gl. 8vo. 3s. 6d.
—— THE ODES IN A METRICAL PARAPHRASE. By R. M. HOVENDEN, B.A. Ext.fcp.8vo. 4s.6d.
—— LIFE AND CHARACTER: AN EPITOME OF HIS SATIRES AND EPISTLES. By R. M. HOVENDEN, B.A. Ext. fcp. 8vo. 4s. 6d.
—— WORD FOR WORD FROM HORACE: The Odes Literally Versified. By W. T. THORNTON, C.B. Cr. 8vo. 7s. 6d.

JUVENAL.—THIRTEEN SATIRES. By ALEX. LEEPER, LL.D. New Ed. Cr. 8vo. 3s. 6d.

LIVY.—BOOKS XXI.—XXV. THE SECOND PUNIC WAR. By A. J. CHURCH, M.A., and W. J. BRODRIBB, M.A. Cr. 8vo. 7s. 6d.

MARCUS AURELIUS ANTONINUS.— BOOK IV. OF THE MEDITATIONS. With Translation and Commentary, by H. CROSSLEY, M.A. 8vo. 6s.

SALLUST.—THE CONSPIRACY OF CATILINE AND THE JUGURTHINE WAR. By A. W. POLLARD. Cr. 8vo. 6s.—CATILINE. 3s.

TACITUS, THE WORKS OF. By A. J. CHURCH, M.A., and W. J. BRODRIBB, M.A. THE HISTORY. 4th Edit. Cr. 8vo. 6s. THE AGRICOLA AND GERMANIA. With the Dialogue on Oratory. Cr. 8vo. 4s. 6d. THE ANNALS. 5th Edit. Cr. 8vo. 7s. 6d.

VIRGIL: THE WORKS OF. By J. LONSDALE, M.A., and S. LEE, M.A. Globe 8vo. 3s. 6d.
—— THE ÆNEID. By J. W. MACKAIL, M.A. Cr. 8vo. 7s. 6d.

Into Latin and Greek Verse.

CHURCH (Rev. A. J.).—LATIN VERSION OF SELECTIONS FROM TENNYSON. By Prof. CONINGTON, Prof. SEELEY, Dr. HESSEY, T. E. KEBBEL, &c. Edited by A. J. CHURCH, M.A. Ext. fcp. 8vo. 6s.

GEDDES (Prof. W. D.).—FLOSCULI GRÆCI BOREALES. Cr. 8vo. 6s.

KYNASTON (Herbert D.D.).—EXEMPLARIA CHELTONIENSIA. Ext. fcp. 8vo. 5s.

VOYAGES AND TRAVELS.

(See also HISTORY, p. 9; SPORT, p. 30.)

APPLETON (T. G.).—A NILE JOURNAL. Illustrated by EUGENE BENSON. Cr. 8vo. 6s.

"BACCHANTE." THE CRUISE OF H.M.S. "BACCHANTE," 1879—1882. Compiled from the Private Journals, Letters and Note-books of PRINCE ALBERT VICTOR and PRINCE GEORGE OF WALES. By the Rev. Canon DALTON. 2 vols. Med. 8vo. 52s. 6d.

BAKER (Sir Samuel W.).—ISMAILIA. A Narrative of the Expedition to Central Africa for the Suppression of the Slave Trade, organised by ISMAIL, Khedive of Egypt. Cr. 8vo. 6s.
—— THE NILE TRIBUTARIES OF ABYSSINIA, AND THE SWORD HUNTERS OF THE HAMRAN ARABS. Cr. 8vo. 6s.
—— THE ALBERT N'YANZA GREAT BASIN OF THE NILE AND EXPLORATION OF THE NILE SOURCES. Cr. 8vo. 6s.
—— CYPRUS AS I SAW IT IN 1879. 8vo. 12s. 6d.

BARKER (Lady).—A YEAR'S HOUSEKEEPING IN SOUTH AFRICA. Illustr. Cr. 8vo. 3s. 6d.
—— STATION LIFE IN NEW ZEALAND. Cr. 8vo. 3s. 6d.
—— LETTERS TO GUY. Cr. 8vo. 5s.

BOUGHTON (G. H.) and ABBEY (E. A.).— SKETCHING RAMBLES IN HOLLAND. With Illustrations. Fcp. 4to. 21s.

BRYCE (James, M.P.). — TRANSCAUCASIA AND ARARAT. 3rd Edit. Cr. 8vo. 9s.

CAMERON (V. L.).—OUR FUTURE HIGHWAY TO INDIA. 2 vols. Cr. 8vo. 21s.

CAMPBELL (J. F.).—MY CIRCULAR NOTES. Cr. 8vo. 6s.

CARLES (W. R.).—LIFE IN COREA. 8vo. 12s.6d.

CAUCASUS: NOTES ON THE. By "WANDERER." 8vo. 9s.

CRAIK (Mrs.).—AN UNKNOWN COUNTRY. Illustr. by F. NOEL PATON. Roy. 8vo. 7s.6d.
—— AN UNSENTIMENTAL JOURNEY THROUGH CORNWALL. Illustrated. 4to. 12s. 6d.

DILKE (Sir Charles). (See pp. 24. 29.)

DUFF (Right Hon. Sir M. E. Grant).—NOTES OF AN INDIAN JOURNEY. 8vo. 10s. 6d.

FORBES (Archibald).—SOUVENIRS OF SOME CONTINENTS. Cr. 8vo. 6s.
—— BARRACKS, BIVOUACS, AND BATTLES. Cr. 8vo. 7s. 6d

FULLERTON (W. M.).—IN CAIRO. Fcp. 8vo. 3s. 6d.

GONE TO TEXAS: LETTERS FROM OUR BOYS. Ed. by THOS. HUGHES. Cr. 8vo. 4s.6d.

GORDON (Lady Duff). — LAST LETTERS FROM EGYPT, TO WHICH ARE ADDED LETTERS FROM THE CAPE. 2nd Edit. Cr. 8vo. 9s.

GREEN (W. S.).—AMONG THE SELKIRK GLACIERS. Cr. 8vo. 7s. 6d.

HOOKER (Sir Joseph D.) and BALL (J.).— JOURNAL OF A TOUR IN MAROCCO AND THE GREAT ATLAS. 8vo. 21s.

HÜBNER (Baron von).—A RAMBLE ROUND THE WORLD. Cr. 8vo. 6s.

HUGHES (Thos.).—RUGBY, TENNESSEE. Cr. 8vo. 4s. 6d.

KALM.—ACCOUNT OF HIS VISIT TO ENGLAND. Trans. by J. LUCAS. Illus. 8vo. 12s. net.

VOYAGES AND TRAVELS—*continued.*

KINGSLEY (Charles).—AT LAST: A Christmas in the West Indies. Cr. 8vo. 3*s.* 6*d.*

KINGSLEY (Henry). — TALES OF OLD TRAVEL. Cr. 8vo. 3*s.* 6*d.*

KIPLING (J. L.).—BEAST AND MAN IN INDIA. Illustrated. 8vo. 21*s.*

MACMILLAN (Rev. Hugh).—HOLIDAYS ON HIGH LANDS. Globe 8vo. 6*s.*

MAHAFFY (Prof. J. P.).—RAMBLES AND STUDIES IN GREECE. Illust. Cr. 8vo. 10*s.*6*d.*

MAHAFFY (Prof. J. P.) and ROGERS (J. E.).—SKETCHES FROM A TOUR THROUGH HOLLAND AND GERMANY. Illustrated by J. E. ROGERS. Ext. cr. 8vo. 10*s.* 6*d.*

MURRAY (E. C. Grenville).—ROUND ABOUT FRANCE. Cr. 8vo. 7*s.* 6*d.*

NORDENSKIÖLD. — VOYAGE OF THE "VEGA" ROUND ASIA AND EUROPE. By Baron A. E. VON NORDENSKIÖLD. Trans. by ALEX. LESLIE. 400 Illustrations, Maps, etc. 2 vols. 8vo. 45*s.*—*Popular Edit.* Cr. 8vo. 6*s.*

OLIPHANT (Mrs.). (*See* HISTORY, p. 11.)

OLIVER (Capt. S. P.).—MADAGASCAR: AN HISTORICAL AND DESCRIPTIVE ACCOUNT OF THE ISLAND. 2 vols. Med. 8vo. 52*s.* 6*d.*

PALGRAVE (W. Gifford).—A NARRATIVE OF A YEAR'S JOURNEY THROUGH CENTRAL AND EASTERN ARABIA, 1862-63. Cr. 8vo. 6*s.*
—— DUTCH GUIANA. 8vo. 9*s.*
—— ULYSSES; or, Scenes and Studies in many Lands. 8vo. 12*s.* 6*d.*

PERSIA, EASTERN. AN ACCOUNT OF THE JOURNEYS OF THE PERSIAN BOUNDARY COMMISSION, 1870-71-72. 2 vols. 8vo. 42*s.*

PIKE (W.)—THE BARREN GROUND OF NORTHERN CANADA. 8vo. 10*s.* 6*d.*

ST. JOHNSTON (A.).—CAMPING AMONG CANNIBALS. Cr. 8vo. 4*s.* 6*d.*

SANDYS (J. E.).—AN EASTER VACATION IN GREECE. Cr. 8vo. 3*s.* 6*d.*

STRANGFORD (Viscountess). — EGYPTIAN SEPULCHRES AND SYRIAN SHRINES. New Edition. Cr. 8vo. 7*s.* 6*d.*

TAVERNIER (Baron): TRAVELS IN INDIA OF JEAN BAPTISTE TAVERNIER. Transl. by V. BALL, LL.D. 2 vols. 8vo. 42*s.*

TRISTRAM. (*See* ILLUSTRATED BOOKS.)

TURNER (Rev. G.). (*See* ANTHROPOLOGY.)

WALLACE (A. R.). (*See* NATURAL HISTORY.)

WATERTON (Charles).—WANDERINGS IN SOUTH AMERICA, THE NORTH-WEST OF THE UNITED STATES, AND THE ANTILLES. Edited by Rev. J. G. WOOD. Illustr. Cr. 8vo. 6*s.*—*People's Edition.* 4to. 6*d.*

WATSON (R. Spence).—A VISIT TO WAZAN, THE SACRED CITY OF MOROCCO. 8vo. 10*s.*6*d.*

YOUNG, Books for the.

(*See also* BIBLICAL HISTORY, p. 30.)

ÆSOP—CALDECOTT.—SOME OF ÆSOP'S FABLES, with Modern Instances, shown in Designs by RANDOLPH CALDECOTT. 4to. 5*s.*

ARIOSTO.—PALADIN AND SARACEN. Stories from Ariosto. By H. C. HOLLWAY-CALTHROP. Illustrated. Cr. 8vo. 6*s.*

ATKINSON (Rev. J. C.).—THE LAST OF THE GIANT KILLERS. Globe 8vo. 3*s.* 6*d.*
—— WALKS, TALKS, TRAVELS, AND EXPLOITS OF TWO SCHOOLBOYS. Cr. 8vo. 3*s.* 6*d.*
—— PLAYHOURS AND HALF-HOLIDAYS, OR FURTHER EXPERIENCES OF TWO SCHOOLBOYS. Cr. 8vo. 3*s.* 6*d.*
—— SCENES IN FAIRYLAND. Cr. 8vo.

AWDRY (Frances).—THE STORY OF A FELLOW SOLDIER. (A Life of Bishop Patteson for the Young.) Globe 8vo. 2*s.* 6*d.*

BAKER (Sir S. W.).—TRUE TALES FOR MY GRANDSONS. Illustrated. Cr. 8vo. 3*s.* 6*d.*
—— CAST UP BY THE SEA: OR, THE ADVENTURES OF NED GRAY. Illus. Cr. 8vo. 6*s.*

BUMBLEBEE BOGO'S BUDGET. By a RETIRED JUDGE. Illust. Cr. 8vo. 2*s.* 6*d.*

CARROLL (Lewis).—ALICE'S ADVENTURES IN WONDERLAND. With 42 Illustrations by TENNIEL. Cr. 8vo. 6*s.* net.
People's Edition. With all the original Illustrations. Cr. 8vo. 2*s.* 6*d.* net.
A GERMAN TRANSLATION OF THE SAME. Cr. 8vo. 6*s.* net. –A FRENCH TRANSLATION OF THE SAME. Cr. 8vo. 6*s.* net. AN ITALIAN TRANSLATION OF THE SAME. Cr. 8vo. 6*s.* net.
—— ALICE'S ADVENTURES UNDER-GROUND. Being a Fascimile of the Original MS. Book, afterwards developed into "Alice's Adventures in Wonderland." With 27 Illustrations by the Author. Cr. 8vo. 4*s.* net.
—— THROUGH THE LOOKING-GLASS AND WHAT ALICE FOUND THERE. With 50 Illustrations by TENNIEL. Cr. 8vo. 6*s.* net.
People's Edition. With all the original Illustrations. Cr. 8vo. 2*s.* 6*d.* net.
People's Edition of "Alice's Adventures in Wonderland," and "Through the Looking-Glass." 1 vol. Cr. 8vo. 4*s.* 6*d.* net.
—— RHYME? AND REASON? With 65 Illustrations by ARTHUR B. FROST, and 9 by HENRY HOLIDAY. Cr. 8vo. 6*s.* net.
—— A TANGLED TALE. With 6 Illustrations by ARTHUR B. FROST. Cr. 8vo. 4*s.* 6*d.* net.
—— SYLVIE AND BRUNO. With 46 Illustrations by HARRY FURNISS. Cr. 8vo. 7*s.* 6*d.* net.
—— THE NURSERY "ALICE." Twenty Coloured Enlargements from TENNIEL'S Illustrations to "Alice's Adventures in Wonderland," with Text adapted to Nursery Readers. 4to. 4*s.* net.—*People's Edition.* 4to. 2*s.* net.
—— THE HUNTING OF THE SNARK, AN AGONY IN EIGHT FITS. With 9 Illustrations by HENRY HOLIDAY. Cr. 8vo. 4*s.* 6*d.* net.

CLIFFORD (Mrs. W. K.).—ANYHOW STORIES. With Illustrations by DOROTHY TENNANT. Cr. 8vo. 1*s.* 6*d.*; paper covers, 1*s.*

CORBETT (Julian).—FOR GOD AND GOLD. Cr. 8vo. 6*s.*

CRAIK (Mrs.).—ALICE LEARMONT: A FAIRY TALE. Illustrated. Globe 8vo. 4*s.* 6*d.*
—— THE ADVENTURES OF A BROWNIE. Illustrated by Mrs. ALLINGHAM. Gl. 8vo. 4*s.* 6*d.*
—— THE LITTLE LAME PRINCE AND HIS TRAVELLING CLOAK. Illustrated by J. McL. RALSTON. Cr. 8vo. 4*s.* 6*d.*
—— OUR YEAR: A CHILD'S BOOK IN PROSE AND VERSE. Illustrated. Gl. 8vo. 2*s.* 6*d.*
—— LITTLE SUNSHINE'S HOLIDAY. Globe 8vo. 2*s.* 6*d.*
—— THE FAIRY BOOK: THE BEST POPULAR FAIRY STORIES. 18mo. 2*s.* 6*d.* net.

CRAIK (Mrs.).—CHILDREN'S POETRY. Ex. fcp. 8vo. 4s. 6d.
—— SONGS OF OUR YOUTH. Small 4to. 6s.

DE MORGAN (Mary).—THE NECKLACE OF PRINCESS FIORIMONDE, AND OTHER STORIES. Illustrated by WALTER CRANE. Ext. fcp. 8vo. 3s. 6d.—Large Paper Ed., with Illustrations on India Paper. 100 copies printed.

FOWLER (W. W.). (See NATURAL HISTORY.)

GREENWOOD (Jessy E.).—THE MOON MAIDEN: AND OTHER STORIES. Cr. 8vo. 3s. 6d.

GRIMM'S FAIRY TALES. Translated by LUCY CRANE, and Illustrated by WALTER CRANE. Cr. 8vo. 6s.

KEARY (A. and E.).—THE HEROES OF ASGARD. Tales from Scandinavian Mythology. Globe 8vo. 2s. 6d.

KEARY (E.).—THE MAGIC VALLEY. Illustr. by "E.V.B." Globe 8vo. 4s. 6d.

KINGSLEY (Charles).—THE HEROES; or, Greek Fairy Tales for my Children. Cr. 8vo. 3s. 6d.—Presentation Ed., gilt edges. 7s. 6d. MADAM HOW AND LADY WHY; or, First Lessons in Earth-Lore. Cr. 8vo. 3s. 6d. THE WATER-BABIES: A Fairy Tale for a Land Baby. Cr. 8vo. 3s. 6d.—New Edit. Illus. by L. SAMBOURNE. Fcp. 4to. 12s. 6d.

MACLAREN (Arch.).—THE FAIRY FAMILY. A Series of Ballads and Metrical Tales. Cr. 8vo. 5s.

MACMILLAN (Hugh). (See p. 35.)

MADAME TABBY'S ESTABLISHMENT. By KARI. Illust. by L. WAIN. Cr. 8vo. 4s. 6d.

MAGUIRE (J. F.).—YOUNG PRINCE MARIGOLD. Illustrated. Globe 8vo. 4s. 6d.

MARTIN (Frances).—THE POET'S HOUR. Poetry selected for Children. 18mo. 2s. 6d.
—— SPRING-TIME WITH THE POETS. 18mo. 3s. 6d.

MAZINI (Linda).—IN THE GOLDEN SHELL. With Illustrations. Globe 8vo. 4s. 6d.

MOLESWORTH (Mrs.).—WORKS. Illust. by WALTER CRANE. Globe 8vo. 2s. 6d. each.
"CARROTS," JUST A LITTLE BOY.
A CHRISTMAS CHILD.
CHRISTMAS-TREE LAND.
THE CUCKOO CLOCK.
FOUR WINDS FARM.
GRANDMOTHER DEAR.
HERR BABY.
LITTLE MISS PEGGY.
THE RECTORY CHILDREN.
ROSY.
THE TAPESTRY ROOM.
TELL ME A STORY.
TWO LITTLE WAIFS.
"US": An Old-Fashioned Story.
CHILDREN OF THE CASTLE.
—— A CHRISTMAS POSY. Illustrated by WALTER CRANE. Cr. 8vo. 4s. 6d.
—— SUMMER STORIES. Cr. 8vo. 4s. 6d.
—— FOUR GHOST STORIES. Cr. 8vo. 6s.
—— NURSE HEATHERDALE'S STORY. Illust. by LESLIE BROOKE. Cr. 8vo. 4s. 6d.

"MRS. JERNINGHAM'S JOURNAL" (Author of).—THE RUNAWAY. Gl. 8vo. 2s. 6d.

OLIPHANT (Mrs.).—AGNES HOPETOUN'S SCHOOLS AND HOLIDAYS. Illust. Gl. 8vo. 2s. 6d.

PALGRAVE (Francis Turner).—THE FIVE DAYS' ENTERTAINMENTS AT WENTWORTH GRANGE. Small 4to. 6s.

PALGRAVE (F. T.).—THE CHILDREN'S TREASURY OF LYRICAL POETRY. 18mo. 2s. 6d.—Or in 2 parts, 1s. each.

PATMORE (C.).—THE CHILDREN'S GARLAND FROM THE BEST POETS. 18mo. 2s. 6d. net.

ROSSETTI (Christina).—SPEAKING LIKENESSES. Illust. by A. HUGHES. Cr. 8vo. 4s. 6d.

RUTH AND HER FRIENDS: A STORY FOR GIRLS. Illustrated. Globe 8vo. 2s. 6d.

ST. JOHNSTON (A.).—CAMPING AMONG CANNIBALS. Cr. 8vo. 4s. 6d.
—— CHARLIE ASGARDE: THE STORY OF A FRIENDSHIP. Illustrated by HUGH THOMSON. Cr. 8vo. 5s.

"ST. OLAVE'S" (Author of). Illustrated. Globe 8vo.
WHEN I WAS A LITTLE GIRL. 2s. 6d.
NINE YEARS OLD. 2s. 6d.
WHEN PAPA COMES HOME. 4s. 6d.
PANSIE'S FLOUR BIN. 4s. 6d.

STEWART (Aubrey).—THE TALE OF TROY. Done into English. Globe 8vo. 3s. 6d.

TENNYSON (Hon. Hallam).—JACK AND THE BEAN-STALK. English Hexameters. Illust. by R. CALDECOTT. Fcp. 4to. 3s. 6d.

"WANDERING WILLIE" (Author of).—CONRAD THE SQUIRREL. Globe 8vo. 2s. 6d.

WARD (Mrs. T. Humphry).—MILLY AND OLLY. With Illustrations by Mrs. ALMA TADEMA. Globe 8vo. 2s. 6d.

WEBSTER (Augusta).—DAFFODIL AND THE CROÄXAXICANS. Cr. 8vo. 6s.

WILLOUGHBY (F.).—FAIRY GUARDIANS. Illustr. by TOWNLEY GREEN. Cr. 8vo. 5s.

WOODS (M. A.). (See COLLECTIONS, p. 17.)

YONGE (Charlotte M.).—THE PRINCE AND THE PAGE. Cr. 8vo. 2s. 6d.
—— A BOOK OF GOLDEN DEEDS. 18mo. 2s. 6d. net. Globe 8vo. 2s.—Abridged Edition. 1s.
—— LANCES OF LYNWOOD. Cr. 8vo. 2s. 6d.
—— P'S AND Q'S; and LITTLE LUCY'S WONDERFUL GLOBE. Illustrated. Cr. 8vo. 3s. 6d.
—— A STOREHOUSE OF STORIES. 2 vols. Globe 8vo. 2s. 6d. each.
—— THE POPULATION OF AN OLD PEAR-TREE; or, Stories of Insect Life. From E. VAN BRUYSSEL. Illustr. Gl. 8vo. 2s. 6d.

ZOOLOGY.

Comparative Anatomy—Practical Zoology—Entomology—Ornithology.

(See also BIOLOGY; NATURAL HISTORY; PHYSIOLOGY.)

Comparative Anatomy.

FLOWER (Prof. W. H.).—AN INTRODUCTION TO THE OSTEOLOGY OF THE MAMMALIA. Illustrated. 3rd Edit., revised with the assistance of HANS GADOW, Ph.D. Cr. 8vo. 10s. 6d.

HUMPHRY (Prof. Sir G. M.).—OBSERVATIONS IN MYOLOGY. 8vo. 6s.

LANG (Prof. Arnold).—TEXT-BOOK OF COMPARATIVE ANATOMY. Transl. by H. M. and M. BERNARD. Preface by Prof. E. HAECKEL. Illustr. 2 vols. 8vo. Part I. 17s. net.

PARKER (T. Jeffery).—A COURSE OF INSTRUCTION IN ZOOTOMY (VERTEBRATA). Illustrated. Cr. 8vo. 8s. 6d.

ZOOLOGY.
Comparative Anatomy—*continued*.

PETTIGREW (J. Bell).—THE PHYSIOLOGY OF THE CIRCULATION IN PLANTS, IN THE LOWER ANIMALS, AND IN MAN. 8vo. 12s.

SHUFELDT (R. W.).—THE MYOLOGY OF THE RAVEN (*Corvus corax Sinuatus*). A Guide to the Study of the Muscular System in Birds. Illustrated. 8vo. 13s. net.

WIEDERSHEIM (Prof. R.).—ELEMENTS OF THE COMPARATIVE ANATOMY OF VERTEBRATES. Adapted by W. NEWTON PARKER. With Additions. Illustrated. 8vo. 12s. 6d.

Practical Zoology.

HOWES (Prof. G. B.).—AN ATLAS OF PRACTICAL ELEMENTARY BIOLOGY. With a Preface by Prof. HUXLEY. 4to. 14s.

HUXLEY (T. H.) and MARTIN (H. N.).—A COURSE OF PRACTICAL INSTRUCTION IN ELEMENTARY BIOLOGY. Revised and extended by Prof. G. B. Howes and D. H. SCOTT, Ph.D. Cr. 8vo. 10s. 6d.

THOMSON (Sir C. Wyville).—THE VOYAGE OF THE "CHALLENGER": THE ATLANTIC. With Illustrations, Coloured Maps, Charts, etc. 2 vols. 8vo. 45s.

THOMSON (Sir C. Wyville).—THE DEPTHS OF THE SEA. An Account of the Results of the Dredging Cruises of H.M.SS. "Lightning" and "Porcupine," 1868-69-70. With Illustrations, Maps, and Plans. 8vo. 31s. 6d.

Entomology.

BUCKTON (G. B.).—MONOGRAPH OF THE BRITISH CICADÆ, OR TETTIGIDÆ. 2 vols. 33s. 6d. each net; or in 8 Parts. 8s. each net.

LUBBOCK (Sir John).—THE ORIGIN AND METAMORPHOSES OF INSECTS. Illustrated. Cr. 8vo. 3s. 6d.

SCUDDER (S. H.).—FOSSIL INSECTS OF NORTH AMERICA. Map and Plates. 2 vols. 4to. 90s. net.

Ornithology.

COUES (Elliott).—KEY TO NORTH AMERICAN BIRDS. Illustrated. 8vo. 2l. 2s.

—— HANDBOOK OF FIELD AND GENERAL ORNITHOLOGY. Illustrated. 8vo. 10s. net.

FOWLER (W. W.). (*See* NATURAL HISTORY.)

WHITE (Gilbert). (*See* NATURAL HISTORY.)

INDEX.

MACMILLAN AND CO., LONDON.